Two Brothers, One Redhead, and a Stolen Giraffe

Sarah Mandell

Two Brothers, One Redhead, and a Stolen Giraffe

By Sarah Mandell

Cover art by Josh Mandell

No part of this book may be reproduced or transmitted in any form without written permission from Sarah Mandell, except by a reviewer who may quote brief passages for review purposes, with proper credit given.

This book is a work of fiction and any resemblance to any person, living or dead, any place, events or occurrences, is purely coincidental. The characters and story lines are created from the author's imagination or are used fictitiously, except for incidental references to public figures, well-known products and geographical locations, which are used fictitiously with no intent to disparage their products or services.

Copyright © 2016 Sarah Mandell

All rights reserved.

ISBN: 1533088748

For Josh

CHAPTER ONE

"We're gonna get caught," Daniel McElroy repeated for what had to be the fiftieth time. He strained to see the dark country road in front of him, lit by a single working headlight. Dylan McElroy, his brother, younger by just thirteen months, shrugged an unconcerned response from the passenger seat. Dylan was never the one to worry about consequences. Daniel worried enough for both of them.

"It might not be right away, but sooner or later, we'll get busted for this. Ain't nobody legally bound to bail us out no more," Daniel went on, pushing his shaggy brown hair out of his tired eyes.

"I know," Dylan snapped. "It's been ten hours of you saying the same damn thing over and over. Yes, we might get caught. We might get away with it too. Quit being so negative."

"I'm not negative. I'm realistic. But *you*, you're so stupid. You've talked me into some stupid shit before, but this tops everything," Daniel accused, peering ahead into the blackness for some sign of hope, some signal this whole mess wasn't reality. They were in the middle of Nowhere, Nebraska, and had been for hours. The boys had no specific direction in mind other than away from Chicago, quickly and discreetly, and Daniel never anticipated being lost like this in a place where no light existed aside from the silver moon in the black velvet sky above. Disoriented, surrounded by darkness, responsible for his younger brother who was incapable of staying out of trouble, it all made Daniel McElroy very uneasy. Or maybe that had more to do with what was in the back of the modified trailer.

A loud crash echoed against the walls of the enormous mobile container behind them. The boys felt it reverberate in their thinly padded seats. For such a specialized vehicle, a custom-built trailer with an adjustable ceiling for going under whatever the highway might bring, this thing sure was rickety and the cab smelled of hay, dry pellet food and animal feces.

"That's just perfect," Daniel muttered in response to the racket going on in the back. He glanced over at his charge, the clean-cut blond boy in the passenger seat he'd been bound to since birth, who was mostly to blame for their current situation. "We're gonna get caught," Daniel started up again, talking in circles. Usually, that was Dylan's job, to talk, talk, talk till someone yelled at him to shut up, but when Daniel got anxious like this, his lips tended to loosen.

Dylan chuckled once the crashing noises ceased and the trailer settled. "She's gotta be hungry by now. Wanna stop for the night?"

"Where we gonna stop, genius? There ain't nothing out here. You think we can just pull up to some Holiday Inn and ask for a room with a balcony? Sometimes I wonder if you have a brain in your head or just potato chips."

"Look who's talking, Mr. 2.3 GPA," Dylan fired back.

"Like you would have actually bothered showing up for school if it weren't for football practice and girls in tight jeans."

Dylan, not offended by the truth, pointed to a crooked mailbox ahead. It was the first sign of civilization they'd seen in almost thirty minutes. "Look. Pull over. Could be a farm with a barn or something."

"So what if there is?"

"Maybe we can get some rest. Let's at least check it out before you worry yourself into a seizure."

Daniel was exhausted from driving. The initial adrenaline high wore off just thirty minutes into this bizarre adventure, when they were still inside the Chicago city limits. Since then he felt nauseous about this new level of trouble they'd gotten themselves into. There was no turning back now, they were all in, but a rest break would be welcome. Pulling this sizable vehicle off the road and closing his eyes for a spell was something Daniel would give just about anything for at this point, not that he had much to give. His younger brother was eighteen now, certainly old enough to take a turn behind the wheel, but Daniel volunteered to be the sole getaway driver knowing if they got caught, which he fully expected they would, he'd do anything to spare his baby brother from whatever penalty they might face. But what exactly was the penalty for ditching the foster system the day after Dylan celebrated the birthday that made him an adult? And what was the penalty for "borrowing" a highly specialized transport vehicle and failing to stop at a single weigh station? But more importantly, what was the penalty for stealing a sick giraffe from the Northside Animal Park?

Daniel pulled off the two-lane road, onto the gravel driveway, just past the mailbox that had *The Larsens* painted in lopsided script. He turned off the only working headlight for fear of alerting any potential Larsens to their trespassing. Once they passed through the perimeter of trees, which concealed the property from the road, the moonlight gave just enough visibility to see a small farmhouse at the end of the driveway and fields in every direction. The left side of the expansive property looked like pastures for cattle, complete with fences and water troughs, but there wasn't a single animal in sight. The right side of the land was clearly for agriculture, some sort of low-lying crops set in rows. There was no sign of life here, and that made this farm the perfect place to stay the night. All three of them.

Cutting off the engine and coasting down the long driveway, kicking up dust in the heavy air of early June, Daniel guided the clunky vehicle towards the large barn behind the farmhouse. There were two pickup trucks parked out front, but they were so old, so dirty, he wasn't sure they were functional. One truck's bumper stickers read *Save the Bees*, and *I Support the NRA*. The other truck had just one bumper sticker, and that one read *University of Nebraska*. This place looked abandoned, but not overgrown. If somebody still lived here, they either didn't have the means to care for it properly or they didn't have the motivation.

The transport vehicle stopped on the far side of the large barn, out of sight should anyone be living in that small dark house. The boys hopped out, marveling at how stiff their legs were from driving for so long. Dylan, the younger McElroy brother, the good-looking one, grabbed the plastic shopping bag from the front seat. It was filled with food, something they picked up when they stopped to top off the gas tank awhile back. There was a chicken sandwich for his brother and a hamburger for himself, plus some fries to share. Under the cold sandwiches and soggy fries were three chef salads in plastic clamshell containers, but the boys had never been inspired to eat healthy. Raised by their grandmother till they were eight and nine, they'd become experts at avoiding vegetables at all costs. Though ten years had passed since then, tonight would be no different meal-wise, if they had anything to say about it.

Daniel stretched his arms over his head and cracked his neck, silently taking in the brightness of the pinhole stars. He nodded towards the lever that opened the back of the trailer. "Now what are we supposed to do, ask her to come out and hope she understands English?"

Dylan smiled, pleased as can be. He handed the bag of food to his older brother and said, "I'll open the door. You can bait her off the truck."

With their roles designated, Dylan reached for the lever. The back door of the trailer flew open with a loud crash. Daniel winced at the noise. They were supposed to be doing this quietly. He peeked around the barn to see the farmhouse, in case a light had come on in response to the bump in the night, but there was nothing. He returned to his spot by the trailer and squinted his eyes, looking into the rectangular cavern. There seemed to be no sign of life in there either, which was odd, considering all the signs of life thumping around in that very same trailer pretty much nonstop since Chicago.

"Crap. Did we kill her?" Dylan asked, his tone wavering just enough to give away the tightening in his throat. "Millie?" His voice echoed in the metal room lined with hay, but no sound could be heard in response.

Daniel stepped forward and held out one of the salads, just like he was supposed to, while balancing the bag with the sandwiches in his other arm. Sure enough, the smell of food inspired movement. The boys smiled at each other in relief. Millie was still alive back there, concealed by darkness, and perhaps she was hungry enough to follow her dinner down the ramp, off the truck, and into the barn. Surely they could lure her like a kitten. How they got her into this huge trailer was something no words could describe, but how they planned to get her out wasn't likely to be any easier.

A long blackish purple tongue emerged from the dark and licked the salad, pulling out a piece of iceberg lettuce to chew. Daniel, no longer pissed at his brother for thinking up these stupid adventures, was now in awe of the creature before him. Her crooked bottom teeth chomped the lettuce against the flat roof of her mouth, just inches from his hand. Next, she inspected the paper bag that held the sandwiches, curious by what was probably her first up-close sniff of fried food, and Daniel let her, thinking nothing of it. She stuck her whole pointy face in the bag, coming out with Daniel's chicken sandwich. It was still wrapped in wax paper, but she didn't seem to mind. Her jaw slowly opened and closed, rolling in circular motions like a cow, as she savored a meal not intended for her. She ate the paper too.

Daniel laughed and shook his head in disbelief. Speaking to the creature, who was licking her lips over and over, he playfully teased, "What a woman. I buy you dinner and you steal mine. No wonder they was gonna put you down, ya ornery ol' thief."

"Don't say that," Dylan scolded, taking offense on Millie's behalf.

Daniel unwrapped his brother's hamburger, letting Millie get a good sniff. "Here, might as well eat his too so we don't fight over it." Lord knows they had enough to fight about already. The ever-arguing brothers were so connected, so bound by love, but they sure got under each other's skin a lot.

Slowly, Millie leaned her neck out of the trailer. Daniel took another step back, hoping the old creature would follow after that delicious smell. She did. She wasn't in a hurry, far from it, but she did manage to step off the back of the trailer and down the ramp, letting the whole thing bounce a little on its tires, relieved now that its twenty-two-hundred-pound cargo was free.

"I thought giraffes were vegetarian," Daniel commented, continuing his backward path to the barn with Millie's nose magnetically attached to that hamburger.

"They're supposed to be, anyway," Dylan filled in, running past his older brother to slide the barn door open.

"This old girl ain't right. Everyone said so. She's eaten at least three wedding bands this year, right off of people's hands, but she never shits them out. And I think she's bitten about a dozen kids by now. Do you think maybe a part of her knew if she didn't come with us, they was gonna…"

"Maybe," Dylan replied.

At sixteen feet and two inches, Millie was too tall to pass through the barn door standing upright, but she desperately wanted that hamburger so she stooped down and scuttled awkwardly through the passageway. Her long front legs bent backwards, like elbows, while she dragged her hind legs till she was clear of the door. Now, the boys were in a pitch-black barn with a giraffe and no idea what else. Quick on his toes, Daniel pulled out his key chain and used the tiny flashlight, barely illuminating the vast wooden room lined with a carpeting of hay and dust. It smelled of farm animals, but there were none, probably hadn't been for quite some time.

Done with her reward-of-a-burger in only a few bites, Millie accepted some cold French fries from Daniel then moved on to the hay lining the floor. The boys watched her move her front legs apart and dip her body downward to feed, always looking like she could collapse inward on herself at any moment. She was almost thirty-five-years old, which was ancient in giraffe years, even for a pampered zoo creature born in captivity. Millie had been bounced around to seven different zoos over the last three decades. She was born at the National Zoo in Washington, D.C., had a nice long stint at the Philadelphia Zoo, five years at the Piedmont Zoo in North Carolina, then onto the Detroit Zoo, The Animal Kingdom of West Cleveland, Leland Zoological Park in Wisconsin, and eventually Northside Animal Park near Chicago. Millie was a giraffe without a permanent home, without a herd of familiar giraffe faces to bond with or a zookeeper that knew her medical history or personality quirks. She was a lonely girl and it sure seemed to most people, she wasn't quite right in the head.

"Guess we're eating salad tonight," Dylan huffed, selfishly grabbing for the two containers Millie hadn't touched. Daniel got stuck with the top one, where Millie's weird purplish tongue had sampled the lettuce just moments ago. He was so hungry he didn't care about sloppy seconds. Standing in the middle of the dark barn, eating with their hands, the boys consumed every shred of lettuce, every tomato and carrot shaving, every cucumber disk, and every broccoli floret. Their stomachs rumbled still, but that would have to hold them over till morning. They'd certainly slept on empty stomachs before, after their grandma passed and they were placed in the foster system where the only way to protest anything was to not eat. The boys, highly skilled protesters, caused their guardians all sorts of anxiety. The two of them were superheroes together, Indian chiefs, and prisoners of war. They played POW quite often during the early years of their foster care, going on hunger strikes to defy whatever evil empire had taken them hostage, demanding all their national secrets. The McElroy boys were the bravest little soldiers you'd ever seen in mismatched pajamas. They always had elaborate plans of escape, wild adventures to take, and the only thing holding them back was their age. As soon as Dylan turned eighteen, they'd be totally free to take on the world. For them, freedom was only one day old now, the milestone just barely passed, but so far it wasn't as magical as they expected after years and years of building it up, talking it up, and dreaming it up. So far, freedom sucked. It was expensive too.

Daniel found some thick blankets by the light of his key chain flashlight and laid them out. He sat down, knees to his chest, and let his eyes adjust to the dark. Millie could be heard taking a slow step, then another, exploring this strange new place that wasn't like the various zoos she'd spent her whole life in. Everything was new here. She was free too. Her long tail swooshed through the air, cutting through the humidity and entourage of pesky flies.

Dylan sat near his beloved big brother and watched the majestic creature as best he could, keeping track of her in the dark, and quietly asked, "How long are you gonna be mad at me about all this giraffe stealing stuff?"

"I don't know. Least as long as when you put that frog in my bed, you little punk," Daniel replied, getting the heebie-jeebies just thinking about the slimy croaking prank he suffered through a few weeks back.

Dylan snickered. "So…we're talking like…two days?"

"At least," Daniel answered, reaching over to mess up Dylan's short blond hair that realistically couldn't be ruffled, no matter how hard the noogie. In truth, Daniel was already over it. He was used to moving on quickly, keeping his brotherly grudges few and far between. Having a younger sibling like Dylan demanded such grace. "You better hope we don't get caught. Cause if we do, I'm turning you in like the asshole you are."

That got Dylan to chuckle. His big brother was bluffing, no doubt about it. "We won't get caught. We made it this far."

"What're we supposed to do with the truck? It don't blend in on the road too good. And what the hell are we supposed to do with a live giraffe? I mean, how do we even get enough food to feed her? I know she can go a week without water…least that's what I heard. Dammit, Dylan. We didn't think this through. What are we supposed to do with her?"

"Dunno."

"I can't believe we did this." Daniel rubbed his tired eyes once more and pushed his overgrown brown hair away from his ears. "I guess we'll figure the rest of this out in the morning."

"You always do," Dylan replied, keeping all the confidence in the world placed in his older brother, the one person who had never let him down before. Not once.

After a few minutes of quiet, only chewing sounds from above as Millie discovered things she deemed edible up in the rafters, Dylan announced, "I'm tired. Guess I'm gonna...hit the hay?" He laughed at his own bad joke before Daniel had the chance to snap out of his anxious trance. "Goodnight, Daniel. Love you," Dylan began.

"Night. Love you too."

"Don't let me die in my sleep," Dylan continued, just as he did every night since he could remember.

"I won't," Daniel replied on cue, like always, not bothering to tuck in his eighteen-year-old brother who was a good three inches taller than him now and at least thirty pounds heavier with solid muscle. Dylan was grown, as was Daniel, but that didn't mean much when it came to spoken bedtime rituals.

Exhausted, dizzy with uncertainty, worn out from carrying the weight of the world on his shoulders, Daniel laid himself down. He used his tiny flashlight one last time to catch a glimpse of their sixteen foot companion, but the battery was weak. He closed his heavy eyelids and drifted off right away. The hard ground below, the scratchy remnants of hay all around, his rumbling stomach, none of it could stop this boy from falling fast asleep.

Hours later, or maybe it was just minutes, Daniel and Dylan McElroy snapped their eyes open only to be blinded by a billion-watt flashlight aimed in their faces. It might as well have been the sun. They scrambled to their feet, unable to see who or what was behind that blazing white light. They shielded their faces, begging for mercy.

A female voice came from behind the painful brightness. She managed to get out, "What in the hell…" before the beam of light shifted upward, illuminating Millie's unimpressed face. The giraffe's long eyelashes blinked downward, inspecting the people below. Her nubby horns cast strange shadows on the ceiling of the barn. Her ears twitched once or twice, in case more hamburgers had suddenly materialized.

While the beam of light from the girl's torch shone upward still, locking Millie in the spotlight, Daniel got a good look at the person holding it. She was a teenager with fiery red hair all mussed from sleep that fell well below her shoulder blades. Her eyes were pale in color, but he couldn't be sure if they were blue or hazel in this severe lighting. She had delicate features, a snobby little nose, and a pair of pink lips parted in astonishment as she gazed upward at the out-of-place creature. This girl, a member of the Larsen family perhaps, was a pretty thing, but she was not in good spirits being awakened in the middle of the night only to find two strange young men and a reticulated giraffe in her family's barn. She had a shotgun at her side, which she now raised up and aimed at Dylan, all the while keeping the flashlight steady.

Wide-eyed, Dylan could only stare at the barrel. Seconds ago, he'd been looking her over too, just like Daniel had been, noticing her unusual height, her boney wrists, and her atrocious cotton nightgown that looked like something out of the 1980's, complete with a bib of frills, so long it covered her all the way down to her ankles. Dylan wondered if she was in a cult, some sort of strict religious sect that forbade women from showing more than four square inches of skin at any time. Now, with the gun in his face and an angry redhead in charge of the trigger, Dylan could only wonder if this was truly the end of his short life. What about all those crazy adventures he had yet to have?

Daniel cleared his throat, ready to say just the right words to save young Dylan from certain death. Again. "We didn't mean to cause no trouble," Daniel explained, palms open with vulnerability. Following his declaration, the girl re-aimed her flashlight and shotgun in his direction. Daniel, the new target, was just nineteen himself, not much older than his brother, but he'd always been the spokesperson when trouble found them, or more likely, when Dylan found trouble. Daniel was the explainer of the mischievous pair.

"Am I hallucinating, or is that a giraffe?" the girl demanded to know.

"That?" Daniel asked, glancing upward in hopes she was referring to something else. "Uh. Yeah. That would be Millie. Millie the giraffe."

Processing this new information, the girl asked, "Millie the giraffe? You've got to be kidding. Give me one good reason not to call the sheriff."

The boys both shuddered at that word. Getting the sheriff involved would be very bad for them. *Very* bad. Not only had they driven off with a zoological creature that didn't belong to them, this specialized truck they made off with was rumored to be one of only five on this entire continent. Plus, Ed and Melinda Griffin, their most recent foster parents, were surely looking for them by now even though, legally, they had no claim on the McElroy brothers any longer. The boys just ran off. No note, no nothing.

"Please," Daniel began. "We just need a place to sleep for the night. We didn't mean no harm. I swear it. We didn't mean no harm."

The girl inspected him once more, shone her light in his face again so his pupils were nice and dilated, then said, "You didn't mean *any* harm."

"Huh?" Daniel asked, squinting in confusion.

"You meant to say you didn't mean *any* harm," she explained again.

"Are you correcting my grammar?"

"It needed correcting."

Daniel stared at her, half offended, half perplexed.

"Names?"

"I'm Daniel McElroy. That's my little brother, Dylan."

She flashed the light over to Dylan again, then back to Daniel, the representative for the McElroy's. "You two don't look like brothers."

It was true. They looked nothing alike. Daniel had messy brown hair with too many cowlicks, dark green eyes, slightly crooked teeth, a lean build and an average face. He was good looking enough, but standing next to young Dylan, he was a lot less good looking. Dylan had a perfectly proportioned face, a strong jaw line, straight white teeth, dimples, and sparkling blue eyes. His short hair was ten shades of blond, natural of course, and it was always in place, even when he slept on his stomach. Dylan had the body of an athlete, where Daniel had the body of an avid reader. Dylan's frame was strong and broad, his chest was like a soldier's, while Daniel was forever slouching, which a former foster mom explained away by saying he carried the weight of the world on his shoulders.

Daniel glanced over at his brother and explained, "We…have different fathers. It's…kind of a long story."

"How'd you two get here?" the girl went on, ready with her next question.

"We drove. Been driving since the sun went down."

"From where?"

"Chicago."

"Chicago? Are there giraffes running wild in Chicago these days?"

Daniel smirked. "No. She came from the zoo. I worked there…well, I *used* to work there cleaning cages and stuff."

"You stole a giraffe from the zoo?" There was a long pause. Neither brother wanted to correct her so they both remained quiet, keeping their eyes lowered in submission. "You two are a pair of thieves, stupid ones at that. You're gonna get caught so you might as well get caught tonight. I'm calling the sheriff, and animal control while I'm at it." She turned to leave, dead serious.

"Wait!" Daniel called after her. "Please don't do that. We didn't *steal* her, exactly. We...we *saved* her."

"If you're lying to me right now, I have no problem shooting this thing," she said, raising the gun once more. "And my dad will be here any second if I holler for him, and his gun is a heck of lot bigger than this one."

"I ain't lying. I swear."

"You're *not* lying. Ain't ain't a word, city boy."

"What are you, the dictionary police?" Daniel scoffed.

"You mean grammar police?" They stared each other down for a moment before she continued, "My daddy taught me well. You have a problem with that?"

It was all he could do to shake his head *no*.

"You've got one more chance to tell the truth, and if I catch you lying to me, I'll knock out all your brother's pretty white teeth."

"Just tell her," Dylan murmured, afraid now that the gun was back in his face, aimed right at his mouth. He was starting to tremble. Tiny beads of sweat appeared at his hairline. "Jesus, Daniel. Just tell her."

Daniel took a deep breath. He never expected to recount their story in a time and place such as this. He figured it would be at a police station in handcuffs. Clearing his throat, he calmly began the tale that sounded very tall indeed, but it was nothing but the truth.

"I started working at the zoo about five months ago, ever since we got moved to Chicago. I was working nights so Dylan snuck in sometimes with me. Nobody really cared too much, long as the shit got shoveled and the floors got mopped. I don't know much about animals and zoos and stuff, but I know this here giraffe ain't right. She ain't right in the head. She's an old girl, moody too, but we always liked visiting her best. We overheard they was gonna put her down in the morning. She's been causing trouble with visitors. Some folks was gonna sue the zoo on account her being such a nuisance and biting kids. They think she might be sick. She's overweight, but she won't let the vet near her to find out what's wrong. She even head butted the vet one time. She's so old, they was just gonna put her down and be done with it. They brought in a replacement giraffe already, on a breeding loan or something. They drove this other giraffe up from Louisville and unloaded her just yesterday. That's how we got ahold that there trailer out in your driveway. Couldn't exactly put her in a U-Haul or nothing. I don't know how we managed, but we…we got her loaded up and here we are, in your barn, with a giraffe in the middle of the night."

The girl lowered her gun. A tiny curl to her lips hinted she might be the slightest bit impressed. Both boys noticed it right away, that little flick of her mouth. Dylan, the girl-chaser of the family, took the opportunity to step in and make a lasting impression on the pretty redhead with the scowl on her face. "It was my idea to save Millie. Daniel just did the driving. I did everything else. It was all my idea."

Daniel stared at his idiot-of-a-brother now, who had suddenly puffed up with a surprising amount of arrogance. Dylan was smiling his winning smile, showing his straight white teeth, those adorable dimples in his cheeks. He always liked to be the hero of the story, especially if a girl was listening. Scratch that: he liked to be the hero of the story *only* if the girl listening was pretty. Dylan went on to explain how giraffes are normally docile creatures, taking the opportunity to inform the farm girl about everything he knew on the topic, which wasn't much. Even still, he could ramble on about anything.

Daniel could tell by Dylan's easy grin, by his giraffe chitchat, that his brother was quite taken with this nameless beauty, gun and all. Millie, sensing she was being talked about, leaned her face down. She inspected Daniel first, the quiet brother, who, when he actually spoke, spoke with a mish-mash of about six different regional accents thanks to his many temporary homes across the Deep South, Eastern Seaboard and Midwest. Somehow, Dylan only picked up the Pennsylvania accent, even though he was moved around just as much as Daniel and attended the same public schools over the years. The brothers couldn't be more different, even in their speech, but it seemed the giraffe already had a favorite McElroy. Millie licked the top of Daniel's head, mussing up his already messy brown hair with her saliva, searching for something to graze on. He swatted her away when she tried chewing on his hair, the brown hay-like stuff conveniently growing out of the top of his head. "Stop it!" he said to Millie, growing more and more annoyed at the situation. "Cut it out!" he shouted upward once more.

Dylan laughed, the girl smirked, all at Daniel's expense. Millie made a humming sound.

In his own charming way, Dylan pushed his hands in the pockets of his jeans, displaying his well-developed biceps, and looked down at the ground sheepishly. That could mean only one thing: he was about to make a move. "Would it be too much trouble if we stayed here for the night? We won't get in your way. I promise."

"You're already in my way."

"Please?" Dylan begged, trying to be cute with a pouty lower lip.

"You can't stay here," the girl replied, not bothering to think it over.

Daniel folded his scrawny arms, which were toned, but much less bulky than his brother's star feature. Growing tired of standing there, seeing Dylan's flirting was going nowhere, Daniel reached in his back pocket and pulled out his wallet. There had to be a way to satisfy this unmovable girl. He flipped through the scarce number of bills and fast food coupons and said, "We can pay you. What does one night in a barn cost?"

The girl cocked her head to the side. "One hundred dollars."

Daniel looked up, judging her expression to see if she was serious. It seemed she was. Her pretty face was pretty straight. He was tempted to ask if McDonald's vouchers could count, but the girl looked like she hadn't laughed in years.

"Okay," he said, pulling out one fifty, two twenties and a ten, his earnings from cutting grass the day before they skipped town. If he had waited till the end of the week, he would have had his paycheck from the animal park as well, which was far more substantial even though he was essentially a janitor who cleaned up bigger messes than any public restroom could boast, but Millie didn't have until the end of the week.

"Can we at least get some pillows for that price?"

"No," she stated, snatching the money.

"What about the use of a shower in the morning?" Daniel tried, just in case.

"Nope." The girl turned and headed towards the door. "And you two better be gone by the time the sun comes up. My daddy won't be pleased to find a couple of hoodlums and a stolen giraffe in his barn."

"Hoodlums?" Daniel mouthed, slightly offended. Did they really look that rough? The boys were in their standard uniforms, loose jeans and faded t-shirts. They must be in another world out here if they were being mistaken for street riffraff.

"Night," Dylan chimed in, beaming a smile her way as she slammed the barn door shut. He turned to Daniel to say, "I think she likes me."

Daniel rolled his eyes. "What on Earth would make you think that?" he hissed, settling back into the blanket on the ground, grumpy as ever.

"She totally does," Dylan said, looking at the door as though the tall girl was still standing there in her horrible sleeping dress. "She's really cute, huh? I mean...*really* cute. Like, cuter than your ex. God, she's cuter than Angie, or Marissa's sister, or even Miss White."

Daniel closed his eyes. He wasn't in the mood to talk about girls, Dylan's favorite subject. Dylan could fall in love with just about anyone: classmates, teachers, and total strangers. Girls seemed to enjoy Dylan's attention at his old high school, his clumsy flirting, but for all his attractiveness, all his smooth talking efforts to impress the ladies, he still hadn't managed to sleep with one by graduation two weeks ago, much to his regret. He was one desperate puppy. If hopping around on his hind legs wearing a tutu while barking jingle bells would get him a treat, he would gladly submit to any nonsense required of him.

Desperate for nothing but sleep, Daniel rolled over, facing away from his chatty brother in hopes his body language would end the conversation, but Dylan had never taken a hint in his life.

"I bet she's nice," Dylan wondered aloud. "All Midwesterner's are nice."

"I'm gonna go with unapologetically frigid," Daniel wagered.

A silent moment passed. Millie could be heard grinding her teeth, a noise Daniel found utterly disturbing, far worse than Dylan's similar nighttime habit.

"Hey Daniel? Did you get a good look at her tits?" Dylan asked thoughtfully, bringing the conversation back to life in an instant, much to his brother's regret.

"Whose tits?" Daniel mumbled, eyes clenched shut.

"The redhead, dumbass. I didn't get a good look, did you?"

"It was a little hard to see past the gun she had in my face."

"What do you think was with that nightgown contraption? She in a cult or something? Is this some sort of hippie commune? She's probably got a really smokin' body under that thing. You think her dad makes her wear it to hide everything?"

"I don't know. I don't care either," Daniel explained. "She wants us gone by sun up so we best sleep while we can."

"She's really smart," Dylan went on, recounting all the qualities he liked about the nameless girl he just encountered.

"Seemed pretty bitchy to me," Daniel muttered, trying to get comfortable.

There was a buzzing sound outside, the hum of an insect orchestra. It was peaceful white noise, something you simply couldn't experience in the city. Just as Daniel was finally nodding off for the second time that night, Dylan whispered, "I can't sleep."

"Uh huh," Daniel replied, barely conscious, barely caring.

"She's really cute. I can't stop thinking about how cute she is."

"Pleeeeease shut up."

"I think she might be the cutest girl I've ever seen, tits or no tits."

"Stop talking. Sleeeeeep."

"I can't."

Sitting up now, agitated, Daniel barked, "Listen. The only female you need to be thinking about right now is the one who might step on you in the middle of the night. Or worse. Piss on you from seven feet up. Go to sleep!"

CHAPTER TWO

"Wake up, liars," was the first thing Daniel heard the next morning. He opened his eyes to see the girl from the night before standing over him, propped up on her shotgun. From his low vantage point, she appeared to be ten feet tall and particularly moody. "You said you'd be gone by sunrise. Its 7:00 a.m. Get up and get out."

"Morning, sunshine," Daniel growled, sitting up. He considered himself a morning person ordinarily, but being awakened by getting nudged in the ribs by a boot was far from pleasant, no matter what time of day it was.

"Look," Dylan whispered from a few feet away. He pointed up at Millie, whose black eyes were still tightly shut. She was asleep, standing in the middle the barn. Her sides went in and out as she breathed. There was a piece of hay stuck to her nose, quivering as she exhaled, a little evidence of her midnight snacking. "She's beautiful, isn't she?" Dylan marveled, standing up. That was just the thing to wake Millie from her light slumber: a compliment.

The giraffe blinked herself awake then approached the two brothers and the redheaded girl. She leaned down to sniff them, no doubt searching for food. When she got to Daniel, her favorite McElroy for whatever reason, she went after his hair again. That long purple tongue swept over his cowlicks, swirling his hair in every direction. "Oh for cryin' out loud!" he yelled, irritated.

"You must use some kind of girlie shampoo, huh?" the redhead teased. He could only manage to glare at her in return. Was that supposed to be a shot at his masculinity?

Dylan, inching closer and closer to the girl whose cuteness kept him awake for hours last night, mustered up the courage to ask, "Do you think you might have something we could feed her? I know she must be real hungry. She can put away a lot of food in that big belly. One time, she ate the toupee right off a man's head. And another time, she got out of her pen and ate all the ice cream and waffle cones from the cart while the ice cream guy was taking a bathroom break."

The girl nodded, suddenly bursting with compassion. "I'll bring her some apples."

Dylan watched the girl walk across the driveway towards the house, her long red ponytail swinging side to side. When she was far enough away, he gave his cranky older brother a thumbs up. "She totally likes me," he declared, giddy as a child on Christmas.

"She likes the giraffe, not you, asshole," Daniel informed him as he shook out the borrowed blankets and folded them as neatly as he could. They hadn't brought any personal belongings inside so there wasn't much preparation needed for their departure. It was time to go, get on with this crazy adventure, figure out what in the world they were supposed to do with a live giraffe, hope nobody would notice them driving along the highway in an extra tall trailer, and get his lovesick little brother away from the pretty girl before he did anything embarrassing.

Daniel surveyed the barn, the equipment and gadgets. There used to be cows in here, he determined. Maybe the feisty redhead pissed them off and they all ran away to the next farm down the road. Surely her snappy temperament could start an epic stampede.

When the girl returned, she handed Daniel a bowl with sliced red apples. "Here. You do it. She seems to like you, city boy."

As he accepted the bowl, he felt nauseous with hunger. Before he could select a piece to offer the giant, Millie was widening her front legs, awkwardly leaning down, ready to help herself. She crunched the first apple, spit out a piece she didn't like, and then went for the next one. All Daniel had to do was hold the bowl. Millie did the rest. While she was running her weird velvety lips over the remaining apples like a hungry horse, the redheaded girl boldly took a step towards the animal. She cautiously reached out her hand and touched Millie's muzzle. Millie didn't mind her light touch. She kept on eating. The farm girl smiled, something the boys hadn't seen her do just yet. She had a sweet smile, small but clever. Daniel got a better look at her eyes now that the daylight illuminated her delicate features. They weren't hazel or blue, like he guessed last night. They were a cool, quiet gray. She wore all her color in her hair, a bright fiery red, pulled back into a long ponytail, the tomboy hairdo of choice.

"So how much do I owe you for the apples?" Daniel asked sarcastically.

"No charge," she replied, touching the short auburn hair on Millie's front leg.

Taking this to be a good sign, desperate to spend some more time with this nameless beauty, Dylan asked, "Could we get some coffee for the road? Maybe a bite to eat? Just a little something. My stomach's been growling all night."

"Sure," the girl said. "A hundred bucks. Each."

"Are you kidding me?" Daniel scoffed before his brother could respond.

"I don't kid. I make money. If you two are as hungry as you say you are, you'll pay."

"That's extortion," Daniel informed her.

"Oooh. Big word," she mocked. "Actually, it's highway robbery. Follow me if you're hungry. I only accept cash."

"Forget this," Daniel said to his brother. "We'll get something in town."

The girl turned around, having overhead his snippy little comment. "The nearest town is about ninety miles away. Nothing will be open till 10. Good luck with the giraffe."

"Dammit," Daniel huffed.

Dylan smiled at the girl, ready to pay up. He reached for his wallet and pulled out two hundred dollar bills. "My treat," he said to Daniel.

"Where'd you get that?" Daniel hissed, alarmed by his brother's unusual cash flow. The boys never had any money. They worked miscellaneous jobs for minimum wage and still they came up empty handed more times than not. Dylan was in high school up until two weeks ago, so Daniel was the only one working steadily at the animal park and cutting grass, but most of his meager savings already went in the gas tank of the thirsty transport vehicle.

"Graduation money," Dylan explained. "The Griffins were very generous."

"Where the hell was that money at the gas station yesterday? C'mon, Dylan. You want to spend it on breakfast?"

Dylan gave a carefree shrug.

Daniel shot him a look, letting him know how unwise this decision was. Dylan cracked a smile in return, not so interested in being wise at the moment. With that, the brothers followed the redhead across the driveway and up the steps of the farmhouse. As she opened the door and led them into the kitchen, she warned, "If you step foot into any other room in this house, I'll poison your breakfast."

"Yes ma'am," Dylan said sweetly, taking one of the two seats at the kitchen table. The table was sturdy wood, rough cut but worn smooth, and judging by the number of chairs, there were only as many people living here. Right now, the only visible resident was standing in front of a sixty-year old cast iron stove, humming quietly, adding three scoops of something into a dented pot. Poison, perhaps.

Daniel looked around the small kitchen. The fridge was harvest gold, at least thirty years old, which put it way ahead of the stove.

There was no microwave. The enamel sink was deep and white, chipped so badly it almost looked a pattern of hieroglyphics. The wide wooden floorboards creaked underneath as Dylan leaned back in his chair, as if he was a welcome guest here. He was hopelessly crushing on this girl, who appeared to be wearing boy's clothing, watching her stir the pot, even though he didn't yet know her name.

Annoyed and in need of clues, Daniel discreetly snooped through a pile of mail that rested on the windowsill just within his reach. He squinted, straining to read the text from afar. Everything was addressed to Mr. Johan Larsen. There were some bills, something about 4-H, a catalogue with farm equipment, but nothing personal. Then, at the bottom of the stack, he came upon an opened letter from the University of Nebraska addressed to Ms. Josephine Larsen, confirming her withdrawal from the Agricultural Sciences program. There was a refund check too, for one semester's worth of classes. Setting the letter back where he found it, surprised to discover she was about his brother's age, though curious why she dropped out of college after just one semester, he looked down at the muddy work boots beside the door. They looked to be men's size twelve or so, and they were placed perfectly in line with the edge of the door, perpendicular with the baseboard. Daniel determined this Mr. Larsen, wherever he was, must be a perfectionist.

The girl clinked some slop into three bowls. "Pay up."

Dylan handed her two hundred bucks, which she shoved into the back pocket of her loose jeans. Her t-shirt was pretty loose too, hiding whatever femininity she may or may not have possessed. Even still, she was beautiful, now that the daylight revealed her face in all its glory. It seemed she only recently grew out of her awkward stage and didn't appear to be all that comfortable in her body. She was tall for a girl, pushing 5'11" or thereabout. Daniel was just barely 6'0" himself, so when she walked towards him to hand him a bowl of some unknown substance, he was almost eye level with her. Although she was pretty in an approachable kind of way, her unusual height, her supermodel stature, put her into the intimidating category for young Daniel.

The tall girl sat at the table with Dylan, which probably made his whole life worthwhile, and began to eat in silence. Daniel ate standing up, leaning against the front door. Whatever was in his bowl, it was chunky and white, tasteless too, but it was hot. He ate it all, putting it past his tongue and down his throat. The coffee wasn't much better. It was hot, as it should be, an appropriate shade of dark brown, but it was wretched in taste. He considered she did it on purpose, prepared this awful meal just to mess with them, just to get them to leave as soon as they were done eating.

"This is really good. Thank you for your hospitality," Dylan lied in his most cheerful voice, scraping his bowl clean. He could be such a brown noser.

"Yes, Josephine. Thank you for your hospitality," Daniel added flatly.

She stopped her spoon halfway to her mouth and looked up, unnerved. "How do you know my name?"

"Yeah. How'd you know her name?" Dylan echoed.

Daniel didn't feel the need to answer. He liked riling her up like this, pretending he knew everything about her, all her secrets. It was the least he could do after she threatened him with a gun several times last night, took his money, took his brother's money too, laughed at his expense, and fed him the worst breakfast he'd ever had.

"Shit!" Dylan exclaimed, pointing towards the window. "She's loose!"

Outside, Millie stepped over the fence and started strolling around in the cattle field, enjoying the morning air. Nobody closed the barn door so she was free to roam. After looking around the fields, surveying this new place, she chose a direction, straight for the thick tree line about a quarter mile away. With those long legs, it wouldn't take her more than a minute or two to get there.

In seconds, all three of them were standing in the driveway, at a loss. Nobody could get the words out: *what do we do?* Daniel was thinking as fast as he could, weighing options, but the redhead beside him was the first one to offer up a plan. It was like she had gone after an escaped zoo animal before.

"Here. You take that truck. I'll take this one. She'll go with the herd. We have to *be* the herd. Got it?"

Quickly, ready to be a hero, Dylan took a set of keys from her hand. He dashed towards the red pickup truck parked in the driveway and was off, driving towards the wayward giraffe.

"You coming?" the girl asked, jogging towards the white pickup with the University of Nebraska bumper sticker. Daniel nodded and ran to catch up with her. He climbed in the passenger seat and barely had the door shut when she floored it, sending gravel flying out from under all four wheels.

The two trucks set off towards Millie, who turned to see them, and decided it was time to start galloping. She had to be running at least thirty miles per hour by the time she got going. Dylan, in the slightly newer-looking red pickup, got between her and the trees, while the other truck circled around the runaway giraffe. Daniel's heart was thumping, his breakfast was sloshing in his stomach. He looked over at the girl beside him, noticing her freckled nose. She had the most intricate ears he'd ever seen. He wondered if all other girls had so many tiny folds and curves to their ears, or if it was just this girl. Did other girls even have ears? Surely they did, but right now, he couldn't remember. Before he could gaze at her any longer, the driving caught up with him. "I'm gonna be sick," he said, putting a hand over his mouth. After all, they were driving forty miles per hour in a tight circle around a confused giraffe, making the doughnut from hell.

"Hold on to your breakfast just a little longer, city boy," she said, revving the engine again. "We got her!"

Daniel looked up. She was right. Millie was trotting in between the two pickup trucks now, heading back towards the barn, like it was all in her nature. Still incredibly nauseous, he asked, "How did you know that would work?"

"We used to have cattle here."

"And you had to go after them with pickup trucks?"

"Sometimes the bulls would bust through the fence and make a break for it. Usually, they were just wanting to mate the old fashioned way, so they only went as far as the other field where we kept the heifers, but once in a while they'd head down the road and we'd have to herd them back home with the trucks."

That was the most words she'd ever said at once. Her voice was smooth and full, mature despite her youth, and she sure sounded like she knew what she was talking about. Daniel was curious how exactly cows were expected to mate, if not the old-fashioned way, but didn't dare ask.

"How come you don't have cattle no more?"

"*Any* more."

Daniel rolled his eyes as she parked the truck by the barn. "How come you don't have cattle *any* more?" he tried again.

"It's expensive. Takes a lot of money to keep them up. Lots of space too. We're doing some summer crops now, and after a year or two, we'll have enough to try some smaller livestock. I'd really like to raise pigs."

"Pigs? Why? Don't they smell bad?"

"You think thirty-two cows smell any better?" she teased, getting out of the truck. Daniel followed, watching Millie crouch down and enter the barn, all on her own. She was done being ornery for the time being.

"What's so special about raising pigs?"

"They take half as much land. They breed in higher numbers, their food costs less, and you can sell them easier because there's less regulations on the meat. Cheaper to get started too. It's going to take a few years selling vegetables and beans to save up but one day I'm...*we're* gonna have enough."

"Just you and your folks?"

"Just my dad and I. We had to let the workers go."

"Where's your mom?"

"That's none of your business, Daniel McElroy."

He was impressed she remembered his name, his full name, at that, but far more impressed that she and her father could run this small farm all on their own. It seemed like a hard life. By her unmoved expression, Daniel could guess the truth about this girl's mother wasn't straightforward. He could certainly relate to that. He wasn't sure where his mother was at the moment, if she was still getting the life beat out of her by boyfriend after boyfriend, or if she was starting a whole new family somewhere better. He hadn't seen his mother in nearly sixteen years.

Dylan closed up the barn behind Millie, then turned to his brother, his herding partner, and gave an out-of-breath laugh of relief. Still high on the success of corralling an escaped giraffe, he asked the girl, "Is your name really Josephine?"

"It's Jo," she corrected, never missing an opportunity.

"Jo," Dylan echoed, pleased with himself for some reason. "I like that."

"Do you?" she asked, her monotone voice lacked any tone that would suggest she gave a damn.

Before the famously impulsive Dylan could make this mess any messier, Daniel stepped in. "We'll get out of your hair now. Really appreciate your helping us out. Tell your dad we're sorry for all the tire tracks in his field. Thanks for everything."

"You know where the road is."

The brothers watched her leave, watched her hips moving as she walked across the driveway to the house, her long ponytail brushing against her back. She didn't bother going in the house. Instead, she continued on to the field on the other side where the crops were coming in. That was the moment everything went quiet for Daniel. All other sounds were blocked out. It was like someone covered his ears, so he could only hear his pulse and the blood moving through his body. Something deep down inside him started to tense up. He didn't want to leave this place. He didn't want to leave her. Daniel ignored all this and snapped out of this momentary rush of feelings that made no sense, then began walking towards the barn, ready to do the right thing and get on down the road.

"I wanna stay here," Dylan stated, as if it were an option, as if he could hear Daniel's similar thoughts.

"We can't. We're lucky she didn't call the police. We should go before her dad shows up and runs us off. We might not be able to buy him off so easily. I'm outta cash anyway. Hope the Griffins were generous enough with your graduation gift to get us to the next town."

"Um. That was…everything. I don't have any more cash."

"You're joking, right?"

"Nope," Dylan said with a grin, like it was no big deal.

"You spent the last of the money on that horrible breakfast?"

"Maybe we can stay here for a little while. What's the hurry?"

"What's the hurry? We have a giraffe! This was your stupid idea."

"I know."

"Well. I feel so much better now. At least you know. So now what? You just gonna let me clean up behind you, like I always do?"

Dylan was quiet.

Growing more agitated, Daniel stomped off in the direction of the tall transport vehicle, ready to get the beast and go. He opened the barn door to let Millie out, hoping she'd go right into the trailer like a good girl, but in a split second he was knocked flat on his back, watching Millie leap over his splayed body as she made a run for the other field where Josephine currently was. "Dammit, Dylan! Get her!" he coughed with dirt in his mouth.

Dylan chased after Millie on foot, like he had any chance of catching her. Daniel filled his empty lungs with a sharp breath of air, brushed himself off and followed after them. They both ran till they came upon Millie and Jo, who were nose to nose in a field of something with green bushy leaves. Jo held up a long reddish stalk of whatever she was harvesting and Millie was chewing away. "She likes it," Jo said, not taking her eyes off of Millie.

"What *is* it?" Dylan asked.

Daniel was panting, crouched over with his hands on his knees. Unlike Dylan, the star tight end of Dalton High, Daniel was winded after that sprint.

"Rhubarb. She likes it," Jo said again, delighted. She smiled and let out a belly laugh when Millie licked her hand, then her wrist, and all the way up her forearm. That long purple tongue might have freaked out other girls, but not Josephine Larsen.

Now that Millie had tried several stalks of rhubarb, which she sucked on like a peppermint stick, Jo was curious what else this creature might eat. "C'mon, Millie, you sweet thing. Come here," she said, walking towards another patch of vegetables. "Do you like asparagus?" she asked the giraffe, not paying any attention to the boys following after them. Millie carefully walked through the rows of plantings, taking surprising care not to crush things with her enormous hooves. For such a clumsy-looking creature, she took great consideration with her path.

As it turned out, Millie liked asparagus too, but not as much as she liked the kale. This farm was a feast and Jo was generous as she offered the majestic stowaway everything growing on this land. At least Millie got a decent breakfast. The boys certainly couldn't claim that.

Dylan, hands in his pockets again, arms flexed just so, charming smile plastered on his wide face, inched closer to Jo and started chatting her up with giraffe facts again. She was too distracted by Millie to notice him much. Daniel stood off to the side, feeling the early rays of sunshine scorching the back of his neck. It was only the beginning of June, but today was shaping up to be a hot one. Pretty soon, Dylan would be shirtless, on display so Josephine might be captivated by muscles, if she were into muscles, that is. Last year, when Dylan and Daniel went to the pool one rare Saturday when they didn't have jobs to keep them busy, Dylan was approached by a talent scout who worked for a local modeling agency. She gave Dylan her business card, and not a day later he called the number on it. Dylan got through about ten minutes of the initial interview, just to the part when they were discussing headshots and building a modeling portfolio, when the talent scout tired of his heavy handed flirting and asked him to leave. It wasn't the first time he blew a good opportunity by letting his hormones take the lead.

"I have a confession," Dylan said in a dramatic voice. Jo waited, as did Daniel, and when he had held a long enough pause, building suspense till he was satisfied, he said his piece. "We kinda…don't have any gas money. You got pretty much all of our cash. Any chance we can work some of that back? Can we can help you…do whatever it is you're doing?"

Dylan was pleased with himself, his grand plan. Daniel was not. He was ready to get going and find a way to regain control of the giraffe situation. But it was true. They didn't have much money left, not enough to get very far. Josephine, tall and skinny, leaned to one side and put a hand on her hip. She shielded the morning sunshine with her other arm.

"My dad isn't looking to take on any workers right now."

"Please?" Dylan began, keeping up hope, "Just for a few days so we can make enough to get on down the road? We can do all sorts of odd jobs, whatever you need. We're very handy, you know."

Actually, Daniel was the handy one, did most of the work when he and Dylan worked as a team, but Daniel didn't bother bringing that up. They really did need some fast cash and if working in a field for a day or two was the way to get it, then they might as well get started. Daniel swallowed his pride and knelt down in the soft soil. He retrieved his trusty switchblade from his pocket and cut the head of lettuce from the roots. He inched forward on his knees and did the next one. Jo watched him repeat this five times before she spoke. "Cut it a little higher up, flush with the bulk of the leaves, like this." She knelt beside him and showed him how it was done. He caught her scent for the first time, that unfamiliar mix of freshly turned dirt, the faintest hint of girl sweat, and just a note of soap, something citrus. "Yes, exactly like that," she said, now that Daniel was getting the hang of things.

"See? We can do all sorts of stuff," Dylan said from above, though he wasn't actually participating at the moment.

Josephine folded her arms and said, "Alright. Give me your resumes."

"Say what now?" Dylan blurted out, still supervising with his arms folded.

"Tell me where you've worked and what you can do and I'll think about hiring you, if you've any useful skills, that is. Go on, now. Let's have it."

Dylan went first. "Um. I can wash cars."

Jo glanced over at the two pickups in the driveway, absolutely filthy with mud. She laughed, like his skills were utterly useless to her. "What else?" she prodded.

"I...uh...I can run really fast. I played football all four years of high school."

"Anything else?"

"I got on the Dean's list."

She gave him a 'you-can't-be-serious look', then turned to Daniel. "What about you, city boy? Can you beat that?"

"My grades ain't worth mentioning. But I worked at the animal park for a lil' while, just cleaning floors and stuff. I used to cut grass for people too, trim hedges and things like that. Painted some houses awhile back. Um...I'm pretty quick with washing dishes and bussing tables. I know how to cook but I never did it for money or nothing. That's about it, I guess."

Jo looked him over. She nodded once, satisfied, and handed them each a basket to fill. She left Daniel and Dylan to work in the lettuce field while she returned to her rhubarb, working alone. Well, almost alone. Millie stayed with her, leaving the boys for the girl who hummed while she worked. Sweet melodies came from her throat, occasionally making their way to Daniel's ears several yards away, interrupting his brother's constant chatter about how cute Josephine was. Daniel couldn't agree more, she was awfully cute, but they simply couldn't stay on her farm and watch her forever and ever, cute or not. Her dad would be home soon and they'd have no alternative unless their lettuce harvesting skills were impressive somehow.

At noon, Jo brought them turkey sandwiches on a cutting board, which weren't great but they were far better than breakfast. Millie was treated to a sleeve of graham crackers. Jo didn't let on whether or not the boys were doing a good job with the lettuce, and wordlessly went back to the other field, plucking rhubarb and keeping an eye on Millie. Millie wasn't in a hurry to go anywhere now. She just walked around the field, occasionally straying to the edge of the open space to sample the leaves from the trees, then she'd come back to steal a few stalks of rhubarb from Jo's basket. Jo didn't seem bothered by this. As one might guess, she'd never had a giraffe keep her company before.

Daniel glanced around the farm, getting used to all this wide-open space, feeling exposed yet incredibly free. The rickety windmill on the far side of the house turned with the breeze, and he wondered about its purpose, if it was used for drawing water from a well, or if it was just a thirty-foot-tall lawn ornament. A glimmer of light reflecting on the roof of the farmhouse caught his eye, tempting further distraction. Daniel squinted, scanning his eyes over the dark blue glass rectangles positioned at the back of the house, a trio of solar panels that looked so out of place in this rundown rural setting. It appeared as though additional panels had been planned for, judging by the framing and spacing, but the money must have run out before the project was complete, leaving half of the roof naked while the other half was clothed in glossy technology.

At around 4 o'clock, Millie started acting funny, funnier than usual, that is. First, she did a little upward hop, like something startled her into defying gravity, then she circled around Jo four times before setting off running towards the trees. Dylan stood up to stretch, watching the crazy old giraffe flee for no apparent reason, and asked, "What's with her?" He got his answer when his gaze slowly fell and landed on a large black snake that was slithering in his direction. "Shit!" he gasped, stumbling backwards. "Kill it! Daniel, kill it!" he spoke quickly, pointing at the snake as if to accuse it of some heinous act, backing up more and more so that his big brother was between him and the danger.

Daniel grabbed a nearby shovel, held it like a fishing spear, and cautiously approached the legless threat. Just as Daniel was about to strike, Jo reached out and picked up the snake by the head. "It's just a rat snake," she explained in a calm voice, lifting the all-black creature to prove there wasn't anything to fear, unless you happened to be a rat, of course.

The boys watched in horror as the snake wrapped itself around her forearm, soaking up her body heat. "It's just a rat snake," she said again, admiring her new dark sleeve, expertly holding onto its head so it wouldn't bite. "They're harmless," Jo added, defending the creature who had an important role in the circle of life on this farm. Daniel clutched the shovel tightly, still on the offense, while Dylan continued backing away, not really caring what kind of snake it was, only that it was, in fact, a snake. Holding up her reptile-wrapped forearm, Jo asked, "Is this going to be a problem?" By the wide eyes and gaping mouths of the McElroy brothers, she accepted their silent response, rolled her eyes in annoyance, then walked across the field to release the harmless snake into the surrounding woods. When she returned moments later with Millie following closely behind her like a dog, the boys were still standing there at the scene of the almost-crime, completely dumbfounded. "Well? Get back to work," Jo snapped, as if nothing were unusual. The boys did as she said.

By the time his t-shirt was soaked all the way through with sweat, Daniel's scrawny arms felt like they might fall off. He'd been working in that field for almost eight hours straight. Dylan, who took his shirt off long ago so Jo might catch a glimpse of his defined torso, hadn't been keeping up the pace with the lettuce now that her back was turned and she wasn't watching his progress. There was no point in working hard if she wasn't looking.

He couldn't shut up about her either, which was the other reason for his lazy pace.

Daniel brushed the sweat off his forehead and smiled at his slacker of a brother. "Dude. If you can talk about something other than Jo for five minutes, I'll finish your row for you."

Dylan looked down at the rest of his row, a good fifteen feet left to harvest, and took his brother up on the offer. Now, Dylan talked about their mother, how great it would be to find her. She dropped off her two young sons with their grandmother when they were just two and three, and never came back for them. Rumor had it she ran off with her latest boyfriend and headed for Mexico. The boys were in good hands with their grandmother, but she was in her late sixties already, not in the best shape to be running after two rambunctious children. She did her best for almost six years, then she passed away peacefully in her sleep and the boys were picked up by social services and put in the foster system. They'd been bounced around even more than Millie.

Daniel, not wanting to upset his brother as he finished up the row of lettuce, simply said, "I don't think Mom wants to be found. Besides. We're on our own now, like we always wanted. Can't you be happy about that?"

"I am," Dylan reassured. "I just think about her sometimes. I wish I could remember her. Do you think she ever wonders what happened to us?"

"Dunno. What does it matter now?"

Dylan shrugged.

The boys broke from their conversation to watch Josephine leading Millie across the field. The giraffe followed the girl with long lanky legs, similar to her own, all the way back to the barn. The two had bonded already, after just one day. It seemed Jo had a way with animals. Once Millie was secured inside the barn, the girl headed for the farmhouse. Dylan was done working for the day and joined her inside, while Daniel finished up in the field as promised. He tried to think of something to hum, just to fill the silence out there now that he was alone, but came up with nothing.

When he got to the last head of lettuce, he held it up, considered its weight, then tossed it in with the rest of the leafy cannon balls. As he carried the basket back toward the house, he felt a sense of pride he never experienced cleaning cages at the zoo or cutting grass for rich folks.

"So how much does dinner cost?" Daniel asked, entering the kitchen to see Jo and Dylan each draining a glass of lemonade.

"Hundred bucks," she said, filling up a glass for him.

"And how much do we get for a hard day's work in the salad factory?"

"Hundred bucks," she said with a smirk.

"So…if we want a meal, we pretty much broke even?"

"Yep."

"What about a shower? How much does that cost?"

"That's free. You both smell terrible. But you can't use the one in here. There's a water trough by the barn. Here's some soap." She handed him a box of laundry detergent from under the enormous sink.

"You're too kind," Daniel said, accepting the box. He was sweaty enough it didn't matter what kind of soap she offered. He might have used bleach if that was the only option.

"Hang on a minute," Jo said, drying her hands on her jeans. As she stomped her way to the second floor she shouted, "Don't you dare come up here!" They could hear her rummaging around upstairs. Every floorboard in this house seemed to have an awful lot to complain about. Every step was marked with a squeak. This place had to be at least a hundred years old, and his bones were starting to hurt, but that only added character, albeit the character of a wheel chair bound centenarian stuck in a nursing home where nobody visited him, and sugar and caffeine were forbidden. All the old farmhouse really wanted was a light sanding for the floor, maybe some oil for the hinges, and a big family gathering at Christmas. Not so much to ask.

When Jo returned a few moments later, she had a pile of clean clothes in her arms. "Hope you both happen to be 34's." She handed over a pair of well-worn jeans and a t-shirt to each brother. Dylan, who had filled out nicely since puberty, was in fact a 34, but Daniel would have to make do with the loose fit. Unsure who they were borrowing these clothes from, they went outside, ready for a sponge bath in the animal trough.

The boys found the hose, then filled the trough with fresh water. Each took a handful of the grainy detergent, mixed it with a little water to form a paste, then began scrubbing away, starting with those pungent armpits.

Surprisingly refreshed, they put on their borrowed clothing. Daniel had to roll up the cuffs on the jeans, but Dylan was tall enough to get by. This would have to work. It was all they had to choose from. It wasn't like they packed a suitcase for this giraffe-stealing trip. It all happened so fast, so spontaneously, they didn't have anything but the clothes on their backs and the money (that used to be) in their wallets. Oh. And a sixteen-foot giraffe.

As they walked back across the driveway, Daniel gestured towards two doors set on an angle at the base of the house. It was the entrance to a root cellar, some sort of underground storage, but it was secured with five separated chains with five separate key locks, plus a combination lock for good measure. Daniel teased, "What do you think she keeps down there? Dead bodies?"

Dylan smirked and replied, "Maybe that's where she takes her lovers to ravish them at night. Bet she ties them up and everything."

"You wish," Daniel scoffed. "This girl is as prude as they come."

"You think?" Dylan asked, curious what his wise sibling picked up on that he hadn't. Daniel was good with girls, at methodically figuring them out. He even figured out how to get a girl into bed his junior year, regularly at that, which was the most awe-inspiring thing to young Dylan. He of course wanted to know every last detail about his sibling's horizontal adventures occurring every day after school, but his tight-lipped hero of an older brother wouldn't spill. That made it all the more fascinating. Daniel would come home with nail marks in his back and hickeys on his chest, but never a genuine smile on his face.

Daniel replied, "Nobody in their right mind would mess with a girl like her. Too much of a hassle. You can melt ice, but she's a glacier."

"I kinda like her anyway."

"Yes. You've mentioned that about a thousand times today."

Dylan smiled brightly. Then, a wrinkle pressed his forehead upwards, like something serious and potentially devastating just crossed his mind. "You think her tits are done growing? Or do you think maybe she's got a little more filling out to do? I mean, she seems like she could probably go up size or two, right? She's young. Still got some growing to do, right?"

"Maybe you should ask her," Daniel replied, opening the front door. "Jo," Daniel began, "My brother has something he wants to ask you."

Red in the face, Dylan swallowed hard and managed to cover for his cup size curiosities by asking, "Should we wait for your dad to join us?"

Josephine was humming as she fried up something in the skillet. Her hair was wet. She smelled more heavily of citrus now, that sweet soapy scent Daniel noticed in the field. She served up three plates and answered, "He came by while you two were getting cleaned up. Said he's got a dinner date tonight, so we should go on ahead without him."

"So you told him about us?" Dylan asked, curious why her dad didn't come out to introduce himself. Maybe he saw they were bathing and simply wanted to respect their privacy.

"Yeah. He said if you two want to stay on a few days, help me in the fields, you're welcome to. He'll pay you on Friday. You have to sleep in the barn, though. That's the rule."

Dylan grinned, pleased at how well this was all turning out. "We'd like that."

Jo pulled in an extra chair from the living room, a room that was off limits to everyone but her, and they sat for a meal of fried ham and a plate of canned peas. The ham was rubbery and way too salty. The peas were gray, hardly vegetables compared to what was growing outside, but they ate it, chasing it all with hard dinner rolls, satisfying their hungry bellies.

Back in the barn, preparing for another night of sleeping on the ground covered in horse blankets, Dylan said, "Night Daniel. Love you."

"Love you too."

"Don't let me die in my sleep."

"I won't."

CHAPTER THREE

"There you are, you pretty, pretty girl," Josephine said, stepping inside the barn with a bowl full of sliced apples, a box of graham crackers, plus one head of lettuce. "I brought you breakfast in bed, sweet girl."

"Do we get that luxury too?" Daniel teased from his resting spot on the ground, accepting she was more interested in Millie than her hired help. He was dog-tired, his arms were sore from the day before, and he wasn't sure how useful they'd be today.

"You get breakfast in the kitchen," Jo replied, handing Millie an apple slice. After chewing awhile, Millie spit a piece at Dylan. She was a cantankerous beast when she wanted to be, but given her size, she could get away with anything. That old giraffe was a sixteen-foot nuisance.

"Did you eat already?" Daniel inquired, stretching his tender arms above his head to make sure he still could.

"Yeah. My dad and I ate about an hour ago, when you're *supposed* to have breakfast when you run a farm. You two sleepyheads will have to deal with the leftovers."

Daniel glanced at his watch. It was 7:08 a.m. "Do you get up this early every day, or is this a test?"

"If you're gonna get any work done, might as well get up before the sun and get on with it."

Millie polished off the crackers, chomped away on the lettuce, then made a move for Daniel's hair again, but he dodged her searching lips and left the barn, closing the door behind him this time.

He was barely functional this early in the day, and running after an escaped giraffe was something he hoped to avoid in the future. He wasn't built for speed, or endurance, for that matter.

Daniel's heart sank when he saw what was in the bowl on the table. It was the same chunky white stuff again, bland and slimy. What made it worse, he still had no idea what it was supposed to be, but, just like the morning before, he was awfully hungry so he ate it and he got through one cup of coffee as well, trying not to gag on the thick black sludge.

Glancing out the window to the clothesline, Daniel asked, "Are those our clothes?"

"Uh huh."

"You washed them?"

"Uh huh."

"Let me guess," Daniel began. "You're gonna charge us a hundred bucks for doing our laundry."

"Nah," she chuckled. "They were really stinky. A thank you will suffice."

After considering this a moment, Daniel said, "Well...thank you."

The men's work boots by the door hadn't moved since the day before or, if they had, they'd been put back exactly the same way, lined up with the floor boards, perpendicular with the wall. There was only one dirty dish in the sink, just the one coffee mug too. Perhaps Mr. Larsen cleaned up after himself, while his daughter did not. Daniel was getting mighty curious about this invisible father of hers. He must be a peculiar man indeed. There was a photograph of him on the fridge, next to a buck-toothed Josephine. She was probably eight or nine years old when it was taken, right in the middle of her awkward phase. She hadn't grown into her beautiful features yet, but her hair was just as red as ever, daring red. Her father looked pale but strong and, if there were any doubts about his ancestry even with a name like Johan Larsen, the photograph cleared all that up. This man was from a Scandinavian bloodline, no doubt about it. He had a full beard that was so blond it was almost white, twinkling blue eyes like Santa Claus, plus rosy red cheeks to complete his jolly appearance. His cheekbones and brows were sharp and looked more Viking than anything, but didn't make him appear any less kind. Josephine didn't resemble her father other than their small clever smiles.

Another snapshot caught Daniel's interest. This one was of a mother and father with a little baby, sitting on the front porch of the farmhouse. The photo was faded and dated, but the farmhouse never looked better. It was freshly painted, crisp white with hunter green shutters. Nowadays, the house was almost gray and the dingy shutters were peeling. The woman in the photo, an Irish lass perhaps, looked exactly like Jo, right down to the shape of her nostrils and the precise tone of their hair. As impossible as it may have been, they even appeared to share the same constellation of freckles across their upturned noses. It was an uncanny resemblance. Johan looked much younger in this photo without his beard. His hair was long then, whitish blond and wavy. Daniel chuckled at the outfits this family was wearing. It was definitely the late 1980's, not the most fashionable era in history.

Daniel had so many questions about Jo and her fair-skinned family, but they didn't know each other yet and it wasn't clear if she wanted to be known. She was private and wasn't sorry for it. This was her house; she didn't need to share it. This was her father; she didn't need to introduce him to some lowly field workers, especially temporary ones. This was her cooking and, as disgusting as it may have been, it was edible and satiated hunger. She had nothing to prove to anyone.

"I'll clean up," Daniel offered once they'd finished eating. He volunteered mainly because he wanted to be in the kitchen alone for a few minutes in order to investigate the ingredients he'd consumed two days straight. He was pretty sure he knew which container she used to make the meal yesterday, so all he needed was a second or two to open it, smell it, and see if he could identify what was in it. Jo stacked the dishes in the sink for him, then went upstairs without saying a word. By the clamoring way she walked up those stairs, you'd think she weighed over three hundred pounds. Dylan was talking to Daniel about Jo again, not about her heavy-footedness, but speculating his chances of getting her were high since she didn't have a lot of other boys to choose from around here. Daniel wasn't really listening. He'd learned to tune Dylan out long ago.

Jo's loud footsteps were directly above now. The coast was clear. Daniel reached up for the blue porcelain canister, the second one from the left, and opened the lid. It was filled to the brim with twenty-dollar bills, all rolled up neatly and secured with a rubber band. With a wrinkle of confusion stuck in his forehead, he replaced the cash-filled canister and tried the one next to it. Yes, this was the one, full of sawdust. He shook the contents, leaned the container on its side so the sunshine could help him identify the substance, then plucked out a piece of flaky white stuff. "Oatmeal?" he said to himself, surprised at his findings. "That's supposed to be oatmeal?"

"Huh?" Dylan asked from across the kitchen, in another world completely.

"Nothing," Daniel replied, putting the canister back where he found it. As proficient as Josephine may have been with herding animals and harvesting crops by hand, she couldn't cook to save her life. How could her father stand to eat this slop? No wonder he had so many dinner dates and always seemed to be missing from the table at mealtime.

By lunch, the boys were sweaty, a little sunburned, but in good spirits. They had slept well on the thick blankets in the barn, eaten something at the beginning of the day, had a place for their stolen giraffe for the time being, and the promise of gas money in their future. Plus, they had a pretty girl humming sweet songs just a few yards away, her red hair shining in the sun. Dylan was smitten already. He could have been tasked with pulling out his own fingernails and that would have been fine, as long as he could watch Josephine Larsen bent over a basket of string beans. Millie stayed by Jo's side the whole morning, eating about a fifth of whatever Jo pulled from the ground, plus anything that resembled a leaf. She was a hungry giraffe but Jo was glad to share.

The highlight of the afternoon was when an unsuspecting Dylan stood under Millie, making jokes about how she was the only source of shade. While he refreshed himself in her looming shadow, it started to rain. Only, it wasn't rain. Daniel and Jo were cackling hard right from the first drop, while Dylan just stood there, unsure this was really happening. He was so traumatized he couldn't move. Dylan's blue eyes were bulging, but at least he had the commonsense to close his mouth. From a few feet away, Daniel watched in amazement as Millie finished relieving her very full bladder all over his sibling. He didn't feel the need to bail his brother out this time. In fact, he sort of reveled in this. Poor Dylan wasn't used to being the butt of the joke. He wasn't used to getting peed on by giraffes either.

Never missing an opportunity to show off his pecs, Dylan stripped down part of the way, wringing out yellow water from his borrowed t-shirt, and asked Jo if his other clothes were dry yet. Unable to speak, still lost in hysterics, she gestured towards the clothesline behind the farmhouse and nodded. Daniel, finally quelling his laughter, took a rare opportunity to make his brother feel a little worse. "You look...pissed," he teased. Dylan made a big show of flicking him off, forced a cheeky smile, then started walking towards the clothesline.

Stinking of pee, Dylan found his clothes on the line next to some striped sheets. As he unpinned his t-shirt and jeans, he noticed some other clothes too. They weren't men's clothing, belonging to Mr. Larsen. They were all Josephine's, all jeans and t-shirts that a skinny teenager of either gender might wear. Her ugly nightgown was there too, blowing in the breeze with all its length, all its hideous ruffles. He fingered the soft material, wondering if his brother was right about her being a prude. But then, he saw a pair of her underwear. He looked back at the field, wondering if Jo could see what he was about to do, then freed her white cotton panties from the line. They were tiny. Sure, they were plain, nothing particularly sexy, but it was the size of them that intrigued Dylan the most, all the glorious things hidden by such a small amount of fabric. He'd never actually touched a girl's underwear before. This in itself was exciting. He held them to his face, inhaled the clean soapy smell of cotton, then stuffed them into his pocket. Dylan decided then and there this would be the girl he'd finally go all the way with. Though she didn't know it yet, she would be the chosen one. Now all he had to do was impress the hell out of her, be as charming as humanly possible, and pretty soon, she'd be begging him to handle all of her undergarments.

    Daniel and Josephine were working a line of beans together, recovered from their laughter by now. They didn't have much to talk about, so they just exchanged a smile every now and then. It seemed they only spoke when they had something real to say, and, until they did, the silence suited them just fine. Truthfully, it wasn't totally silent. Jo filled whatever void there may have been with her quiet humming, singing softly with her throat, keeping her lips sealed as she carried the barely audible notes. Daniel wanted to tell her he liked her humming, that it made him feel calm, but didn't want to let on he noticed.

    While Daniel worked, he glanced across the field to watch Millie inspecting a grouping of white wooden boxes that were raised up off the ground. Another grouping was placed at the opposite corner of the field, as if to mark the boundaries. He'd noticed the boxes earlier, but wasn't sure of their purpose. There were an awful lot of contraptions and tools around here he'd never seen before. Farm country was vastly different from the city, even the suburbs. Off in the distance, Millie appeared to be sneezing after sniffing these mysterious white boxes, then she set off running and shaking her head like a bug flew up her nose.

"I think she must have found the bees," Jo said, watching Millie's face shake repeatedly, her ears twitching wildly as she trotted away from the white boxes.

"Bees?" Daniel asked.

"Mr. Wessel's bees. Those are his hives."

"You let someone keep their beehives on your farm?"

"The bees like our crops and the crops need those bees. Mr. Wessel comes by every now and again to scrape out the honey and check on the queen, but other than that, we don't bother the bees and the bees don't bother us. We help each other. Everybody wins."

"Everybody except that there trouble-making giraffe. Bet she was after the honey. She eats everything, I don't understand why. Look at her, I think she got stung on her face."

"Did you get stung, sweet girl?" Jo asked Millie, who was approaching and looking sorry for herself. "Gotta leave the bees alone, ya hear me?"

Millie snorted a response and shook her head again, making her ears flop in annoyance. She swayed her long neck backwards and used her nubby horns to scratch her haunches, tending to one of her many bee stings.

Jo scratched Millie's front legs, offering sympathy to the old girl who couldn't seem to stay out of trouble. Jo nodded towards her basket of freshly picked green beans and said, "I think I'm gonna go into town and drop all this off."

"Can I go with you?" Daniel asked, a bit too eagerly. More coolly this time around, he added, "It's just…we need some stuff. Like toothpaste and shaving cream and shampoo. Stuff like that."

"Um…okay. But just you, not your brother."

"Sounds good to me," he said, glancing over at Dylan who was rinsing his urine-soaked hair in the water trough by the barn. He needed a break from the chatterbox.

With a brief explanation as to where they were headed and instructions on finishing up the string beans, Dylan was left on his own. Jo locked the front door to the farmhouse so he wouldn't be tempted to snoop. She didn't trust him, or anyone else for that matter. Maybe she had a right to. Thinking only of impressing her, of all the things that might happen if he played his cards right, Dylan got back to work on the beans, knowing how proud she'd be if she came home to see he'd done the rest of the patch all by himself. He was bound to win her over.

In the white pickup truck, loaded up with baskets of rhubarb, beans, and lettuce, Daniel and Josephine drove towards the town of Morton. The road looked so different in the daylight. The last time Daniel was on this road was the night before last, when they had no idea where they were in the vast state of Nebraska, with a hungry giraffe in the back. They passed by some trees, then more rolling farmland. It was beautiful out here, a part of America that demanded pride. After just fifteen minutes or so, they arrived. It wasn't much of a town, but it was their destination, as evidenced by Jo pulling off the road into the parking lot near the market.

"I thought you said the nearest town was ninety miles away," Daniel said, a little ticked off, but mostly amused by this discovery.

"Did I say ninety?" she asked playfully. "I meant to say nine."

"Who's the liar now?" he teased, unloading a basket of lettuce from the bed. Jo took a load too, although it looked to be a bit heavy for her to manage, though she never asked for assistance, and then led Daniel towards a frail looking man wearing overalls. The man smiled with his crinkly brown eyes and greeted them.

"Oh Josephine. You get purtier and purtier every time I lay eyes on you," the old man said, patting her cheek. "You tell your daddy he better watch out. He's gonna be running off your boyfriends pretty soon." The man looked over to Daniel now, narrowing his eyes as he scanned him from head to toe, and mumbled, "Maybe this is one of the boyfriends who needs running off."

Jo explained, "This is just Daniel. He's helping us with the harvest. Don't you worry, Mr. Ulrich."

"Mmm hmmm," Mr. Ulrich replied, his tone suggesting intense disapproval. He motioned for Jo to come with him, but not Daniel. While the old man used his shaky hands to count out a hundred and seventy dollars in cash for the produce, he took the opportunity to share some wisdom with the young girl he'd watched grow up over the years. "You best be careful, Ms. Josephine. Boys these days. Nothing but trouble. You just gotta be watchful. They go after one thing and one thing only, and I don't have the heart to tell you exactly what that is."

Jo smiled at the old man, looked into his cloudy eyes. He had about four hairs left on his head, which shivered as a warm gust of wind blew across his sun-damaged scalp. "I'll be very careful. I promise. Whatever he may or may not be after, he won't be getting it from me."

"That's my girl," the old man said, patting her shoulder this time. "You tell your daddy we need to go fishing soon, after he's done with the fields. We haven't been since last fall. I miss his dirty jokes. Don't tell him I said that." The old man gave a cheeky grin and went back to whatever it was he did all day at the market, sorting vegetables, weighing goods, paying farmers for their bushels and selling to grocers from other towns near and far. He was also a bookie when it suited him.

"The drugstore's on the other side of town," Jo explained to Daniel.

He opened the door to the truck, ready for a drive.

She laughed and crossed the street, pointing to a sign that read *Dickerson's Drugs Since 1934*. Daniel smirked and closed the door, catching up with her. By the other side of town, she meant the other side of the street. The town had one traffic light, that's all. From where he was standing, he could see a church at one end, another church at the other end, a bakery café, an auto repair shop, a restaurant, a doctor's office, a grade school, and a store that had all sorts of odd things for sale on the sidewalk: everything from tractor parts to cooking utensils to ladies' dresses and light bulbs. All of these little shops, sandwiched in between dueling houses of God.

Before going inside, Jo gave Daniel a quick tour of Morton, Nebraska, just by pointing her finger. "My parents got married in that church," she said, gesturing down the two-lane street towards a white steeple. "My momma sang in the choir." She gestured toward another building, working her way down Main Street. "I went to school there till fifth grade, then my dad home schooled me." The grade school was a flat roofed building with a playground beside it. There wasn't a bus drop-off zone, like the public schools Daniel attended over the years. He'd never been in such a small town before, a compact area of civilization. Jo continued, "That café is where you go if you want to know everyone else's business, and that restaurant over there is where you go when you want your secrets to be safe. At least that's what my daddy told me." She let a small smile press her lips upward, as though this verbal tour of her hometown was against the rules. "That school over there, it may not look like much but it's the only real-deal tornado shelter around here. You wouldn't think it, but downstairs…it's like a vault. I've been in it twice."

"You get tornados here?"

"This is the Midwest. Course we do." She pointed up at a lamppost to the dated-looking warning siren covered in carcass-filled cobwebs.

Jo opened the door to the drug store and began filling a hand carrier as she roamed the narrow aisles. Daniel got to work gathering things for him and his brother: a stick of deodorant, a bar of soap, a razor, some girlie shampoo, a tube of toothpaste, and a toothbrush to share. They always shared everything, including germs. Besides, Daniel had less than twenty dollars to spend, a small advance from Jo, so whatever he chose needed to come in under budget. Luckily, the prices in this store weren't up to market rates, probably hadn't been in twenty years, so when Daniel checked out at the register he was pleasantly surprised by his $8.75 total.

Jo spent a little more. She bought some hair elastics, a three-pack of Cherry Chapstick, two hoses for a houseplant water sprayer, a small scale for weighing goods in ounces, some latex gloves, a box of gallon-sized plastic baggies, and a pack of Marlboro Reds.

The woman at the register handed over the cigarettes and said, "You're so sweet getting your daddy's smokes every week." Her nametag read Brenda even though everyone in this town knew everybody else. Nametags were a formality.

"You know he can't start the day without one," Jo replied lightheartedly.

Brenda smiled, her gaudy pink lipstick creasing deep into every wrinkle of her seventy-something-year-old mouth. "You tell him we're still waiting on him to look at the AC unit. If anyone can figure out what's wrong with it, it's your daddy. He's so good with that stuff."

"I'll remind him. He's awfully busy lately. I'm sure you understand."

"Course I do, sugar." Brenda handed Jo her change. "Is he going to the protest in Lincoln next Saturday?"

"I'm not sure," Jo replied, looking a little uneasy.

"I know he and Art Buford and Mr. Sullivan and all them are real passionate about the...the...what's it called, with the bees goin' missing?"

"Colony Collapse Syndrome," Jo replied, much more self-assured this time.

"That's the one. I know your daddy's wantin' to get that bill passed to ban them pesticides."

"Yes, ma'am." Jo clutched the bag, ready to depart and keep the conversation pleasant, but then she turned back to the counter and the old woman standing behind it, gathering a little courage to speak her mind. "Ms. Brenda, it's not just the pesticides. It's all the monocropping the government is forcing on everyone around these parts. It's bad for the land, it's bad for the bees, and it's bad for us, for all of us, not just the farmers."

"How do you figure, sweetheart?" Brenda asked, adjusting her glasses.

"If everyone grows just one kind of crop, soybeans, corn, whatever, the bees don't have much to live off of so they die or they move on. Then, more pests come, they don't care about variety, like the bees do. More pests mean more pesticides. Pesticides kill what's left of the bees. They hurt the soil too. Pretty soon, some of these big shot commercial farmers around here are gonna be sitting on a hundred acres of dead earth. It's only a matter of time."

Brenda shifted a little, not wanting to debate politics or any other hot topics in her old age. "Well, if the land goes bad, they can just raise cattle on grain, like you and your daddy used to do."

"Yes, ma'am. I suppose they can do just that," Jo said, offering an apologetic smile as she turned to leave. "Have a good day, Ms. Brenda. I'll see you next week."

On the way home, Daniel dared to ask, "What does your dad do?"

"He's a farmer."

"I mean...what does he do during the day? Does he usually help you in the fields or does he leave you alone a lot to go protest bills and things?"

"I like working on our farm and I don't mind being alone."

"Me too. I like being alone too. But Dylan's always around."

"Does he always act like this?"

Daniel exhaled a laugh. "Like what? Like he's never seen a pretty girl before?"

Jo's gray eyes peeked over at him, but her face remained forward. She cleared her throat and said, "Essentially."

"Um. You know. He's...totally harmless, just a little goofy sometimes. I think he may be a little love struck with you, that's all. Is he getting on your nerves?"

"I've never heard somebody talk so much."

"Know what you mean. I wish his mouth had a zipper."

"You two are pretty close, huh?"

"Sometimes we wanna kill each other but…yeah, we're close. He's all I have. We're a family, just the two of us. We'd do anything for each other."

"I can tell."

"What gave it away? Helping him steal a giraffe?"

"You only bought one toothbrush and I don't think its 'cause you forgot to get a second one for your brother. You have to be pretty close with somebody to share a toothbrush."

That was it. That was all they had to say for the time being. Jo hummed a little, nothing recognizable, just a soft tune she probably thought nobody could hear but her. The window was cracked, letting a slight breeze pull strands of red hair away from her ponytail and blow them in her face. She was so peaceful just then. Daniel snuck a peek at her side profile, her upturned nose, those delicate ears.

When she turned to catch him staring at her, Daniel quickly found something to talk about. Picking up the blue plastic gadget that was haphazardly wired to her tape deck, he asked, "What is this thing. Is this like…an iPod or something?"

"It's my music box," Jo said with a grin. "Yes, it's like an iPod, if by that you mean an MP3 player. It's not the fancy kind you probably have back home."

Daniel wished he had an iPod. He wished he had a cell phone too, and a newer watch that actually kept time, and maybe a warmer winter coat for those cold days in January up north. There were a lot of material things Daniel wished he had, but he didn't dwell on that too much, like Dylan was prone to do and even beg for from time to time. "What kind of music do you listen to?" he asked, trying to operate the gadget that was the size and heft of a block of cheese. This music box of hers was ancient in technology years, and it probably belonged in a museum. He could only guess what kind of computer it would hook up too. No flat screens around here, no high speed Internet. In this year, 2007 A.D., it seemed the Larsen's were not the type to save up their pennies for silly things such as these.

"Little bit of everything," she replied. "I really like Doug Burr. He has the most soulful voice I've ever heard."

"Don't know him."

Jo took the music box and punched a few buttons so Daniel could hear this soulful voice for himself. "This one's called 'Always Travel Light'."

What an appropriate selection. Daniel always traveled light, from foster home to foster home, and now to Josephine's farm in the Heartland of America. It was so easy to leave his last home, just days ago. There was nothing in that spacious brick Colonial other than a few drawers full of clothes, a couple of overdue books from the library, and an alarm clock on the shared nightstand that his brother could sleep through despite its obnoxious volume. He wouldn't miss any of it.

Rolling down the long gravel driveway, just beyond the gate of old growth trees, Josephine nodded towards the shirtless Dylan in the field who was diligently dropping beans into the baskets she left for him. He looked up to see the truck and started working even faster.

"He's working hard today," she said, not impressed, just stating the facts.

"How unusual."

"You mind helping him finish up? I've got another errand I need to run before it gets dark out."

They parted ways. Daniel met back up with his brother in the field and put his fingers to work plucking beans. Millie was over by the trees, munching away, recovered from her bee stings. She was totally free here, free to roam. The forest and underbrush surrounding the property was too thick for her to pass through easily, so the only way she could escape was if she went down the driveway, where the trees had been cleared out to form the narrow passage, and she hadn't figured that out just yet. Or maybe she just liked it here, had no intention of making a break for it. The boys kept an eye on her anyway. The only thing to steal Daniel's attention was catching a glimpse of Josephine on the far side of the field, opposite the house. She disappeared into the trees, slipped into this other world, and he looked up just in time to see a flash of her pale yellow t-shirt. Where was she going?

Far too curious about this quiet girl and her very private life, Daniel excused himself for a bathroom break, at least that's what he told Dylan, and followed after Jo. The forest was much darker than the field, a thick canopy gave a cool shade from the late afternoon sun. His footsteps were soft as he picked up her trail, heading deeper and deeper into the woods. For a moment, he lost her. It wasn't until he heard the sound of somebody sniffling that he was able to locate her once more. The faint smell of burning cigarettes confirmed she was back there.

Quietly approaching from behind, Daniel stopped when he was able to see Josephine clearly. She was kneeling on the ground in front of a large rock, which was about the size of a pumpkin. There were no other rocks like this one in the forest. It was out of place, white with gray veining, something from a quarry. A small bouquet of pink wild flowers was set in front of this strange boulder, like an offering. A lit cigarette lay atop the rock, slowly becoming ash as it burned itself down all on its own, like a stick of incense. He watched Josephine's shoulders shaking as she hugged herself and remained low to the ground, staring at the rock. Daniel noticed the dirt beside the rock, the long area of forest ground that had been disturbed at some point, dug up and filled back in, but not too recently.

Josephine turned at the sound of a branch snapping.

Daniel looked down at his foot, to the disloyal branch beneath it, split in two. He looked back up at Jo, knowing full well he'd been busted. At a loss for words, he approached her, ready to explain himself and apologize for his snooping. As he got closer, he could see just how bloodshot her eyes were, the flushing on her tear-stained cheeks. Slowly, she stood up and wiped the salt water from her face. Then, she gave a small laugh of disbelief, like she had a hard time wrapping her head around what was about to be unveiled.

After fidgeting with her thumbs for a moment, Jo lifted her arm towards the gravesite, then let it flop back to her side. She took a deep breath and said, "Daniel McElroy, I'd like you to meet my father."

CHAPTER FOUR

"He's...dead?"
"Yes."
"He's...not going to the protest in Lincoln over the weekend?"
"No."
"He...didn't eat breakfast with you this morning?"
"I haven't had breakfast with him in months."
"Holy crap," Daniel said, taking it all in, feeling dizzy as he started to grasp this elaborate web of lies she'd been spinning with such attention to detail. "How did he die?"
"An accident." Jo was always succinct, painfully so at times.
"Here?" Daniel asked, gesturing toward the grave.
She shook her head. "No. He was bringing the cattle in. I was in the barn cleaning. When I came out, he was being dragged by one of the bulls."
"Didn't he scream for help?"
"The ropes were around his neck. I think it must have happened pretty quick."
"Geez," Daniel said, scratching his cheek. "That's terrible. And you...you buried him here, all on your own?"
"Uh huh. He loved it back here. It's so peaceful." She was calm as she surveyed this serene place. Jo fiddled with the hem of her t-shirt, looking shy once more. Her fingers were so slender, elegantly

long, but her fingernails were short and ragged. They had dirt underneath them too. Those fingers said so much about this quiet girl.

"When did all this happen?" Daniel asked, moving closer still, letting her know he didn't think any less of her for lying by closing the gap between them.

"December 19th."

"Of this past year?"

"Yeah. Right before Christmas. It was snowing."

Putting the pieces together, he asked his next question only to be sure he had indeed put the pieces together correctly. "And you haven't told anyone in town?"

"You're the first to know the truth and I barely know *you* at all."

Daniel tilted his head back and looked up through the canopy. The trees rustled overhead, sending that shimmering sound of untouched nature right through to his bones. This was truly a peaceful place, layered with secrets and sadness, but also refreshment. The trees blocked out most of the sunshine, letting only a few dappled spots hit the forest floor. They swayed and rustled again, carrying whispers from leaf to limb. Those old growth trees kept Josephine's secrets all this time, gave her father shade in his final resting place when he could no longer protest on behalf of the bees.

"So you've been out here by yourself for almost seven months, running the farm on your own and letting everyone in town think your dad is just a busy, busy guy?"

"Pretty much."

"How? How're you doing it?"

"I had to sell the cattle. I couldn't handle them on my own. We had some workers too but I had to let them go, so nobody would catch on."

"So you traded in cows for crops?"

"We've always had some crops as a little side business. Now those crops are the main source of income. When I was ten, my dad asked me what I wanted to do with the farm because it was my farm too, and one day it would *all* be mine. He inherited it from his father but he never liked raising cattle much and he didn't expect I would either. I told him I wanted to grow things and raise smaller animals. I wanted to do both. He liked that idea. I love animals and I'm good at growing lots of stuff. My daddy said I'm a natural."

"I believe that. But does it pay? Can you get by?"

"Been getting by okay. Pretty soon I'll have enough money to start over with the livestock. I've got a plan."

"Pigs."

"Precisely."

"How long will it take you to save?"

"A few years. There's only so much I can grow in the fields. It looks like a lot of land, but it's not. Half of its being wasted right now, since the cows are gone. It's just gonna take some time, some money, but I've got a plan. I want lots of pigs and a blue barn, and fields full of vegetables, and hives full of bees. It's not so much to ask, but it's a lot to save for."

"What about the mortgage? What about bills?"

"I'm managing."

"By eating canned food and oatmeal?"

She cracked a smile. "It's edible, isn't it?"

"Barely."

Jo chuckled. "I care about getting those pigs and that barn more than I care about a decent meal."

"You're either the most persistent person I've ever met, or the most stubborn."

"Why? Because I'm not afraid to work hard and go after what I want?"

Daniel shrugged. He was stuck somewhere between pity and awe. She was one tough girl, inspiring in her independence.

"I'm from a long line of go-getters."

"I believe that too."

"My ancestors came over from Sweden, they were pioneers. They worked their tails off. But they got what they wanted in the end, they made a home and they earned money and lived well. I'm no different. I want to prosper here. I was born in that house and I'll never give it up. That's why you gotta swear to keep this a secret. Nobody can know about my dad. If they find out he's gone, I'll lose it all."

"You can't fool this town forever. They'll figure it out."

"I know. I'm lucky I've gotten away with it this long. Buying him cigarettes every week has been a good move. My dad smoked a cigarette when he woke up and one before bed, and if he didn't get a pack of Marlboro Reds every week from Brenda Neilson at Dickerson's Drugs, she'd know something was wrong."

Daniel stood close to her now, watching her blotchy pink eyes fill up with tears again at the very thought of giving up her home. "So how long are you gonna keep up the charade?" he asked with caution

"Till my eighteenth birthday."

"When's that?"

"Month and a half. Then I'm old enough to inherit the farm so it won't matter about my dad, long as I can keep making the payments. I did all the legal research, I have his Will and everything, but none of it matters if I'm underage. I have to be eighteen, there's no way around it. If anyone finds out he's dead before then, the bank will sell the house at auction and the state will put me in a home for unwanted kids and orphans, something awful like that."

Daniel smiled in understanding. "I know first-hand how unappealing that is, believe me."

"Oh," she said, taken by surprise. "I'm sorry, I didn't...I didn't know. I didn't mean to offend you." She looked up, truly sorry for her comment. She folded her arms, hugging her small frame. "I didn't realize you...were...um. I'm so sorry."

"Hey. It's okay. I'm free now, my brother too, so...yeah. It's okay." He stepped forward and rested his hand on her boney shoulder. It was the only way he could think of to let her know it was truly okay, no hard feelings. "I know all about the countdown to your eighteenth birthday too. My brother just turned eighteen the day before we showed up here and we left right on the mark. We'd been waiting on that day for so many years, waiting, waiting, waiting, bouncing from one foster home to the next, staying in homes with other unwanted kids in between."

She wiped her tears once more and looked Daniel in the eye. In a soft way, she asked, "Please don't tell anyone about all this. Not even your brother. Please. Swear you won't tell a soul."

"I swear it." He spit in his palm and held it out, ready to seal the deal with this childhood gesture of secrecy. The McElroy brothers were regular users of the spit handshake, ever since they were little. It was a gross thing to do, but it worked. They never told each other's secrets, never tested their loyalties. Saliva was like glue for loose lips.

Jo spit in her own palm then slapped her hand to his and squeezed. The spit between their hands made a squishy noise as they gave one firm shake. A slimy bond of trust had been made. Each of them wiped their palm on their jeans after that, then laughed once more at what they'd done. It seemed a little silly, considering.

"You have to tell me a secret now, it's only fair," she said.

"Hmmm," he hummed, pretending he had thousands of them. "Better sit down for this," he teased, taking a seat on the forest floor. She sat beside him, eager to get some dirt from Daniel. "Should I tell you about how I played with action figures in the bathtub till I was thirteen, or about the time Dylan and I stole our caseworker's car keys and went joyriding?"

"Tell me a real secret. Something nobody else knows."

Daniel thought about it. Yeah, there was one that came to mind. But did he really want to say it out loud? It was something he never discussed with anyone. Heck, Dylan didn't even know about it. He wasn't 100% sure it was true, but deep down, he was fairly certain it was. Daniel looked over at Jo, her trustworthy gray eyes waiting on him. He bent his legs and rested his elbows on his knees. "I think my mom might have been raped. I think…that's I how I got here…in the world, I mean."

Jo's sweet face turned serious. "Why would you think something like that?"

"I was really young when she left us, I hardly remember her much, but I remember her taking me to some sort of support group one time, and I sat on her lap, and everyone was looking at me real strange. I remember them other women saying how brave she was. They said that word over and over: *brave*. And when I was a little older, I remember my grandmother saying something once about how people can be blessings in disguise. She told me I was one. She said good things can come from horrible circumstances that should never happen to nobody. I never really understood that till a few years ago, long after Grams was gone, and there wasn't nobody else for me to ask. I don't blame my mom for giving me up. I think I would have done the same thing if I was in her shoes. I'm just glad to be alive, really. Of all the mothers who ain't ready to be mothers, specially with the way it happened, I'm just glad she went through with me."

Jo had nothing to add. She pulled her knees to her chest, just the way Daniel had done, keeping herself protected physically and emotionally. She scraped the toe of her boot with her other foot, smearing dirt in a line along the inside. "So I suppose you never knew your dad?"

"Nope."

"What about Dylan's dad?"

"He stuck around for a little while, but then he left too, just like all them other boyfriends. He was really rough with my mom, with me too. I don't remember much about him but I remember figuring out how to wedge a chair under the door handle at night to keep me and Dylan safe. My mom had a knack for picking these kinds of guys."

"What else do you remember about your mom?"

"She was beautiful. I remember that perfectly. She had blue eyes, like Dylan. She had brown wavy hair, like me. But she cried all the time. She wasn't happy. I think…we made her unhappy. Me and Dylan. We ruined her life. She didn't know what to do with us, she didn't want us."

Jo shifted, hugging her thin arms around her knees. She watched Daniel, waiting for him to finish his story.

Daniel bit at a hangnail on his thumb. The forest all around him was quiet now. The wind died down so he could continue, uninterrupted. Jo, all these trees, they were all waiting for him to speak again. "When she had enough of us, my mom took me and Dylan to our grandmother's house. She lived in Harrisburg. That's in Pennsylvania."

Jo cracked a smile, quickly flashing her teeth in a silly grin at his sharing of facts, then forced her face back to its normal neutral expression. She knew where Harrisburg was. She could probably name the state capitals in alphabetical order too. "My grandma knew she was taking us in. She knew my mom wasn't coming back. I was almost four, Dylan was barely talking yet, but my grandma took us anyway. She was such a sweet lady, my grandma. She could cook like...like...I don't even know. She was an amazing cook. I remember sitting in her kitchen watching her make stuff, mostly cookies and sweet things like that. The house always smelled like a bakery. I miss that smell. I miss her."

"Did she pass?"

"Yeah. She passed away in her sleep. She was so old. I don't think she'd ever been young a day in her life. I can't picture her any other way, other than old and wrinkly with her white hair pulled back in a bun."

"Was she sick?"

"Not sure. She was seventy-three when she passed. I was nine by then, Dylan was about to turn eight. Dylan found her. He thought she was napping, he got into bed with her like he did sometimes after school. I guess he figured it out, that she was dead, but he never screamed or nothing. I came in to complain about how hungry I was 'cause it was past suppertime, and Dylan was just sittin' on the bed, biting on his nails, rocking back and forth, starin' at her. He's still afraid he's gonna die in his sleep."

"That's so sad," Josephine said quietly.

"Really? I dunno. I think it's the best way to go. I hope I die in my sleep when the time comes. I don't want to be old or get sick. I just wanna slip away in my bed, tucked in forever, with someone sleeping next to me who loves me, even if it's a little brat like Dylan."

"I guess considering the other ways to die, it sounds okay. Better than being strangled to death by a cattle lead. Or a toxic lump in your breast."

Daniel stopped biting his thumb and looked up. He wasn't sure she meant to say that last part so he asked, "Who's got a lump?"

"My mom."

"Is she getting treatment?"

Jo smiled and shook her head no. "She's long gone. I don't remember anything about her." Something changed in her face just then. Her brow furrowed, her jaw tightened, and tears spilled from her bloodshot eyes once more. "I will never understand why she did what she did. I'll never understand her."

"What do you mean?"

"She refused to get help. She had a lump and she could have gotten some help. This was in 1990, it wasn't like chemo wasn't available. She could have gotten help. But no. She thought God gave her that lump for a reason and she had no right to take it out. She didn't believe in medicine, only faith. Guess what. God put that lump in her to kill her. God didn't like all the prayers she was praying for healing. God didn't want me to have a mother to braid my hair or sing me to sleep."

Josephine's tears poured faster now. Her breathing turned erratic and choppy. She put her hands over her face, hiding her pain, and let it all out. Every sob was heavier than the last. Unsure how to comfort a crying girl who lost both her parents so tragically, Daniel scooted closer to her and wrapped two strong arms around her shoulders, holding her tight enough that each time she shook, he shook too. He could feel her hot tears soaking through his t-shirt as she moved her head and nestled her face into his chest.

Every so often, she sniffled, inhaling her snot back before it could leak out onto poor Daniel's borrowed shirt. He wouldn't have minded. Being soaked in her nose runoff would have been fine if it helped comfort her in some way.

They stayed like that for quite some time. He let one hand stroke her pointy elbow and the other one stroke her boney backbone. Soon, her shoulders stopped shaking and her sobs lessened. Still, she didn't move from her spot, wrapped up in Daniel's arms with her cheek to his chest. When she did finally move her face away, Daniel got a good long look at her wet gray eyes, surrounded by blotchy pinkness. Her gray eyes were the color of a thunderstorm, of river stones, of his favorite flannel shirt. They were the saddest eyes he'd ever seen, but they were by far the prettiest.

Before he realized what was happening, Josephine's lips were on his, warm and tender. He felt a wisp of air from her nose pass over his cheek, a breath of relief like she wasn't sure his lips would be there to meet hers. After a few seconds of being surprised and unprepared for her sudden kiss, Daniel finally closed his wide eyes and reached up to cup the back of her head under her red ponytail, then pressed her face closer to his. His thumb traced over her jaw, right in front of her delicate ear. Feeling brave but mostly nervous, he took a cautious taste, then another, and another. She tasted like Cherry Chapstick, sweet and uncomplicated.

It had been almost two years since Daniel kissed anyone like this, what he liked to call an all-or-nothing-kiss, not since his high school sweetheart gave him one final kiss goodbye before she broke his heart at the end of the summer, saying college was for new beginnings. Daniel didn't have a new beginning. He had one more year of high school to finish, Dylan had two, and he wasn't going anywhere without his brother, no matter what. His brother was his everything.

Oh shit. His brother. Dylan Michael McElroy. The handsome young man with an amusing lack of commonsense, who shared half of his genes, loved the female race and had a major thing for the girl Daniel was currently kissing. Daniel quickly pulled his mouth away, leaving her with parted lips in the air, eyes still closed. She wasn't expecting the kiss to end so abruptly.

"What?" she asked, barely a whisper. "Do you have a girlfriend or something?"

"No," Daniel replied, standing up quickly. He had to get away from her, fast.

"Then what?" she tried again, her cheeks turning pink with embarrassment.

Daniel was speechless. What words was he supposed to use now? How could he tell her he liked her, that this kiss, albeit brief, was the best thing to happen to him in a long, long time? How could he tell her he thought she was the prettiest girl he'd ever seen, a whole new level of beauty he wasn't familiar with and had no words to describe? How could he tell her he enjoyed her humming, that he was intrigued by the way she pulled plants from the ground, that he adored her thin wrists, her pale skin, the folds of her ears, and her smell, even when she was a little sweaty? He liked her, plain and simple. But he couldn't like her. He wasn't allowed to like her. Dylan liked her first.

"I can't...do this. My brother...he...I can't...I'm such an asshole."

Daniel closed his eyes and ran his hands over his face then covered his mouth, removing the dampness from his lips, regretful of what he'd already done. That kiss would crush Dylan if he ever found out. How could he do something like this to the one person he loved, the one person he'd ever cared for, the one person he could put up with? Dylan was his life. The messes his little brother made were his messes too. They shared toothbrushes, punishment, and glory, but never girls. Never *ever* girls.

"I'm sorry. I don't know what else to say." With that, Daniel left her there in the clearing and walked off into the dense forest. She could sit there and cry about it to her dead father. Whatever. As much as Daniel may have liked that kiss, liked the girl attached to it too, he *loved* his brother and that mattered more than some silly girl and her sweet, sweet lips. Dylan was his one and only brother, they were blood, after all. "Bros before hos", they'd always sworn. His heart was thumping wildly as he pushed branches out of the way, walking as quickly as he could before the all-seeing trees could throw things at him for being such a jerk, for treating Josephine in such a way. He put his arms up over his head, shielding himself from the trees that were surely watching him, preparing to throw branches, jagged seedpods, even small sharp-toothed animals at him to ensure he never entered these sacred woods again. He started to run, fleeing this peaceful place. He wasn't welcome here anymore.

CHAPTER FIVE

"And another thing about giraffes..." Dylan went on, scraping his soup bowl clean without breaking from his chatter. "The females are the only ones with hair on their horns usually. The males don't have it cause it wears off or something."

"Male pattern baldness transcends the animal kingdom," Jo deadpanned, barely looking up. Her voice had never sounded so dry. She was just a lump, sitting at the kitchen table, probably wishing she was alone in this house and that she'd never met Daniel McElroy.

Unphased, Dylan continued, "Wanna hear something gross?" Nobody replied, but that didn't stop him. "Did you know a male giraffe will taste the pee of a female giraffe in order to tell if she's in heat? That's pretty gross, if you ask me. Can't the female just wink or something?"

Daniel and Josephine both glared at him for that last one. He'd been offering up all sorts of giraffe related facts throughout dinner, using words like 'ossicones', spitting back bits and pieces he picked up from re-reading the information plaques at the animal park every night while Daniel cleaned cages. Dylan was keeping the one-sided giraffe conversation going all on his own, talking with his mouth full. Jo had hardly anything to say. Neither did Daniel. But Dylan, as it turned out, had a whole lot to say and it didn't matter if anyone was actually listening. Josephine and Daniel quietly ate canned chicken soup, occasionally clinking the sides of their bowls to add background noise to Dylan's rambling and slurping.

Eventually, Josephine finished her soup. Staring at Dylan, watching him go on and on about nothing, she shook her head in disbelief. Then, she cracked a smile and stood up, walked behind Dylan, and clapped her hand over his mouth. He was quiet now, mostly in shock from her touch. She leaned in to whisper, "Shhh," into his left ear, sending tingles down his spine, making his blond hair stand up on end.

Jo glanced up at Daniel, exchanged a smirk with him, then removed her hand from Dylan's mouth. Dylan was awestruck by that soft whisper echoing in his ear. Never in a million years would it occur to the younger McElroy that he ought to be quiet once in a while.

Daniel crumpled up his napkin and tossed it across the table at his baby brother. "Usually, I just throw something and tell him to shut up. I'll have to remember your way, Jo, it's much more effective."

"Up yours," Dylan said, throwing the napkin back at his brother. In a sarcastic voice, Dylan said, "*Sorry* you're too stupid to think of something to talk about. *Sorry* I know a lot about giraffes. So *sorry* I…"

Jo was back, her hand muffling his words once more. "Shhhhh," she hissed, less gently than before. "You're giving me a headache."

"But I…" Dylan tried, but her hand cut him off again.

"You used up your words for the day. What will it take for you to be quiet?"

Daniel was amused. Watching Jo silence his annoying little brother was kind of sexy. He had never been one to beat up his younger sibling, or rat him out, but letting him get teased once in a while was different, especially if Jo was the one doing the teasing. Ready to add to his own amusement now that Dylan was in the hot seat, Daniel said, "Little brother, little brother, I bet…if you keep your mouth shut till ten o'clock, Jo will give you a goodnight kiss."

Dylan's eyebrows shot up with hope. Jo, still standing behind Dylan with her hand over his mouth, shook her head, declining. She looked a little surprised the same boy she kissed just hours ago would even offer such a thing, as if he had the right to pawn her off.

Knowing his brother all too well, Daniel tried again. "C'mon, Jo. If he can go the next three hours without speaking, you can't give him one little peck on the cheek? Seems like a good trade. I mean, we're talking…three…three hours of nothing, not even a peep. The last time he went that long without making a peep he had an umbilical cord."

Dylan mumbled something from behind Jo's hand. She moved it, letting him protest properly. "That's not true! What about when I'm asleep?"

Daniel chuckled. "Dude. You talk in your sleep. Always have. You grind your teeth too."

He could have disclosed more, telling Jo that Dylan cried in his sleep sometimes, that he passed gas like crazy, but Daniel wouldn't dream of humiliating his baby brother, especially in front of his crush.

Jo squinted at Daniel, processing it all. She turned to Dylan, "Okay. Just a kiss on the cheek, but you can't say anything, no noises either. Total silence or the deal is off."

Dylan grinned from ear to ear. He was finally going to get somewhere with Jo tonight. He closed his mouth, pretended to zip it shut, and threw the invisible key in the direction of the stove. The challenge was a go.

Jo gathered the dishes, smiling at the silence. Maybe a kiss would be worth it. This house had been quiet since her father's passing and she'd grown to love that. Kissing a chatty young man might be a good trade off to get that peaceful silence back for a while. Daniel took over at the sink, saying, "I don't mind cleaning up. You cooked."

"Thanks," she said, filling up a glass under the tap before giving him some space. "Are you two okay working through the end of the week? I can get you your money on Friday."

"Yeah, sounds good," Daniel replied for them both.

Since it was only Tuesday, this was marvelous news for the temporarily mute Dylan. He'd have three more days to impress her to death, and since she didn't seem all that impressed with his giraffe know-it-all or string bean harvesting skills, or even his ability to be quiet when bribed, he could use this extra time to figure out another way to win her over. Plus, a few more days of paid labor would be good too, since they were flat broke and stranded here till they could afford to move on. Jo told them a hundred bucks a day was what her dad could offer, and even though that worked out to be less than minimum wage since the hundred dollars was for both of them, they accepted. A hundred big ones was better than nothing. Plus, they got free room and board for the remainder of the week. It wasn't much, a blanket on the ground in an old barn and food that was barely palatable, but it was something. Millie was safe here too, which sweetened the deal somewhat.

"Look at her," Daniel said, nodding out the kitchen window as he rinsed a pot. Millie was moseying around the barn now, sniffing the roof, sticking her long prehensile tongue in the gutter to pull out some moss. She could pass for elegant sometimes, even if she was cleaning out a gutter with her face. Her long slow movements happened with such care, such deliberate measure, because everything took more effort to do at her size and age, even walking at her slow gate. Her beautiful patterning of auburn shapes outlined with tan edges made for a map of some unknown territory with landlocked countries butted up against each other, set just right to fill in all her terrain. Her dark eyes were so caring, always inspecting, and those long, long eyelashes were incredibly feminine, even on a creature that was anything but. Daniel smiled to himself, squeezing the soapy sponge. Millie the giraffe and Josephine the farm girl had a lot in common. They were both quiet girls, old souls with a red mane and long thin legs, who were drawn to Daniel for some reason, though he couldn't guess why. Neither Millie nor Josephine thought much of the other McElroy brother, though Dylan was the first to take an interest in each of them. The girls had a strong preference, a clear favorite between the boys, but thankfully Jo wasn't the type of girl to urinate on somebody she didn't like.

"Hey Dylan," Jo began, leaning on the counter. "You think you could help me get started on the spinach tomorrow? You were really quick with the beans today."

Dylan lit up. "Of course!" he blurted out. Then his face dropped. "Crap," he huffed, knowing he just blew his chance for a good night kiss.

Josephine gave him a wink from across the kitchen, pleased with herself. Some things were just too easy around here.

Daniel, done with the dishes, took the opportunity to mess up his brother's hair and console him. "Ooooh. Tough break, kiddo. You almost had it. Just another two hours and fifty-seven minutes and you would have gotten that kiss. Better luck next time."

"That's not fair," Dylan stated. "She asked me a question. That doesn't count."

Jo spoke in a wise-woman voice, "I believe the rules were...not a peep?"

"This is a stupid game," Dylan growled, folding his arms like a spoiled little brat. "I want a re-match."

"Nope. It was a onetime only offer," Jo declared.

"C'mon. In school you can re-take a test if you do real bad on it."

Jo scoffed, "What kind of school would that be?"

Dylan shrugged, "You know. Public school. Aren't you in high school?"

"I finished up last spring. Tried college for the fall semester but...the timing didn't work out. Got too much to do around here now so I didn't go back."

Daniel joined the conversation, speaking his considerations out loud. "Wait a sec. Did you graduate high school a year early? You're still seventeen now…soooo…you were only…"

Jo smirked and let Daniel put the pieces together on his own. When he did, he gave her an approving nod. A moment later, Dylan was still having trouble grasping what was being said and asked Josephine, "Are you super smart or something? Like, smarter than the average bear?"

Jo cackled once and left the kitchen, not in the mood to talk about her high aptitude or chart-topping SATs. It was probably for the better. She would have just made the boys feel dumb.

Dylan turned to his brother for an explanation, because in his mind, his big brother knew everything and anything that needed knowing. Daniel folded his arms and said, "Yes, Dylan. She's smarter than the average bear."

With a wide smile, Dylan informed him in a delighted whisper, "I told you she was smart!"

The boys left the farmhouse for the night and took a late evening wash-up in the water trough by the barn. They enjoyed the bar of soap instead of laundry detergent this time, plus the feeling of having clean teeth after a few days of less than stellar hygiene. They both shaved, using the side view mirror of the nearest truck. Daniel used the toothbrush first, while Dylan dried off his face. When Daniel was done with his oral hygiene routine, he rinsed the toothbrush, reapplied some toothpaste, then handed it to his little brother. Dylan accepted it, began his turn of brushing, while Daniel swiped some deodorant under his arms to keep himself smelling fresh for a little while longer. He'd already learned when you work on a farm, fresh doesn't last very long.

"Guess I need to buy some more soap," Daniel said, hands on his hips, watching Millie chew the bar of Irish Spring. "That can't taste too good," he said to the creature, who rolled the bar of soap on her tongue once more like a Starlight mint, then swallowed the soap just to spite him. Daniel half expected her to start hiccupping bubbles. She was such a strange animal.

The sun went down and the boys retired to the barn. Millie was resting on her knees in the center of the room, one of her big beautiful eyes was shut, the other watched over the boys suspiciously. She took a heavy sigh and lowered her head a little, like she was falling into a deep sleep. They'd never seen her do that before, she always slept standing up, at least since they took possession of her. She seemed unusually tired, pretty worn out for some reason. Maybe she was finally getting some real exercise on a piece of property that fit her scale, unlike all those years in the various zoos. Maybe she knew this day was a gift, that she was supposed to be put down that morning and had escaped death by injection when she climbed into that cramped trailer with the two well-meaning brothers who had no idea what they were doing. Maybe she really *was* sick. Maybe her mind was gone. Whatever was bringing her to this new level of exhaustion, it was winning, and it made the boys tired too.

Daniel and Dylan used to stay up talking when they were younger, sometimes under a fort of sheets by the light of a flashlight, other times hanging upside-down from their bunk beds, but now, as mostly grown men, they had less and less to talk about. They used to talk about girls and driving flashy cars. They used to talk about their mother, going over what they knew about her as if to make her more real. Sometimes, if they were living with a particularly strict foster family, Daniel and Dylan would make up elaborate plans of escape, usually involving tying sheets together and climbing out the window like in the movies, but they never followed through. Even still, they got into a lot of trouble together, but at least they were together, just as they were now.

Dylan, on his back, covered in a navy blue blanket on the floor of the barn, pulled something out of his pocket. It was white piece of cloth. When he unfolded the fabric to display the true shape, it became perfectly clear to Daniel what he was holding: a pair of girl's underwear, size small.

Wide eyed, Daniel said, "Those better not belong to who I think they belong to. Damnit, Dylan. Those better not be…"

With a sheepish grin, Dylan said, "They sure are," then laid the white underwear across his face like a sleeping mask. He was lost in some dreamy world of hormones and stupidity. With the lantern close by, Daniel could see the thin fabric fluttering with his brother's inhaling an exhaling.

"How did you get them?" Daniel inquired, getting a sick feeling in his stomach. What if he had recently kissed a girl his brother had also kissed? That was a cardinal rule that two brothers could never break.

"Took them off the clothesline. Think she'll notice?"

With private relief, Daniel found it in his voice to be angry now. "You just don't think sometimes. You do stupid stuff and don't think about the consequences. She's gonna think we're a bunch of perverts. Go put them back right now."

Dylan peeked one of his blue eyes through a leg hole and said, "Can't. She already took the rest of the laundry in. They're mine now."

"You can't take personal stuff like that. They don't belong to you."

"Neither does she," Dylan said, gesturing towards the sleeping animal a few yards away.

Frustrated, Daniel stood up and grabbed the underwear from his brother, ending his foolishness. "Fine. *I'll* go put them back. You're not keeping these."

With his face exposed once more, Dylan looked up at his brother hovering over him and grumbled, "Killjoy."

"Do I look offended?"

Still drugged by his thoughts of Jo, Dylan said, "Just smell them. Take a good long whiff. What is it about her that smells so good? God, I want her to have my baby!"

"That's not funny," Daniel snapped, slightly hurt, but more angry than anything.

"Sorry," Dylan conceded, knowing his baby comment was way out of line.

"When you say things like that, it makes me wonder if there's something seriously wrong with you."

"Nothing's wrong with me. I'm in love, that's all." Dylan shrugged, like he just couldn't help himself.

"You're not in love. You've known this girl for all of two days now. She's gone out of her way to let you know she ain't interested in you but you're too thick to realize that. Besides, she's way the hell out of your league."

"She's just playing hard to get, that's all. She'll give in pretty soon, they always do, right? She's gonna fall in love with me. Just you wait." Dylan paused to grin. "And you know what happens when you fall in love." He started pumping his hips up and down. "Pretty soon, *I'm* gonna be the one coming home with hickeys on my neck and nail marks in my back."

Daniel rolled his eyes. He may have once been the only high school junior who could have sex ten times a week and not brag about it, not even now, two years later. He was one lucky bastard, in every sense. "You're going to be sorely disappointed."

"With sex?" Dylan questioned, stopping his below-the-belt nonsense.

"With Josephine. She's not like other girls. She's…not gonna be won over by you clowning around. You can't impress a girl like her, nobody can. Don't waste your time trying."

"But Veronica was like that at first, she played hard to get better than anyone at Dalton. Remember how bitchy she was when you first asked her out? How many times did you have to ask her before she said yes? You didn't give up and look where you ended up. I mean…you know what I mean. *Before* she got knocked up."

Daniel hadn't heard that name in so long. Veronica. She was the girl who broke him in pieces before she left for college after a ten month romance complete with I love you's, matching mood rings, and unprotected sex. What broke his heart the most was that she didn't even bother telling him about her abortion until the end of the summer, many months after the fact. At the tender age of seventeen, just a year younger than Dylan was now, Daniel had unknowingly fathered a child halfway through his junior year. Veronica was a senior at the time, president of the French club, supposedly on the pill to clear up her skin, and on her way to Brown University in the fall with an enormous amount of pressure from her parents. Veronica Caldwell, along with Mr. and Mrs. Caldwell, had killed that unborn child and then gone out to Red Lobster afterwards. Veronica didn't even miss a day of school, or going to the spring formal with Daniel for that matter, never letting on what she'd done without any input from him other than what he'd already given her day after day following their walk home from school.

Daniel grew up fast after finding out about her decision, a decision he knew Veronica didn't think through all the way because her parents did all the deciding for her. Mr. and Mrs. Caldwell didn't think much of the always polite but fairly scruffy Daniel McElroy or his poor grammar, but they did feel awfully sorry for him because if he had a set of *real* parents raising him right, they would have taught him not to go around getting pretty girls pregnant, especially pretty girls with scholarships. Daniel cost them several thousand dollars in medical bills, not to mention the hassle of having to take off work and drive to a clinic in a different city for privacy's sake.

At the end of summer, Veronica had explained to Daniel, "It was early, it was just a bundle of cells," to which he replied, "*You* used to be a bundle of cells, *I* used to be a bundle of cells," before he walked away forever with a deep sense of loss and a heavy guilt. Daniel truly carried the weight of the world on his shoulders after that, slept twelve hours a day on average, and lost ten pounds he really couldn't afford to lose. He was fired from his part-time dishwashing gig for being late one too many times, his C average tanked, he didn't speak to anyone except his brother for about three months straight, and he kindly turned down all six girls who asked him to the senior prom the following spring. To those six young ladies, the brooding and detached Daniel McElroy had become quite the catch ever since he showed up single at the start of twelfth grade, especially since he was rumored to know what was what under the sheets thanks to Veronica's BFF's who couldn't keep anything to themselves. Daniel didn't want any part of anything, no relationships, no friendships, no nothing. Somehow, that just added to his appeal around Dalton High. Veronica and her scraped out uterus had really done a number on him emotionally, thrust him into some new level of manhood he really wasn't ready for.

All that was two years ago. He was over Veronica by now, forgiven her for what her parents had talked her into, though she never indicated she might be sorry. He'd been on a handful of first dates since graduating but not many seconds, and he did everything he could not to remember that curly-haired girl from his past or what they'd done at her house after school while her parents were at work. Those afternoons were all blurred together now. He could barely remember the details of Veronica's face but he could still picture the wood grain patterns on her headboard in perfect detail.

With a heavy sigh, Daniel grumbled "I told you I never wanna talk about that, I never wanna talk about *her*."

"Lighten up, asshole," Dylan snapped.

"*You're* the asshole." It sounded immature coming from such a mature boy, but it was all he could come up with.

"Geez. You got your period or something? What the hell's your problem?"

"You. *You're* my problem, as always," Daniel fired back, storming out of the barn with Josephine's underwear in his hand.

He headed towards the house, hoping she hadn't locked the door this time. He couldn't exactly hang up a single pair of underwear on the line, otherwise she'd know somebody put them there and that would spell disaster for him and his idiot brother. He'd cleaned up after Dylan so many times over the years but returning someone's underwear without them noticing was something he hadn't attempted as of yet.

Daniel held his breath as he tried the front door. To his relief, the lever released and the door pushed inward towards the darkened kitchen. Knowing full well the floorboards would not be on his side, he took off his shoes and set them next to the deceased Mr. Larsen's work boots by the door. Letting his eyes adjust to the lack of light, he tried to think of something to do with the underwear, but came up blank. Surely the only place he could stash them where they wouldn't raise any red flags was upstairs. He crept towards the staircase and just as he was about to take his first step, sure to be a creaky one, he glanced in the living room, lit only by the moonlight pouring in through the sheer white curtains.

There, in all its saving grace, sat a laundry basket full of folded clothes and sheets. He was off the hook this time, Dylan too. All he had to do was place the folded underwear under some of the other clothes in the basket and she'd never know. When she came to them in the morning, she'd think they'd been there the whole time, not draped over some horny teenager's face. Relieved, Daniel changed his course and stepped into the living room, a room that was supposed to be off limits. Quickly, he plunged the white fabric in his hand under the sheets and towels, and his task was done. Now, all he had to do was get out of the house without making a sound.

He stood in the living room for a moment, looking around in the dimly lit space. There was a couch in front of the fireplace and two chairs on either side, surrounding a coffee table. No TV could be found, but there was an old record player on a console by the window. A clock on the mantle ticked, keeping rhythm in the quiet house. Beside the couch sat two beat-up looking instrument cases, one for a banjo, one for something else, something wide and deep. He slowly turned in his spot, since the floor boards seemed to be settled here, and scanned his eyes around the back of the room. His lips parted in awe as he saw an enormous bookcase overflowing with volumes and volumes of books. Being a literature junkie, a lover of all things written, he stepped closer, hoping these books were one's he'd recognize, not something boring like farm animal reference books, or manuals on how to raise crops.

With minimal creaking, he got to the bookcase and plucked a hardback from the shelf. It was so dim he could barely make out the words *Moby Dick*. This was one of his favorites. He flipped through a few pages, smelling the musty paper that bore one of the greatest tales of all time, then returned the book to its slot. He ran his fingers across the shelf and stopped at *The Crucible*. That was a good one too. Next, he discovered *Call of the Wild*, followed by *Ivanhoe* and *Oliver Twist*. *War and Peace* turned out to be a false book, the center was cut out to make a hiding place where several rolls of cash were stashed, a little more than what was squirreled away in the canister in the kitchen. Daniel put it back and continued searching the shelf. A book-like shape wrapped in red Christmas paper with a gold ribbon around it was placed between *Swiss Family Robinson* and *David Copperfield*. He pulled it out and read the gift tag. In neat evenly spaced handwriting was *To: Dad, From: Jo. Merry Christmas!* Johan's gift would never be opened now, only Jo knew what book it was.

    Daniel continued reading the spines, working his way down the line of books that were organized in a way that made absolutely no sense to him. When he got to *A Farewell to Arms*, a piece from Hemingway he'd always wanted to read, he heard swift footsteps coming down the stairs.

    He had time to shut the book and widen his eyes, but nothing more. When Josephine turned on the lamp beside the couch, just a few seconds after descending the stairs, Daniel was caught red-handed, though not with her underwear as he'd entered the house, but holding one of her precious books in a room he was forbidden to enter. There, in her atrocious nightgown, hair cascading over her shoulders, Jo stared at her discovery: a wide-eyed Daniel McElroy. After cocking her head to the side, as if to decide how to punish him for disobeying her orders, she put both hands on her hips. This angry gesture did something unexpected. It pulled all that loose fabric tight to her body, showing she had some curves under there after all. She hid them all day and all night too, by the look of it, but they were there none-the-less. Dylan would be thrilled.

After several moments of silence, just the clock tick-tick-ticking, Josephine nodded towards the book and asked, "Have you read that?"

"This?" he asked, holding up the book his nervous palms were sweating all over. "No. Have you?"

"Yeah. It's good. It was one of my dad's favorites. These are all his books. Most of them are first or second editions."

"Wow." Daniel stood back and surveyed the bookcase again. Every shelf was stuffed with classic literature. Some rows of books had other books piled horizontally on top, filling the gap between the spines and the shelf above. There had to be five hundred novels or more. They were probably worth a fortune too, if they were really such rare editions, like she said. Surely she could sell them all and have an easier life financing her farm dreams instead of laboring over every green bean in that field all summer long.

"I don't get to read much anymore, only when it rains," she said, joining him in front of the bookcase. "I finished *Sons and Lovers* last week. I think next on my list is *Tender is the Night*. I love Fitzgerald."

"Yeah. He's pretty great. What about Joseph Conrad? Do you like him?"

"He's okay. *Heart of Darkness* didn't inspire me, but it was alright. I liked *Inheritors* a little better but nothing I'd read twice." Josephine was relaxed now, ready to talk literature all night long. It seemed whatever rejection she'd felt after that kiss in the woods was replaced by excitement over talking books with someone. She probably hadn't *really* talked to anyone about anything in quite some time, let alone the endless topic of fiction.

Daniel said, "I really liked *Almayer's Folly*. That was Joseph Conrad's first novel. I've read it five times."

"Don't think we have that one here," she said, scanning the bookcase.

Daniel flipped open *A Farewell to Arms* once more, just because.

"You can borrow that, if you want."

"Really?"

"It's gonna cost you," she teased, ready to charge him a hundred dollars per loan.

Taking in the bookshelf's size once more, Daniel replied, "Then I'd like to start a tab, please. Will work for books."

"I didn't know you were such an avid reader."

"I uh...I sorta...um...I used to get sick a lot. My Grams would make me stay in bed all day, whenever I did. There's not much to do when you're stuck in bed other than reading."

"Oh," she said, processing his words.

Daniel cleared his throat, ready to lighten the mood. "I used to read stories to Dylan before bed every night but I think I enjoyed it more than he did."

"How many books a week?"

"Back then, or now?"

"Both."

"'Bout a book a week back then. Now, none."

"Why'd you stop?"

"Wasn't by choice. I didn't have time no more. I had two jobs before we left town. Hate to say it but I sorta miss high school. At least in high school you get to read as part of the homework and stuff. I never did too good on the tests but I always loved the reading part."

"*Well*. You never did *well*." She couldn't resist correcting him, especially if they were going to talk academics.

"You just proved my point for me. I ain't no scholar," he said, just to rile her up a little more. It worked, she chuckled at his words, pleased he could make a joke at his own expense. "So...you and your dad must have looked forward to rainy days, what with all these here books just waiting inside."

"These books were my dad's best friends, mine too. My daddy always said books will never talk about you behind your back, or judge you, or hurt your feelings. When I turned fifteen, he told me books are better than boys too."

After considering this a moment, Daniel replied, "I guess it depends on the book."

"Or the boy," she added quietly.

Now that it was clear she wasn't going to retrieve her shotgun to run him off, he knew it was time for a heartfelt apology. She deserved it. "Look. I can't tell you how sorry I am about what happened earlier this afternoon. In the woods. I'm really sorry."

"It's okay. I guess." She looked uncomfortable standing there in her own living room, and dug her big toe into the area rug just to have something to do. "Let's just pretend it didn't happen."

"Okay." He led a painfully long pause before adding, "You're a really good kisser."

She closed her eyes and smiled, blushing by the light of the table lamp. "So are you," she whispered to the floor.

Silence now. A window rattled as a nighttime breeze pushed the glass against the frame, over and over. The clock forgot to tick for a second or two, lagging behind, slowing down time. A floorboard cried out as Daniel shifted his weight from one leg to the other. Out of the corner of his eye, he saw something moving by the ash bucket beside the fireplace. Jo saw it too. It was a little brown field mouse, out for a late night excursion in search of crumbs. Daniel's eyes widened and his arms stiffened, afraid to move in case the mouse might attack. Calm and collected, like she'd done this hundreds of times, Jo found a small plastic bowl in the kitchen and carefully placed it over the mouse. She scooped him up, saying, "I suspect you'll be much happier out in the fields."

Daniel followed her outside to the edge of the lettuce patch, and watched her release the little mouse by the light of the moon. Together, they observed the miniscule creature as he set off running down the dirt freeway in between the rows of lettuce. The animal made it about ten yards, twelve at the most. That's when a ghostly barn owl swooped down without making a sound and snatched him up, right before their eyes. "Shit!" Daniel gasped, shocked and horrified. He turned to Jo, to confirm what had just happened.

Jo put her hand over her mouth, muffling her own gasp, and stared at the empty crime scene. After a moment, she started to laugh. It wasn't a loud laugh, but it was hearty nonetheless. Daniel started to laugh too, finding the humor in this animal release gone morbidly wrong. To the night sky, he said, "Yeah, you're welcome. Bon appetit," in the direction the owl had flown.

Jo headed inside, leaving Daniel to find his own way back to the barn for the night. Before he went inside, he searched the dark sky for any sign of the owl, but it was gone without a trace. Had it ever been there at all?

"What happened? Where've you been?" Dylan asked, sitting up in his makeshift bed, looking genuinely concerned as Daniel walked in. "I was starting to get worried."

"Everything's fine."

"Well? What did you end up doing with them?"

"With what?" Daniel was so disoriented. There was a reason he went over to the house at such a late hour, he just couldn't remember now.

Dylan shot him a look. "The underwear? The thing you confiscated like a teacher with a pole up your butt and supposedly returned?" Dylan's scowl softened, he let a mischievous dimple appear next to his mouth. "Or did you change your mind?"

"Huh?"

"You did! You took one good whiff and decided to keep them for yourself, you greedy pig! See? You're just as big of a pervert as I am."

Daniel frowned. "I put them in her laundry basket."

"Oh." Dylan looked a little let down. His brother had willpower he couldn't begin to fathom, especially when it came to attractive females.

"Don't you dare do anything like that ever again. I'm tired of cleaning up after you all the time. You gotta grow up and quit pulling stunts like this. I'm sick of it."

Daniel didn't bother going into detail about how Josephine caught him snooping in her dad's library, or about how they talked books and authors for a good while, or the story of the owl that ate the mouse, or about how he made her blush with his little comment about her kissing. Now, Daniel had several secrets to keep from his brother: Jo's father's untimely death, and that telling kiss they shared by his grave. He didn't relish keeping things from Dylan, but these two secrets could never be revealed. Daniel watched his little brother get settled back in for the night under the blanket. He heard the familiar words, "Good night, Daniel. I love you," and knew it was true. His little brother looked up to him, loved him, and trusted him.

Daniel swallowed hard, his saliva turned thick with guilt. He tried to keep his voice sounding normal as he said, "I love you too, Dylan. Goodnight."

"Don't let me die in my sleep," Dylan continued through an unassuming yawn.

Daniel smiled to himself and replied, "Have I ever?"

"Just say it. Say it right." Dylan didn't want any deviation tonight.

"I won't let you die in your sleep."

CHAPTER SIX

"Rise and shine, slackers!"

Dylan pulled the blanket up over his face, hiding from the morning light pouring through the barn door, filtering through Jo's red halo of hair. "Please, Jo. Just ten more minutes. Please," he begged from under the covers.

Daniel, bright-eyed and bushy-tailed for a change, got up and ran his fingers through his messy brown hair, as if that would subdue it. Millie was already awake, she only slept in ten-minute bursts anyway, and now she was taking a slow lap around the barn, searching the rafters for something to munch on. During the night, she'd eaten part of an old leather saddle, some more soap, and an owl's nest that was situated in the corner rafter, eggs and all. It wasn't like Jo and the brothers didn't provide a healthy dinner for her, it just seemed she couldn't help herself and was too darn curious when it came to food, or anything else she could sink her flat teeth into.

Watching her sniff the rafter, then move on to a new spot with such great hope each time, only to be let down again and again, got Josephine to thinking. "After breakfast," she began, "We're gonna make her a feeder up there. She could use a water bucket too, something hanging from the roof so she doesn't have to keep bending over like that."

They all watched Millie spreading her front legs apart, awkwardly dipping down to reach a bucket of water on the ground. The old girl was having a tough time for sure, but not for much longer now that Jo had a plan. "We'll hang it from there," she said, pointing up at a long beam that ran down the center of the barn.

"You gonna climb up there?" Daniel asked, stretching.

"Yeah. Unless you want to," she said, far too perky for this hour.

"I wouldn't dream of taking over your project."

"Afraid of heights, are we?" Jo wasn't really asking. She smiled that little sideways smile of hers, playful as can be.

Daniel cleared his throat and explained, "I'm not afraid. I just have a strong preference for being on the ground."

"You're afraid," she taunted, turning to leave.

Dylan followed closely behind her, like a puppy. Today was a new day. Somehow, he was going to win her over. Maybe if he talked some more about giraffes, that would do the trick. She seemed to like Millie, who happened to be a giraffe, and if Dylan talked about something she liked, then maybe she'd like *him* in the end. It made all the sense in the world. She was sure to drop this hard-to-get act soon enough.

In the kitchen, on the sturdy wooden table in the center of the room, was a new pair of jeans for each McElroy brother, plus a clean t-shirt. They were being shown hospitality today, fresh clothes from the closet of unused men's attire upstairs that once belonged to Johan Larsen. Dylan took the pile with the red t-shirt, the color that demanded attention, while Daniel scooped up the white, the color that wasn't really a color at all. After breakfast, they would freshen up and change clothes before getting started with another day of hard work in the fields.

"Is your dad joining us for breakfast?" Dylan asked, pouring himself a cup of coffee, then one for Josephine, forgetting all about his older brother.

Standing by the stove, Jo answered, "No. He made a run to Omaha today. Had some business to take care of."

"But his truck is outside, isn't it?" Dylan filled in. "He drives the red one, right?"

Jo wasn't expecting that. She stopped moving for a moment. Then, when she had formed her lie, she began moving again and explained, "He got a ride with his business partner."

"Huh," Dylan replied. "I feel bad we haven't met him yet."

Daniel and Josephine locked eyes across the kitchen. She was telling fibs, keeping up her story, but Daniel knew the truth now. He knew everything. Her face, pale and smooth, was looking uneasy so Daniel did what he had to do. He played along with her tall tale and flat out lied to his brother.

"I met him yesterday," Daniel said, gaining Dylan's attention. "I guess you were still working the string beans when he came by."

"You did?" Dylan asked, trying to remember if he'd noticed anyone from afar.

"He's a really nice guy," Daniel continued, getting a smirk out of the farm girl. "Jo, tell him how pleased your dad is with the bean harvest. I know Dylan would love to hear that."

She took his lead and said, "He was really impressed. You did a great job."

Dylan smiled wide, then he shrugged like it was no big deal. "Well, I try."

He bought the lie. All it took was a compliment. Relief washed over Jo in a noticeable way. Her boney shoulders, tense just moments before, relaxed and loosened up. She turned her attention back to breakfast, reaching for the blue canister on the shelf, the third one from the left. Oatmeal.

"Hey! How bout I make breakfast today," Daniel blurted out, desperate to save himself from eating that slop for the third day in a row. "You've been taking such good care of us, how bout you take the morning off?"

"Oh," she said, caught off guard. "Uh...okay."

Daniel pulled out a chair for her at the table, encouraging her to sit down and back away from the oatmeal. Dylan knew exactly what his older brother was up to and gave him a subtle nod of thanks. At the table, Dylan occupied Josephine with his usual chattering while Daniel got to work at the stove.

The water was already boiling. He added several scoops of dry oats and stirred. He grabbed a whisk from the drawer and continued making circular motions, getting a nice even consistency. He added another scoop of oats, and kept stirring till there were no more lumps. Once the oatmeal flowed like thick pudding, he opened some cabinets in search of seasoning. Daniel poked through the spices, taking the cinnamon, allspice, and clove from the shelf. After discovering another money stash behind the cornmeal and discreetly putting it back, he found the sugar and added some, then a little butter from the white porcelain dish. "Do you have any honey?" he asked, rummaging through the nearest cabinet once more.

Jo chuckled to herself, "Do I have honey…" and reached over to open the pantry door to reveal the stash of mason jars filled with golden yellow sunshine. There had to be eight or nine stacked in there, all filled to the brim with raw honey. She grabbed a jar and tossed it to Daniel, adding, "It's local," with a smirk. "Mr. Wessel's a little too generous sometimes."

"Is it supposed to have chunks in it?" he asked, inspecting as he stirred.

"Yes. And for the record, *good* honey doesn't come in little plastic bear bottles."

Daniel took a small taste, curious what those bees on the other side of the field were capable of. Savoring the taste, he conceded Jo was right and added a tablespoon to the oatmeal.

Pleased with himself, he served each of them a ladle full of his special recipe, steaming hot and smelling like a Christmas treat. After blowing on a spoon full of breakfast, Jo took a bite. She actually closed her eyes as she swallowed, savoring the flavors.

Dylan spoke up, saying, "This is how Grams used to make it. Daniel helped her in the kitchen a lot. He's the girlie one of the family. You should make one your pies, Daniel. Bet Jo will lend you her apron and everything."

Happy to be made fun of in exchange for a decent breakfast, Daniel scratched his cheek with his middle finger, aimed at his devilish little brother. Dylan could be a brat sometimes, but Daniel had accepted that long ago and learned to deal with it. He sure loved that brat.

Jo didn't offer any critique or compliment until her bowl was scraped clean. When she finished, she asked, "Can you make it like this again tomorrow, so I can learn?"

"You bet," he said, filling his coffee cup. Maybe tomorrow he could show her how to brew a proper pot of coffee too, if she was up for improvement. Lord knows she needed it.

Her terrible cooking made sense to Daniel now. It was obvious her father was the one who did the food preparation in the Larsen household and it seemed Jo never learned, never took an interest. Now, with nobody to feed her but herself, she had to figure it out on her own. It wasn't her gift, like caring for animals and growing healthy crops, so she did her best but her best was pretty awful in this department. Even a girl as book-smart as Jo had some things to learn.

The morning went by quickly, but the fields were left untouched. Instead of kneeling in the dirt getting soil under their fingernails, they were in the barn working on a feeding apparatus for Millie, the most ornery giraffe on the planet. Jo fashioned a crate for hay with wide gaps so Millie could feed easily, with a long rope on each end to secure it to a beam high up in the barn, about eye-level with the long-necked lady. Before she was ready to hoist the crate in place, Jo found a wide plastic tub to use as a watering bucket. She tied that to a rope as well, so they could simply raise and lower it to refill each day. Back at the animal park, Millie went through ten gallons of water and nearly sixty pounds of food every day.

When the crate and tub were ready to be raised, Jo climbed the ladder to the loft, then onto the crossbeams in the ceiling. Daniel tossed her the ropes, and she inched her way out on the beam, one leg on either side, straddling it till she was in a decent spot to tie them off. She was a good eighteen feet off the ground, higher up than Millie's horns, but she was in her zone working hard, tying expert knots. Millie, curious to have someone near eye-level with her for once, inspected Jo's feet and tried to remove her boot with her creepy lips, as if it were edible. That giraffe was always hungry, always testing and tasting things with her velvet lips and long pointed tongue. Josephine reached down and scratched the top of Millie's lumpy head, nice and hard, and Millie closed her long eyelashes as though she was thoroughly enjoying the rub down.

Below, Dylan had positioned himself just right to see up Jo's loose t-shirt whenever she reached out. She was quite a ways up there, but even that far-off forbidden glimpse of skin and hints of her bra was enough to make Dylan a very happy young man. Catching on to his sneaky little brother, Daniel said, "Come here and help me with the crate."

Still gazing upward, Dylan waved him off and said, "Yeah, just a sec." Jo reached out again to check her knot, unaware of what Dylan was able to see from his strategic vantage point. Satisfied with her knot, she pulled her arms back in, ending the unintentional show. Disappointed, Dylan yelled upward, "You sure it's tight? Check it again."

Daniel stepped in, speaking loud enough so Jo would hear, "I'm sure it's fine." In a quieter voice, he scolded, "Come over here, you little perv."

Dylan spoke upward again, "Just check it one more time."

"Don't! Jo, don't check it one more time! It's fine!" Daniel shouted upward.

Confused, Jo questioned, "What's going on? Do I need to check it again or are we good?"

Dylan offered, "Better safe than sorry!"

Jo shrugged in agreement then reached out one last time, pulling the rope to ensure it was secure. Daniel refused to look up. He kept his frustrated gaze focused on Dylan, who was biting his lower lip through a grin, his blue eyes enjoying what he could see above. "Hot," Dylan mouthed.

The boys tested the ropes, lowering the tub and crate to the ground, filling them up with hay and water, then pulled with all their strength to raise them back up again. It worked. Millie began feeding almost immediately, pulling clumps of hay from in between the boards of the crate. She slurped some water, sending quite a bit of it dribbling down her chin, her long, long neck, and onto the ground below. Dylan, who had learned his lesson about standing too close to a wild animal like this, especially the back end, was far against the side of the barn now, out of the way. He was in the mood to stay dry and urine free today.

By the time they were done and Jo was back on the ground looking satisfied, it was lunchtime. Daniel privately wondered why they went through all this trouble for Millie if they were just going to leave in two days and get back on the road as soon as Jo paid them for their work this week. Maybe this was her way of asking them to stay, telling them it was okay, that she liked the company and having help in the field. Or maybe this was her way of adopting the giraffe, which she'd grown quite fond of. Perhaps Jo was getting Daniel and Dylan McElroy off the hook for their stupid spontaneous adventure that involved stealing a thirty-four-year-old giraffe from the Northside Zoo. The boys had no idea what to do with Millie, nowhere to hide her, so maybe Jo was taking over for them, making their rash decision right somehow.

The afternoon was spent back in the fields, for Daniel and Dylan at least. They got a quarter of the way through the spinach, which was pretty good for two novices. Jo had other things to tend to, she said, so she showed them what to do, how to harvest the crop, and returned to the farmhouse for chores. With the boys working the summer harvest, she had twice as much time as she used to. The afternoon sun beat down on the brothers. Daniel was working on a nice tan from his short sleeves down, and from his collar up his neck. A farmer's tan, as it were. His shirtless brother, on the other hand, had a nice even tan over his defined torso, his muscular back. Dylan's blond hair was getting lighter in the sun too. He was looking more and more like an All-American surfer.

When a few raindrops hit Dylan's bare back, he said, "I guess it's quittin' time," as he looked up to the dark clouds approaching. He was right: a storm was coming in, pretty fast by the look of it. The grass in the fields was blowing in one direction, bending with the wind that rolled over the flat land without anything to stop it. Jo was nowhere to be seen. They picked up their bushels and headed for the farmhouse. As they approached, Jo materialized from the root cellar. The brothers looked at each other, curious what she was doing down there, and continued their path. By the time they were within speaking distance, she'd already secured all the locks with the keys around her neck and gave a good spin to the combination dial as well. Whatever she kept down there was valuable.

Dylan, the bold one of the pair, or maybe the foolish one, dared to ask, "So what's in there? You making moonshine or something?"

Jo gave him a never-you-mind kind of smile. "Don't be such a nosey bugger."

Dylan liked that, being teased by a pretty redhead. She must really have it bad for him if she's teasing him like this, surely she must. Just to play along, he set down his bushel and pretended to rattle the chains on the root cellar. Jo's eyes widened for a moment, then she relaxed, seeing he would never be able to get in without all five keys and those lived on a chain around her neck, right in between her breasts, and that was a place Dylan would never get the privilege of seeing.

That night, Jo did something unthinkable. She let the boys sit in the living room after dinner. Daniel had cooked, did what he could with some turkey hash he found in the freezer, and since the rain was coming down heavy now, they were waiting it out as the evening rolled on. By nightfall, the rain still hadn't let up, and the boys were not looking forward to dashing to the barn since they'd surely get soaked to the bone, so Jo let them stay a little longer, gave them each a bowl of ice cream. With nothing to do, no TV to watch, no board games to play, Jo took a book off the shelf and got cozy in one of the armchairs. Daniel did the same, asking permission with his eyes. Dylan was bored to tears. His brother was occupied, so was his love interest, and he just wasn't much of reader. He was tired though, and laid his head down on a pillow. He was tired enough to be quiet.

The clock on the mantel chimed twelve times at midnight. Jo had fallen asleep in her chair with the book in her lap. Dylan was asleep on the couch, had been for over an hour, so Daniel had taken the opportunity to watch Josephine dreaming away since nobody was awake to notice. She looked so delicate when she slept: her snobby little nose, her soft eyelashes, her bottom lip that was just barely separated from her top. Jo opened her groggy gray eyes as the clock finished ringing in the new day, and looked around like she was confused. It was midnight and the brothers were in her living room. This was unusual indeed.

"Has the rain stopped?" she asked through a yawn.

"Died down a little, but still going," Daniel quietly replied.

Dylan was out cold on the couch, his left arm hanging off the furniture at an uncomfortable-looking angle. Dylan could sleep hanging by one toe if he had to. He once slept with half his face in a bowl of cold cereal when he was four, woke up with a Cheerio stuck in his nose that five-year-old Daniel had the unpleasant task of dislodging. If anyone could risk drowning in a bowl of milk, it was definitely Dylan McElroy.

"We'll just make a run for it. I know it's late," Daniel said, marking his place in the book he'd gotten halfway through during the course of the rainy evening.

"Okay. See you in the morning," she said, standing up and yawning again.

"Wake up, asshole," Daniel said to his baby brother, poking him in the forehead in that loving way only a sibling could.

Dylan twitched his nose and came out of his heavy slumber at a second poke in the forehead. He didn't open his eyes, but he was undoubtedly awake.

"C'mon. Time to get you tucked in for bed," Daniel said, poking rapidly this time to hurry his brother along.

"Ssssstop," Dylan groaned. "I'm going. I'm going. Quit being such a dick."

Dylan was so tired he teetered as he walked, like a drunkard. Daniel kept a strong arm around him, keeping him upright, and guided him through the kitchen towards the front door. The light drizzle outside revived Daniel during their short walk to the barn, but not Dylan. He was walking with his eyes closed. Fieldwork was pretty tiring, it turned out, requiring even more energy than football practice.

Dylan didn't bother changing clothes or brushing his teeth. He flopped onto his blanket and was snoring and mumbling before Daniel had even closed the barn door behind them. In a whisper, Daniel spoke to his sleeping brother, "Goodnight. I love you, Dylan. I won't let you die in your sleep. I promise."

Daniel lay down and closed his eyes, ready for sleep, then snapped them open again. The barn was leaking, dripping rainwater onto his face. His blanket was soaked. The rain picked up just then, sending more water through all the cracks in the roof. Millie didn't seem to care as she happily chomped on some hay from the crate above, getting a shower while she did so. Daniel tried to sleep through his discomfort, tossed and turned under that wet blanket, but he was so cold and clammy sleep was never going to happen. Without waking Dylan, he walked back to the farmhouse. When he got inside, he whispered up the stairs, "Jo. It's me. I'm sorry to bother you but…the barn is leaking. Do you have any dry blankets we could use?"

A sleepy-looking Jo appeared in her long ruffled nightgown. "Oh," she said, rubbing her half-closed eyes at the top of the steps. "Um. Okay. Yeah. I've got some extras." After a moment, she added, "Aw hell. I guess you guys can sleep on the floor in the living room, if you want."

"Really?"

"No funny business, okay?"

"No funny business. I promise. Thanks for...making an exception...just this once."

"That'll be..." she paused to yawn, "a hundred dollars."

"I wouldn't expect to pay anything less."

Within minutes, Daniel managed to drag his half-conscious brother back to the house and settle him in on the same couch he'd been sleeping on not ten minutes earlier. Jo passed Daniel a dry quilt and he laid it over his brother's sleeping body. As he took the second quilt for himself, ready to lay down on the floor, he had an overwhelming urge to give Jo a good night kiss. She was so adorable standing there, so sweetly tired after a long day's work. He resisted and said, "Thank you," then nothing more. Jo went upstairs, creaking her way back to her warm dry bed.

Alone now, wanting only to be free of these wet jeans, Daniel took off his clothes, right down to his underwear. He was about to turn off the light when he became aware of somebody standing in the room. It was Jo. How she'd come back down the stairs without making a sound was something he couldn't fathom. The warning system built into the creaky floorboards must have broken, failing at the most inopportune time. Josephine was holding two pillows, her reason for returning, but now she was staring at Daniel and his skinny body with the funny tan lines, thanks to his current employment outside. After another moment of staring at the half naked boy in her living room, she snapped out of her daze and said, "Here," as she passed him the pillows.

"Thanks," he said, feeling more and more awkward. He used the pillows to cover his scrawny torso, wrapping his arms around them tightly.

Jo turned to leave but before she did, she asked, "What does it mean?"

"What does what mean?"

"Your tattoo. I didn't mean to stare...I was just...I wasn't sure..."

"Oh," he exhaled. He shrugged his right shoulder up and glanced down at the small ink drawing that had been there since he was sixteen. "It's a compass rose. So I know where I'm going."

Jo nodded once in understanding. She fiddled with her thumbs, looking down at them to avoid eye contact. "Are you always…*going*? Or do you ever stay?"

"Staying…it's not really an option. My brother and me, we don't get to stay nowhere for too long."

"And you're okay with that?"

"I dunno. I guess so. That's just the way it is. We're used to it. Just like you're used to staying in one place, you're used to this farm and things being the same. We're used to…things changing all the time, everything from the mattresses we sleep on to the way the tap water tastes, not to mention the people."

Dylan mumbled something in his sleep, interrupting them. He twitched a little under his blanket, unknowingly breaking the tension building up around him. Daniel and Josephine both laughed quietly, relieved they could abandon this loaded topic. Sound asleep, Dylan's nose scrunched up, he swatted at something, nothing real, then rolled over onto his back. He looked like a little kid, a blond boy with rosy cheeks and a trouble-making soul.

Daniel looked over at his snoring sibling and said, "It's really tempting to get a feather and put shaving cream in his hand, isn't it?"

"It sure is," she said in return. "Or put makeup on him."

"Been there, done that."

"Have you really?" she questioned, failing to hide her cheeky grin.

"Yep."

"That's cruel," she said, grinning even more.

"Nah. It's funny."

"Maybe a little funny. But you said no funny business tonight," she reminded him with a sly smile.

Dylan snorted loudly, waking himself up. He opened his blue eyes just a slit, then closed them again. He only needed to see the blur of his big brother through those slits in order to feel safe. He hadn't noticed Josephine standing on the other side of the couch, over by the stairs. In a murmur of a voice, Dylan slurred, "Goodnight, Daniel."

Daniel smirked, ready to repeat his lines for the second time. "Night, Dylan."

"I...love you," Dylan went on, barely able to talk as he drifted off.

"Love you too."

There was a long pause. Dylan forgot the last part, it seemed. Suddenly, he snapped back to consciousness and finished with the most important words of this whole routine.

"Don't let me die in my sleep."

"I won't."

CHAPTER SEVEN

"What're you doing up?" Jo asked, joining Daniel in the kitchen. It was only 6:15, well before Daniel's normal waking hour. Not only was he awake, he looked it.

He shrugged. "I guess I slept better in here."

"You made coffee?" she went on, glancing over at the full carafe.

Daniel nodded. He was reading a book at the kitchen table, nursing a hot cup himself. He was really starting to like this place.

"This tastes…different," she said, cautiously slurping.

"Tastes better, or just different?"

"Better."

"Good," he said with a smirk.

"I said better, not good," she teased back. "Guess I'm gonna go feed the tall girl."

"Already done."

Jo looked surprised. Her thin eyebrows wriggled with skepticism.

Daniel turned a page and said, "I made *you* breakfast too."

Jo glanced at the stove. There was a stack of pancakes on a plate, next to the cast iron skillet. He had already washed the mixing bowl and spatula. They were drying on the wooden dish rack next to the sink. She fixed herself a plate and sat across from Daniel. He slid the syrup her way, before she even mentioned it.

"Why're you doing all this?" she asked suspiciously, drizzling some amber liquid over her breakfast. "Why are you being so nice?"

"I like to be nice once in a while, just to make sure I still can."

Not a moment too soon, Dylan emerged from the living room. He wore his jeans and waited until he was in the kitchen then he pulled the clean t-shirt over his head, just to remind the only female for miles of what a fantastic physique he had. "Morning," he said brightly to Jo. "Morning," he said less brightly to Daniel.

Jo kept her face unchanged as she read the word written in black marker across Dylan's forehead. There was just one word written there, and it was *Asshole*. Daniel had considered writing *douche bag*, but wasn't entirely sure how to spell it, so he went with the obvious. Jo glanced over at Daniel, the culprit, who was keeping his face perfectly blank. Silently, with just one look at each other, Daniel and Jo both swore not to laugh. There was no telling how long Dylan would wear this title on his face. Totally oblivious, Dylan poured himself a cup of coffee. Daniel, who was finished with his breakfast, pulled out the other chair so his brother could sit and eat. He wasn't being chivalrous, he was doing it to make things difficult for Jo, to make her burst out laughing since she was now stuck looking right at the Asshole. Daniel hadn't counted on Josephine's remarkable ability to keep a straight face. She didn't even crack a smile as she ate her way through her stack.

"Why's everyone so quiet?" Dylan mumbled, mouth full of pancakes.

From across the small kitchen, Daniel replied, "Just waiting on you."

"How'd you sleep?" Jo asked, as if nothing was unusual.

"Really well. That couch is comfy."

"You're a pretty sound sleeper, huh?"

"I guess so," he said, adding more syrup. "Why?"

"No reason," she said with a wink.

Dylan's heartbeat sped up. She just winked at him. She was flirting with him. Finally! This was going to be a good day, he just knew it. He finished his breakfast at a quickened pace, feeling flutters of puppy love run through his belly, mixing oh-so-well with his pancakes.

Out in the fields, hands deep in wet spinach leaves, the three of them enjoyed the cool of the morning. It was overcast. The leftover storm clouds brought a few extra hours of relief from the heat. The ground was almost too soggy to work with. Millie the tall girl was part of the group, watching over them as they labored below. Occasionally, the giraffe would regurgitate some of her food, chew it further, then swallow once again, just going about her regular duties as a ruminant. Jo was fascinated by this, and pointed in amazement as a lump of pre-chewed food visibly rolled up Millie's long throat, and once it reached her mouth, she began working on the cud. All Dylan could do was cringe. He was not nearly as fascinated by this digestive phenomenon. Millie made a sound that was almost like a cow's *moo*, which got Jo and Daniel to laugh. Dylan had to think quick and find a way to steal the attention back, before Millie kept it too long.

"Did you know a giraffe can decapitate a lion with it's hoof, if it kicks hard enough?" That was another factoid he'd read over and over those long nights he kept Daniel company at the zoo while he cleaned. Dylan never dreamed of chipping in to get the job done faster. The cages were disgusting and he wasn't the one getting a paycheck to deal with it.

Next, Dylan went on a rant about Northside Animal Park, how they were fools to have such light security. He said if he wanted to, he could have walked out of there with an elephant. He wondered aloud if anybody would even look for Millie, or if her disappearance was welcome and saved them the trouble of having to dispose of her. Neither Jo nor Daniel had much to say in return, not that they had a chance to get any words in.

"Hey Dylan," Jo finally interrupted. "How fast did you say giraffes can run?"

"Fast."

"I know *fast*...but how fast? You think you could outrun her?"

Dylan stood up. That sounded like a challenge, a way to show off his impressive athletic skills for Jo, though he could never dream of running thirty miles per hour. "Let's race. You and me against Millie."

"Nah."

"C'mon," Dylan begged, brushing himself off, ready to run faster than he'd ever run. "Don't be such a..."

"Such a what?" she demanded to know.

Dylan smiled and shrugged. The handwritten word Asshole was still clear as ever on his forehead. He wasn't working hard enough to sweat away the ink yet. "C'mon. Race me. Forget the giraffe. You and me and Daniel, to the trees. Last one there is a rotten egg...which will be Daniel, since he's slower than molasses."

Daniel stood up too. "Am I being invited to get my ass beat just for fun?"

"Always," Dylan replied in his own snarky way.

"One two three go!" Daniel yelled, already running toward the trees, ready to start this ridiculous race and get his defeat over with. He looked a little silly when he ran, like it took an awful lot of effort to move his lanky legs and arms.

"Cheater!" Jo shouted, running after him. She looked a little more natural, like a gazelle maybe, using her long legs to gain on Daniel quickly.

"You two better run faster than that!" Dylan added, giving them a nice long head start. It wouldn't be hard to catch up, not at his top speed.

They were all sprinting, racing across the field. Just about the time they were neck and neck, right when Dylan was about to overtake them both, Millie whizzed right past them. The herd was running, so she ran too, but for her, fifteen miles an hour was just a light jog, only half of what she was capable of. The crazy old giraffe kept going but the three runners stopped, unable to run and laugh at the same time. They each doubled over, exhausted, cackling at

Millie's victory. She was over by the trees now, having a snack of leaves to celebrate her unmatchable speed.

"Show off!" Daniel shouted at the old girl, panting. He dropped to his knees to recover.

Catching her breath as well, Jo playfully pushed Dylan. "I had you."

"No you didn't," he said back, giving her a lighthearted push in return.

"Yeah. I did," she said again, straightening up now that her lungs were full of air like they were supposed to be. Her cheeks were flushed pink and her ponytail was a little disheveled, but she looked beautiful regardless.

"No. You didn't," Dylan said again. Was this play-fighting considered flirting? He wasn't sure. He hoped it was and beamed a smile her way.

"I had both of you," Daniel said from his knees, though it wasn't the least bit true.

They started walking back across the field, energized rather than worn out. They got about halfway across the field when Millie trotted over to catch up with the herd. The four of them walked side by side, like heroes from a war movie.

Josephine ran her hand across the back of her neck, wiping the sweat away. Her eyes widened and she stopped walking. Without explanation, she dropped to her knees and started feeling the ground, searching for something. Before long, she was mumbling words the McElroy brothers had never heard fly from her lips before. Cursing, crawling on the ground on all fours, Jo was distraught.

"What's wrong?" Daniel asked.

"My necklace. I lost it. It must have fallen off when we were running."

"The one with the keys to the root cellar?" he clarified, joining her on the ground.

"Yeah." She continued crawling and cursing.

"What are we looking for?" Dylan asked, realizing this was more serious than he first thought. He swatted away one of Mr. Wessel's beloved bees.

"Her necklace. With the keys. You gonna help us look or just stand there like an asshole?" Daniel asked. Dylan, with that very word scrawled across his forehead for all the world to see, dropped to his knees and started feeling around.

After an hour of searching, the necklace was nowhere to be found. The field was huge, and there was no telling at which point during the footrace the necklace came loose and slipped off her slender neck. Jo was determined to find it. When silent tears started streaming down her face, Daniel asked, "What do you keep down there? Why are these keys so important?"

"They just...*are*," she said, frustrated. "What does it matter what I keep down there. I need those fucking keys!"

Dylan whistled a don't-blow-your-top kind of whistle. "Want me to try and pick the locks?" he offered, like he could do anything if he set his mind to it.

"No!" she shouted back.

"Geez. Okay," he replied, backing down. Jo was not in a good mood. She was angry and upset, frustrated as she continued to search.

"Shit, shit, shit," Jo muttered again, like she couldn't believe this was happening.

They didn't stop for lunch, which Dylan whined about. Finding those keys was Jo's top priority. They were almost to the far side of the field now, still inching their way through the damp dirt in hopes the chain and keys might catch a glimmer of sunlight and reveal themselves.

"I'm hungry," Dylan whispered to his brother again. He sounded so boyish, even more so than usual.

"I know. But we gotta keep looking," Daniel replied maturely. "This is important to her. We gotta keep looking."

"But I'm really, *really* hungry."

"So am I. Soon as we find them, we'll eat. Okay? Keep looking."

And so they did. Two o'clock rolled by, as did three. Jo's tears had dried up by then, her cursing stopped too, but now she looked totally drained. This searching had sucked the life out of her. Maybe those keys unlocked more than just a musty old root cellar underneath the house. Maybe they were her future, and without them, she had none.

Daniel crept forward beside Dylan, continuing to touch every square inch of the field. Then, at the exact same moment, the boys both laid eyes on the item they'd been combing for. The two brothers reached out to claim the chain, both pulling at it. The keys clinked together, but Jo was far enough away that she didn't hear that glorious sound of rattling metal, proof the treasure had been found. The boys each kept a firm grip on the chain, unwilling to release.

Dylan spoke through gritted teeth, "Let go."

"You let go," Daniel shot back.

"I said *you* let go!"

The intense look on his younger brother's face was unnerving. Daniel watched the vein pulsing in Dylan's neck, a sign he was truly serious, that he wanted this chain and the keys on it and he would do whatever it took to get his brother to let go. Dylan said it again, this time in a low whisper. "Let go."

Daniel looked down at his hand, watched his own fingers open obediently and the chain slide away. What did it matter? They found it. The search was over now. What difference would it make which brother took the credit? To Dylan, it made a huge difference. Now that the necklace was in his possession, Dylan's tense expression melted into a victorious smile. He shouted, "I found them!" and held up the chain to prove himself.

Jo whipped her head around and stood up, elated. She ran over to him to accept her necklace, but Dylan held the keys up over her head, just out of reach. "What are you gonna give me?" he wanted to know.

Jo looked at him, furrowed her brow and said, "I'll say *thank you very much* and that's it."

"Not good enough," Dylan teased, like it was all a game.

"Just give them to her," Daniel chimed in from a few feet away.

"I want a kiss," Dylan stated.

"No," Jo snapped, growing angry once more.

"No kiss, no keys."

"Just give them to her," Daniel said again.

Josephine crossed her arms, unwilling to cave in. "If you don't give me those keys, I won't pay you tomorrow. All the money you earned this week, it's gone."

"You can't do that," Dylan argued. "It's *our* money."

"And those are *my* keys."

"Just give them to her already!" Daniel ordered.

"Don't tell me what to do! You're always telling me what to do!" Dylan shouted at his brother. With that, the boys were fighting again, wrestling on the ground, trying to pin each other in whatever way necessary. Dylan was bigger and stronger, but Daniel could certainly hold his own. Dirt rose from the ground as they disturbed it with their tumbling bodies. They never threw punches, never bloodied each other up, but they got into matches like this a few times a year, usually over stupid stuff.

While the brothers tried to overpower each other without actually inflicting harm, Jo took the opportunity to snatch the keys from Dylan. After they were secured around her neck, back where they belonged, she shouted, "Just stop this! You're both being ridiculous!"

The two boys were stuck in a stalemate and stopped their forceful tangling. They exchanged a look, making sure if one stopped, the other would stop too. Meeting eyes, they came to an unspoken agreement. Dylan let go of Daniel's neck and Daniel let go of Dylan's t-shirt. From the ground, they watched as Josephine walked toward the farmhouse by herself.

Eventually, Daniel and Dylan brushed themselves off and headed toward the house as well. They were hungry before the wrestling match, but now, they were famished. No words were exchanged as they moved across the field. There was nothing to talk about, really.

Inside, Jo was fixing lunch. "Sit. Both of you," she said, putting two plates on the table. She didn't have any intention of joining them this time but the boys obeyed anyway. "Well?" she began. "Are you gonna apologize to each other or what?"

Dylan spoke first. "I'm not apologizing to him. He's an asshole."

If only Dylan knew how ridiculous he sounded, calling his brother such a name when that exact name was still written on his own forehead. If only he knew. Josephine took pity on the youngest McElroy, how pathetic he looked just then. She grabbed the shiny silver toaster, unplugged it from the wall, then placed it in front of him so he could see his own reflection. Dylan looked furious at first, seeing the backwards letters in the toaster. Then, his fury turned to heartbreak. His older brother, the one guy he looked up to, had done is to him while he slept and let him walk around all day like this.

Daniel went first, offering an apology. "I'm sorry I wrote that on your forehead. It was just a joke. I had to get you back for the frog in my bed, right?"

Dylan had nothing to say, no forgiveness to offer, no smile to crack.

"It was just a joke," Daniel repeated. "I'm sorry."

Dylan was silent. He got up and stormed off to the bathroom, ready to wash his face. Jo followed after him. She knew Dylan would need her, whether or not he admitted it. When she entered the bathroom, Dylan's blue eyes were red and puffy. He was scrubbing furiously at his forehead but had no luck getting the letters to fade using just soap and water.

"Can I help?" Jo asked in a quiet voice.

Dylan sniffled once. "No."

"Don't be so stubborn," she said, reaching into the medicine cabinet. She emerged with a tube of toothpaste and squeezed some onto a cotton ball. Without his permission, she reached up and dabbed the letters, starting with the A. In no time at all, the ink was gone. It was like magic. Dylan watched her, took in the sight of her face so close to his. It was nice to be cared for like this, in a motherly way.

Just as Jo was wiping down his forehead with some cold water, cleaning off the aqua foam, Dylan said, "I was just kidding about the kiss. I mean...I was gonna give the keys back either way. I just thought...maybe...I dunno. I was kidding around."

"It wasn't funny."

Dylan took a deep breath. "Jo, I think you know by now...it's pretty obvious I like you."

She said nothing in response.

"I think you like me too. You don't have to admit it...just...well maybe you and I could...will you be my girlfriend?"

She shook her head, declining.

"Why not? Is it because I talk too much?"

"No. It's because there's no point. You two are leaving tomorrow. Once I pay you, you'll be on your way."

"I want to stay. Ask your dad if we can stay longer. We can keep working. I don't want to leave, but Daniel...screw him. He can leave. I don't care."

"Don't say that."

"I mean it. I'm tired of him. I don't want a brother anymore. I just want...you to be my girlfriend."

"I don't want that. I don't want to be anyone's girlfriend."

After a long pause, Dylan followed up with, "Not even Daniel's?"

"Not even Daniel's," she replied flatly. "You two shouldn't fight like that. You're family, you're blood. You should be watching each other's backs."

"He's always telling me what to do. I hate that. He's only thirteen months older, it's not like he's my dad or something. What gives him the right?"

"He's just looking out for you."

"I don't need looking out for."

Finished with her cleanup job, Jo replied, "We all need looking out for."

Back in the kitchen, Jo sat with Daniel and ate her sandwich. Daniel hadn't touched his food; his stomach was sour. Not only had he gotten into a fight with his brother, the boy he practically raised and watched over every night of his life, but Jo had witnessed the whole thing. Daniel was left with nothing but regret now, regret and an untouched turkey sandwich.

"Thank you…for everything," Daniel said quietly. "And I'm sorry for everything too. Thank you and I'm sorry."

She nodded, acknowledging she heard him.

"Sorry you had to see that. Sometimes…we just go at it. But we always get through it. By the end of the day, we'll be brothers again."

"You're brothers right now. You should act like it. You have no idea how lucky you are to have someone so close to you. You don't have to be alone, not ever. Don't take that for granted."

Dylan joined them in the kitchen a moment later. He began eating his sandwich. His forehead was pink, a little irritated from all the scrubbing, but at least there was no longer a message written there. Dylan asked his brother, "Can you pass the mayo?" and Daniel did. They were already making progress on patching things up.

It was getting to be late in the afternoon. Not much work had been done today, just a lot of emotional damage. Jo glanced out the window at Millie, who was strolling around like the whole state of Nebraska belonged to her, and said, "I need to drop off the spinach in town. Either of you want to come with me?"

"I do," both boys said in unison.

"Fine. We'll all go," Jo said, unwilling to let another fight happen over nothing.

"I'll put her in the barn," Daniel volunteered, taking responsibility for Millie.

Dylan sat in the middle of the truck's bench seat, Daniel was on the passenger side, and they all headed towards Morton to drop off their pickings at the market in exchange for some cash. Dylan got to meet Mr. Ulrich for the first time, got to feel the old man's judgmental eyes scanning him over from head to toe like Daniel experienced earlier in the week. Jo got to hear the old man's words of warning about how all young men were after one thing and one thing only. She reassured the man, told him her daddy wanted to make plans to go fishing in August, then wished him well till next time.

"Since this is your last night in Morton, you guys wanna eat out?" Jo asked, gesturing toward the café across the street. The brothers shook their heads up and down, always hungry, always ready to eat whatever was in front of them.

This town was so small, the sight of sweet Josephine Larsen at a table with two strange boys was enough to inspire lots of gossip throughout the café. People were wondering where her daddy was, casting strange glances, exchanging whispers, developing wild rumors, but Jo didn't care. She may have had fair skin, but it was thick. People could say whatever they wanted. They always talked about her daddy, ever since he yelled at a persistent pastor in front of the entire congregation and called him a 'soul collector' and a 'headhunter' and 'God's gift to televangelism' among other insults. After that infamous Sunday morning outburst so many years ago, Johan, who was awfully young to be a widower, left the church with a screaming redheaded toddler and never came back. He kept to himself for the next decade and a half, and became less and less present over the last six months, which only fed the rumor mill around Morton. Like her father, Jo didn't take any of that speculative talk personally. Around here, speculative talk was one of the few forms of entertainment.

"So where are you two gonna go next? You'll have plenty of gas money tomorrow," Jo said in a positive voice that was almost believable.

"Dunno," Daniel replied, fiddling with his napkin.

Dylan took a turn to speak. "Jo, do you think we could talk to your dad, maybe ask if we could stay and work another week or two?"

"I don't think so," she said, tracing her finger over the rim of her water glass.

"Maybe if we could meet him, and he could see we're not a bunch of freeloaders, he'd let us work for a while longer," Dylan went on.

"I don't know," she mumbled.

"Please?" Dylan begged.

"For how long? How long would you want to stay?" she asked tentatively.

"Few more weeks?"

Daniel chimed in, speaking to Jo to keep the pressure off her. "It's okay. You don't have to agree to anything. We can leave tomorrow if you want us out."

Jo thought about it. A wrinkle appeared in her forehead, indicating she was thinking quite hard at the moment. "Just a few more weeks? Till the harvest is done?"

"Yeah. Just a few more weeks," Dylan echoed, pleased how this conversation was turning around.

"I'll ask my dad," she said, looking up to Daniel who knew darn well she couldn't ask her dad. "You two might be able to stay a little longer. But no more fighting."

The brothers looked at each other and nodded, agreeing to her terms.

While Jo excused herself to the ladies' room after they finished eating, Dylan told Daniel, "I asked her out today and she said no. Do you think it was too soon?"

Daniel was surprised and it showed. "What do you mean you asked her out?"

"I asked her to be my girlfriend. She said she didn't want to be anyone's girlfriend, not even yours."

"Why the hell did my name even come up?" Daniel's face turned red and his throat closed up a little. He started tearing his white paper napkin into tiny bits.

"I don't remember," Dylan said. "So do you think she just wants, I don't know, like…a friend with benefits sort of thing? Since she doesn't want a boyfriend? Do you think she's a free-love hippie? Doesn't want to get tied down?"

"If she said she didn't want to be your girlfriend, or anyone else's girlfriend, then I think that's exactly what she meant. I'd leave her alone, if I were you."

"But I think she likes me. I really do. She just doesn't know how to let herself like me back. Ya know?"

"That makes zero sense."

"It makes all the sense in the world. She'll come around. A few more weeks of working with her in the fields, and she'll come around. I wish I could meet her dad. Winning over her dad would be a huge gain. She seems like a daddy's girl and if her dad likes me, she'll feel comfortable liking me back. I know she does deep down. I can just tell. It's a sixth sense."

Daniel shook his head, not wanting to argue anymore. If his brother was so disillusioned, so be it. Dylan was staring beyond Daniel now, watching something or someone move across the café. He nudged Daniel in the ribs and nodded towards the waitress who'd been taking care of them. "Look at her tits. Now that's what I'm talking about."

Daniel frowned. "What about Jo? You over her already?"

"Nah. Jo's great. I'm crazy about Jo. I'm just saying…that woman over there has a really nice rack. Don't you think? What if Jo had a rack like that? She'd be perfect."

Daniel didn't reply. Jo was already perfect, but what was he supposed to say in response? He was too busy thinking to speak out loud, too caught up processing what his brother was saying, not so much about certain body parts Dylan had a preference for.

Dylan drained his water glass and said, "Will you help me with Jo?"

"Huh? Like...how?"

"Help me get her. Help me win her over."

"She doesn't want to be won over, Dylan. She's made that perfectly clear."

"She's just playing hard to get. That's all it is and you know it just as well as I do. And you're good with stubborn girls. So you gonna help me or not? You owe me for the asshole thing."

"No. I did the asshole thing to get you back for the frog thing. We're even."

Dylan shook his head, disagreeing. Putting a frog in Daniel's bed a few weeks ago was funny, a little mean, but Daniel's harsh retaliation was uncalled for. With a single nod, Daniel gave in and replied, "Yeah. Alright. I'll help you get the girl. Then we're even."

CHAPTER EIGHT

Friday was much like the other days. Routines were easy to form on the Larsen farm. Breakfast was at 6:30 a.m. in the small kitchen, where Daniel prepared his sweet spicy oatmeal recipe and black coffee. These were his responsibilities now, part of his morning duties, and they were all better off for it. After eating, they got right to work in the fields, watching over Millie as they did so. As usual, Dylan did more talking than working, while Jo and Daniel did the opposite. The three of them, even counting the lazy one, could get an awful lot done as a team, much more than Jo could ever manage on her own. Today, they finished up the spinach at an impressive rate. It was payday, which probably helped the boys keep a little pep in their step. They were owed five hundred dollars total, a hundred bucks each day for all five days they'd worked. That was more money than they ever had before, and they didn't even have it yet. Just the thought of so much money was enough to inspire the boys.

"So when do we get paid?" Dylan asked over supper.

"Don't be rude," Daniel chastised, even though he was thinking the same thing.

"Don't tell me what to do," Dylan snapped back.

"Stop it. Both of you. Stop it. Can you get through one meal without arguing?"

"Sorry," Daniel said to Jo.

"He started it," added Dylan.

"What are you? Eleven?" Jo asked him, annoyed.

Dylan shifted in his chair, ready to defend his maturity. "I'm eighteen. Technically, I'm older than you."

"Then act like it," she went on. Jo let a quiet moment linger before she continued speaking. "Anyway. About the money. I'm going to the bank tonight. I probably won't be back till late so I'll just give it to you in the morning, if that's okay."

"It's seven o'clock. You got banks open at this hour in that little sleepy town of yours?" Daniel inquired, clearing the dishes from the table. "Not that there's any rush. Tomorrow's fine for the money."

"I'm going to Omaha."

"Can I go with you?" Dylan chimed in from his spot by the stove. He would never dream of clearing the table after dinner.

"Nope."

"Why not?" he persisted.

"Because I didn't invite you."

"Please? I promise not to argue with Daniel."

"Oh? So what, now Daniel's coming too?"

"No. I don't know," Dylan said, shrugging his shoulders.

"Neither of you is invited. I've got a hot date tonight."

The brothers looked at each other from across the kitchen, trying to determine if she was pulling their leg. It seemed she wasn't. Before they could ask any follow up questions, she went upstairs, keeping all the mystery intact. Josephine Larsen had a secret for every hour of the day.

Annoyed once again, Dylan asked his brother, "Does she really have a boyfriend? She said she didn't want a boyfriend. What the hell?"

"Dunno," Daniel replied, pretending he was less shocked than he was. If she really had a boyfriend, why hadn't she mentioned that yet? If she really had somebody special, why did she kiss somebody else by her father's grave? The phone never rang at the

Larsen house, there were no love letters coming in the mail from a long distance admirer. Jo didn't appear to have any friends out here, let alone a boyfriend.

Dylan folded his muscular arms and demanded to know, "If she really has some boyfriend, what the hell am I supposed to do? Steal her away?"

"She just rejected you yesterday. I mean, it's been twenty-four hours. Give it some time, Dylan. Then…try again, if you must. You have to be patient with girls, you can't just chase them till they give in from exhaustion. You gotta earn their trust, and I mean really earn it."

"Earning somebody's trust can take forever. I don't want to wait. This is taking too long. She's taking too long to…to…why can't she just…I don't know…change her mind about me?"

"Quit bugging her to death and talking her ear off, and quit bickering with me while you're at it, and who knows, maybe things will fall into place by the end of the harvest."

Dylan rested his face in his palms. He rubbed his eyes and admitted, "Sorry. I'm being a really big asshole, aren't I?"

"Only a little bit."

"Do you ever wish you were an only child? Do you ever wish you could get rid of me?" Dylan questioned.

Daniel sat down with his brother. "Do you know how many times I could have gotten rid of you? Do you know how much effort it took to stay with you all this time? They wanted to split us up and send us to different homes. It's hard to place siblings, not everyone can take two. Do you know how many times I had to persuade them to keep us together? And what about the last year? I could have left. I was old enough to leave, but I didn't. You piss me off like nobody else but I love you. So don't stay stupid shit like that, about me wanting to be an only child. Got it?"

Dylan cracked a smile. He needed to hear that.

Daniel continued, "C'mon. We better get washed up. It's getting dark out soon."

The boys headed outside. The whole parcel of land was lit up with the last rays of the golden sunset. The perimeter of trees looked even darker now, in contrast to the fields. In the shadow of the farmhouse, the boys took off their shirts and jeans and tossed them into a washtub beside the screened-in porch, the Larsen version of a laundry basket, then proceeded to the watering trough by the barn, the Larsen version of a bathtub. Millie was roaming around near the barn, stopping to drink some of the bath water from the trough while the boys splashed her for fun, then she went about her business looking for moss in the gutters again. Since Jo was inside, out of sight as she primped for her mystery date, Daniel and Dylan stripped down the rest of the way, getting 100% clean this time with their sponge bath. They weren't shy about Millie standing there, the tall girl getting a good view of everything. She wasn't impressed. In fact, Daniel could almost swear the creature just scoffed at him and his naked self. Each brother hung up his boxers on the fence near the trough and continued washing, lathering up and rinsing down. Dylan's hair was as short as his attention span, and he typically used a bar of soap to wash his head. Daniel, on the other hand, always took the extra minute and spent the extra buck on shampoo, something sweet smelling, though if you asked him flat out, he'd deny it and say something like "I just use whatever's in the shower", which was only a decent excuse when you share a bathroom with a foster family member of the opposite sex. As Daniel rinsed off the tropical suds from his head, Dylan rolled his eyes and teased, "Pretty boy," though his big brother was anything but. Daniel was doing well if he could remember to shave a few times a week and even when he did, he looked fairly scruffy with his overgrown hair and wrinkled clothes.

By the time the boys realized Millie had their boxers in her mouth, she was halfway to the farmhouse. They were stark naked out there, several yards away from the rest of their clothes. Daniel and Dylan looked at each other, wide eyed and alarmed, then back at Millie who had just played an exceptionally devilish move. A giraffe had their underwear sixteen feet off the ground and she wasn't interested in returning it to them any time soon.

"See?" Daniel said through gritted teeth. "It's no fun to get your underwear stolen, is it?"

Dylan laughed, amused for the time being. Then, his face dropped when he glanced back at the farmhouse. Millie's head was peeking in the second story window of the farmhouse, and wouldn't you know it, Josephine was hanging out of that same window, petting Millie's head from her bedroom.

"Whatcha got there, sweet, sweet girl?" Jo asked Millie, eye to eye, tugging on the fabric in the giraffe's mouth. Millie released the underwear, almost on command. She only listened to Josephine, it seemed, not those silly boys who rescued her from certain death at the zoo. Jo looked up at the brothers once she realized what she was holding. Her jaw dropped too.

"Shit!" Dylan exclaimed, and ran for cover in the barn, showing his white rear end to the world as he dashed several yards in a blur of nakedness. For such an exhibitionist, always wanting to display his perfectly toned body in front of girls, he sure ran fast now, shy as ever. There was just one part of him he wasn't ready to display yet.

Now, it was just Daniel standing there, only partially covered by the trough. He grabbed a dented washtub, used it to cover himself, and made the walk of shame towards the farmhouse. When he got below Jo's window, he looked up at her and the prankster giraffe. Millie, unimpressed as usual, batted her long eyelashes as if to taunt him further. Her long wispy tail swung, adding to his torment. Josephine wasn't much better. She was twirling his boxers on one finger while smirking a sexy little smirk.

"Are these yours? Or are they Dylan's? I can't decide which one of you would wear alligator boxers."

He cleared his throat and tightened his grip on the washtub so expertly placed to cover up his most private of parts. "Those are mine," he admitted, only half embarrassed. He knew those alligator boxers she was currently twirling, his favorite ones, had a huge hole on the side, right at the waistband seam. Jo noticed it immediately.

"Want me to sew these up for you? It'll only take a second," she said, knowing full well he wanted them back now, hole or no hole.

"That's okay. Just…toss em' down, would you?"

"What about Dylan's?" she asked, holding up the plaid pair in her other hand.

"You can keep his, that little chicken shit." Daniel glanced back to the barn where his brother was peeking from behind the door, hiding his body shamefully while watching to see if his sibling could smooth talk his way into getting their underwear back.

"Don't be silly. Let me sew these up for you. It'll just take a second," Jo said again, intent on mending his underwear right then and there.

"No. Jo…" he started.

She left the window briefly and returned with a needle and thread, looking believably domestic, even for a tomboy. She gave Millie something, candy, perhaps, which she chomped away on and gave Daniel a look from above that showed just how much she preferred this redhead who slipped her tasty treats. Hanging out the window once more, Jo got to work stitching up the hole in the threadbare alligator fabric, while Daniel waited patiently below, holding onto that washtub for dear life. This was very uncomfortable indeed. Desperate for something to focus his eyes on other than Jo above, Daniel glanced over at the setting sun, just beyond the corner of the house. A bundle of cables and wires crawled down from the roof, carrying captured energy from the solar panels. Daniel let his eyes follow along the cables, tracing their route from the roof all the way to the door of the root cellar.

Jo couldn't cook, but she could sew. The rip was mended in no time at all and she let the boxers float down. A breeze threw them a few feet off course, so Daniel had to find a way to bend down and get them while keeping the washtub exactly in place, all the while Jo watching from above. It was anything but graceful.

"Thanks. I owe you," he said sarcastically, retrieving his boxers from beside Millie's enormous hoof.

"That'll be a hundred dollars, city boy," Jo teased as she handed Dylan's plaid boxers back to Millie to do with whatever she pleased, and closed her bedroom window once more.

Daniel kept the washtub over his front and held his boxers over his backside, then scampered back to the barn. Dylan was more than a little pissed his brother hadn't retrieved his boxers too, but Daniel felt Dylan needed to learn to do things for himself sooner or later. This was a lesson learned, for sure. As Daniel pulled on his boxers and inspected Jo's handiwork, he couldn't help but laugh. The rip was such an odd shape that her stitching looked like the letter J. J for Josephine. How appropriate.

"So what am I supposed to do?" Dylan whined, buck-naked in the barn, both hands well placed like he was protecting himself for a penalty kick.

"I'm sure Millie will tire of your boxers soon enough."

"I hate you," Dylan growled.

"No you don't."

"You're right. I don't. But I should."

"That's more accurate," Daniel said, pulling on a pair of clean jeans. He shook his wet hair, spraying water like a dog. He really needed a haircut, it was getting long, overgrown around his ears, turning wavier and wilder each day.

Daniel pulled a fresh shirt over his head, covering his tattoo and the rest of his skin and bones. Dylan started dressing as well, everything but the boxers. He looked uncomfortable already. Feeling sorry for his baby brother, unable to pull off this tough-love deal for very long, Daniel went outside to track down the batty old giraffe and reclaim what didn't belong to her. Luckily, Dylan's boxers were right there on the ground, just beside the water trough. She practically put them back where she found them, quite the unpredictable creature.

"How come Jo won't let us use the shower inside?" Dylan asked.

"Dunno. It's her house, her rules."

"Do you think it has something to do with her dad?"

"Maybe," Daniel replied, pretending to wonder about a man who wasn't alive anymore to wonder about. "Maybe he's strict."

"Maybe," Dylan hypothesized. "Did you really meet him?"

"Course I did," Daniel lied.

"What's he like?"

"Quiet."

"Like Jo?"

"Even more quiet. Hardly spoke at all," Daniel filled in. "Seems like a nice guy though."

"Think he'll be here for dinner tomorrow night?" Dylan went on.

"Probably not. He's got a lot going on. He's really active with protesting bills and saving bees and things like that. Jo can take care of the farm so he handles other stuff. That's the impression I get, anyway."

"I just…I think it's a little weird he's never here. Don't you?"

"No. Not really. Jo's fine. She's totally capable. She's…mature."

Dylan let his lips curl up in a smile as he swooned, "I like that about her."

Daniel wanted to say me too, but he kept his mouth shut. He already promised to help his brother win her over, even though she wasn't up for being won over. He made a promise to his brother, and that was all there was to it.

Through a crack in the barn, Daniel watched Jo go into the root cellar and bring up two soft black bags, overnight luggage perhaps, then load them into the cab of the white pickup. She had changed clothes. She didn't look like a farmer's daughter anymore. She looked like a trendy teenager in her tight jeans and black tank top. Her hair was down, still wet from her shower, but released from its usual ponytail. It looked like she might be wearing eye shadow, maybe a little liner too. She was even wearing a watch and had a slim pink cell phone stuffed into her back pocket. This wasn't the plain-Jane Josephine running a farm anymore. This was a girl dressed to kill.

Surprised by his sudden swell of jealousy, Daniel started to wonder about this supposed hot date happening tonight, somewhere in Omaha. Did she really have some bull-riding boyfriend who was going to take her out for nice medium-rare steak, then line dancing with friends, followed by a few beers in some city park after dark? Was he going to kiss her Cherry Chapstick lips and run his fingers through her soft red hair? Would he get those tight jeans off her tonight in the front seat of his oversized pickup truck and run his rough hands all over her porcelain skin? Whoever he was, this fictional boyfriend Daniel just dreamed up, he wasn't good enough for her. Neither was his girl-crazed brother, for that matter. And when he thought about it a little more, as much as it pained him to admit to himself, he wasn't good enough for her either. Nobody was.

CHAPTER NINE

It was 7:45 a.m. on Saturday morning. Jo hadn't come to wake them yet, but there were plenty of songbirds willing to fill in for her. Daniel rolled over and watched the sun sneak through cracks in the barn and illuminate the ground in a striped pattern. He had just rubbed his eyes open the rest of the way when it hit him. Jo wasn't home. Something was wrong. Wide-awake now, Daniel sat up and peered through the cracks in the rough wood walls to see if Jo's white pickup was in the driveway. It wasn't. Adrenaline shot through his chest at the mere thought of something bad happening to Josephine.

Daniel woke up his brother, needing someone to share in his panic. "She never came home last night," he said quickly.

Dylan made a confused face. "You think she slept over at her boyfriend's?"

"She doesn't have a boyfriend."

"How'd you know?"

"Gut feeling."

"So now what?" Dylan wanted to know, though he wasn't willing to get up just yet and clutched his blanket protectively.

"I think something happened to her. We need to go look for her. Get dressed. C'mon. We gotta go find her."

"Okay but... we don't have a lot of gas. We won't make it to Omaha. Well. I don't know, actually. How far is that from here?"

Daniel shrugged. It didn't matter. He just wanted to get this search party up and running as soon as possible. The thought of Jo stranded on some deserted highway with a flat tire flickered through his mind, followed by a flash of Jo's body all bloody in the truck upside down in a ditch. "C'mon! Hurry!" Daniel said, rushing his brother. They left the barn without feeding Millie. She would have to deal with the leftovers from her dinner last night, if there were any.

Just as they pulled the transport vehicle around to the other side of the barn, Jo's white pickup truck turned at the mailbox and rolled down the gravel driveway. She was alive. She was home. Desperate for an explanation, Daniel stopped the truck and got out. He was at her driver's side window before she even put the thing in park.

"Where the hell have you been?" Daniel blurted out, just as she opened the door to exit. "We was worried about you. We thought...you was in an accident or something."

Jo looked tired. Her eyeliner was slipping, smudged after a long night of doing whatever it was she was doing in the city. There were two empty coffee cups in the cup holders. Daniel stared at those two cups for quite some time. Those two empty cups proved everything. She and her boyfriend had coffee together in this truck last night. What else did they do in here? Did they talk? Did they make out? Did they go all the way? Daniel's heart sank. Then, he perked up a little when he noticed a box of caffeine pills on the passenger seat. She was trying to stay awake for the drive. She had two cups of coffee and some caffeine pills to help her stay alert on the road. Surely that would explain it. The opened box of pills was next to the black bags she took with her last night. The bags were empty now, sagging in on themselves. She went on some strange date, that's for sure.

Dylan joined his brother beside the truck. "Are you okay?" he asked sweetly, without a trace of anger in his voice.

"I'm fine," she replied with a smile. "Really. I'm fine."

She looked happy but tired. The smile on her face was one a girl might have after spending the night with an exceptional lover, a satisfied but worn out kind of smile. Daniel took a deep breath, discreetly smelling the air around her, hoping to find some clues like aftershave, some distinct male aroma. Nothing. It didn't smell like she'd been drinking either. It just smelled like coffee, like she'd been intent on staying up all night for some reason.

"How was your date?" Daniel inquired, watching her face closely.

Jo blinked and looked away. "Fine," she said.

Daniel smiled to himself because that little blink gave her away. There was no date.

She reached across to the passenger's seat to retrieve something from her bag. "Here. I have your money." She pulled out one of several rolls of cash that was the diameter of a beer can. She unwrapped the rubber band and counted off five hundred dollars in twenties, then handed it over to Daniel, hoping to erase any suspicion. He accepted it, looked down at the gas money they'd been working all week to earn, then he looked back at her thick roll of cash which was one of four rolls. Even though she just parted with five hundred bucks, it hardly changed the diameter of her roll. She had to be in possession of several thousand dollars, easy. He had never seen that much cash in all his life.

Jo passed between the boys without further explanation and went into the house. She didn't explain where she'd been or how she'd gotten all that money. She certainly wasn't making that much selling rhubarb. All the cattle had been sold months ago, right after her father's death, so Daniel wracked his brain about what she was doing or selling that brought in such high quantities of currency. Maybe she was slowly selling off her family's heirlooms, her father's things, putting away the money for her future in pigs, hiding it all over the house in every nook and cranny, every canister and hollowed out novel. Perhaps there were a few less rare books on those packed shelves after all. Maybe that's what was in the bags. Or maybe, maybe she was selling something else. Something unthinkable. Daniel felt nausea creep in. Surely there were several thousand dollars worth of scumbags in Omaha who'd pay a seventeen-year-old girl for some dirty deed in the front seat of a pickup truck. Daniel started to feel lightheaded now. Maybe she had more than one hot date last night.

When Jo was inside, out of earshot, Dylan turned to his brother and said, "She's so pretty, I wish she would dress like that every day," like nothing could possibly be wrong. He wasn't having the same sickening thoughts as his sibling.

Flabbergasted, Daniel replied, "Are you kidding me? Did you see all that money? Doesn't that disturb you in the slightest way?"

Dylan shrugged, not concerned about it. "She's a farmer's daughter. They probably don't have bank accounts and stuff. She probably keeps it under her mattress."

Daniel rolled his eyes, though he wouldn't have been surprised if there was cash under her bed. "She has a cell phone and an MP3 player from God-knows-when. I think she's modern enough to have a checking account, Dylan."

"What does it matter? She paid us, like she said she would. Her dad said we could keep working a few more weeks. We can make a few thousand dollars by the end of the summer."

"Yeah. Maybe," Daniel said flatly.

He left his naïve little brother and headed towards the farmhouse, expecting Jo to be in the kitchen. He was ready to confront her, ready to demand an answer. If she was selling her body to keep this farm running, Daniel was prepared to talk her out of it. There was no way it was worth it. He opened the door, gathering the words he'd use, but she wasn't in the kitchen. "Jo?" he spoke, but heard no reply. Daniel found her on the couch, sound asleep. She hadn't even made it up the stairs. Her little upturned nose was producing some un-lady-like snoring sounds and her black tank top had ridden up a little, exposing her navel. Her tummy was perfectly flat, perfectly smooth, and about the palest skin tone Daniel had ever seen on a living human being. Her belly button was smiling at him, a toothless, jolly smile.

Watching her dream without a care in the world or a wrinkle of shame on her face told Daniel all he needed to know about her nighttime adventures. There was no way she did anything degrading last night, no sign of shameful encounters was present on her peaceful expression. Jo's head flopped to the side as she fell further into the unconscious realm. She looked like a child, innocent and perfect. Watching her sleep with her neck crooked like that made Daniel wince. She'd be in agony if she slept like that for too long. Carefully, he slid his arms under her knees and shoulders, and lifted her up. She weighed hardly anything, just a string bean of a girl.

Breaking the rules, Daniel ascended the creaky stairs. Josephine didn't stir, she was passed out, even the screaming stairs couldn't rouse her. Her room was the first door Daniel came to. Ever so gently, he placed her body on her bed and covered her with the green and white quilt that was crumbled at her feet. It looked like she wasn't one to make her bed or clean her room, not today, not any day. It was a mess, a disaster of Jo's belongings. There were clothes all over the place, stacks and stacks of books. Perhaps this was the one and only perk to being an orphan. There was nobody to nag her about cleaning up.

Surrounding a mirror over her cluttered dresser was an impressive collection of brightly colored prize ribbons. Her 4H victories were numerous. She'd showed many a winning cow in her day. A photo of young Josephine wearing two braided pigtails lured Daniel closer for a better look. She appeared absolutely ecstatic in the photo, all of her too-large teeth were showing in a proud grin as she clutched a blue first place ribbon close to her chest, draping her arm over the massive neck of the brown cow beside her, as though the two had been best friends all their lives.

By the window, next to an old-looking computer monitor that was nearly two feet deep, there was a pyramid of Marlboro Reds, all empty packs. These were her father's cigarettes. She'd been buying a pack a week since his death in order to keep the shopkeepers from getting suspicious, so by Daniel's calculations, there were about thirty packs neatly stacked by the window. She was a good girl, didn't smoke them herself, only lit them and let them burn at her daddy's grave, as if to entice him to rise from it. The collection of small red and white boxes was piled with such care, stacked in such a particular way. It didn't fit with the chaotic state of her bedroom. Everything, with the exception of those cigarette boxes, was carelessly tossed, but those empty packs were meticulously placed. It must have been a special ritual of hers, adding another box to the stack, marking another week without her father. It must have been her way of paying her respects.

Tempted to look through her things and find out more about her now that he was in her room and she was out cold, Daniel resigned himself to leaving her be. She needed to sleep, not have some nosy young man going through her drawers. Before leaving, Daniel gently touched the corner of her pink mouth with his thumb, remembering what her lips felt like. They had to be the softest substance on the planet. He couldn't resist leaning over to deliver one gentle kiss to the tip of her button nose. Dylan would never have to know, and neither would Jo.

The brothers ate breakfast alone. Dylan wasn't too concerned about Jo's mysterious disappearance last night, but more about how to impress her today. He was scheming ways to knock her socks off when she woke from her current state of exhaustion. He was ready to try some new tactics, more than just his charm and chatter. It was time to get out the big guns.

"I wanna get Jo some flowers," Dylan declared, like it was the best idea a man could have.

"Flowers?"

"Do you think the market has some? We could go into town, maybe. We need soap anyway."

Daniel watched his brother, read his determined expression. Dylan was serious. He thought flowers were the way to her heart. Even though Daniel knew there was a lot more to it than that, he would have to be a good older brother and help pull this off. They had a deal, after all.

"Yeah. We can go get some flowers," Daniel started. "I think Mr. Ulrich can help us out. But let's finish the far field first, before it gets too hot. Then we'll go. Okay?"

"Okay," Dylan said with a grin.

"What kind are you gonna get?" Daniel inquired, raising his mug to his lips, sounding old and wise.

"Red roses."

"Really? That's kind of...predictable. Don't you think?"

"All girls like red roses."

"But she's not like other girls, remember. She's in a whole different league."

"What about...what were the one's Grams used to like?"

"Tulips."

"Right. Tulips. Maybe those. Or what are those ones that are real pretty but smell bad? You know, the orange ones?"

"Tiger lilies."

"Those are nice too. What do you think?"

Daniel thought for a moment, hiding a smile. "She's more of a...wild daisy kind of girl, if you ask me."

"Huh," Dylan hummed, processing Daniel's advice. "Why do you think that? Why do you think she's a wild daisy kind of girl?"

"She's simple and sweet. She's not fussy or high maintenance. She likes nature the way it is. She's delicate but...hearty." Daniel could have gone on and on, using words like 'pure' and 'perfect' and 'unexpectedly uncommon' but he stopped himself.

Dylan nodded his head slowly, considering this idea. "But wild daisies don't cost money. I gotta actually buy her something for this to count."

The morning was spent in the fields, as in mornings past, just without Jo this time around. They remembered to feed Millie several hours later than usual, which annoyed the old girl, but they made up for it with some extra kale and got her satisfied before they left for Morton. They borrowed Jo's white pickup instead of taking the stolen transport vehicle with the adjustable roof, since it would be less conspicuous. She rarely drove the other truck, the red one that once belonged to her father. The white one with the University of Nebraska sticker on the bumper was her truck of choice and it had a Cherry Chapstick wedged in the ashtray to prove it. The thing had over 200,000 miles on it, 204,199 to be exact. Surely she wouldn't mind them using it for an hour to run this errand.

Daniel took the liberty of playing her music box, getting another taste of this Doug Burr person she liked so much. When they made it downtown, they headed for the market, taking time to chat with Mr. Ulrich for good measure. This old man seemed like he had connections and spies all over Hooker County, so if the boys wanted to stay here for the time being and stay under the radar, they needed to be nice to this old geezer no matter what. There were a lot of "yes sirs" in the conversation the boys carried on with the man. They'd never been so polite.

Roses. That's all the market carried. Just roses, any color you could dream up, but no other variety of flower. It was slim pickings out here. Dylan was ready to settle for a dozen pink ones and call it a day, but Daniel told him he could do better. They were in the process of driving to the next town over when Daniel screeched the breaks and pulled over. A patch of wild daisies lined the side of the country road, beautiful and white. The boys gathered up a huge bouquet and headed back to the Larsen farm, full of pride, but each for very different reasons. After arranging the daisies in an old watering can, as well as two young men could manage, they called it a job well done.

Jo didn't wake up till almost three in the afternoon and would have slept longer if it hadn't been for the ever-impatient Dylan chucking little pebbles at her bedroom window from the driveway. Annoyed, she got out of bed and pulled back the curtains to see Dylan and his masterpiece that just couldn't wait any longer. That afternoon he'd decided to go all out, to do more for her than just pick flowers from the side of the road. He and Daniel had spelled out JOSEPHINE on the gravel driveway, using nothing but vegetables from her fields. She cracked a smile as she peered down at the message, then burst out laughing when Millie came up from behind Dylan and started eating the top of the S. Daniel was sitting on the porch, watching his love-struck brother run off the giraffe yelling "You greedy ol' bitch!" Jo glanced down to see Daniel and gave a shy wave. He waved back. She disappeared from the window and reappeared on the porch moments later. This shadow on the front steps was Daniel's place to stay while Dylan took all the glory and kept the spotlight.

With a jar of Mr. Wessel's raw honey and a pack of graham crackers in her arms, Jo plopped down next to Daniel on the top step. She opened the lid and dipped half a cracker in, then tilted the jar towards Daniel, wordlessly sharing her favorite snack. "What's all this about?" she asked, nodding in the direction of Dylan's vegetable message.

He shrugged, buying himself time to finish chewing. "You'll have to ask Dylan. It's all him."

"Is he responsible for the flowers on the table?" she inquired, watching Dylan chasing after Millie like she was just an oversized puppy.

"Yep. That's all him." It was a lie, but he was determined to be a good brother and help Dylan get the girl. Daniel McElroy was on a selfless mission now.

Jo smiled and hugged her knobby knees. "Maybe he's not as dimwitted as I thought."

"He's a good kid," Daniel explained, sucking a drop of wayward honey from his thumb. "Just a little…goofy sometimes."

"And chatty," she added.

"And chatty," he agreed. "He has a pretty big crush on you. I guess you already know that. Do you think…is there any way you might…reconsider?"

"Reconsider?"

"About being his girlfriend. I know we've only been here a week or so…but maybe after a few more weeks…after you get to know him a lil' better, could you give him a chance? That's all he's asking for. He's a good kid."

Jo watched Daniel's eyes, searching for something. He was pleading on his brother's behalf, the same boy he wrestled to the ground the day before.

Cautiously, Jo asked, "Does he kiss like you?"

Daniel exhaled a laugh. "Dunno. I've never kissed him."

Jo chuckled at that.

The two of them looked out across the driveway to see Dylan climbing up the side of the barn, coaxing Millie to come closer. He was holding onto a drainpipe, leaning his arms out toward the animal. Before it occurred to Josephine or Daniel what he was up to, Dylan was on Millie's sloped back, holding on to her thick neck.

"Dylan! No!" they both screamed from the porch.

Dylan waved at them, proud as can be for having mounted a giraffe, bare back, no less. Millie wasn't fond of this. She started running at top speed, galloping across the pasture while Dylan held on to her neck for dear life. He looked like the stupidest cowboy that ever lived. All this, just to impress a girl.

Daniel was in awe of his brother's idiotic demonstration unfolding before his very eyes. He was frozen on the front porch next to Jo, neither sure this was really happening or how to end it. Typical Dylan had figured out a way to do something showy and reckless, got on Millie's back seven feet off the ground, but he hadn't thought through how to dismount. Unfortunately, Millie decided for him. She bucked like a bronco and Dylan went flying through the air. A cloud of dust rose up from the ground where he landed.

"Awwwf!" That was his first scream. "Fuck! Fuck!" he went on, rolling onto his side as Millie left him to writhe in agony after noticing some tasty looking trees. "I broke my fucking arm!" Dylan continued yelling.

Josephine sprinted to his rescue, followed by Daniel at a slower pace. When she came upon the boy in the dirt, she feared he was right. His left arm, which broke that long fall he just took, was likely damaged. He held it close to his body with his other arm and groaned in pain on his back. Dylan was trying so hard not to cry, now that Jo was crouched down close to him. He had to be brave for her and act like breaking an arm was no big deal, like it happened all the time. He had to be tough.

"I'll be right back," Jo said firmly, turning back for the house.

Alone with his brother now, Daniel whispered, "You stupid little punk!" as he knelt down to comfort his moronic sibling, though he was really tempted to give him a hard kick in the ribs. "You are so stupid!"

Through gritted teeth, Dylan asked, "Did she see me? Did she see me before I fell off?" The poor kid, he was only concerned that breaking his arm by falling off a galloping giraffe hadn't been for nothing. "Did she see me?"

Daniel smiled and shook his head in disbelief. "Yeah. She saw you."

That made his little brother smile, put him at ease for the time being. Seconds later, Jo pulled up in the white pickup and helped Dylan into the cab. They all squeezed in and got on the road, going for medical attention, presumably. A mile down the country highway, something occurred to Daniel. "Uh. Jo? Is there someplace we can take him that's not a hospital?"

"Huh?" she said, watching the road ahead. A large bug splattered on the windshield just then, ending its life with a brown smudge.

"We sorta...ran off from our last foster home. I don't know if they're looking for us or what. I mean, legally we didn't have to stay there no more, since we're both over eighteen now. But I...I was thinking...if we go to a hospital, we'll have to do paperwork and stuff, and they'll ask for his ID."

"Oh," she said, catching on. "Good call." She made a U-turn in the middle of the road and headed back in the other direction, passing by the farmhouse and onward. They passed wheat fields and barley fields, some cattle ranches too. After a thirty-minute drive listening to Dylan trying to control his breathing, they turned off the main road. This plot of land they were driving through was mostly fenced in. There were a dozen horses roaming the green pastures, ranging from brown to black, to reddish auburn. The house at the back of the property was even smaller than Jo's and the roof was in need of repair, however, the barns looked immaculate. It seemed the horses were the top priority here.

"Whose house is this?" Daniel asked, careful not to disturb his brother's arm as he helped unload him from the truck.

"Ms. Olsen. She's a sweet lady. She'll help us out."

Ms. Olsen was already standing in the doorway, her long dark hair braided to the side. It seemed she wasn't used to visitors all the way out here, but glad to have some for a change. She looked concerned, her forehead wrinkled when she saw Dylan grimacing and clutching his arm. "Come in. Come in," she said, opening the door for the girl she hadn't seen in a year and two boys unknown.

"He's broken his arm. Can you help us?" Jo said, not bothering with introductions. They were here and they needed help. No need to beat around the bush. The woman was in her late fifties, she had a tabby cat circling around her ankles, and she had the most compassionate smile this side of Yellowstone.

"Sit down, child," Ms. Olsen said, gesturing to a chair in her dining room. Dylan took a seat, as instructed. The woman inspected his arm, touched his tender skin till he yelped. "It might be fractured but it's not split through," the woman informed Jo and Daniel. "Let me see what I have to fix him up with."

Ms. Olsen left the three of them in there, surrounded by dizzying red and white floral wallpaper. The wood table in the center of the room was hand-built, simply crafted, and looked like it might weigh eight hundred pounds. It was solid. Daniel thought the woman might have Dylan lay down on the table, like in a doctor's exam room. Was this woman even a doctor?

With a bottle of Jack Daniel's Tennessee Whisky in her left hand, and a bucket of supplies in her right, Ms. Olsen returned. First, she poured a shot of whisky for herself, downed it, then refilled the little glass for Dylan. He looked up at his older brother, wordlessly asking if it was okay to take it. Daniel nodded. It was probably in Dylan's best interest to be a little out of it. With his good arm, Dylan raised the glass to his lips and cautiously sipped it. He made a disgusted face.

"Just throw it back, son. The quicker the better," Ms. Olsen said, pulling items from her bucket and getting set up for the work to come.

Dylan drained the glass, made a face like his throat was on fire, then a small smile crept to his lips. "Can I have another?" he asked Ms. Olsen and his brother, all at once. Daniel nodded. The woman poured again, and Dylan drank it. Now, they were ready to get down to business. Jo and Daniel watched from the same side of the dining room table as Ms. Olsen unrolled bandages next to Dylan.

"Owww!" Dylan shrieked, when Ms. Olsen moved his elbow.

"Ahh!" he screamed this time, when she flexed his wrist.

"Shhh!" she hissed, then moved it again.

Dylan bit his trembling lower lip, trying to keep quiet. He was doing his best to be courageous, gritting his teeth down hard every time the pain shot through the left side of his upper body. Ms. Olsen got to work wetting plasters and putting them over Dylan's forearm. He couldn't help the few tears rolling down his smooth cheek, the handful of sniffles escaping from his nose. Daniel could almost feel his brother's intense pain. Every time Dylan flinched, Daniel flinched too. Seeing this sensitive brotherly reaction, Josephine reached for Daniel's hand and squeezed it reassuringly. He looked over at her, grateful for the small gesture of comfort.

"You're almost done," Ms. Olsen said, sliding a sling over Dylan's head and under the cast on his forearm. "Now tell me, young man, how did this happen?"

Dylan looked at his brother to bail him out, as usual. He couldn't tell the truth, that he fell off a reticulated giraffe while trying to impress Josephine Larsen. Daniel, not wanting to lie to this woman he hadn't officially met yet, passed off the responsibility to Jo with a glance. Josephine had no choice. She was up.

"He fell off the back of my pickup. We were all just being silly, riding around and he fell off when I turned a little too tight. It was stupid."

"Yes. It was stupid, Miss Josephine," Ms. Olsen confirmed. "Your daddy didn't raise you to horseplay like that."

"No, ma'am."

"And you won't be going round doing nothing like that in the future, I reckon?"

"No, ma'am."

The woman changed her serious expression and poured herself a shot of whisky for a job well done. "That's the first time I ever set a bone for a person," she said, proud as can be.

Dylan's face dropped. He looked pale now, like his arm might fall off. Ms. Olsen wasn't a doctor, it turned out. She was a vet. Daniel started laughing. He asked, "Ms. Olsen, how much do we owe you? Would you say he was comparable to setting the broken leg of a jackass? Or more like a mule?"

Ms. Olsen chuckled. "With all his screaming, it was more like a Billy goat. They make such racket when they get banged up."

"We'll pay you fairly. What do you normally charge for setting the broken bones of Billy goats?" Daniel inquired, pulling out his wallet.

"Oh, hundred dollars or so," Ms. Olsen replied.

Daniel's head popped up, hearing that familiar charge. "You two related or something?" he asked, glancing back to Jo. "Everything in this town costs a hundred dollars."

"Hell, just give me ten," she said. "For the whisky."

Daniel paid the woman, thanked her again, and led his patched-up brother back to the truck. Dylan's arm was secure in a white sling. He was carrying the bottle of Jack in his other arm, though it only had a little bit left by now. Ms. Olsen told him to self-medicate tonight, that he should take a swig every hour or so, just to take the edge off the pain. Dylan was delighted by the doctor's orders. He'd never had alcohol before, he felt like a man now, like a sailor who had traveled the world and bedded hundreds of women. He also felt a little wobbly as they returned to the Larsen farm.

When they pulled in, they all noticed the barn door was open. Nobody put Millie inside before they left in such a hurry. She was nowhere to be seen. That crazy old giraffe had finally done it. She escaped. Jo looked to be the most upset. Her eyes misted over. Millie had become her charge, her pet, and now she was off and she wouldn't likely return. Daniel scanned the tree line, hoping a giraffe-shaped head might peek over the tops, but he saw nothing. With a heavy heart, Jo and Daniel helped Dylan to the living room and settled him in on the couch.

With plenty of whisky in his system by now, he was fast asleep in minutes. Daniel leaned over him and released the bottle from his grasp. He whispered, "Goodnight Dylan, I love you. I won't let you die in your sleep, you stupid, stupid idiot."

Daniel took the cap off the whisky, took a small swig for himself to speed up the forgiveness of his brother's dumb antics, then tilted it in Jo's direction. She looked down at the floor, and shook her head no. "I don't drink," she explained, as though she was nothing but a disappointment.

Together, Daniel and Josephine went outside to the barn to close it up for the night without Millie. "Want me to go out looking for her?" he offered, holding his lantern up as they walked. "How hard can it be to find a giraffe in Nebraska?"

Jo managed a defeated smile. She put her hand on the door to the barn, ready to slide it shut, but stopped when she saw who was inside. With astonishment and joy, she said, "Not very hard, apparently." Jo pointed into the dark barn, just barely lit by Daniel's lantern.

Millie was in there, right where she was supposed to be. She'd put herself to bed, brought herself in for the night without any apple bribes, without any trucks rounding her up. For once, she was a good girl, not a wild animal. She was swaying ever so slightly as she slept with her head near the hay trough, high above everything else, with one eye open and one eye closed, just like always. As ornery as she may have been every other day of her life, Millie had found it in her twenty-three-pound heart to come home tonight.

"I'll keep her company," Daniel said, gazing up at the beautiful beast.

"You can sleep in the living room again, if you want."

"It's okay. I don't want to be…*any* trouble."

"You won't be *no* trouble at all," she said with a wink, borrowing Daniel's poor grammar since he was improving after just a few days' worth of her corrections. "It's okay if you want to sleep inside. I know you don't want to be apart from Dylan, especially after a day like this one," Jo offered.

"I think maybe it's better we spend a little time apart."

"Why?" she questioned. Josephine hugged herself, like she was cold, even though it was a warm summer evening. The insects outside were humming away already, singing their melodies all at once.

"Because I like you. I like you a lot. And he likes you too. A lot. And that's not good."

There, it was all out in the open. All that honesty in a few short words.

Jo didn't say anything in return. She looked from his left eye to his right, searching for something. She must not have found it because she turned to leave without speaking and closed the barn door behind her, but not before glancing back one time.

CHAPTER TEN

"Jo! Wake up! There's something wrong with Millie!" Daniel was standing at her bedside and the hour was 2 a.m. "There's something really wrong with her," he said again, in case she wasn't truly awake the first time.

Josephine rose from her bed, ready for combat. Her giraffe wasn't well; no time could be wasted. Loudly, she thumped down the stairs and stepped into a pair of dark green rubber boots that clashed with her ugly nightgown oh-so-spectacularly. She grabbed a flashlight and raced out the door and Daniel followed after her with a camping lantern. Dylan continued sleeping in the living room with the bottle of Jack sitting on the coffee table sympathetically watching over him.

In the barn, Millie paced around. She was agitated. For a normally silent creature, she was making an awful lot of noise, a variety of low hums and annoyed huffs. Millie dropped to her huge knobby knees, then stood back up. She couldn't get comfortable, didn't know whether she wanted to kneel or stand.

"She's sick," Daniel began. "I think her stomach is upset. She's been eating a lot of soap lately, she ate three whole bars since last week. I bet that's what it is. She's been like this for two hours, she's gone to the bathroom like…a hundred times…it's gotta be her stomach. But I wasn't sure, that's why I woke ya up."

"Her stomach's upset?" Jo questioned, stepping closer to the animal.

"Think so. Look," Daniel said, pointing towards her big belly just as a muscle twitched oddly. "Do you think she has...gas...or something?"

"I don't know," Jo said, watching the strange convulsions happening around the swollen belly of the giraffe. Suddenly, something shifted in Millie's body. Her bulging belly flexed again, her tail raised up too. "She's in labor," Jo gasped.

"She's in what?" Daniel questioned, but Jo was already springing into action.

Jo ran over to the giraffe's backside and pointed up. "She's gonna have a baby!" The excitement in her voice was something Daniel had never heard before. She wasn't afraid of what was about to happen to this old girl, she was thrilled. "Millie's gonna be a mommy!"

Millie huffed another heavy breath as if to say I'm ready. Daniel, who was not ready for this by any measure, croaked, "What do we do?"

"We wait. She'll do it all on her own. We just wait now."

And wait they did. Daniel and Jo found a spot below the loft and watched Millie continue her pacing, and after about a ten more minutes of this, they watched something start to emerge from her womb. It was a foot, a round hoof about the size of a saucer, followed by a scrawny leg, all contained in a thin white sack. The process was slow. Daniel and Jo remained where they were, letting Millie and Mother Nature work things out. Daniel reached for Jo's hand, wanting his palm on hers for comfort as they watched this miracle unfold before them.

By 3:05 a.m., two legs and a head were out. They dangled lifelessly from Millie, who was getting tired, it seemed. She was so old, this had to be tough on her. At one point, she even closed her eyes, as if to take a nap, a little break from her delivery. Each time she tried to push, her front legs quivered. Daniel and Jo held hands, waiting, waiting, waiting. The miracle would happen in its own time.

When 3:45 a.m. rolled around, Jo's magical expression slowly vanished. She released her hand from Daniel's. "Millie stopped pushing, and I'm pretty sure it's coming out all wrong," she said, approaching the giraffe and her half-born offspring. "Her baby won't be able to…its neck is…we have to help her finish or the calf will suffocate."

Daniel believed her every word. This almost-newborn giraffe couldn't remain like that: half in, half out. For the second time that morning, he asked Josephine, "What do we do?"

Hands on her hips, ready for a fight, she spoke firmly, "Go get the ladder. It's by the root cellar."

Daniel went at once. He ran towards the house, located the ladder by the moon light, and dragged it to the barn. He made quite a racket doing this but there were more important things to worry about. When he next laid eyes on Jo, she had on rubber gloves up to her shoulders. Now, he truly understood what had to happen and was thankful he wasn't going to be the one to do it.

They placed the ladder behind Millie, praying she wouldn't decide to back up any time soon. Jo climbed to the top with her long rubber gloves on, and Daniel spotted the ladder, ensuring it wouldn't sway too much. There was nothing he could do should Millie move suddenly, but he felt better about holding it in place rather than standing around idle while Jo did all the work up top.

"I helped my dad with a breech calf last spring. This should be just like that. Only seven feet off the ground. Right?" Her voice was nervous, unsure she could really do this. She took a deep breath and lifted Millie's tail out of the way. The tired mother-to-be turned to look at Jo curiously, but didn't move or protest. She still wouldn't push and if she wasn't going to push, it was time to pull.

Jo cringed as she dug in. Daniel cringed too. With all her might, Jo pulled and pulled, inching the baby into the outside world. The helpless creature dangled still, covered in white mucus. It was dark brown and scrawny. Jo was up past her elbows now, still pulling, using all her strength to free this enormous baby that was probably twice the size of the calf she helped birth with her father's supervision. "C'mon Millie. Help me out here," she said, gritting down her teeth as she pulled some more. Millie refused.

Once the calf was two thirds of the way out, gravity took over and it went plunging to the ground with a splat. What a way to be born. It toppled over on its head and flopped to its side. Jo gasped in horror. She wasn't expecting to catch the thing, but she wasn't expecting it to crash to the floor of the barn like that either. It made a weird squishy thud when it hit the ground, a sound everyone heard and would never forget.

A voice spoke from the other side of the barn. It was Dylan's. He was joining them at the most peculiar time. "Oh my God. That's disgusting," he said, before he turned to throw up on Daniel's blanket. Just then, the placenta fell and burst along with a surprising amount of fluid, and Dylan gagged, "That's even more disgusting," and threw up again. It could have been the whisky catching up with him, but most likely it was the sound of slime hitting the floor which turned his stomach in such a violent way.

Daniel wasn't feeling so good himself, looking at what was on the ground in front of his feet. He'd never seen a newborn anything, but this strange long-legged mess covered in all sorts of stuff wasn't particularly appealing to look at. Before the nausea could catch up with him as well, Jo spoke from above.

"Is it alive?" she yelled, backing down the ladder. "Is it alive?"

"I can't tell," Daniel replied, watching the creature for signs of life.

As soon as both feet were firmly planted on the ground, Jo removed the soiled gloves and crouched down to inspect the newborn. With her bare hands, she pushed away some of the mucus from the giraffe's nostrils, clearing a passage for air. "It's a boy," she said. On cue, Millie turned and leaned her head down to smell her brand new baby. She stamped her hoof once, letting Jo know she needed to give her and her baby boy some space. Jo obliged, glad some motherly instincts had finally caught up with Millie.

Now that Dylan was done retching, he joined his brother and Jo by the door, watching, waiting for something to happen. Millie used her nose to nudge the body of her calf, as if to wake him. Nothing. No movement. Jo's eyes turned glossy. All her hard work pulling that baby free was for nothing. It wasn't showing any signs of life. Mother Nature could be so cruel sometimes.

Daniel put his arm around Jo and squeezed her shoulder. "You did everything you could. You were awesome up there."

Jo sniffled now, the reality sinking in as each long minute went by. Millie, this old giraffe who was so out of place on this farm, who was not sick or overweight, as it turned out, had become incredibly special to her, and this baby was a total surprise. If only he could be alive now. He was perfectly still, his ribs weren't moving up and down, his eyes weren't open either. Millie sniffed her baby again, licked him with her long rough tongue, and still, there was nothing to prove he had made it. After nearly ten minutes of nervous anticipation from the group and no movement from the creature on the floor, Jo gave up hope and buried her face in her hands and turned away. Daniel started to reach out to comfort her, but stopped himself. Standing beside his brother, wishing there was something he could do, he watched the sad pile of giraffe on the floor, totally still. But then, he saw an ear twitch.

Daniel whispered, "Look," and Jo lifted her head. "Watch his ears."

After a moment, the ear twitched a second time. Jo's eyes lit up. "He's alive," she said quietly, as if to keep her voice from frightening the poor thing. His fur was dark brown, wet with birth, and his ears were flopped over like a dog's, but they were moving all right. Josephine clasped her hands together and jumped once, silently bursting with excitement.

They all watched in awe as the baby opened his eyes and lifted his pointy head. He looked so frail, all disorganized on the floor, just four long legs and a deflated body. After looking around for about fifteen minutes, surveying his environment, the baby wriggled and tried to stand, but failed. Millie licked the newborn some more, then smelled him again. Each time the baby tried to stand, he failed and fell back to the ground, letting gravity win every time. Jo wanted so badly to help him, support his body so he could try out those lanky legs, but Millie was circling around him protectively, ready to stomp at any potential predators, even Josephine.

In just over an hour's time, the scrawny newborn finally stood up. He had fallen over about twenty times in a row, once he even ended up with all four feet in the air, far too weak to use his legs. Now, he was finally upright, as wobbly as can be. Millie continued licking him, furiously cleaning her boy, getting acquainted with her offspring. The pre-dawn sky gave the barn a pinkish cast. Out of everyone watching, Millie included, Josephine was the proudest. She smiled so widely as the baby put one hoof in front of the other. Now, tears of joy filled her tired eyes where tears of sorrow once were. This truly was a miracle, although if you asked Dylan, he might not agree.

"We should name him Yoda," Dylan said, pausing to yawn. "He looks just like him, except not green."

"Since Jo acted as midwife, I think she should name him," Daniel added.

Jo liked that offer and it showed. She smiled, cocked her head to the side and watched the baby teeter towards his mother, waiting for just the right name to inspire her, which didn't take long. "Napoleon," she said, and that was that.

Daniel smirked. "That's perfect. Napoleon and Josephine. An unlikely match, it's true, but one of history's greatest love stories. Suits him."

Napoleon was helpless but tireless. He was walking well by 5:30 a.m., able to keep himself from toppling over. Before long, he was standing taller and searching his mother for milk, which he found, and helped himself to a great deal of. Millie took a nap, letting Napoleon feed while she did so. She was awfully tired after such a night, especially since she was so advanced in her years. It was no wonder the animal park didn't know what was wrong with her. She was too old to worry about her breeding successfully, so she got away with a fifteen-month gestation period while everyone just thought she was moody or sick, and maybe a little chubbier than she should be. She wouldn't let anyone near her to find out what she was growing in her big belly.

The entire morning was spent in the barn, watching Napoleon grow up before their eyes. He was dry now, his mother licked him clean and he was a beautiful shade of auburn. His patterning was a small-scale map of lines, simple shapes that fit together perfectly, just like his mother's borders and boundaries. Napoleon's big black eyes were glossy, so dark you could almost see another world in them. His face was still wrinkly, pruney from being in the womb for so long. His little pointed mouth was just a dopey smile as he looked around, taking in the world. There were two hair-covered nubs for horns, but they weren't yet upright, still leaning inward in these first few hours. The line of hair down his neck, his short-cropped mane, was bristly and darker red than the rest of his fur. His face had more white than Millie's, even his long eyelashes were light in color. His kneecaps were way too big. He would have to grow into them.

"He's going to be a handsome devil," Jo declared.

After a quick break for lunch, and a change of clothes for Jo, they all came back to the barn to watch Millie and Napoleon, giving them plenty of room to feel safe, but unwilling to miss this magical first day of the baby giraffe's life. So much was happening every hour. Napoleon was walking perfectly now, even running a few yards at a time, after just a half day's practice, and he was hungry as can be. He was also starting to get curious about the three humans by the barn door, who had been watching him since he opened his eyes. Scanning over them with his funny little face, he started to approach, but Millie stamped a hoof in front of him, letting him know it wasn't safe to wander off just yet. Obediently, he stood under his mother, ears askew, a smile on his fuzzy face.

Dylan asked, "Did she have that…uh…udder thingy before?" gesturing towards his own lower abdomen, giving Millie's under belly a weird look while Napoleon fed.

Jo cocked an eyebrow. "It's called a teat, Dylan," she informed him. She knew he'd find it funny, as immature as he was, and she folded her arms waiting for him to burst out laughing, which he did in about two seconds flat. Daniel just shook his head, amused by his predictable brother. As he stood there watching Napoleon guzzle his mother's milk, Daniel searched his memory for something that would explain why in the world the keeper at Northside Animal Park had neglected to notice anything peculiar about his female giraffe. The keeper had been known to show up to work hung-over fairly regularly, and he had certainly fallen behind on her medical records because he fully expected her to drop dead at any moment, which Daniel knew first hand having worked with the careless keeper for the last few months. Even still, the circumstances were all quite unexpected. First there was one stolen giraffe, and now there were two.

Everyone slept in the farmhouse that night, now that the barn was a nursery. Millie wasn't comfortable having anyone get too close to her baby. She was extremely protective of him. Daniel's blanket had been puked on by his brother and stunk of whisky and vomit, so it was time they upgraded to the living room and some new linens too. Dylan slept on the couch, like before, and Daniel managed with a quilt on the floor. At night, the boys looked up longingly at the ceiling as if they could see Jo up there.

Dylan quietly spoke, "You think her dad knows about the giraffes?"

"I'm sure he must by now."

"He's a pretty cool guy, if he's okay with all this. Don't you think?"

"Yeah. He's a pretty cool guy."

Dylan pulled the blanket up to his chin. "Goodnight, Daniel. I love you."

"I love you too."

"Don't let me die in my sleep."

"I won't."

Two days after giving birth, Millie was finally comfortable enough to let her young calf meet the humans, his new extended family. Jo was tall for a girl, but Napoleon was taller, especially since his horns were upright now. He came right up to her and sniffed her face. He was about six feet already. His big black eyes looked into Jo's gray ones, and they understood each other. A silent bond formed in an instant. Cautiously, she reached up to touch his long neck, waiting to see if he would startle, or if Millie would object. It seemed both giraffes were okay with this gesture, so she gently rubbed his fur, smoothing it downward.

It was only fitting that Napoleon meet the two boys as well, after he got a nice petting from the girl who helped birth him. He sniffed Daniel next and went right for his sweet smelling hair. Daniel let him chew for a while, let him slobber all over his messy brown mop, just to humor the little guy. "You're just like your mamma," he said, grossed out and amused. Jo told Daniel his hairdo was stylish, once Napoleon finished giving him a lopsided faux-hawk with his long purple tongue.

Next, the not-so-little giraffe wandered over to Dylan, who was still in his sling and would be for a few weeks. "He looks just like Yoda, doesn't he?" Dylan said for the hundredth time, taking in this funny little face before him. Napoleon's eyes were wide set, his gigantic ears stuck out sideways. He had a weird mouth and velvety lips that were always moving around. He was hairy too, short brown hair covered every part of him, even his eyelids.

After one sniff of the youngest McElroy brother, the giraffe lost interest and turned back to Josephine. She was much more interesting. While Jo petted his skinny neck again, Napoleon relieved his bladder all over Dylan, just like Millie had done that day in the field, only a lot less urine. Dylan's luck with the back ends of giraffe's hadn't changed and wasn't likely to.

"You are so gonna pay for that," Dylan told Napoleon before heading outside to the water trough to change clothes and clean up.

He had a heck of a time taking a sponge bath with the cast on his left arm.

While Dylan was outside, Daniel and Jo met eyes. She continued rubbing Napoleon's long neck, since he seemed to enjoy it, and Daniel sent an easy smile her way. She smiled back. There was something unspoken going on here, with a two-day-old giraffe standing in between them, who also appeared to be smiling if you looked at him straight-on. Daniel grinned again, feeling a little silly for doing so, and Jo blushed. Just then, Dylan came back with wet hair, wearing fresh clothes, and Daniel wiped the boyish grin off his face. Jo returned her attention to the animals, pretending Daniel didn't exist.

On the fourth day after his birth, Napoleon followed Millie out of the barn for the first time. He was a timid little guy, staying under her shadow. There were no predators here, no lions or crocodiles, but he knew in his little giraffe core that staying with his mother was all that mattered. He didn't take an interest in the vegetables or grass, or even the saplings at the edge of the property. For now, mother's milk was all he wanted. He needed a lot of it too, because by the seventh day, he was running at top speed. His little trot wasn't as elegant as his mother's gallop, but he could outrun Jo and the brothers already. For fear he might get curious about the road beyond the driveway, they always kept a close eye on him. Millie never ventured up that way but Napoleon was young, inexperienced at life as a giraffe, so they didn't yet trust him to choose well for himself.

Dylan also couldn't be trusted to choose well for himself. Even though his left arm was wrapped in hard plaster and set in a sling, he still found ways to do stupid things to impress Jo. He hadn't learned his lesson, which made Daniel uneasy. There were a lot of other bones that could get broken at this rate. Plus, his brother had a tender heart and that was bound to get crushed sooner or later. Dylan simply couldn't see that Josephine wasn't interested in him. He couldn't even fathom it. Every night before telling his brother goodnight, and that he loved him, Dylan talked about Jo and how pretty she was, how smart she was. For Daniel, it was tough to listen to. His own feelings had multiplied, and it seemed Josephine might share them, but there was a significant thing keeping things from going further, and his name was Dylan.

On Friday night, Jo transformed herself from a farm girl who birthed zoo animals, into the well-dressed seventeen-year-old with a pretty rockin' body. She wore her tight jeans again, a dark wash, which were made for those boney hips of hers. She wore an airy little top that showed off her shoulders and the freckles on them, plus a touch of lip-gloss on her pouty lips. The collection of small keys that unlocked her underground storage room hung on the chain around her neck and lay under her white blouse, as though they were part of her trendy outfit. Once more, she loaded up her truck with two black bags from the root cellar, and drove off for the night. This time around, Daniel refrained from panicking when she didn't show up for an early breakfast on Saturday morning. Though he didn't know where she went, what she was doing, or who she was doing it with, he trusted she would come home safe.

When he borrowed her truck to run a field's worth of turnips to the market in town on Saturday afternoon, and spend a little of his payday cash on some more soap and chewing gum, he noticed her odometer. Last week, it read 204,199. Now, just eleven days later, after a week of hardly any use other than her Friday night excursions due to all the excitement with Napoleon's birth, it read a staggering 205,987. Omaha was only 370 miles from Morton. Where on Earth did she drive to?

On Sunday, he had the courage to ask, "Where do you go on Fridays?"

"The city."

"What do you do there?"

"I go sight-seeing. I meet people."

"In the middle of the night?"

"Lots of things to see, lots of night owls in the city."

"Do you really have a boyfriend there? Is he one of the night owls?"

"No," she chuckled.

"Then why did you say you had a hot date? Was it to get Dylan off your back?"

"And to make you jealous. Did it work?"

Daniel didn't reply.

CHAPTER ELEVEN

"Does anyone actually eat these things?" Dylan asked, holding up a stalk of rhubarb with his good arm. He inspected the thing like it was from some foreign planet, apt to explode at any minute.

Wiping sweat from her brow, Jo said, "You'd be surprised."

"I wish you grew good stuff, like blueberries and strawberries. Seems like all we harvest around here is healthy stuff nobody likes."

"I'm gonna make one of Grams' rhubarb pies tonight. Remember those?" Daniel chimed in from a few feet away, diligently plucking rhubarb at a faster rate than his invalid brother.

"Mmm," Jo hummed. "I think Daniel gets a raise. He's the master chef around here."

"What about me?" Dylan pouted, pointing to his sling to remind her of his need for sympathy. "I should get worker's comp."

"You didn't get injured on the job. You got injured because you didn't use the brain in your head the way it ought to be used."

That hurt. Dylan passed off a teasing grin, like it didn't bother him. He told himself she was just playing hard to get, that her constant rejection was a good sign because girls only did that when they really liked a guy. Girls in grade school teased him mercilessly, but, as he found out if he stayed in the same school till the end of the year, those same girls were more than willing to give him a sloppy kiss at recess behind the playground. Females made zero sense to him, especially now, but oh how he desperately wanted to be with one in the most intimate way.

The straw hat Jo had been wearing to keep the sun out of her face blew off her head, right past Daniel. Quick on his toes, though not so quick for long distances, Daniel chased after it. Seeing him running inspired Napoleon to run as well, practicing his running-with-the-herd instincts. He was so fast, the giraffe, that is. He could break ten miles an hour already, just two weeks into his young life. Those stick legs of his were functioning well, growing stronger by the day on his mother's nutrients. Out here, on this wide-open farmland, he was encouraged to get plenty of exercise. With the swift breeze at his back, Napoleon galloped back towards his mother, not wanting to get too far from her just yet. Daniel caught up with the hat, caught his breath too, then walked back to the rhubarb patch where Jo and Dylan continued their work, letting Mr. Wessel's bees fly peacefully overhead.

"Thanks, hot shot," she teased, accepting the hat. She didn't bother to put it on her head again since the breeze was too strong now, knowing there was only so much Daniel McElroy could do in a day with his well-read physique. She let the lightweight hat hang on her back, the leather cord tight to her throat, keeping it in place. Another updraft put dirt in Dylan's blue eyes. As he wiped it away with the only hand he had available, Jo looked up at the clouds. She looked beyond Millie and Napoleon in the far field, then back to the barn, and eventually scanned her eyes over the farmhouse, making sure things were as they were supposed to be. The weather vane was going in slow circles, unsure which way to settle on. North. East. South. West. Repeat. The afternoon sunshine was giving way to some dark clouds over the horizon. Millie seemed to sense something in the air. She stared off into the distance at nothing, ignoring her baby as he nudged her front legs for attention.

"I think there's a storm comin'. I'm gonna see if I can get them inside the barn and fed before it starts raining," Jo said, standing up. She walked over to the white pickup truck, in no hurry at all since the clouds were pretty far off, and began her routine of herding the giraffes by way of an old Toyota 4x4 that had no horn, no working AC, but excellent turning abilities. Those tight turns came in handy when corralling the animals into the barn for the night. Millie was being difficult today. She didn't cooperate like she usually did. It took Jo a few extra passes in the truck before Millie finally went into the barn. Before shutting the door, Jo asked Millie "What's gotten into you today?" Millie just stared off into the western sky, like she was waiting on her spaceship to come.

The brothers were still at it in the rhubarb patch when Jo returned. She tried to focus on the task at hand, on her precious purple crops, but she was more than a little distracted. Pieces of her red hair blew in her face, whirling off her head and out of her ponytail. She kept looking up from her work, scanning the horizon. Something was unsettling to her. The dark sky was getting closer and closer, eating up the fluffy white clouds. Still, it would probably take some time for the storm to reach them. The flat landscape was excellent for seeing what weather was coming. Surely they had time to finish up their rows before calling it quits and baking that rhubarb pie. Jo looked back at the weathervane spinning wildly. West. South. East. North. Repeat. It had changed directions. The copper rooster on top was getting dizzy. She watched him spin till he turned blurry.

Then, she saw it.

Beyond the farm house, just to the other side of the tree line, was a funnel cloud dropping down. The skinny gray finger from the sky brought darkness with it from the west, towing angry air along to wreak destruction on anything in its path. Right now, the Larsen farm was *directly* in its path. Jo stood up, dropped her stalk, and opened her mouth to yell but in her sudden panic, she'd forgotten what the word was. Tornado.

Daniel noticed Jo, and stood up as well, but his back was facing the danger. Still speechless, she pointed, watching as a second funnel cloud appeared next to the first one. Daniel's eyes widened when he saw it and he yanked his brother up by the t-shirt, accidentally pulling on his sling.

"Ow!" Dylan yelped, clutching his arm and scowling at his brother. Then he saw it too, and the shooting pain in his arm was washed away by a flood of adrenaline. Miles away, the warning sirens went off just as the two tornados joined together, making one enormous column of furious wind and debris. It seemed those sirens were caught off guard as well, blaring their warning just a little too late.

They all ran towards the house, leaving their baskets of crops behind. Mid-stride, Jo pulled the necklace with the keys from beneath her t-shirt. She fumbled to get them into the locks that secured the root cellar. It took her shaking hands several tries to get the combination right. Just as she opened it, she grabbed Daniel by the shoulders to say,

"What about the animals?"

Daniel shook his head, "We can't get them in here. They're too big. We don't have time."

"We can get Napoleon," she said, already sprinting back towards the barn. She was running *towards* a tornado, fearless and full of fear, all at the same time. She was going to save that little giraffe, with or without the help of the McElroy brothers.

"C'mon!" Dylan pleaded, one foot in the root cellar already. The wind was wild now, blowing his neat hair all over the place. He squinted up at his brother, trying to keep dust from getting in his eyes, and pleaded again, "C'mon! Get in! Daniel, c'mon! Let's go!"

Daniel set off running after Josephine. He'd never moved so fast in his life. His plan was to catch up with her and talk her out of it, tell her there was nothing they could do for the giraffes other than let them loose and hope they ran in the right direction, but when he got to the barn, he had no choice other than to join her mission. Jo was pushing the stubborn baby out the door, and Millie was stamping her hooves, very displeased by all this. Napoleon wouldn't cooperate and locked his legs to protest, so Jo could only move him by shoving his hind quarters so that he slid like a statue. The young creature was too scared to go along with Jo, too stirred up by his mother's rare display of aggression. Millie swung her whole neck backwards, winding up in preparation to bash her head into Daniel. She was ready to do whatever she had to in order to protect her baby. She didn't understand Daniel and Jo had the same mission, that they were putting their lives on the line to save Napoleon. Daniel dodged Millie's first swing, the horns on head she was attempting to use against him.

Before she could wind up for another try, Daniel looked at the baby giraffe, then at Jo. There was only one way to do this and no time to discuss it. "Alright. On three. One. Two. Three!"

The both groaned as they lifted Napoleon off the ground. He was well over a hundred and ten pounds already, and not only that, he was kicking those dangerous hooves as he was carried across the driveway toward the root cellar. There was no decent place to hold onto him, but they did their best, despite his squirming. Perhaps Napoleon was kicking so hard because he was being separated from his mother for the first time, and in such a violent way. Or maybe it was because he was the only one to see what was coming through the trees, plucking them out of the ground and sending them flying like toothpicks.

With much difficulty and plenty of cursing, the two of them got the six-foot giraffe lowered into the root cellar. Jo pulled the doors shut above her, struggling against the fierce wind that desperately wanted to take them away altogether. She took one last look outside, checking to see if Millie had in fact left the barn and made a run for it as she hoped, but Millie was nowhere to be seen. There, in the dark underground, they huddled together with Napoleon in the middle, eyes clenched shut. The baby giraffe made whimpering noises that sounded like crying, worried sounds they'd never heard before from an animal or a human. Then, they heard nothing other than the freight train overhead. The air pressure changed in their hiding place. Daniel's ears popped and he felt like his head was going to explode. With Jo to his right, and his brother to his left, he put one arm around each of them, begging this to be over quick. He would never let go.

The freight train continued on down the tracks, leaving howling wind in its wake, and then it was dead silent. That was probably the scariest thing of all: hearing nothing. Nobody moved, for fear the gray pillar from the sky would come back if it knew anything survived, and destroy them all for good. Daniel, Dylan and Josephine each had their eyes sealed tight so nothing could get in, no dirt, no horrors, no nothing. The first one to feel safe again was Napoleon.

The young creature started licking Daniel's hair, chewing on it. They could hear the noises from his funny little mouth. Daniel let out a breath of relief, thankful for a moment of humor after so much fear. "We made it," Daniel said, hearing his voice echo in a way he hadn't expected. This room must have been a heck of a lot larger than he thought. There was a strange smell too. Not a musty damp smell, but something fresh, something lively. He inhaled, catching the now familiar smell of soil, but there was something else too, something he recognized but couldn't quite put his finger on.

"Is there a light down here?" Daniel asked.

"Please don't turn it on," Jo said with a shaky voice.

"Jo, don't be silly."

"Please," she begged.

Dylan didn't care about the conversation going on between Jo and his brother, or about her strange request for darkness. He felt around for the light switch and illuminated the space. The darkness went away instantly, replaced with bright lighting that had a greenish cast. Daniel's eyes widened as soon as he opened them to take a peek at his surroundings. Now, he recognized that fresh grassy smell. He had smelled something similar just once before at a party in high school, and not since then. Staring at the distinct leaves on the plants, slender and pointed, he knew this wasn't some basement full of kitchen herbs. It was a cave for growing marijuana, and a lot of it too.

"Holy…" Dylan started, finally recognizing what was surrounding them. "Holy shit. Is that…holy shit. Holy shit!"

Daniel turned to Jo now, for some sort of explanation. She looked ashamed. Her secret was out, her business plan exposed. She wasn't making thousands of dollars a week selling your standard produce. While the boys scanned their eyes over what looked like acres and acres of the stuff, Jo looked at the ground, at her feet, because she couldn't bear to look them in the eye just yet. Her head snapped up when she heard chomping noises coming from the baby giraffe. Napoleon was having a taste of the lush green leaves all around him. He'd never had anything other than his mother's milk until now, but it seemed these leaves were quite palatable. "Stop! Stop eating that!" she said, trying to grab the leaves from his velvety lips. Napoleon refused and swallowed just to spite her.

She put her hands over her eyes, hiding her face, knowing this was a complete and utter disaster. Pretty soon, this baby giraffe would be raiding her fridge looking for cheese whiz and cookie dough, he'd be swaying to the rhythms of Bob Marley with his eyelids half shut, he'd be laughing at things that weren't really all that funny. "Stop it!" she hissed again, when Napoleon took another mouthful, a good hearty serving.

Daniel could hardly find his voice to ask, "Is this what you do Friday nights?"

Jo turned her attention to Daniel now, letting the giraffe get as much of that green stuff as he wanted. "Yes. I grow and I sell. But I don't *do* it."

"Yeah right," Daniel said, exhausted from processing all of this.

"I swear I haven't. I've never smoked a joint in my entire life and I don't plan to."

"They why grow it?" Daniel scoffed.

"Because I'm good at growing things. This pays better than beans and rhubarb, I'm sure you can understand that. It's just for the extra income right now."

"Jesus, Jo. What the hell have you gotten yourself into?"

"A lot of money."

"I bet," he said sarcastically, trying to guess at how many hundreds of plants were down here under these eerie grow bulbs powered by the sun.

"I'll be able to start buying pigs in less than two years if I keep going at this rate. Then I'll stop growing. I'll let it go. I just want the cash to get started. That's it. I swear that's it," Jo went on, offering up more information in hopes of keeping her friends.

"Where…how did you even learn how to do all this?" Daniel managed.

"YouTube," she replied with a straight face. Several seconds of silence followed. Jo knew there were more questions coming and there was no getting out of answering them so she waited.

"Who are you selling this stuff to? Gangsters?" Dylan chimed in, sounding more naïve than ever.

"I'm the start of the chain. I just do the growing, then I pass it off to the distributors and dealers."

"You could go to prison for this," Daniel stated, taking in the size of the room.

"I know," she said in a serious voice. "I could get up to fifteen years if I get caught. I know that. I knew that from the start, but I have to say it's been well worth it."

"Why on earth would you risk it?" Daniel questioned, astonished this book smart girl could get caught up in something so devious.

"I only have to get away with it for another year or two, then I'll quit growing. I figure my odds of getting caught in that time are pretty low. I work alone, my power source comes from the panels so my electric bill isn't suspicious. Plus, I'm really, really careful. I play this game on my own terms."

"It's Russian Roulette." Daniel drew a deep breath. "And it's not a game."

"I know what I'm doing, Daniel. I can handle it. I'm making so much money. You wouldn't believe how much. I'm taking a big risk, I know, but the payoff is more than I could ever dream. I'm gonna get my pigs and start running this farm the way I want to in no time at all. I won't have to harvest crops all spring and summer. I'll have a better life."

"You'll have a better life *if* you make it that long."

Daniel gave her a serious look, letting her know just how dangerous he thought this side job was. She swallowed hard in response. She knew it was dangerous, and now that Daniel and Dylan McElroy knew about it, the whole thing just got more dangerous than ever. Part of her security was that nobody suspected a girl like her could pull something like this off. Nobody knew where she lived or how she did it. Now, two people she hadn't known very long were privy to this highly sensitive information.

"Does your dad know?" Dylan inquired.

Jo didn't quite know how to answer that one, so she offered the truth, though not all of it just yet. "They're *his* plants. He started everything, then I took over."

Daniel warned, "I never thought you'd do something like this. I didn't think you could stoop this low just to make your dreams happen a little quicker."

"I guess you don't know me very well."

"I guess I don't."

"This farm means everything to me. This house…it means everything."

"It's just a house," Daniel said.

"It's *not* just a house. You wouldn't understand. You've never had a real home before! How could you possibly understand?"

As if on cue, the lights went out, a bit delayed as the last bits of large debris from the tornado smashed into the solar panels on the roof. Unwilling to stand there in the dark and argue about whether or not he ever had a real home, or whether or not selling pot to finance your dreams at an expedited pace was acceptable or not, Daniel turned and blindly felt his way to the steps and left the root cellar. Dylan followed after him. Jo waited for them to clear the doorway above, take a minute to breathe the fresh air and hopefully lessen their anger, then she emerged as well, guiding the stubborn little giraffe.

Standing at the mouth of the underground cavern, all three of them remained completely still, surveying the land, or what was left of it, at least. The house was still standing behind them, but other than that, there was hardly anything familiar. Huge chunks of trees were missing from the thick perimeter of forest. Some of those trees were in the old cattle pastures now, others among the crops. One tree was lying across the driveway, blocking the way out for the vehicles. It didn't matter though. Nobody was going anywhere because both trucks were missing.

Jo could see one nestled up in a tree, just a white hunk of metal hanging like a Christmas ornament. The other truck, the red one her father used to drive, was on its side among the radishes. The extra tall transport vehicle the boys had borrowed to drive all this way from Chicago was upright, but it was not where they left it next to the barn. It was up near the road now. But that wasn't what stirred them up the most, it wasn't what brought tears to Jo's gray eyes and a lump to Daniel's tight throat.

"Where's the barn?" Daniel asked in a monotone voice.

There was a mess of wood planks, scraps of metal, pieces of the roof, and an array of items that had once been inside the barn, strewn all across the piece of land where it used to stand. This wasn't a small barn, it was almost twenty-five feet high with a hayloft, but it was gone, utterly removed from the face of the Earth. The tornado just barely missed the farmhouse but it went right through the only other structure on the property.

Jo took a raspy breath and asked the question Daniel knew was coming next but couldn't bear to answer. "Where's...Millie?"

CHAPTER TWELVE

Josephine led the search party. She stomped off across the field, then she started to run, growing more desperate with each urgent step. The brothers jogged after her, and Napoleon galloped alongside them, trotting along with the herd. The sky was a brilliant blue now. Wisps of pink and yellow painted the canvas as if no dark cloud had ever trespassed there.

Jo ran along the perimeter of the property, peering into the woods, looking back across the field and scanning for any sign of Millie. Maybe she had indeed made a run for it, they left the barn open, after all. It was her only chance. Where was she? How far had she run? Even when Millie would wander to the edge of the farm, she was always visible, a bonus to being so large in size. But now, there was nothing that resembled her anywhere in sight. Still hopeful, Josephine moved towards a clearing in the woods that hadn't been there previously. These woods were so thick, so dense, this new clearing changed the lighting so dramatically it looked surreal.

In the center of this new open space was Millie, collapsed and broken. She'd been carried a half a mile and dropped here, thrown at the ground by the funnel of destruction. She'd hit the earth so hard there were piles of dirt all around her, a crater from her impact. Her big black eyes were closed forever, her eyelashes gently sealing them. Those long, long legs of hers were splayed out like they were nothing but rubber. Jo knelt down beside Millie's mouth and touched her fuzzy horns. She started to weep with her whole body.

With bloodshot eyes and a voice that wasn't her own, Jo instructed, "Take him away, don't let him see his mamma like this. Take him back to the house."

Daniel knew she was talking to him. He was the only one capable of action during a time like this. Dylan was just standing there staring. Josephine started to sob harder now, hiccupping with grief, so Daniel guided Napoleon away, hoping to spare him from nightmares, if he was even capable of dreaming. With no barn to put him in, Daniel led him up the front steps to the screened-in porch. It wasn't a lot of room for a baby of this magnitude, but it was tall enough for him to stand up all the way. Napoleon would have to wait on the porch by himself till there was a better option. Daniel just hoped the little guy wasn't so clever that he'd figure out the screens weren't very secure and he could probably break through them if he tried.

As he walked away from the farmhouse, Daniel could feel Napoleon's sad black eyes following after him. This two-week-old creation was motherless now. It was that heavy thought which pushed Daniel over the edge, drew the first salty tears from his emerald eyes. He hadn't cried in years but he knew what it was like to be motherless, how hard life could be even with the best of stand-ins. He wiped those tears away, walking straight through where the barn used to be, but more tears quickly replaced the ones he just ran off with his wrist when he remembered how young Jo was when her own mother had passed. They would all have that in common now: orphan-hood. By the time he made it back to Millie's remains and his brother and Jo, his face was damp from his cheekbones all the way to the stubble on his chin.

Josephine didn't even look up when he stepped closer. She was humming something, crouched down and rocking ever so slightly, petting Millie's soft head in a comforting way. Dylan was beside her, gently rubbing her back in hopes of getting her to stop crying, but it didn't do much for her. For Jo, she might as well have been the only person on the Earth. Growing tired of Dylan's tender gesture, his palm on her back, she pushed him away. She wanted to be left alone.

Dylan gave his older brother an I-don't-know-what-to-do look, some combination of a shrug and a cringe. Seeing a girl cry like this was something that made young Dylan incredibly uncomfortable. Daniel gave his clueless brother a nod, telling him to give Jo some space. Dylan backed away, obeying this silent order. They all were quiet now, except for Jo's crying. With Millie on ground level, her size was even more impressive. She was quite a creature.

With nothing better to do in that moment, Daniel pulled out his pocketknife and cut off some of the long dark hairs at the tip of Millie's tail. Her fly swatter, they used to call it. He smoothed the hair, about six inches worth, and began to braid it, keeping it taught as he worked his way down.

Daniel sat on the ground next to Jo when he was done. Gently, he took her by the wrist and tied the black braid around her thin wrist. "I'm so sorry, Jo," he whispered, wishing he could make all this pain go away. She'd been through enough pain already, enough to last a lifetime, if not several. Though it was Dylan who first fell in love with the giraffe, seeing her at Northside Animal Park as she caused all kinds of trouble in her pen, it was Jo's giraffe. Everyone knew she was Jo's.

Dylan took the opportunity to be insensitive and mocked, "Where's my bracelet? Huh? It was my idea to save her and now she's gone. I'm sad too!"

"Just shut up," Daniel said. "Just shut up, for once in your life!"

"Up yours," Dylan retorted, scowling at his older brother.

"Fuck off!" Daniel shot back.

Jo's small voice interrupted the harsh words being thrown back and forth. Sensibly, she said, "We should get some gasoline. We can't move her. We have to cremate her right where she is. We should do it soon. The vultures will be here any minute."

Leaving the boys to fight or argue or whatever brothers did when they were at their wits end, she walked back towards her home, the house she was born in. The whole farm was a mess. She passed by a swing set that didn't belong to her, a tire, a doghouse, a rocking chair, and even a hay bale, none of which were there just an hour ago. People's belongings became debris. The red gas can was found near the house, and once she grabbed some matches from inside, she couldn't help but stay with Napoleon for a few minutes on the porch. She hummed to him, stroking his neck with the hand that bore a piece of his mother's tail.

While Jo was gathering supplies for the bonfire, Dylan and Daniel were about to have a tense conversation. Boiling up with all sorts of emotions, Dylan pushed his brother forward with one arm, letting him know he was not pleased with him.

"What the hell was all that about?" Dylan began.

"What?" Daniel said, stumbling a little and catching himself.

"You know exactly what."

"The bracelet?"

"Yeah, dickhead. The bracelet. Is something going on with you two?"

"No," Daniel swore.

"Whatever happened to bros before hos?"

"For one thing, she's not a ho."

"So you're defending her now?"

"We're just friends. I swear. I just wanted her to know I was sorry for her. She's never looked so sad before. I just wanted her to know I was sorry for all this, that's all. We're just friends."

"You sure about that?" Dylan asked suspiciously.

"Positive. You can ask her yourself if you don't believe me."

"You know I like her. You've known all along that I like her. You're supposed to be helping me win her over. And as big of an asshole as you can be sometimes, going after the girl I like would really top the charts!"

Before Daniel had the chance to defend himself, the sound of a gunshot cracked through the air, followed by a wavering echo that seemed to carry on for miles. Startled, the brothers ducked instinctively, unsure which direction the danger was coming from. Another gunshot was fired, accompanied by a distant voice shouting "Fuck you!" Two more shots, two more fuck you's, and Daniel cautiously rose to confirm it was Jo responsible for both.

Halfway across the field, Jo set down a red gas can beside her feet, aimed and fired again at the sky, only pausing a second or two for each outburst of shells and profanity. For a moment, Daniel thought she was taking her anger out on God, attempting to send a shot of frustrated revenge all the way to the clouds in response to the life taken on this day, but then he looked up and saw her real target, the trio of vultures circling above the trees. In the distance, six more large bodied birds were approaching, ready to join in the inevitable feast. It was like they stalked the tornado, like they knew there'd be a larger than usual carcass waiting for them on the Larsen farm. Jo reloaded and shot again, her voice growing more raspy and desperate with her two word message for the scavenger birds who were forming a black feathered tornado of their own up in the sky, getting hungrier with each patient pass. Finally out of shells, seeing the birds were growing in numbers by the minute, fearless of her shots and shouts, Jo threw the shotgun to the ground and wiped her tears away.

Dylan was cowering on the forest floor, covering his ears in preparation for more gunshots. Jo didn't speak, she didn't acknowledge the boys as she approached the scene with her red gas can. Silently, on her own, she spread gasoline over Millie's brown patchwork hide. It seemed Jo didn't want any help with this task. It was her giraffe, after all, so this was her responsibility.

Daniel knew this wasn't her first time laying a body to rest. She'd had to dig her father's grave, move him to it, and bury him with no assistance whatsoever. She had to place that white rock and mourn for him, with nobody to comfort her. The hardened look on her face as she finished off the gas can over Millie's neck was a look Daniel could barely recognize her through. Her whole face changed, distorted with anguish.

Satisfied with the soaking, ready to get on with it, she tossed a match and stepped back. They all watched as the flames spread over the animal, quickly up her mane, singeing the hair, then more slowly over the rest of her. After a minute, they had to step back even more, because the heat was so great. The smell wasn't so great. Hair and flesh were consumed by the flames, sending smoke up into the dusky sky, deterring the vultures. The birds gave up and flew east, where they began circling over Ms. Olsen's horse farm.

In only a few hours, the bonfire in the forest at the edge of the Larsen property was just that, a massive fire with no recognizable shape, just bright red and yellow ribbons of flame extending from the charred mound.

The amount of smoke must have been more than they realized, because pretty soon a fire engine showed up. The well-equipped vehicle drove over the fields, right up to the edge of the forest where the fire was burning.

"Miss Josephine, you okay?" the first fireman asked, quickly approaching. With a head full of white hair, he looked like he might be a little too old for this profession. It was easy to see his back was hurting him.

"How could anyone be okay after something like this?" she said quietly. "The storm, I mean. How can anyone be okay after a storm like that one?"

The older fireman, now beside three others dressed exactly the same but at least thirty years younger than him, spoke firmly as he instructed, "You best move back and we'll get this fire out for you."

"No!" she yelped. The four firemen all looked at each other, then back at Jo. "It's fine. It'll go out on its own. Just leave it alone."

"Josephine, we can't just leave you here with a big fire like this. It'll spread before long. We've got a lot of other fires to put out, so we best be getting to work on this one. Did a propane tank land here or something? Do you know what started it?"

"Doesn't seem like propane to me," one of the younger firemen added. "It would be blue fire if it were propane. Besides, there would be shrapnel, don't you think?"

"Pretty sure I smell gasoline," another voice offered.

After another moment of silence, Jo choked out an answer. "I set the fire. It was a steer. Must have been from Mr. Berger's farm. The tornado came from the west, so yeah, it had to be his steer. I didn't know what else to do. I would have called Mr. Berger…but the phone lines are down."

"You done alright, Miss Jo," one of the fireman said, resting his hand on her shoulder. The decision was made to get to work and send a column of water towards the burning pile. As the firemen did their duty, Jo, Daniel and Dylan looked at each other uneasily. What if there was some shred of evidence left that would blow their cover story?

In order to keep them from looking too closely at the soaking wet black mud, buying a little more time for the sun to set and leave no incriminating light, Jo asked the firemen lots of questions. "Are there any casualties? Did everyone in town make it?"

"Far as we know," the older fireman replied. His sooty face was lined with pink creases where his wrinkles were free of ash. "Where's your daddy? He safe?"

"He's not here," she said. "He's in Topeka till the end of the week. Visiting some old friends. Glad he wasn't here for this."

"I'm sure he's trying to call you to see if you're alright. Soon as the phones are up, you best give him call and put his mind at ease. Ya hear?"

"Yes sir."

The fireman and his crew continued on their way without delay. There were disasters waiting all over Morton and the outlying areas. As the firemen drove the engine through the grass on the side of the driveway, since the gravel path was blocked by an uprooted tree, the older one looked back at the farmhouse and saw something very strange on the front porch. He squinted his dark eyes, trying to make it out in the twilight. It looked an awful lot like a giraffe, a small one.

He shook his head and rubbed his tired eyes once more. He'd seen a lot of strange things that afternoon, since the tornado hit. The whole town was shuffled around and things were showing up where they weren't supposed to be. So far, all five hundred and forty-one residents of Morton, Nebraska were alive, but every last one of them was shaken up. The firemen were shaken up too, getting delirious with exhaustion as they continued their duties through the night until reinforcements could be sent. Before they would finally go home for rest, they would see a live horse stuck in a tree, a frightened man stuck under a collapsed house, a confused heifer inside the café, and a screaming child on the roof of the church. Every rescue was stranger than the last and the illusion of a small giraffe on the front porch of the Larsen farmhouse wouldn't be all that memorable by the time they were done. The farmhouse was dark now. Jo and the brothers found flashlights, lit candles, and did their best to illuminate the space. There was broken glass everywhere. More than half the windows were shattered. While Dylan marveled at the damage, Jo and Daniel actually did something about it. She got to work taping cardboard over the broken windows and Daniel did his best to sweep up the glass. Jo wasn't humming while she worked, like she normally did. Her silence showed the extent of her fragility. The only sound she made was a quiet clink of the keys she wore around her neck.

They'd been working for hours cleaning up the first floor by candlelight, when Jo made the wise observation about the refrigerator and its lack of power. "We better eat anything that's gonna go bad. The power won't be back on for a few days."

"I'm starving," Dylan said, right on cue.

"Let me," Daniel said, taking action. "It's a gas stove. All we have to do is get a match to start it and we'll be good to go."

"You don't mind?" she questioned, looking grateful and tired.

"Of course not," he said with an understanding smile. "Just sit, take it easy. I got this."

She handed him some matches and watched as the stove produced a small flame that lit up the dark kitchen. Jo sat at the table and stared at nothing, Dylan talked about how awesome it was to have survived a tornado, while Daniel got to work cooking, using up whatever would go bad. He made scrambled eggs, bacon, turkey hash, sautéed chicken strips with herbs, vanilla pudding, milk biscuits with melted cheese over top and some fruit punch that combined the orange juice, cranberry juice, and the pitcher of lemonade. It was a feast. To top it all off, Daniel found a bushel of rhubarb from the field, and made that famous rhubarb pie he promised to make, using up all the butter. He was talking about making that very pie just six hours ago when they were in that field without a care in the world.

They ate like kings. It was a seven-course meal. Candles were placed all around the kitchen on every ledge, every flat surface, giving the small space a cozy feel. One of the two windows was boarded up now but the one facing front by the door was still intact and a curious giraffe face peered through it, watching the three of them eat at the table. He looked lonely out there, like he wanted nothing more than to be with his mom, or at the very least, the rest of the herd.

"Do you think he'll eat any of this? He's probably hungry," Jo said, finishing her piece of pie.

"Worth a shot," Daniel replied.

"He's too young to be weaned. He really needs his mamma."

"Maybe he'll drink some milk? We gotta try something," Daniel said, sharing Jo's anxiety about the health and well being of this funny little fellow who was now an orphan.

"There's still half a carton of whole milk in there. I could only think of so many things to do with it."

"You did great," she said, cracking an almost believable smile.

Josephine gathered up the milk and a sampling of the food from dinner, a little bit of whatever they had including the vegetables, and opened the front door to try her luck feeding the poor creature standing out there by himself. Millie would eat almost anything. She'd eaten a variety of homegrown veggies from the field, plus fried food, meat, paper, wood, soap, leather, bird's nests, and hair, in addition to hay, oats, and grass. Surely her offspring would accept something from the plate Jo had made for him.

"I have some milk for you," she said, setting down the flashlight so she could use both hands to support the bowl. Napoleon just stared at her, confused.

"No milk?" she asked, holding the bowl higher. "I know, you just wanna skip right to the food, huh? Let's try some beans first. Do you like beans?" she asked the giraffe. He sniffed them, and turned his head away.

"Okay. What about rhubarb? Do you like this?" Again, he refused.

"How about chicken?" He didn't even bother to smell it.

"Biscuits? Everybody likes a cheese biscuit." Everybody, with the exception of Napoleon, liked cheese biscuits.

Losing hope now, Jo asked "I bet you like pudding, right?" Napoleon took a small taste, but it turned out he didn't like pudding either. Nothing appealed to his velvet lips or tempted his purple tongue. Not one thing. Daniel watched her try again, patiently offering each item one more time to the hungry giraffe, in case he changed his mind the second time around. He had to eat something, sooner or later. Perhaps he was on a hunger strike, like the McElroy brothers used to do.

"He's a picky eater," Jo said, finally giving up.

Daniel had an idea. "What about the bale of hay. Maybe it landed here for a reason."

"We can try."

Daniel took a flashlight and set out looking for the massive roll of dried grass that had blown here from another farm. It was theirs for the taking and Napoleon needed to eat. He was too young to go without nourishment. He'd lose his strength quickly if he didn't feed, and eventually, his life too. In the pitch black, Daniel had trouble locating the hay among the other miscellaneous things strewn all over the property. By the time he returned, pushing the thing end over end, Jo had discovered the unlikely food item Napoleon couldn't resist: ice cream.

Mint chocolate chip, to be exact. He had pale green slop all over his muzzle. Jo smiled broadly, holding the carton for him as he helped himself to the dessert that was already starting to melt. "He loves it, look at this," she said, amazed.

Daniel left the hay bale by the front steps and joined them on the porch. Napoleon started licking faster, as if Daniel was a threat to his food source. And what a delicious food source it was! The hungry baby slopped his mouth around the carton, desperate for just one more taste, but it was all gone. Now, Napoleon focused on getting whatever remained on his face into his mouth by using his extra-long tongue to lick it all up.

"I knew it was gonna start melting, so I made myself a bowl," Jo began, "And he just started eating it so I went back in and got the carton."

"Well, I'd say it's a success," Daniel said, trying to encourage her after such a terrible day.

Dylan, on the other hand, was too tired to encourage Jo, or help feed the giraffe, or tidy up from dinner, or do his share to clean up the broken glass inside. He had a rough day. All he could think about was what a rough day this had been as he got comfortable on the couch for the night. His arm was broken and he had survived a tornado. Poor him. He felt awfully sorry for himself. Jo and Daniel stayed on the porch, keeping Napoleon company on his first night as an orphan. Napoleon was settled on his knobby knees, comfortable enough with Josephine there to let his guard down against the predators his brain was wired to fear. This girl who fed him such a delicious dinner could surely protect him until his mamma came back.

"He won't go to sleep. He just keeps looking at me like I'm supposed to do something," Jo explained, shaking her head like a new mother without a clue.

"Maybe he wants you to sing to him," Daniel suggested.

"I already tried that."

"Maybe he wants you to read him a bedtime story," he said, sitting down beside her with his back to the house.

"I don't know any. My dad never read to me, I read to myself. I don't know any bedtime stories. Do you?" Jo's gray eyes were still bloodshot, and now, they were lined with bags. She was so exhausted but couldn't find it in her heart to fall asleep until Napoleon did first.

"I know some poems," he said quietly.

"Do you know any Frost?"

"Nah. Better than Frost. My Grams made one up for me and Dylan."

"Really?"

"Yeah."

"Let's hear it then."

Daniel cleared his throat. "I feel kinda cheesy doing this. But...here goes." He shifted once, getting comfortable before speaking the words he heard every night before bed for six years straight, though he hadn't heard them spoken out loud for close to ten years now. Still, they were fresh in his memory, just like the smell of his grandmother's kitchen. "The day is over, it's time for rest. Sleep all night, tomorrow you'll be your best. Teeth are brushed, pajamas on, dream away until the dawn. No more bouncing on your beds, time to lie down and calm your heads. Another day of fun will come again with the rising sun."

Napoleon let out a long breath, as if bored by Daniel's lines. He was a rude giraffe, kind of like his mother. After a few more quiet moments, Napoleon gave a big yawn, showing off his oddly shaped mouth.

"Bouncing on the bed, huh? You two were a handful," Jo teased.

"'Fraid so. I guess we still are, a little bit."

"Your grandmother's poem was way better than Frost. I mean, I'm a big fan of the one about the two roads, and taking the less traveled one but...'."

"I'd be a faker if I recited the one about choosing which road to take. I never got to choose. It was always chosen for me."

"Because you're always looking after Dylan?"

"Yeah. Sorta. But it's not his fault. He just…doesn't think. His spontaneity is such a pain in my ass but I love him anyway. He's chosen the road for us this time. And I'm glad. I'm glad we are here. I'm glad I'm sitting next to you right now, even after everything that's happened. This was the better road. Not sure what road is next. Guess I'll just wait and see what trouble my brother can find and we'll go from there."

"'Til he does, this is your home. Okay?"

Daniel looked at her cheek, her profile. "It feels like home."

Clueless she was being stared at, Jo continued, "How many times have you moved?"

"A lot."

"How many states have you lived in?"

"A lot of those too."

"How many? For real. I've never been anywhere other than Nebraska, South Dakota and Kansas. I'm a little…jealous."

Thinking it over, Daniel started listing them off, all these places he'd once called home with all these families that didn't work out in the long run. There were so many. It was going to be awhile, but it seemed Jo was in no hurry to leave. "I was born in Jackson, Mississippi. Dylan was born in Atlanta. We lived in Tampa for a while, then moved to Greenville, South Carolina. My mom took us to live with Dylan's father for a few months, that was up in Annapolis, Maryland. They broke up, we moved to Richmond, then my mom dropped us off with Grams."

"In Harrisburg," Jo interjected with a wink. "And that's in Pennsylvania."

"Smart ass."

"Then where?" Jo was fascinated by his travel log. She wanted more. She was asking for a bedtime story of her own.

"We were in Harrisburg for a while. That's the longest we've stayed in one place. When Grams passed, we were sent to Philly, to a boy's home for a few months 'til a foster family took us. They were in Pittsburgh, but we weren't there long. Got sent to Dayton, Columbus and Cleveland, and caused the state of Ohio a whole lot of trouble." Daniel chuckled, remembering just how much trouble he and Dylan got into when they got caught shooting at squirrels with a borrowed BB gun from the roof of their foster parents' house, which was located in a dense suburban community where people didn't usually fire guns, let alone from a rooftop in the middle of the night.

"Then where?" she asked, begging him to continue.

"I guess we bounced around Kentucky awhile. We were in Evansville for a grand total of three months. We spent some time in Elizabethtown but I don't really remember much about that. We stayed in Nashville for almost two years. That's where I graduated high school. Can't believe all my stuff transferred. They probably could have held me back or something. I think maybe it was easier to let me graduate than deal with me another year. Nashville's probably the place I feel like I come from the most, out of all of em'. So much happened during those two years. When we got moved there, we was kids. When we left, we wasn't kids no more."

"What's Nashville like?" She fiddled with her black woven bracelet, turning it over and over on her wrist absent-mindedly. It seemed this part of Millie was a great comfort to her now.

"Lots of music, lots of barbeque, lots of bars, lots of cowboy hats. Lots of pretty girls too."

"I bet," she said, elbowing him in the ribs. "Did you have a pretty girl?"

"Yeah. I guess I did."

"What was her name?"

"Veronica."

"That's a pretty name."

"Yeah. I guess it is."

"What happened to her?"

"She went off to some fancy college and left me behind." Daniel looked over at Jo. He wasn't sure why, but he wanted to tell her the whole truth and knew deep down he could trust her. "I thought I loved her. I really did. She had…an abortion. It was mine. She didn't even tell me nothing 'til it was all too late."

With a tinge of shock in her expression, but with a calm voice, Jo asked, "Why didn't she talk it over with you first?"

"'Cause she knew I would have never let her go through with it. And I guess not going through with it wasn't really an option for her since she had scholarships and stuff. Her parents never liked me much and they talked her into…ending things. I always wondered if it had been someone else's baby, someone with better grades, or a closer shave, if they would have let her keep it."

Josephine's eyes fell to the porch. "Oh," she said in a quiet voice. "Did you…want to be a father? You had to be awful young."

"I was your age. And no. I didn't wanna be no father but I didn't want no kid to get killed neither. I could have helped her find a nice family to take care of it or something. We coulda figured something out, you know? I mean, hell, if anyone shoulda had an abortion, it was my mom, like I told you. I'm just happy to be alive, even if I didn't get raised by my own mother."

Jo shook her head up and down, but not in a knowing way, just a sluggish bob. She started biting at her thumbnail, out of words at the moment.

Not wanting to dwell on that tangent any longer, Daniel picked back up on the verbal map of his life. "Anyway, Dylan and I lived in Springfield, Peoria, and Danville after that. And about six months ago, we got transferred to a family near Chicago. They was real nice but we just didn't want parents no more. We was tired of parents. We had hundreds and hundreds of parents and were grown enough not to need em' no more."

Jo snickered.

"Sorry. Any more. I gotta get better with speaking and stuff if I'm gonna be round you all the time, huh?"

"Long as you're in Morton, Nebraska, you ain't gonna get away with poor grammar, city boy. My daddy won't stand for it."

"Messin' with the ghost of your daddy's something I'm not sure I want to do."

"Better improve that grammar then, or he'll haunt your dreams."

"All them fancy words don't suit me much. I guess I'm a simple guy. Anyone can see that. Can't your daddy see that from where he is?"

"So what does a simple guy want out of life? What's your pig farm with the blue barn?"

"I want Dylan to be happy. And safe. Wish we got along better too."

"What do you want for yourself? Not what do you want for Dylan."

"I want a happy family and I guess he's all the family I got." There was a long, long pause after that. Even the grass stopped moving in the night breeze.

"I miss my family," she finally spoke. The melancholy she carried was heavy. For the first time, Daniel saw how lonely she was. Up until now, he thought she was independent and tough, that she didn't need anybody. Sure, she could get by on her own, but she wanted to be known.

"What was your dad like?" he asked, treading carefully. "Mr. Ulrich told me about his nickname. I'm awfully curious about…The Swearin' Swede."

She smiled at that. Her daddy was a foul-mouthed farmer, the second generation American-born in his bloodline. He smoked and drank, and his politics were a little wacky but he wasn't ashamed of them. He loved his books, his records, his wife and his tomboy daughter.

"He was a good man. This whole God-fearing town just misunderstood him."

"How so?"

"He liked his liquor. He liked using the F-word when it was the right word to use. He liked having his diversified pesticide-free crops and keeping the bees happy, and keeping the politicians off his farm. He didn't like the church so much because the people around here just wanna pray a prayer with you so you can get saved while it's on their watch. They wanna have a list of all the people they led to Jesus so they can point at it when they die and get themselves a spot in heaven. My daddy called them 'scalpers' and he just didn't have the patience for that kind of shallow faith. He went every Sunday till a year or two after my momma passed. He blamed God for taking her away so there wasn't much point in going after that, especially after the new pastor came to town and started preaching different things. Everybody talked about what he was preaching, how it wasn't really from the Bible, but my daddy was the only one with the nerve to say anything about it. The day he stood up to that pastor, that's a day in Morton history."

"How old were you when your mom passed?"

"Just a baby. I was having my first birthday when she found that lump. Guess she was about to turn…forty-two. She was almost twenty years older than my daddy. She taught him in grade school. It was quite the scandal when they got married but my grandpa gave them the farmhouse anyway, as a wedding gift, along with the cattle. After she got sick, my daddy took care of both of us, a colicky baby and a dying wife. When she passed a year later, he had to take care of me all by himself. He was alone, he lost the woman he loved. He started drinking bout that time. I guess he drank a lot, if you ask people in town."

"What if I ask you? Did he drink a lot?"

"Sometimes. But he never hurt anyone. He just did it to get through the day and help him sleep at night. There was an awful big hole in his life after my mom passed and bourbon filled it up okay. And all those church people pestering him to stop drinking and come back to the Christian way of life, that just pushed him further away. He got help, he was in AA for awhile. I never asked him to, but he did it after he got into an accident. He drove off the road into a tree and had to call me in the middle of the night to come get him. I was only fourteen. I wasn't supposed to be driving yet. That whole thing was a major wake up call for him, he was so upset. He cared for me and loved me just as much when he was drinking as when he was sober. My daddy was a good man, whether or not he drank or attended Sunday service. He was a good man and I miss him. That's all there is to it."

CHAPTER THIRTEEN

The sun was up. Josephine's head rested on Daniel's shoulder, just the way it did all through the night. He had one arm around her, keeping her safe as she slept, and despite spending the night sitting upright on the front porch, propped up by the house behind them, sharing the space with a zoo creature, he had slept incredibly well. Daniel was the first one to stir. He heard something in the distance, the crunch of gravel.

Opening one green eye to take a peek, he saw a truck stopped halfway down the driveway, right where the tree lay. That displaced tree was going to buy him the time he needed to wake Jo and get the giraffe out of sight. "Hey. Someone's here," he said, shaking her a little to bring her into the land of the living.

"Hmm?" she asked, barely conscious.

"There's a truck coming down the driveway. We gotta move Napoleon. You think he can go in the house for a minute?"

Jo watched the truck taking the detour around the uprooted tree and replied, "Yeah. He can hide in the bathroom."

Somehow, they did it. They got the miniature version of Millie off the front porch, through the kitchen and living room, and into the only bathroom in the house. Daniel woke Dylan and shoved him into the bathroom to watch over Napoleon.

"How long do I have to stay in here?" Dylan whined.

"I don't know. Just…please cooperate for once. Please," Daniel said, shutting the bathroom door.

From inside the bathroom, Dylan yelled, "Well, if you're locking me up in here, I'm taking a bath!" The water started running. He wasn't kidding. The rule about using the bathtub inside was being broken, but Dylan felt it was only fair.

Meeting Jo in the kitchen, Daniel said, "It's safe."

Jo opened the front door to greet two men in their fifties, one bald, one about to be.

"Morning, gentlemen. How'd you fair the storm?"

"Done alright," the taller one said. "We was worried 'bout you out here. Mr. Frank said he come out here for a fire last night after the storm. He said your daddy's in Topeka?"

"Yes, sir."

"Well, we come to make sure of you, see if we could help clean up or repair anything that might need repairin'."

Josephine smiled, onto their motives. "Did the church ladies put you up to this?"

The two men exchanged a guilty look. There was no sense lying about it. The short fat one grinned and said, "You know they after your daddy's soul and if they hafta build him a new barn to get him to come back to church, and get good and saved, then a barn they'll build."

"I'll tell him you stopped by. Thanks, Mr. Gregory."

"Miss Jo, wait," the taller one said, halfway out the door. "You mind stepping out of doors for a moment? I got a little something to ask but it's of a private nature."

"Of course," she chirped, pretending to be friendly as she followed the men through the porch with her springy red ponytail bouncing behind her as she walked.

Being alone now made Daniel very uncomfortable. These old timers didn't like the looks of him and his brother, didn't want them staying in this conservative town any longer than they had to. He inched closer to the window in hopes of overhearing any gossip or warning these men might start up.

"Miss Jo, we all know why your daddy left the church. Losing the woman God gave you is a terrible thing, but it's his drinking we're worried about. Drinking is the devil's work, especially for so many years now. I know you wouldn't hurt a fly and you're a good girl, so you can tell me the truth 'bout your daddy and his liquor," Mr. Gregory asked, taking over for the taller gentleman by his side. "We all want him to come back to the church and if we need to do an intervention…"

"He's not drinking anymore. I promise you that. He hasn't had a drink since December."

"Is that the truth?"

"Yes, sir."

"But…Mrs. Norma said she sold him whisky just last week."

Jo laughed out loud. This town could make up so many grand stories to pass the time. The small population was blessed with wild imaginations and an addiction to scandal. They could turn two people pumping gas at the same gas station into a whirlwind affair. They could take a woman who was looking a little pale and turn her into a mother-to-be. Those citizens who didn't show up for the Hooker County Fair every July 4th were Communists. The people who paid Debra at the drugstore using large bills were dubbed gamblers. Just last week, Charles Hopkins, the owner of the cafe in town, had to close early because he wasn't feeling well and the very next day people were telling him how sorry they were about his brain tumor. The man just had a headache.

"We're worried about him raising a sweet girl like you. He's been so reclusive lately. And what with him selling all the cattle this spring, we just want to make sure he's caring for you properly."

Jo used her most convincing voice to say, "I'm fine. Everything's fine."

Moving on to the next topic of disapproval, Mr. Gregory brought up those two boys who'd been hanging around for almost three weeks now. "Are those boys causing you trouble? Where'd they come from anyhow?"

"They're my cousins."

"Didn't know you had cousins."

"Yes, sir. We didn't know about them either. There's a whole branch of the family tree we're just learning about now."

"On the Swedish side?"

"No, sir. The Irish."

"I see. So they come to visit you and your daddy?"

"We had a lot to bring in this season, now that the cattle's gone, and we just couldn't do it on our own."

"And they've been helping you and your daddy?"

"Yes, sir. They haven't been causing any trouble at all around here."

"Well. They been causing trouble in town."

The two men exchanged a look. "The taller one…with the blond hair…he seems up to no good, if you ask me. Seems like he's looking for mischief. You just let your cousin know his Irish mischief isn't welcome round here."

"Did he do something?" Jo asked, knowing full well Dylan could find trouble wherever he went, including the sleepy town of Morton.

"Mr. Ulrich saw him snatch a peach right from the stand. He just went on and took it and didn't pay up."

"Oh goodness," Jo said, feigning utter shock. "A peach?"

"Yes. A peach."

"Well, I'll let my father deal with him when he gets back from Topeka. He won't stand for such things."

Satisfied, the men nodded and wished Josephine well, telling her everyone in the town was pitching in with the storm clean up, so if she wanted some help, it was most certainly available. They also told her if anything blew onto her property that wasn't hers, to put it up by the mailbox. Everyone was doing this, so they might locate their lost items. Everyone trusted everyone else to be honest and return what wasn't theirs.

"Miss Jo," Mr. Gregory said, pausing his exit. "Your daddy gets back when?"

She tried to recall what lies she'd already told in order to keep spinning this web as neatly as possible. So many people asked about her father on a regular basis, including Dylan, who was starting to get awfully curious about this invisible man. Each time Jo fabricated yet another excuse for his absence, she risked it all falling apart.

"Should be back Saturday. Just a few more days now. I'll tell him you came by."

"Alright, lil' Miss. You take care now. And watch after your cousins."

"Yes, sir." Jo went inside. She marched right back to the bathroom and opened the door without knocking. Napoleon was partially blocking the door but she managed to squeeze her slim body through. Dylan was in the bathtub surrounded by bubbles. He grinned up at her like this was all a joke. Irritated, she knelt down. Dylan thought something wonderful was about to happen when she reached her hand into the sudsy water right between his legs. He held his breath for a moment, waiting for good things to begin. She must really want him bad, being so forward like this. Dylan was more than ready to forgive her for being so forward. His heart sank when she jerked up the drain, ending his luxurious bath.

In a stern voice, Jo warned, "Don't steal anymore peaches from Mr. Ulrich. You got that?"

Covering himself as the water disappeared and exposed his body, he nodded his head profusely, urging Jo to believe him and leave before the last of the bubbles went down the drain. "It was just a peach," he defended.

"It wasn't your peach." She turned to Napoleon and said, "C'mon, you." She had to ask twice, but the young giraffe did eventually follow her through the house and back out to the porch, while taking the opportunity to sniff the ceiling fan and knock over a vase on his way.

For the next two days, the crops went neglected. Daniel and Dylan helped Josephine get the farmhouse back together as best they could. They managed to get the red pickup truck back up the way it ought to be, with all four tires on the ground. They used a chain saw and a couple of heavy-duty clippers to cut the fallen tree into manageable pieces, freeing a path down the driveway. All the odd belongings that landed here from somewhere else were placed at the mailbox for the rightful owners to claim. Everything except the hay bale. They kept that for Napoleon because other than hay, he refused to eat. Jo made a special run to Seneca, the next town over, and picked up a large cooler and several bags of ice in order to bring back four gallons of mint chocolate chip ice cream. The giraffe ate well, while the rest of them got by on non-perishables.

One morning, Daniel and Dylan were startled awake by a series of loud banging sounds on the roof. It was Jo up there, hammering away at the loose shingles. Once they realized who was responsible for the morning racket, that there was no cause for alarm, Dylan flopped back on the couch and covered his face with the pillow to block out the noise. "Does she have any idea what time it is?" he groaned.

Daniel got up and got dressed. He headed outside to check on her, and climbed the ladder up to the roof. Jo was getting the last remaining solar panel back into place. She'd lost the others in the storm, the glass was visibly fractured, and one of the panels was missing altogether, probably sitting in some kid's sandbox in the next town over. How much power she'd get from a single panel was unknown, but she wasn't going to give up just yet. "Do you need some help?" he asked, joining her on the roof.

"No," she said, then nothing more. It was clear by her clenched jaw she'd been frustrated, but was taking care of things as best she could. Daniel knew better than to insist on helping her when she clearly didn't want to be bothered, but he stayed on the roof with her anyway until she was done, just to keep her company. The sunrise was beautiful shades of pink and yellow, lighting up the perimeter of trees. Eventually, Jo came over and sat next to him and leaned on the chimney, finished with her task, and watched the sky brighten with each passing moment.

"Was this land all trees before?" Daniel asked, nodding across the western pasture.

Jo knew the answer; she knew the entire history of this land. "You've heard of the Dustbowl, right?"

Daniel nodded, then shrugged, not so confident in his final answer.

"There were lots of low lying shrubs and a few more trees when my family first settled here, but they kept the forest around the edge of the property and only cleared out what they needed to open up the fields, just enough to build the house, really. I guess they had a sense about how the climate worked because just a generation or so after they came here, a lot of farms all but blew away. Everyone else around here cleared their land so they could maximize their farm, but then there was no brush or deep roots left for hundreds of miles, nothing to hold down the dirt, and the whole Midwest got blown all the way to New York City. My family lost crops just like everyone else, but they didn't have to pack up and leave. Those trees kept a lot of the dirt and dust from destroying their crops. They survived."

"So how many people were born in this house?" he continued, knowing full well he could never stump her, not with her own family history.

"Including me…seven." Jo smiled to herself. "My dad was born out in the woods, actually." She gestured in the direction of his grave. "He came early. My grandmother was out picking blackberries, she thought she had another month to go, but then there he was all of a sudden, clawing his way out into the world because he had things to do. Legend has it she was only in labor for about five minutes."

"Wow," was all he could say in response. They were sitting atop a building with so much history, so many stories, looking out at land that had sustained so many generations. It was no wonder it meant so much to her.

Later that day, Mr. Wessel came by to check on the beehives. The tornado hadn't obliterated them, surprisingly enough, but he told Jo the population wasn't what it should be. The beekeeper, a broad-chested man with a head full of gray hair and a beard to match, cleaned up the white boxes at the corners of the field. The tornado had sandblasted the sides of the boxes, but hadn't ripped them from the ground, which wouldn't have been much of a challenge for winds of that speed. The tornado could do what it wanted; it could pick and choose what to destroy. Jo and Daniel watched as Mr. Wessel puffed some smoke from a little metal contraption filled with slow burning rope into the hive in order to calm the bees before carefully opening the top to find the queen. To Daniel's horror, Mr. Wessel pinched off her head. "Time for a new ruler," the beekeeper explained, and pulled out a canister from his pocket, which contained the new queen, the hope for the future colony. What a strange circle of life, what a difficult kingdom to rule over.

Daniel and Dylan were permitted to go upstairs that night, but only to help mend the walls and clean up the mess of glass and debris left by the storm. Jo's room was untouched. The only tornado that ever passed through it was her, leaving clothes and shoes all over the floor. Her window was perfectly in place. Nothing had been wrecked by the forceful winds. Her father's room, on the other hand, was trashed. Both windows had been blown out, the curtain rods were ripped from the sheet rock, and there was a part of the exterior wall that was see-through now. A large flying object had sliced through the siding at a hundred and thirty miles an hour, all the way to the gray paint on the inside. The only remedy was to hammer plywood over the gap.

Her father's room was tidy, or at least it had been up until the tornado came through. The furniture was simple dark stained wood with little ornamentation. There was a trunk at the foot of the bed and a small writing desk by the blown-out window. The ladder-back chair that normally sat at the desk was on its side, too lightweight to withstand the wind once the room was no longer sealed. Daniel noticed a photo of Jo's mother on one side of the bed, a portrait of a woman with long red hair and gray eyes. He watched as Jo retrieved each displaced item and put it back exactly where it had been for the last decade and a half: the perfume bottle on the dresser, the fuzzy slippers by the far night stand, just the way her mother had left them, just the way her father continued to leave these things. The fuzzy slippers Jo was setting down with measured accuracy on the rug looked old, but not because they were worn through or in bad condition. The closet door was slightly ajar since one of the hinges had popped when the house shifted during the storm, giving Daniel a glimpse of the woman's clothing hanging inside. Dresses, all outdated and belonging to Josephine's mother, hung there like she still lived in this house. Not only was her memory still here, so were her things. Mr. Larsen hadn't moved anything, but the storm had. Jo picked up each precious possession and replaced it exactly where it had been since her mother's passing in 1990. It seemed she'd carried on this tradition with her father's things as well, keeping everything just the way he left it.

By Thursday night, the power still hadn't come back on and there were doubts it would for a few more days. The tornado was an F-2. It hit Morton hard, but the town due west, Whitfield, got the worst of it. Five people had been killed. One of them was an eight-year-old girl. Even Millie's tragic death, a secret except for the three people living in this house, just couldn't compare.

Josephine was still sad, as expected. Nobody pressured her to snap out of it, she deserved to be blue as long as she wanted. She wasn't sulking, exactly. She was just quiet. She was pretty quiet anyway, but now she'd reached a whole new level of silence thanks to the storm and all the damage done. She stopped humming. Even her footsteps were muffled as she padded around the house. When she fell asleep in the tattered green armchair holding a copy of *The Turn of Screw*, she didn't snore like she usually did.

When Friday came, Daniel helped Jo load up the truck with two black bags full of freshly picked marijuana leaves. "This doesn't mean I approve," he said.

"I know."

"Be careful, okay?"

"I always am."

She was off, dressed like a city girl, carrying three pounds of greens, which would bring her several thousand dollars by the time she off-loaded it. Daniel stood by the porch with Napoleon and watched her truck drive away. He gave a wave too, the only way he could support her, because he couldn't not support her now. This was her livelihood. He couldn't take that away. He couldn't snuff out her dream of raising pigs in a blue barn. She was risking so much to get it. It meant everything to her, so he kept his fear and judgment to himself.

"Jo's dad is supposed to come home tomorrow," Dylan said, settling in for the night. He pulled his blanket up to his chin and fluffed a pillow behind his head.

"Right," Daniel said, lying on the floor, dealing with a less fluffy pillow.

"Guess I'll finally get to meet this guy, huh?"

"Sure. I guess."

"What's your problem?"

"Nothing," Daniel said. "Goodnight, Dylan."

After a moment of confusion, Dylan replied, "Goodnight, Daniel. I love you."

"Love you too."

"Don't let me die in my sleep, okay?"

"I won't."

The next morning, Daniel woke up to the distinct sound of a truck driving over gravel. Either more people from the church were here for Mr. Johan Larsen and his wayward spirit, or Jo was home from her Friday night business dealings. He perked right up and dressed quickly, eager to welcome her back. As Jo emerged from the truck with two empty black bags and a thick wad of cash, he could see she had something else too. It was a brown paper bag from a fast food restaurant and it was full of hot breakfast food.

"That smells so good," Daniel said.

"Thought I'd treat. We can have a little something special since there's not much cooking to be done with what's left in the pantry."

"And I see you brought our funny little friend some breakfast too," Daniel said, watching Jo lift a large cooler full of ice cream from the bed of the truck.

"He needs to eat. He can't afford to lose any weight and if this is the only thing he'll eat, well…that settles it."

Daniel, Dylan and Jo ate their egg biscuits and hash brown patties in the kitchen. They each drank coffee from a paper cup. They hadn't enjoyed coffee since the morning the storm hit, so this was a welcome indulgence. Jo was in good spirits as she fed Napoleon, after feeding herself. She must have had an exceptionally profitable night.

"Goodnight," Jo said, heading upstairs at 8:45 a.m. for her make-up rest. "Wake me up for lunch?"

"Sure thing," Daniel said, smiling up at her. "You want us to keep working on the fields or make another pass for debris and stuff?"

"It's the weekend. You can do whatever you want," she replied sleepily.

With Jo asleep upstairs, Dylan was ready to be lazy and stay in, but Daniel wouldn't have it. "C'mon. There's a lot to do out there."

"But it's the weekend. She said we didn't have to work." Dylan was about as mature as a twelve-year-old, where Daniel was more like a thirty-year-old. Though they were just a year apart, which technically made them Irish twins, they were at opposite ends of the spectrum.

Daniel explained, "If this was your land, your house, and a tornado did this to you, wouldn't you want help getting it back the way it used to be?"

"You're right," Dylan said, catching onto something Daniel wasn't actually saying. "She'll be really impressed. So will her dad, when he gets home."

With a sigh, Daniel replied, "Exactly." It was easier to go along with it.

The boys continued their outdoor cleaning efforts, picking up pieces of trees, leaves, parts of the farmhouse, and other miscellaneous things that blew onto the property. After several days of combing the land for odd bits and filling at least twenty trash bags full of everything imaginable, the farm was looking better. They were confident enough in their clean up job to let Napoleon back outside where he could roam freely without concern for what jagged shrapnel he might step on or try to eat. Napoleon appeared to be looking for his mom, wandering a little further than they were comfortable with. They kept a watchful eye on him.

With all the storm related chaos, the Larsen driveway was having a lot more traffic than usual. People kept stopping by, and each time, they barely got Napoleon back into the house. The last thing they needed right now was to get caught with a three-week-old giraffe and no believable explanation as to how they acquired it.

"Look!" Dylan hissed, pointing to the black sedan rolling down the driveway.

The boys jumped into action, pushing Napoleon inside and through the living room. They shut him in the bathroom once more. This little trick of hiding a giraffe wouldn't work for much longer, not at the rate he was growing. With the baby beast hidden away, Daniel went upstairs to wake Jo.

"There's some people here," he said, trying to wake her with words and nothing more. She was asleep on her stomach, still wearing the clothes she wore last night.

With a groan, she rolled over. "Is it lunch time?" she asked, looking disoriented.

"No. There's some people. You got some more visitors."

"Where's Napoleon?"

"Bathroom. He's fine."

She nodded once, then sat on the edge of her bed. Just as she stood up, there was a knock at the door. Curious who these drop-in visitors might be, Jo went downstairs and opened the front door. It was Mr. Miller, a farmer of barley, who lived three miles down the road. He'd come by to visit his friend, Mr. Larsen, The Swearin' Swede.

"I been hearing things round town about your daddy. Heard he took a long trip and left you home with your cousins. Heard he's drinking again too," Mr. Miller said.

"He's fine. He's not drinking. You can come look at the liquor cabinet if you like." Jo was serious. She led the man into the living room and opened the cabinet doors revealing a few shelves of specialty glasses for scotch and after dinner drinks, but no liquor. "He got rid of it all in December. Didn't want it around the house anymore."

"Can I talk to him? They said he was coming home today."

"Who said that?" Jo asked, ignoring the crashing sounds coming from the bathroom.

"You know. Mr. Gregory. He told everyone your daddy would be home today. That's your daddy's truck is out front, isn't it? Is he working the fields?"

"He's upstairs," she said, almost out of breath.

"But it's just barely midday."

"He's not feeling well."

"How do you mean?"

"He's just a little under the weather, that's all."

The man watched her face, searching it for truth. He must have found it because his expression turned concerned. "I'll have Mrs. Miller send over one of her pies. He'll be feeling better in no time. Soon as the power comes back on, she'll get to baking it. She had to get the electric stove. I told her gas was better, but she had to get the electric."

"That's not necessary. He'll be better soon. Thank you though."

"I insist."

Mr. Miller left and two days later, when the power came back on, they discovered he wasn't kidding about that pie. Mr. and Mrs. Miller showed up just after lunchtime. Jo had been in the root cellar tending to her underground crops, so Daniel and Dylan had the task of hiding the giraffe in the bathroom again. Jo accepted the pie, told the kindly couple her dad wasn't up for visitors yet, and they went on their way. To her regret, they said they'd be back in the morning to check up on him and hoped he'd be feeling better.

"Jo, where is your dad?" Dylan asked. "How come you said he's upstairs?"

Jo took a deep breath. It was time to tell him the truth. "He passed away. He's dead. I'm sorry I lied."

"Are you joking?" Dylan asked with wide eyes.

Daniel stepped in and said, "She's not joking."

"Why…how come…I don't understand," Dylan began, taking it all in.

Josephine went through all the details for the youngest McElroy brother, and Dylan listened just as carefully as Daniel had done that day by the grave. Dylan was impressed she kept this a secret for so long and managed the farm on her own. His crush got a little heavier, his heart a little fuller. She really was something special.

Dylan wasn't mad at Jo for lying, but he was mad at his brother. After all, Daniel knew the whole truth for several weeks now, and never filled him in. What kind of a brother did that? How could he keep that kind of thing to himself all this time? Dylan was ready to give Daniel the silent treatment for several days, not that he could have actually stuck to such quiet revenge, but when Jo asked a favor of him, he quickly forgot about anything else.

"I need your help," she said to Dylan. "This is never gonna end." Jo realized this web of lies was spinning out of control now. "There's gonna be visitor upon visitor coming for my daddy, and they're not likely to stop till they see him. I need them to believe my dad is alive for another four weeks, till my birthday passes."

"Sounds like you have a plan," Daniel interjected.

"I do. It involves you, Dylan. Tomorrow, when the Millers come back to check on my daddy, I want you to be him."

"You want me to be your dad?" Dylan clarified.

"I do. I need a body under some covers. Your hair is almost the right color, you're about the right height too. I need some sickly groans. I need you to keep your face hidden, but move around under the covers some. You on board?"

Dylan looked thrilled. He was going to be a hero. He nodded his head, happy as can be. There was a secondary element to his happiness, not just this incredible chance to save the day for Josephine Larsen. Now that he knew her father was dead, he felt a little more comfortable going after her. Without an overprotective father to work around, there was nothing stopping him now. He slept a lot better that night.

The next day arrived and it was time to pull off this simple yet elaborate plan. If the stand-in for Mr. Larsen failed, Jo would have an awful lot of explaining to do. Not only that, but she might lose the farm and the house she was born in. Getting the Millers to believe what Jo wanted them to believe was critical. Just as instructed, Dylan went upstairs and covered himself with the sheets in her father's bed. As Jo helped him get prepared to pass for her sickly guardian, he reached up from his spot on the bed and tried to pull her on top of him. She caught herself on her elbows and stared at the boy below her, alarmed. She didn't know what to say, whether to slap him, scold him, or laugh. She chose to do nothing. Jo headed downstairs and waited for her neighbors to come back again, just as they said they would. Napoleon was already in the bathroom with Daniel keeping watch, so they were all set to pull this off.

Josephine escorted the elderly couple up the creaky stairs and into the bedroom. Mr. and Mrs. Miller were in awe of the storm damage, the boarded up windows, but they were more worried about Johan Larsen who was under the sheets sounding terribly ill.

"He's doing worse today. I know he's just not feeling like himself," Jo said, looking at the lump in the bed. Dylan's groans were a little much. He was trying too hard, sounding more like a cat in heat than a sickly farmer. Thankfully, the Miller's bought it.

"Goodness," Mrs. Miller gasped, hand to her heart.

"He might be contagious so don't get too close now," Jo added.

The husband and wife exchanged a worried glance. Mr. Miller cleared his throat and said, "Well, we best be going. Don't want to keep him from resting up."

They were suddenly very anxious to leave, already moving towards the steps to make a speedy exit before catching whatever virus was lurking in that bed. Mr. and Mrs. Miller wished him well, a quick recovery too, and left the house like they were going to be late for the church bingo.

Watching the black sedan roll back up the driveway, Jo knew the coast was clear. "We did it!" she shouted with elation. Her plan was a success and would likely get this town off her back for another month so she could keep her secrets safe till she was officially an adult. "Home free!" she added, doing a little victory dance.

"We are awesome!" Dylan sang from the bed. He got up and was about to hug her, just to celebrate successful teamwork, but she moved away, not up for another sloppy move from this boy.

"Not only are we awesome, but there's another peach pie!" Jo said, leading the way downstairs. The steps squeaked as usual, the wood creaked to applaud her.

The three of them celebrated their victorious charade with Mrs. Miller's fine baking and gave Napoleon a little extra mint chocolate chip ice cream as a reward for behaving so well in that cramped little bathroom. Everyone played their part perfectly.

In fact, the next day they discovered just how convincing this whole thing had been. The town doctor made a house call, ready to aid the contagious Mr. Larsen. The doctor was a young man, just thirty or so, with mousy brown hair and nervous eyes that always glanced around instead of meeting one's own. Especially Jo's. She made him exceptionally nervous.

"Hello, Josephine," the doctor said, breaking a sweat. "May I see your father?"

"No, you better not. He's finally asleep. If you wake him now, he won't be happy. He's doing better today. I think he's gonna get through this just fine."

"Oh," Dr. Holbrook said, setting down his traveling case filled with things he might need, most importantly, latex gloves and a mask to keep himself protected from whatever horrible virus Johan picked up in Topeka last week. "But I heard…well…people in town were saying…he's got boils all over his face."

"Boils? On his face?" Jo almost laughed out loud. If somebody claimed they saw Johan Larsen's face with boils on it, they were quite the teller of tall tales. Nobody had seen anyone's face in that bed the day before, let alone a face with nasty pustules. "Boils," Jo repeated, letting this disgusting detail validate her story. "Maybe you could recommend an ointment for him?"

"Yes. I brought some. I'd just like to see him for myself, if you don't mind."

The doctor glanced around the room as if he were following a fly buzzing from one corner of the ceiling to the other. His glasses sat crookedly on his face, tilting more to the left. As nervous as he might have been in the living room with the pretty redhead, he was not likely to leave this house without seeing the deathly ill Johan Larsen, whose stand-in was up in the bed and under the covers, just like yesterday. Jo needed a major distraction to keep the doctor downstairs since Dylan's face would never pass for her father's.

"Dr. Holbrooke. Can I ask you something?" she began, taking a seat on the couch. She patted the cushion beside her, inviting him to sit as well. Whatever medical school he attended, they hadn't taught him much about how to act comfortable with his profession or his patients. He was the most uptight man Jo had ever met, who also happened to have the posture of a ladder back chair.

"Of course, Josephine. You may ask me whatever you like." He tried to smile but his mouth just didn't know how to do it well. It looked more like a wince. Dr. Holbrooke was used to treating the old folks around Morton, who couldn't hear him anyway, so he never needed much in the way of conversational skills. He lived alone, never dated, and sat by himself in the front pew at church every Sunday.

"It's embarrassing but…you're a doctor so…"

"There's nothing to be embarrassed about when it comes to the human body," he said matter-of-factly. He folded his hands over his stomach, waiting.

Jo swallowed hard, preparing herself for what she was about to do. "I think I might have a lump."

"A lump?"

"In my breast."

The doctor's cheeks turned red. "In your breast?" he repeated, out of breath.

"Like my mom had. Will you…check it?" She started unbuttoning her plaid shirt before he could respond. The doctor looked like he'd been smacked in the head with a canoe paddle from behind. He wasn't blinking or breathing. Jo finished opening her shirt. She turned her body to face him, then slid one bra strap over her shoulder. The doctor hesitated for a moment, but then, because this young girl's health was in desperate need of his expertise, he reached out. His hands were cold as he felt around, squeezing, holding, searching for something that wasn't actually there. He made damn sure it wasn't there, for about forty-five seconds, the longest breast exam in history.

Satisfied this small-chested girl wasn't headed for an untimely death, Dr. Holbrooke pulled his hand away and took off his glasses. Jo put herself back in her bra but left her shirt unbuttoned.

"Everything feels fine to me. You're perfectly well."

"Are you sure? Do want to check the other one?"

"Oh. Uh. I suppose I should."

Jo let him.

After another long moment of awkward probing, the young doctor cleared his throat and said, "That was one healthy breast."

"Thank you, Dr. Holbrooke."

He almost thanked her in return but caught himself.

Taking the opportunity to end the doctor's visit, Jo buttoned up her shirt and said, "Well, I appreciate you coming by. I guess I'll see you in town. Or perhaps the county fair?"

"Oh. Yes, of course. Have a pleasant evening, Josephine."

The young doctor left the farmhouse, totally out of it, forgetting all about the original purpose of his house call. He left his glasses on the coffee table, but Jo quickly ran them out to him before he drove off half blind.

The legend of the sickly farmer lived on. The whole town was concerned for Johan Larsen. According to the doctor, this virus was something highly contagious. That kept visitors away but it didn't stop the onslaught of baked goods and flowers and get well wishes from showing up on the doorstep. They were to the point of keeping Napoleon indoors from early afternoon till dusk, due to the high chance somebody would stop by. Napoleon didn't seem to mind much. He was like a giant puppy, content to be around his master, the redheaded girl who fed him ice cream and scratched his neck. Somehow, he even learned to hold his bladder till he was led outside when the hour was safe. The three-and-a-half-week old giraffe was house trained, something nobody could explain.

On Sunday, Napoleon was free to roam outside all day long. The whole town of Morton was at Sunday school and church in the morning, then Sunday dinner. Visiting the sick was the Christian thing to do, but not if it messed with Sunday dinner. Or bingo. Sundays were sacred to Johan Larsen when he was alive, but not because of church. He used to love Sundays because he could walk down Main Street without seeing a single soul. On Sunday mornings, he could stop and toast the church full of people from the middle of the road if he liked, with or without clothing, hungover or still intoxicated from the previous night. On Sunday mornings, he could stand in front of the store with the pretty dresses in the window and remember his beautiful wife, with no worry of judging eyes watching him. He could take Jo fishing without having to find an unclaimed hole. He was a man of simple pleasures. Bourbon was one of them.

CHAPTER FOURTEEN

"I can't believe you're going again. Feels like you just went," Daniel said, helping Jo load the only remaining truck with bags of high quality leaves after supper on Friday.

"This week has been unusual, huh? Sorta flew by."

"Yeah. Guess it did. Be careful tonight, okay?"

"I always am."

"I know you are. I just feel better when I say it."

Once again, she was off, and once again, Daniel watched her go, waved to her as she turned left at the mailbox. Each time she headed out, he missed her a little more, the warmth in his belly faded with her absence. She always came home Saturday morning, so he worried less and less each time, but he couldn't deny that he missed her. It seemed Napoleon missed her too. Whenever she left, he was a fussy little devil. Daniel had his hands full trying to feed him. The young creature was being raised on mint chocolate chip ice cream, but it seemed he had a strong preference for having Josephine feed it to him.

"Oh come on," Daniel said, trying again with the ice cream. "Just eat it already."

A few days ago, they tried some other ice cream flavors, just for variety, but Napoleon turned up his nose. The main problem with his picky eating was that the modest-sized market in Morton only stocked up on so much of his favorite flavor. He was eating such high quantities that the three of them took turns driving to Whitfield and Seneca, the towns on either side of Morton, to clear out whatever mint chocolate chip ice cream was in the store's freezer section. Sometimes he ate a little hay to offset all the ice cream but, all in all, he was doing great, looking healthier and stronger every day.

Napoleon used his face to knock the carton out of Daniel's hands again, toying with him, perhaps. He was already shaping up to be an ornery creature, just like his mamma. Pretty soon, he'd start stealing from their bushels as they worked the harvest, but for now, all he wanted was ice cream, which made for more productive afternoons in the fields. Everything they picked counted now and their payoff with Mr. Ulrich was a little higher too. Still, it couldn't compare to the payoff on Friday nights. Those long-leafed beauties growing underground paid astronomically better but, for appearance's sake, they continued meeting Mr. Ulrich's expectations.

With Jo out for the night and Dylan tucked in for bed in the living room, Daniel recited his grandmother's poem for Napoleon, just the two of them out there on the porch, keeping up the bedtime routine. It was nice to have a routine again. It was nice to have a home. Daniel never slept so well in his life.

In the morning, Daniel looked out the kitchen window, beyond the sleepy-headed Napoleon who was standing there with his eyes shut, to see the red truck parked outside. She was home. The warmth was already returning to his belly. It was automatic now, whenever she was near. With other girls, Daniel got flutters, the feeling of little butterflies in his stomach, but with Josephine Larsen, it felt more like a cup of hot tea warming his belly on the coldest day of the year.

Daniel poured her a cup of coffee, ready to welcome her back. What was taking so long? She was still in the truck several minutes after pulling in. Daniel wondered if she'd fallen asleep out there. She was always dog-tired after her city runs. He took a sip of coffee then walked across the driveway, ready to rouse her and help her get to bed to catch up on a lost night of sleep.

When he opened her door, he noticed the bruise on her cheek, the scrape on her forehead above her eyebrow. The blood was dry, but the fact that she'd been bleeding at all was enough to thrust him into panic-mode. "What happened?" he asked hurriedly.

She raised her eyelids slowly and shrugged. As if to apologize for her condition, she reached for her roll of cash and pulled off five hundred dollars, a week's pay for the brothers. Her roll of cash was significantly smaller this time, about a fifth of its usual size. Josephine looked weak sitting there, totally removed from reality.

"Did something go wrong?" Daniel asked his obvious question, getting a sick feeling in his empty stomach. He put a tender hand to her face, inspecting her wounds. She flinched. "Talk to me, please?"

"I guess I got what was coming to me," she spoke in a tired voice.

"Tell me what happened. All of it." Daniel was stern as he spoke, in the mood for nothing but the truth from her.

"I got taken." She closed her eyes again. "One of my big drops…there were a bunch of people there, I should have known better. Usually, I meet with one person at a time at a place I decide, and that's the end of it. I should have known better. They took it. They took everything I had left. I only got paid for the first two drops and now the other dealers who were expecting a load last night are wondering where the hell their stuff is. And I'm three thousand dollars out of pocket."

"C'mon," he said, helping her exit the truck. Daniel led her to the bathroom and sat her down on the edge of the bathtub. He drenched a washcloth and knelt in front of her. Gently, he wiped her face down. Too tired to avoid his questions or his care, Jo sat there and let him.

"How many were there?" he asked.

"Five," she said. "They had guns. They knew I wouldn't go to the police. That's a pretty safe assumption on their part. After I handed the bags over, one of them pushed me to the ground just to give them some time to run away, as if I'd actually chase after them. Guess I got a little scraped up, huh?"

Stuck on a very important detail, Daniel repeated, "They had guns?"

She nodded. Before Daniel could ask anything else, Dylan poked his head into the bathroom and said, "Geez. What happened to your face?"

Jo glared at him, as did Daniel, who was in the process of cleaning her off. Her scrape wasn't that bad, it just bled a lot, like head wounds often do. "I had a bad night," Jo replied, not wanting to recount the details again just yet.

Dylan went on, "Man. That looks...how long will it take to heal?"

His lack of sensitivity inspired Daniel to shut the bathroom door right in Dylan's face. Jo smiled at him, now that they were alone. It was a defeated smile, but full of thankfulness. Daniel wiped the last of the dried blood from her cheekbone, finishing his duties. He set down the washcloth and ran his damp fingers over her chin, his thumb over her bottom lip. Her scent crept up his nose, that smell that couldn't be described in words and made his brain a little fuzzy. Carefully, he moved closer, ready to brush his lips over hers, just once, just barely. They were so close, their eyes were closed now, their lips were parted, they were breathing the same air, but that kiss never happened.

From the other side of the door, Dylan yelled, "Hey, Martha Stewart! Can I eat these muffins or what?"

"You made muffins?" she whispered, just an inch from his mouth.

He said, "Hope you're hungry," and pulled away. That was a close call.

In the kitchen, Dylan had already helped himself to the muffins Daniel baked at sunrise to welcome Jo home after a busy night. She picked at one, putting small crumbles of blueberry muffin in her mouth, too shaken up to eat the thing in a rushed manner.

"I don't want you doing this anymore," Daniel began maturely, hands wrapped around his mug. "You're gonna get yourself killed. You've gotta stop. Next time, it might not be bumps and bruises, so there's not gonna be a next time. Okay?"

She set down a morsel of muffin and argued, "You can't say things like that. It's not up to you. I'm fine, I'm gonna keep doing it. You know I have to."

"Then I'll slash your tires. Whatever I have to do to keep you from risking your life every Friday night is fine with me."

"This is my choice. I'm not gonna stop just because a couple of jerks got greedy last night."

"I know you're not," Daniel said. "That's why I'm gonna take over the drop-offs. It's not safe for you and I know you're too stubborn to adjust your business plan. I want you to have your pigs and your blue barn, but I want you to be alive and well too."

"What?" she questioned in disbelief.

"You keep doing what you're doing down there, using your green thumb and what not, and I'll take over the drop-offs."

"I'll go too," Dylan said, joining the conversation. "Me and Daniel can do the running around. Nobody's gonna mess with us like they messed with you and if they do, they'll be sorry." His chest puffed right up, his courage and boldness visible in his determined expression. Never mind his broken arm, he was invincible.

Daniel was about to tell Dylan he would have no part of this, but then he looked over his brother's strong build, his broad shoulders. Thugs might mess with Daniel if he was on his own, but they wouldn't mess with Daniel if Dylan were there too. Dylan was a bull, solid and ready to fight, forever geared up to put his raging testosterone to good use on a moment's notice. Maybe doing this together, taking on a dangerous job as a pair instead of alone, might bring them back together and reaffirm their weakening bond. Ever since they got here, they'd been at each other's throats. Now, they could come together as outlaws and share a common quest: keeping Josephine safe.

Fiddling with her black braided bracelet, Jo thought it over. It might be nice to have some help, actually. "Okay," she finally said. "But it's gonna go like this."

The boys looked at each other, pleased she was giving in, but a little nervous about her house-rules. Sitting at the head of the heavily worn table, Josephine was the CEO of her illegal enterprise. She was serious as she listed off her requirements, told her new employees how this would work if they were in fact joining her company. She had their full attention and it showed.

"In the mornings, we'll work in the fields. Mr. Ulrich will get suspicious if I stop sending a truckload of summer crops twice a week. After lunch, one of you will go to the root cellar and tend the plants with me. The other will stay up top with Napoleon and keep a lookout for nosey townspeople. If you see someone coming, you'll knock on the cellar doors three times, then take Napoleon inside. On Thursdays, one of you will help me pull leaves for bagging. You'll wear gloves. You will never ever try it. On Friday nights you'll both help me pack up what we've picked and all three of us will head to the city. I'll make the calls and choose the drop points. Dylan, you're the muscle. Daniel will do the talking. You do not give anybody anything until there's money in your hand. You will only accept twenties. Do not take bigger bills. Ever. I'll stay in the truck while you do the drop offs, and I'm gonna start taking the shotgun just in case. Once we use a drop point, we never use it again. I have a system and it works. After we do Omaha, we do Lincoln and Sioux Falls. When I can, I try to get out to Topeka and Des Moines. It's far, so having two extra drivers will be good. We can take turns sleeping and driving. Did you get all that?"

The boys exchanged a look and nodded to confirm.

"Here's the most important thing I'm going to say," she began. "You do not tell anyone where we came from. If anyone figures it out, it won't take long to find us here."

"Is that why you always look so nice on Fridays?" Dylan asked. "Cause you're trying not to look like a farm girl?"

Daniel swatted his brother's good arm, making sure he knew that was a jerk of a question.

"Yep. Gotta pass for city folk," she said with a grin. "Sometimes, if my runs are done early, I go to the Walmart in Jefferson City. It's open 24 hours." Her eyes were lit up, her face was beaming, because Walmart was something magical to her. Having grown up several hours away from the nearest Walmart, it was like Mecca, a place she stood in amazement on the rare occasions she walked through those sliding doors and into the fluorescent light from Heaven above. Her daddy once protested the building of a Walmart closer to home, but now that he was gone, she indulged in this guilty pleasure once in a while.

Daniel chuckled. As savvy as she may have sounded telling them the rules of selling unprocessed marijuana leaves, she just lost all credibility of being remotely street-smart when she got to the topic of Walmart.

Everyone was onboard. They kept to the plan. Mornings in the field, afternoons in the root cellar, switching between brothers. Jo upped their earnings, now that they were trustworthy and efficient with her precious plants, not just the crops growing in the fields. She started humming again too.

On Friday afternoon, Daniel was taking his turn in the root cellar, wearing latex gloves, filling his last baggy with leaves. He weighed it on the small scale, then added a few more leaves to hit the target number. Jo, who was busy germinating seeds in damp paper towels, smiled at him, pleased with her helper. Her smile dropped when she looked up to see something peculiar. It was Napoleon's long neck and it was reaching down into the cellar, where his busy little face munched happily on the taller plants he could reach from above. "Dylan!" she yelled, more upset with the bad babysitter than the bad baby. "You're supposed to be watching him!"

Napoleon chewed away. Jo snatched the leaves from his mouth but it was too late. Several plants were completely bare of leaves. How long had Napoleon been standing there eating? Long enough.

He'd eaten about eight ounces of leaves, and that was enough to do some damage.

"I think he's stoned," Daniel said, watching Napoleon take a wobbly side step.

"I think you're right," Jo agreed, once they were above ground.

Daniel loaded the truck while Jo went to yell at Dylan for falling asleep on the job. He was looking mighty relaxed on the porch swing, taking an afternoon nap. Though he was still in his sling looking helpless, she didn't spare him a few choice words about responsibility. When Napoleon toppled over on his side and sent a cloud of dry brown dust into the air around him, Dylan started laughing. The giraffe was high as a kite but Jo wasn't so amused.

After supper, they managed to lure Napoleon onto the porch with some ice cream. He had the munchies, after all. After that, he had the nerve to push the front door open and enter the kitchen without an invitation. He had a dopey smile on his fuzzy face. It was easy to see he was up to no good.

"Maybe one of you should stay here tonight. We can't leave him like this," Jo said, watching Napoleon sleeping on the kitchen floor, where he just collapsed moments ago. It was getting late. They needed to get on the road. People were expecting them.

"Honestly," Daniel began, "I bet he sleeps it off. I think he'll be okay. I doubt he'll notice we're gone. Let's just say, he's in a happy place."

Jo agreed to let the giraffe sleep where he was, with his neck bent sideways like a handle so his head was on the floor. There was no hope in waking him or moving him. Normally, he slept standing up or on his knees, out on the front porch, but now he was splayed out in the kitchen from the front door to the stove. One of his hooves was in the living room. He was getting so big. Jo dropped a potholder onto his face, just to see if he would notice. No such luck.

"Alright. Let's get on the road," she said, stepping over the giraffe, ready for a busy night.

Jo took the first shift behind the wheel. Dylan sat in the middle, probably to be closer to her, and Daniel sat on the far side, like a bookend. Tonight, they were headed for Lincoln first, 271 miles away. It took them four and a half hours. When they got into town, it was midnight and the streets were mostly empty. Jo pulled out a book called *Things to Do and See: Lincoln*. She also had one for Omaha, Sioux Falls, and four other Midwest hotspots where marijuana was in demand. She flipped the book open *to Fairview: Home of William Jennings Bryan*. This was her system, using tourism books to determine her drop points, then texting the address and time to a phone number she had scribbled in the back of the book. About half of the Lincoln sites had already been crossed off, used once as a meeting point and never to be revisited.

"William Jennings Bryan," she began reading aloud as they waited for their client to show up. "Served two terms in Congress and was U.S. Secretary of State and Democratic nominee for President in 1896, 1900, and 1908. His historic residence has been restored to its early 1900's grandeur. Open 10 a.m. to 4 a.m., Monday through Friday. Closed Thanksgiving, Christmas Day and New Year's Day."

The clock blinked over to 12:14 a.m., well past visiting hours. She didn't mind. Each time she made a drop in the city, she learned something new, saw something she'd never seen. This farm girl was getting out of her tiny hometown for about twelve hours a week and she was making the most of it, even from this far off vantage point.

"There he is," she said, pointing toward a figure walking across the street.

Daniel grew nervous. He was on.

"I can totally take him," Dylan said, as if a fight was guaranteed with every drop off. He clenched his fists to prove himself, even though he just had the one fist available.

Daniel and his brother got out and took the smaller bag out of the black luggage in the cab. It was an ordinary looking shopping bag that had *Thank You* printed about fifty times in red script. It was stuffed with two gallon-sized plastic bags containing nothing but leaves inside, which were concealed in empty graham cracker boxes. Jo didn't handle anything other than growing and harvesting. The dealers she delivered to would have to take it from there, dry it, process it, and divide it up for resale.

The man approaching, the first client of the night, was wearing a black baseball cap. His clothes were loose, which made him look even skinnier than he probably was. He needed to shave and he smelled like cigarette smoke, but he had a promising roll of green paper in his left hand, ready to trade.

"Where's the girl?" the guy asked, looking over Daniel's shoulder.

"She's in the truck, with the gun."

"Right," the guy replied. He eyed Dylan's mending arm.

Dylan noticed and pompously said, "You should see the other guy," as if this was a war wound.

The buyer smirked, then turned to Daniel. "Okay. Give me a hug."

"What?" Daniel huffed.

"Give me a hug. I'm gonna put the cash in your pocket. C'mon, I don't have all night."

Dylan watched his older brother hug a man he'd never met before. Feeling the cash drop into his pocket, knowing it was enough by the weight, Daniel quickly peeked to make sure they were all twenties, then handed the guy the generic-looking bag. Jo had run some training sessions before letting her novices take over. She trained them on the weight of cash. Since she called the shots with her dealers, she always requested twenty-dollar bills, nothing larger, nothing smaller. She sold gallon-sized bags, no portion thereof. Each bag was to be traded for a roll of cash, a specific amount so she wouldn't have to stand there and count it.

Before leaving Lincoln, they visited the Thomas P. Kennard House, the Lincoln Statue, and the Historic Haymarket. It was almost 1:30 a.m. when they headed for Omaha. There, they saw the Veteran's Memorial, the outside of the Bone Creek Museum of

Agrarian Art, and the Great Platte River Archway. Everything was going incredibly smooth. Nobody tried anything funny, everyone paid in full, and by 2:45 a.m., they were done and headed for Sioux Falls with some high quality plants. Here, they saw St. Joseph's Cathedral, the USS South Dakota Battleship Memorial, and the Delbridge Museum of Natural History, all from the truck, of course.

"Are we done yet?" Dylan asked. The clock read 4:02. He was tired and cranky but Jo was wide-awake after such a productive night with her new team.

"I'm thinking…Walmart," she said with a teasing smile. Since it was her turn to drive, the boys had no choice. As usual, Dylan was the only one who minded the detour. As if to protest, he went to sleep. When Jo pulled into the vast parking lot forty-five minutes later, they decided it would be better to leave Dylan in the cab while they went inside. Neither wanted to wake the cranky kid just to drag him through the store unwillingly. That would ruin the whole experience.

Once she passed through the automatic doors and stood in the brightly lit space station that was Walmart, Jo's energy tripled. Daniel was amused by her giddiness, that magical look in her eye as she scanned the endless aisles. "I love this place," she said, taking it all in.

And I love everything about you, Daniel wanted to say, but he knew better than to speak such words. Dylan was still after Josephine, blindly crushing on her. She was supposed to be off-limits to Daniel. He never meant to fall for her, it just sort of happened. She was perfect, everything about her was fascinating. The only part of her that was a problem was that she managed to attract the very determined Dylan McElroy, and that was a pretty big problem indeed. She never cast out her line for Dylan, but he was hopelessly hooked. The only way to get rid of him would be to cut the line altogether.

Daniel followed her through the aisles, watched her pick up things, consider buying them, then return them to their proper place. It seemed she just like the idea of so many choices, not necessarily purchasing anything. She passed through the makeup aisles and picked up a bottle of pale pink nail polish. It seemed she had a girlie side after all. Holding up the bottle, she said, "It's so pretty, but it always gets chipped. I wish I could wear it but it doesn't even last a day on me." With a sigh of resignation, she added, "I'm never going to have hands that look like they belong to a girl."

"What about on your toenails?" Daniel suggested.

A small smile crept to her lips and Revlon's "Cotton Candy Shimmer" went into her basket.

The next aisle over, Daniel held a Nebraska road map about four inches from his face, straining to read the tiny text, curious how far they had driven that night. Jo caught him, cocked her head to the side, and said, "You need glasses."

"Maybe," he admitted, pulling the map further away to see if everything went blurry like it usually did.

"C'mon," she said, leading him to the end cap across the way where an assortment of reading glasses were displayed. She handed him one pair, and asked, "Better or worse?"

"Worse," he said, unable to read anything at all on the map in his hands. She handed him another pair and asked the same question. "Uh…better, maybe?" She continued handing him different ones with different numbers on them, until finally the map was as clear as day. "Yes! Better," he said in amazement. Jo looked happy at first, then guilty. "Those are women's glasses," she admitted, searching again for something else. When Daniel asked, "Does it really matter," he could tell from her expression he must be wearing some exceptionally feminine glasses. When he pulled them away to look, he realized there were little rhinestones in the side corners, and that the color of the plastic was actually purple, not gray like he originally thought. Fortunately, Jo found a suitable pair, and added them to her basket with Daniel's approval.

When they got to the electronics section, Daniel tuned in a radio station through the static of nothingness and held out his hand, asking for a dance. The song playing at this early hour was "Strange Currencies". He wondered how many other people were actually listening right now. It felt like they might be the only two.

"Who sings this?" she asked, taking his hand.

"REM," he replied, pulling her close. "It's from a long time ago." Slowly, in an uncoordinated slide, they moved their feet on the vinyl tile ground, under the bright fluorescent sky, surrounded by the forest of racks and shelves. His nose pressed against her neck, he breathed in that glorious smell of her skin and determined then and there this particular spot on her neck, just below her ear, was the source of that intoxicating scent she probably had no idea was present or the affect it had on his ability to think.

At one point during the song, while the shaking voice continued on the radio, Jo looked up at him, her face close to his. Her expression was easy to read: *Aren't you going to kiss me now?* The hot tea feeling in his stomach spread up to his chest. It was the perfect time to kiss her mouth, tell her everything she needed to know without saying a thing, but he didn't.

CHAPTER FIFTEEN

"It's your turn to go get ice cream," Josephine said from her spot on the couch. It was a rainy Sunday morning and two out of three of them had their noses in books so she volunteered Dylan, the lazy one, to put those lazy bones of his to good use. Napoleon finished off the last of the mint chocolate chip ice cream that morning, which was the only thing they kept in the freezer these days. He was a growing boy, helping himself to six to eight gallons a day. He barely made a dent in that hay bale outside.

"I went two days ago," Dylan protested from the floor, where he lay on his back looking utterly helpless. He still had his sling, but that wasn't what made him look so helpless. It was that pouty lower lip, those *why-me* eyes that rolled with annoyance.

"Exactly," Jo confirmed. "Daniel went the day after that and I went yesterday. It's your turn again," she explained, flipping a page. Today, she was almost through one of her favorite books for what had to be the hundredth time: *The Great Gatsby*. Daniel debated starting *The Brothers Karamazov* that morning, once it was clear they wouldn't be working the fields, but settled for something a little more approachable: *Uncle Tom's Cabin*. It was his first time reading with his new glasses, and even though his brother made fun of him for 'trying to look smart' he now realized he probably should have gotten his eyes checked a long, long time ago. Books were that much better when they weren't blurry.

"C'mon. It's not like you're doing anything," Daniel added, not bothering to look up. "Make yourself useful for a change."

"I *am* useful," Dylan mumbled his argument, getting himself upright. "I'm gonna go to the movies or something. You bookworms are such a drag," he teased, playing with Jo's ponytail as he stood next to the couch, vying for her attention. "You wanna go with me?" he asked nonchalantly.

"I'm perfectly happy being a bookworm, thank you very much. Have fun," she said, her eyes following along the rows of text, not slowing as she spoke. She swatted him away from her ponytail. She was the lemonade and Dylan the tireless fly.

"Do *you* wanna go with me?" Dylan tried his brother this time, his second choice. All he got was a headshake in return, declining the offer.

Dylan was on his own today, left to entertain himself in this land where entertainment was simple, as were the natives. A nomadic boy such as himself who'd called twenty cities home in the last ten years, would have to drive forty minutes and plunk down eight-fifty to catch a matinee if he wanted to enrich the next few hours of his life with something thrilling. There was nothing thrilling on this farm, and that was how it should be. When the sky was kind, like it was now, offering gentle rain for the crops and no funnel clouds, and Napoleon wasn't being fussy, and Jo wasn't interested in anything but her book, and his brother wasn't pissing him off, and there were no crops to harvest today, there just wasn't much to do out here. His need for excitement re-ignited on Friday night when they did their illegal deeds miles away from here. He'd forgotten how much he liked civilization.

Seeing that sense of excitement missing in his brother's face, Daniel put down his novel and said, "I know that look. That's the look you get right before you get us into trouble. If you come back from the movies and have more than six gallons of ice cream, say…a hippopotamus or something, I'm going to be very disappointed."

That got a sheepish smile out of Dylan. As much as they got under each other's skin on a daily basis, his brother knew him better than anyone. "Yeah, yeah," he muttered through his grin. With a nice chunk of cash in his pocket, his cut from Friday night as well as his earnings from the week prior, Dylan took the keys to Jo's truck and said, "How would you feel about a rhino?" as he headed out on his own.

On this gloomy day, the first day of July, it looked like it might be the grayest day of winter except for the trees full of green. You could smell the dampness, feel the shiver in your bones. The fields were quiet, nobody was working, no giraffes were bounding around, just rows of crops and dirt soaking in the water from above. This was the most rain they'd had in almost thirty years. The McElroy brothers brought record-breaking weather when they came.

After tossing the cooler for the ice cream into the bed of the truck, Dylan drove up the long gravel driveway and turned left, heading away from Morton, off on an adventure without his brother telling him not to do this and not to do that. He was a little blue Jo wasn't with him. Going to a movie with her would have been just wonderful. Sitting in the back of a dark theater, surely she'd let him put an arm around her, maybe more if he played his cards right. He knew she liked him. She *had* to like him by now. What was not to like?

As he got the truck up to speed on the wet country road, he decided to add one more stop to his list of errands today. After the movie, but before the ice cream pick up, he would buy Josephine Larsen something expensive, because all girls like expensive things. Maybe a necklace. Maybe a bracelet. Maybe earrings. Did she even have her ears pierced? He couldn't remember her ears, whether or not they were adorned or untouched as nature made them. A bracelet might be good, get her to replace that black braided one, which was kind of gross in his opinion. She was wearing the hair of a dead animal, all day every day. Yuck. If he bought her something lovely from a jewelry shop, something shiny and valuable, she'd be thrilled to upgrade and throw that other thing in the trash where it belonged. He was ready to try again with the whole will-you-be-my-girlfriend thing and having a little something to sweeten the deal, like a bracelet, would be just the ticket.

Back in the living room, it was quiet. Only the sound of a page turning every now and then interrupted the steady drops of water on the roof. Daniel looked up at Jo, snuck a peek at her reading. She was almost done, just a few more pages left. He continued his own story. Jo took a turn to look up at him, just to make sure he was still there, then back down at her book. Daniel glanced up again, taking in her beautiful face and vibrant hair, then let his eyes fall to the black text below. Sensing she was being watched, Jo moved her line of sight just past the top of her book, and before she could look away, Daniel's gaze finally caught hers. Busted.

It took Jo twenty minutes to read the last five pages, all because of this little game going on. Daniel wasn't even reading at this point, just staring at the pages when he wasn't staring at Jo. Their shy eyes alternated looking across the living room, getting caught, retreating to the words waiting to be read, then starting all over again. Finally, Jo closed her book. She stood up with confidence, as if she'd made up her mind about something big.

Daniel closed his book too, not bothering to mark his place, and watched her cross the small room and extend her right hand toward him, encouraging him to stand. After a lingering moment, she turned and pulled his hand along with her, and he didn't fight it. She led him up the creaky stairs and into her bedroom. The rain was louder here. So was his heartbeat.

She let go of him and nervously brushed some stray hair out of her face. Unsure what to do with her fingers now, she started picking at her thumb. She may not have known what to do with her hands but she knew what to do with her mouth as soon as Daniel confidently stepped forward and pressed his lips to hers. It was what she was waiting for, her reason for bringing him up here.

He wasn't sure at first, but now, he was positive. This was exactly what she wanted. A few nervous breaths of air escaped her nose, and she eventually raised her right hand to touch his face, his unshaven cheek. Her delicate fingers ran over the short stubble, a contrast in textures. Even though she worked her hands hard in the fields running the farm, they were the softest things Daniel had ever felt. He realized this was the first time he'd ever kissed a girl who matched his height. It was only weird for a second, then he realized how much he treasured having her mouth line up exactly with his, without needing to crane his neck. Her lips were right there, totally accessible.

Without warning, Jo broke from his kiss. "I've had sex before," she blurted out, backing away from him like he had a bomb strapped to his chest.

"Oh," Daniel exhaled, caught off guard by her abrupt departure more than her statement.

Jo bit her thumbnail nervously then added, "Just once."

"Um. Okay," he said, giving a small smile since she was acting so jumpy all of a sudden. It wasn't like he made a move or anything. All they were doing was kissing. He would be glad to get back to the kissing any time now.

"I didn't really like it," she added.

"What?"

"Sex. I didn't like it. The one time. I didn't like it at all."

Daniel squinted and nodded, taking in her strange details, details he never asked for. "We don't have to…do anything. I would never…I wasn't trying to…we can just…"

"No. I *want* to," she stated, cutting him off. "I want to."

"Oh," he breathed, accepting her words. His brother might have sold his soul to hear those words from Jo, but for now, Dylan wasn't his concern.

Jo considered something for the first time and her head popped up as she asked, "Do *you* want to? I mean, I just thought…oh my God, I feel so stupid now. You *don't* want to. I feel so stupid. You don't even think about me that way, do you? I'm such an idiot."

Daniel smiled, amused by her. "I never said that."

"Soooo...you *do* want to?"

"Very much. But there's no rush, and I don't want to do this if you have any doubts. Any doubts at all. Are you sure this is what you want?"

"I'm sure. No doubts...just a little nervous."

"Me too," he admitted quietly. It was an honest answer. He was quite nervous indeed. It had been so long since he'd done any of this stuff, and Jo was so perfect, so worthy, so beautiful and clean, he wanted to get it right. Now that they'd established they both wanted the same thing, Daniel found the nerve to ask, "So, what uh...what didn't you like about it before?"

She made a funny face, like a disgusting thought just entered her mind. "I didn't like the guy."

"I see," Daniel offered, unsure what else he was supposed to say.

"He was...really sweaty, disgustingly sweaty and...I didn't really want to, I mean I *did*, but I didn't. You know? "

"Oh," he managed. His cheeks felt hot already.

"Sorry," she said, blushing a little. "When you...before...did *you* like it?"

"Uh huh."

"Did *she* like it? The girl you were with? Or...*girls*? Plural?"

"Not plural," he reassured.

Jo didn't look any less relieved he'd been with just one girl. She was more concerned about whether or not it was good, and patiently waited for an answer.

"I'd like to think she enjoyed it," he replied, feeling a little ridiculous for this awkward conversation happening in Jo's bedroom. Her total lack of seduction was rather endearing to him now. She was naïve, but not completely.

With a quick glance out her window to the dreary world, Jo asked, "Should I take off my clothes, or do you want to do that?"

"Oh. Uh…" he began, surprised how fast things were moving. "It uh…it doesn't matter, I guess. I uh…no…it doesn't matter. Whatever you want."

Realizing the extent of her gracelessness, she offered an apology. "I'm sorry I'm not very…you know. *Sexy*."

"Sexy is overrated."

Hearing that, she smiled, the first true smile she'd managed since they made it upstairs. Feeling more at ease following his little comment, she unbuttoned her shirt, put it on a nearby chair, and stood in her jeans and camisole. Her naked feet had wriggling toes, antsy from everything spinning through her head.

"Are you sure you want to do this? Cause we don't have to do anything. I like you a lot, Jo. You know that. I've liked you from the start."

"No you didn't," she said with a smirk. "You thought I was bitchy."

"Who told you that?" he shot back.

"Your brother."

"That little snitch!"

"It's okay. I wasn't very welcoming."

He bit the side of his lower lip, unsure what was supposed to happen next. The rain fell harder, filling the silence. "We could just lay there together, clothes on, and that would make me very, very happy, Jo. You have no idea how happy that would make me."

She put a condom on the nightstand, pulled back the covers of the un-made bed, then lifted her pale pink camisole over her head, letting him know his counter offer just wouldn't cut it. In her white bra, the plainest piece of underwear Daniel had ever seen, he felt his insides melting already. She was so pretty, her tall skinny body, her disheveled red hair, her collection of simple cotton coverings. Jo slid off her loose-fitting jeans and let them lay in a puddle on the floor. Nobody spoke. She unhooked the chain around her neck, and set the keys on the nightstand. With a deep breath, gathering courage, she took off the rest and stood there, letting him look while he remained fully clothed, protected from such vulnerability.

Josephine, the slender girl with no dramatic curves or overemphasized angles, was breathtaking. Everything about her was subtle and soft. She had a few freckles on her chest, on her shoulders, which ordinarily remained covered by clothing but were now exposed. There were so many things he wanted to say, but he said nothing.

After about ten seconds of this, an eternity if you're the naked one, Jo lost her nerve and got into bed under the covers, hiding her skin and bones. She put a pillow over her face, as if to suffocate herself, and murmured, "I can't believe I just did that."

"I'll just let you know right now, I'm not nearly as brave as you." He sat down on the bed, then took off his shirt and balled it up, facing away from Jo, who had the covers pulled up to her chin in an effort to hide. "I…uh…I'm gonna have to do the rest of this under the covers," he said, getting under the sheets before taking off anything else.

From there on out, things went more naturally. The rain lightened up and so did their anxieties. After that initial gasp, that first sensational shock, they both relaxed and found an unhurried rhythm. It wasn't overwhelmingly passionate, nothing you'd see in a perfectly-lit scene in a movie, it was just *them*, two young lovers under the covers, breathing hard on a rainy day. After Daniel whispered "Are you okay, do you want me to stop?" three times in a row, Jo whispered back, "Please stop asking me that," and gave him a smile so bright and confident it made his eyes sting with the threat of tears. She was sure, he was sure.

When it was over, when every muscle in his back tightened and Daniel stuttered out a breath of pure pleasure for the first time in over two years, Jo closed her gray eyes and smiled wide. From her pillowcase, she was beaming, utterly at peace. The rain finally stopped waltzing on the windowpane above the bed. Daniel rolled over on his back, right next to her, and looked up at the ceiling.

Once his breathing steadied, he turned his head towards her, feeling shy again now that it had actually happened. When they briefly made eye contact, Jo's cheeks turned pink and she looked away. "Oh sure, *now* you blush," he quietly teased, noticing the flushing on her face didn't stop at her neckline. "I tried really hard not to sweat," he whispered through a smirk, attempting to put her at ease.

She laughed, shaking the bed a little. "Yes. Thank you for that."

After a long moment of silence, Daniel asked, "Was it…okay?"

She made a funny grin and nodded. "Do you think we could do it again?"

That was awesome news for Daniel. He wasn't as rusty as he feared and this wasn't going to be a one-time only type of thing. Maybe tomorrow afternoon they could fit in a session while Dylan did his duties in the field. Maybe they could sneak out to the bed of the truck tonight and make love under the stars. All these beautiful scenarios including Jo, this glorious dance they'd just done, and a wide-open future, flashed through his blissful brain. If only he knew how soon in the future she had in mind.

"Right now?" he questioned, watching her crawl over him.

"Yeah," she said, looking down at Daniel in a carefree way, tracing her thumb over his belly button.

"I…uh…I need a minute," he explained, surprised he had to explain at all.

"For what?" she questioned, totally oblivious, ready to go.

Daniel cocked an eyebrow, waiting to see if she was serious. He rested his hands on her boney hips and chuckled at her, this sweet, sweet girl above him, who knew so much about animals and crops and little about men.

After the second time around, once the flushing from their cheeks faded away, they were both a little silly. For two quiet people, reserved in their laughter most of the time, they were certainly laughing a lot now. The floodgates had opened. The river of cackles and animated chatter filled the space between them. In that bed, naked as the day she was born, Josephine had never talked so much in her life. And Daniel, who normally kept things pretty serious out of habit, was right there with her, laughing so hard he got tears in his eyes. The two of them had quite a different take on basking in the afterglow.

At that very same moment, downstairs in the kitchen, Dylan McElroy fiddled with the silver horse dangling from the charm bracelet he paid just shy of three hundred dollars for about an hour ago. He was sitting at the table now, listening to the laughter coming from upstairs. He dug his thumbnail into the silver horse's body, trying to break it in half. The sterling piece wouldn't even dent. If the stupid thing would just dent, he'd feel better, more powerful. He pushed harder, sending all his anger through his thumb into that tiny horse he picked out for the girl he was certain he loved, who he was *almost* certain might love him back. He took such pride in this bracelet, a gift for his crush. When he walked up the stairs to the farmhouse just minutes ago, he showed the charm bracelet to Napoleon and gloated, "She's gonna love it." Napoleon didn't look impressed with his big black eyes, he just looked hungry, ready to dig into the ice cream already. Dylan fed the giraffe and dropped the bracelet into his pocket, absolutely pleased with himself for remembering her saying she wanted to raise horses one day.

Of course she didn't want to raise horses, she wanted to raise pigs, but it was all the same to young Dylan. When he entered that farmhouse, he was so tall, so proud, so ready to sweep her off her feet, but when he heard the two voices up there, giggling and carrying on, *he* was the one who was swept off his feet. His knees got rubbery so fast he was lucky to find a chair in time. Gravity pulled him down and his stomach turned sour. Now, sitting in that same chair that caught his fall, he was just going to wait. They couldn't stay up there forever.

Daniel, being as ridiculous as he'd ever been, was showing Jo he could fit her whole fist into his mouth. She didn't think he could do it, but he was proving her wrong. He was almost there, pushing her balled-up hand further into his cheeks, while she shrieked in delight, half disgusted, half impressed. When he succeeded in his outrageously weird demonstration, Jo gave a shout of congratulations. She couldn't clap for him, given one of her hands was wedged between his molars at the moment. Once her hand was freed from the cavern of his mouth, she took great pleasure in wiping all his slobbery spit on his bare shoulder over his tattoo, which he avenged by digging his fingers into her ribs and tickling her mercilessly till she snorted. Any embarrassment about their naked bodies, any jitters about being with somebody for the first time, they were long gone now.

Hearing another loud burst of laughter carry down the stairs to his jealous ears, Dylan stood up, opened the front door a few inches, then slammed it shut again, making damn sure they'd hear it this time and would stop whatever it was they were doing up there.

The whole house shook when Dylan slammed that door. It reverberated through the floor, rattled the pictures on the wall, and wiped the smiles off Daniel and Josephine's faces. They looked each other in the eye as if to make plans to escape through the window. Daniel started to feel lightheaded. He took a deep breath, gave Jo a quick peck on the cheek, and started getting dressed beside the bed.

Josephine watched him from her place under the covers. She asked, "Should I stay up here?"

"Yeah," he said, buttoning his fly. "Just…give me a few minutes to talk to him. It'll be okay." As he pulled his t-shirt over his head, he added, "I hope."

Jo looked tense. She pulled the quilt tight to her thin frame, comforting herself. "Maybe I should talk to him," she said in a concerned voice. "I thought he could take a hint but…"

"Dylan? Take a hint? Yeah right."

Daniel leaned in once more to kiss her, a quick kiss to tell her it would all be okay, then left the bedroom for the creaky stairs. Each step announced his dishonor, a sharp cry of brotherly disgrace with every floorboard he disturbed. He started to break a sweat. This wasn't going to be an easy conversation, but there was no way out of it.

Before Daniel had the chance to say anything at all, having finally descended the stairs, a silver charm bracelet bounced off his forehead, leaving behind a thin red line where a tiny horse hoof dug into his flesh.

"Did you have a nice nap up there, you fucking asshole?" Dylan yelled.

Stunned, unable to speak or move, Daniel stared at the bracelet on the floor near his feet. When he had the nerve to look up, the sight of his heart-broken brother was nauseating. Dylan had a tear streaming down each of his smooth cheeks. His blue eyes were glossy and bloodshot; he had never looked so vulnerable. It seemed everyone knew Jo wasn't interested in him, *except* for him, and now he was nothing other than crushed. He was stuck somewhere between humiliation and boiling fury, and for so many reasons. After all, his one and only brother broke a cardinal rule.

Daniel had to say something. But what? This was his baby brother standing here now, the blond kid he'd grown up protecting no matter what trouble he got them into. This was his best friend, albeit a best friend he wanted to strangle sometimes. "I'm ... sorry," Daniel managed, though he didn't say for what specifically. He wasn't sorry for having feelings for Jo, or for what they'd done upstairs under those covers, but he *was* truly and utterly sorry his brother had to get hurt like this.

Dylan shook his head, letting Daniel know the apology wasn't accepted. "You're sorry?" he mocked. "I'm the one who's sorry! I'm sorry I have a low-life for a brother! I'm sorry I fell for a carrot-headed, flat-chested, simple-minded slut! I'm the one who's sorry!"

Daniel stepped forward now, finding some anger of his own. "Outside! Now!"

Daniel grabbed his brother by the shirt and dragged him through the front door, passed the startled giraffe with minty green slime all over his lips. Out in the driveway, Daniel pushed his brother in the chest, getting him ready for the fight they were about to have.

Dylan had the nerve to ask, "So, does the carpet match the …" but Daniel popped him in the mouth before he could finish his crude inquiry. Never in his life had Daniel *really* hit his brother like this, hard enough that his knuckles throbbed in pain after the punch was effectively delivered. "Go ahead! Hit me back!" Daniel taunted, wanting a fair match.

Dylan, with only one arm to fight with, didn't take a swing. He looked as shocked as Daniel felt at that moment, both surprised by that punch. His lip was split open, blood spilled from his mouth.

"Hit me, you stupid asshole! Hit me!" Daniel screamed again.

"I don't wanna hit you," Dylan growled in Daniel's face. "I wanna *kill* you!"

Nose to nose, Daniel looked into the hateful blue eyes of his brother, knowing full well he didn't mean that. By Daniel's unchanged expression, Dylan saw his bluffing was pointless. His brother knew him too well. With a one-armed shove, Dylan pushed Daniel over.

"Have you two been fooling around the whole time we've been here?" Dylan all but accused, wiping more tears from his face, then blood from his chin.

Daniel shook his head no, though he wasn't sure how much his honesty was worth now.

Dylan continued, "Why did you do it? Huh? I liked her first! You knew I liked her!"

In a much quieter voice, Daniel replied, "But she never liked you back."

"Oh? Is that a fact? Then why didn't you say something! Huh?"

"I did! A thousand times! But you wouldn't listen to me! You never listen!"

"You did this to get me back, didn't you?" Dylan tried to make sense of it.

"God no. Are you nuts? It has nothing to do with you!"

All Dylan could do was shake his head, denying it all. He reached down and flung some wet gravel at his older brother, who was still sitting where he landed moments ago. Dylan hurled more tiny rocks, waiting for Daniel to shield his face each time, and grumbled things like "I hate you, I hate you to the fucking core! I'll never forgive you for this, I hope it was worth it!" Having said his piece, Dylan stormed off toward the transport vehicle, which was parked where the barn used to be. Daniel picked a small rock out of his chin and watched his brother take the license plates off the stolen vehicle, leave them on the ground, and drive away.

CHAPTER SIXTEEN

"What're you looking at?" Daniel snapped at Napoleon on his way through the screened-in porch. Napoleon had nothing to say in return. The giraffe wasn't moved by the fight he just witnessed in the driveway. He may not have noticed anything at all other than the ice cream drippings on the floor.

Daniel sat at the kitchen table and covered his eyes with his hands. He felt awful on so many levels. The creaking stairs announced Josephine's fast-approaching arrival. Quickly, before she made it down to the kitchen to see his face, Daniel wiped the bubbles of tears from his eyes before they did anything rash like run down his flushed cheeks. Whatever happened, he didn't want to cry in front of her, not over something like this.

As soon as she met his bloodshot eyes, she knew everything. Instead of asking the obvious questions, she took a seat at the table and waited for Daniel to say whatever he felt he needed to say, in his own time. Instead of speaking, he started cooking dinner, just for the two of them. Dylan wouldn't be coming back tonight, maybe not ever.

"Let me help," Jo offered, standing up to assist. Daniel passed off the potatoes to her and she started peeling in silence. By the time dinner was ready, Daniel had come to terms with the situation. His brother was the foolish one here, and if he wanted to part ways because he didn't get what he wanted this time, so be it. Daniel was done sacrificing for a selfish little brother who had a one-track mind and a heart full of hormones.

Once they finished eating, Jo quietly pleaded, "Say something. You haven't spoken a word in almost an hour. Just…say something. Anything."

Daniel smiled once to put her at ease. He was about to ask her if she could smell that odd smell, something like cleaning chemicals and peaches wrapped in wet newspaper, but when he tried to move his mouth to speak, he couldn't. His tongue felt thick, swollen, way too large for his mouth. Something wasn't right. He was sure he smelled peaches, but there were none. And what was wrong with his tongue? Why was it nailed to the roof of his mouth? Daniel looked across to the redheaded girl, whose name he suddenly couldn't think of. She was looking at him in a concerned way. "Daniel?" she said, her voice echoing as though she was at the bottom of a well. "Daniel? Are you okay?" the girl spoke again. Who was she? Where did she come from? How did she know his name?

The last thing Daniel saw before succumbing to the electric convulsions spiking through his brain were his own hands turning into tight fists. When he came to, when the seizure had run its course for several minutes, his short finger nails had managed to dig into his palms. It felt like he'd been asleep for years, like a whole lifetime had gone by. He was on the floor now with his head in Jo's lap. She looked frightened but continued stroking his forehead as if she was waiting on his return. It was so good to see her face. With some difficultly, he moved his hand up toward her cheek, wanting only to show affection and gratefulness. A smear of blood from his palm stained her chin. Next, he slowly wiped his mouth, the foam on his lips. He was beyond embarrassed. At least he hadn't hit his head, or knocked anything over, or worse. So far, all the seizures he'd had during his lifetime had been clean and damage free.

Following a sniffle, Josephine said, "You never told me you were epileptic. You should have told me, Daniel. You should be wearing a medical bracelet or something."

When he regained control of his fingertips, Daniel reached into his pocket and pulled out his medical bracelet, which had been broken for years. He had never gotten around to repairing the chain, but that was mostly on purpose. The engraved metal plate revealed what he was, that awkward title he could barely spell, the permanent branding he'd had since the first time he had a seizure when he was just six years old. Jo took the broken bracelet and shook her head in disbelief. "How often do you get them?" she asked.

"Not very. The…last one…" he started, trying to remember how to talk. "Three years ago."

With a look of relief, she said, "Is there anything else I need to know about you, Daniel McElroy?"

He closed his eyes, feeling more and more like himself with each passing minute, then replied, "My feet are two different sizes."

Jo chuckled. "Mine too."

That night, after they got Napoleon settled in on the porch, Daniel lay on the couch and rested his head in Jo's lap once more. She'd already fixed the link on his medical bracelet, so he had no excuse not to wear it now. Daniel was recovered, just feeling that certain kind of exhaustion and dizziness that always followed one of his seizures. What he didn't tell Jo was that the last time he had a seizure was the day he and Dylan were in a pretty serious car accident. The time before that, he had a seizure following a fight at school where he ended up with a broken nose after trying to calm things down between Dylan and two thugs he'd managed to piss off in the cafeteria. And the time before that, it was the day his grandma died. It seemed Daniel McElroy saved up his seizures for particularly bad days. But today wasn't all bad, just the part when his one and only brother left him in a flurry of anger. Before the fallout, this had been one of the best days of his life, all because of this gorgeous redhead who was swiftly taking over his heart.

"Is Dylan epileptic too?" she asked, in another world altogether.

"No. At least…not yet, not that we know of."

Sweetly, she ran her fingers through his messy brown hair. "Should we go out looking for him?" she asked.

"I don't want to go anywhere."

He meant that. This was the only place he wanted to be. For once in his life, he wanted to stay put. Lying there with his head resting in Jo's lap, with her fingers in his hair, was the best place in the world. It felt a little weird without Dylan by his side, but sooner or later they would have to lead separate adult lives. He just never imagined it would be so soon. Dylan was barely an adult.

Jo spoke quietly above him. "I'm sorry…if I…"

"Shh," he said. "You have nothing to be sorry about."

"Do you think he'll come around?"

"He's too full of himself to come around."

"But he's your brother…"

"And he's a fool."

The following evening, back on the couch with his head in her lap and her fingers stroking his hair just she'd done the evening before, Daniel was in much better spirits. Having the house to themselves for twenty-four hours did magical things for them. Without Dylan's neediness to deal with, they were permitted to be affectionate and speak openly, if they felt like speaking at all. Daniel was finishing up Uncle Tom's Cabin under the shadow of Jo's copy of My Antonia. With one hand, she held her book above his head, with the other hand, she ran her fingers through Daniel's hair, only stopping when a page needed turning. At one point, Daniel glanced over to the beat-up instrument cases beside the couch and asked, "Are those yours?"

"My dad's banjo, my grandfather's accordion."

"Can you play?"

Jo set down her book and said, "I can play the accordion, but I'll never show you, so don't even ask."

"Oh c'mon, why not?"

"Because I look silly when I play."

"It can't be that bad. I really wanna hear you play. I won't watch," he begged, squeezing her leg to persuade her. He had to ask four more times and swear on his own life he wouldn't laugh, before Jo eventually got up and strapped the accordion to her chest. She managed one full blast-of-a-chord before Daniel was caught off guard by his own surprised laughter. He didn't mean to laugh, it just exploded out of his chest uninvited and unstoppable.

"See?" Jo said, stopping the music. "I look ridiculous, don't I?"

Daniel covered his mouth, willing himself to stop laughing, and finally managed, "It's just…your elbows. They're like…" but he couldn't finish. She was so tall and skinny, holding this massive accordion, and the way her bony elbows looked sticking out like that, it was just too much. Jo stuck out her tongue, played a quick little song with her elbows flying wildly through the air, and Daniel laughed freely this time and clapped in time to the music to encourage her. In some small way, he felt like he was bonding with her dead father just then, like Johan could have been sitting across the room in the armchair, laughing along with them, mocking Jo in a loving way. By the end of the fast-paced polka, Jo was laughing too and did a dramatic bow once the instrument was back in its case.

Jo reclaimed her seat on the couch and said, "Yeah, well, you look ridiculous when you run," and Daniel said, "Fair enough." They returned to their usual quiet selves as they read the evening away, just like an old married couple. At one point, she paused to ask, "How long have you been reading that page? Did you get stuck on a big word?"

"Ouch," Daniel replied, appreciating she could tease him. He closed the book and admitted, "You're distracting me."

"Sure, sure," she said, pretending not to believe him. She closed her book and they went upstairs.

From his spot on the left side of her mattress, Daniel watched her float across the dimly lit room in her hideous nightgown, the same one she always wore. He couldn't help but smirk at the sight of this gorgeous girl, the one with all those subtle but perfect curves, wearing something so ugly to camouflage them. She noticed his quick change of expression and asked, "What?" as she took down her hair, letting it fall to her waistline before brushing it a few times, this nighttime routine that was no longer private.

"Nothing," he said, feeling that disloyal smirk giving him away.

"It's obviously something," she went on, rubbing lemon-scented lotion on her forearms and elbows like she did every night before turning in.

Comfortable speaking his mind, though not in the fullest capacity just then, he asked, "Where'd you get that...uh...nightgown?"

"Why?"

"It's...unusual, isn't it?"

"Is it?" she asked, looking down at her bib of ruffles and all the yards and yards of fabric that came after it till the floor mercifully stopped them.

"I don't think I've seen anything like...that...before."

Her face dropped. She was onto him. "You think it's ugly."

Fearing the first fight of their relationship coming on, if they were in a relationship at all, he back-peddled quickly. "No, no. It's just...unusual. You look beautiful, so beautiful I may not let you sleep in anything at all tonight."

She bought it and got under the covers. "It was my mother's," she said quietly, getting settled on her pillow.

Daniel should have guessed. The white cotton nightgown was vintage in a bad way, and all those women's clothes in her father's bedroom hadn't been moved since her mother's death in 1990, with the exception of this one atrocious article. Sure, this thing had deeply rooted sentimental aspects for Jo, but it also slid over her head quite easily, so in the end, Daniel didn't have to sleep next to her wearing it. Tonight, it was just skin on skin. Tracing his fingers along her backbone, he memorized every rise and fall of her rocky spine as if this mountain range was his new home.

Nobody said I love you, or good night, or don't let me die in my sleep. Nobody said anything at all. Dylan was out on his own, sleeping somewhere without his older brother nearby to protect him. The McElroy boys never had so much distance between them, physically or emotionally. This realization kept Daniel awake for hours, or maybe that had more to do with this beauty beside him, a beauty he knew he didn't deserve.

In the morning, before they got out of bed to start the day, Jo propped up on her elbow and kissed Daniel's forehead. She whispered, "Where do you think he went?"

"Who? Dylan?"

"Who else?"

"I dunno. I'm sure he's fine."

"You sure you don't want to go out looking for him?"

"I'm sure. He was ready to leave, but I'm here to stay. I wanna help you raise pigs in a blue barn. If you'll have me, that is."

"You know anything about pigs?" she asked with a suspicious smile.

"No. But I didn't know any about radishes or beans…or marijuana…"

"This is true. I guess you're a fast learner, huh?"

"So does that mean I can stay?"

She nodded. "What are your salary requirements," she teased.

"You have to sleep naked from now on."

"What if I get cold?"

"You won't. You'll never ever get cold," he said, rolling over and covering her body with his, proving himself. As long as he was in that bed with her, she would never have to shiver again.

They didn't get started in the fields till 10 a.m., three hours late. Life around the farm had a different pace now that Dylan was gone. Unfortunately, Napoleon suffered from this. He was starving by the time his ice cream breakfast was served, his substitution for his mother's milk. As soon as Jo opened the lid of the ice cream, she had a hungry giraffe face pushing and slurping fast with his long purple tongue. Today, graham crackers were on the menu as well, but Napoleon hadn't mastered how to keep the whole thing in his mouth and chew at the same time. For every cracker he crunched, half of it fell to the ground, but Jo patiently bent down to retrieve each one and return it to those fuzzy disorganized lips.

One evening before bed, Daniel heard a strange electronic squeal and crackle coming from Jo's room. He found her sitting at the computer, that gigantic beige portal by the window. "You've got some retro internet out here, huh?" he teased, listening to the sounds of the dial up handshake, sounds he hadn't heard in years.

Daniel sat down on her bed and observed the yellow-tinged screen as she searched handyman websites and read three different step-by-step tutorials about how to stop a faucet from leaking. When things weren't working properly in this old house, she was the one to figure out how to fix them nowadays. "I really miss my dad," she said, taking notes on which tools she'd need for the plumbing job she'd tackle first thing in the morning.

When she was satisfied with her new knowledge on how to fix that annoying drip in the kitchen sink, Daniel scooted closer to the computer and asked, "Can you do a search for me?"

"Sure. What keywords?"

"Giraffe. Missing. Northside Animal Park," he said, feeling nervous as she obediently typed.

Jo didn't have to scroll very far. The first hit was a newspaper article from the Chicago Tribune, titled "Sold Out Giraffe Dissection Canceled, Zookeeper Fired."

She covered her mouth in horror as she read. Daniel scooted closer, unsure he was reading this right. He really needed his glasses, the small text was hard to make out. "Oh my God," Jo said, eyes filling up with tears. "Oh my God," she said again, finishing the article. She turned to Daniel and asked in disbelief, "Dissection?"

Daniel was clueless. He had no idea what the zookeeper had been planning after Millie's death. At the start of his evening shift that fateful day, Daniel had discovered the enormous dose of barbiturates prepped in the office, and the zookeeper's hand scrawled calculations based on Millie's height and weight. Sedating a giraffe was a tricky thing and usually avoided unless absolutely necessary. Daniel knew that much. It was a long way to come down, and difficult to get back up again for an animal that large. By the size of the dose, Daniel figured out it was for Millie, that it was intended to end her life because it was three times what the dose should have been, and since the new breeding female had been delivered earlier that same day, it all added up and he and his brother decided to do something about it.

That's how this whole crazy adventure began. Daniel didn't know the full backstory or the zookeeper's intentions, since the man barely took the time to talk to him. All Daniel ever did was clean the floors and fill the feeders in the African exhibits, and cover for his boss when the man had a little too much to drink on the job. The zookeeper hated Millie, she was nothing but a problem for him, even before she managed to swallow his car keys a few months back, which at the time, Daniel thought was pretty funny, even though he was the one who had to search her poo for the next 72 hours until she passed them. The zookeeper had been claiming she had chronic colic, and a mental disorder called "zoochosis" and since giraffe's typically didn't breed successfully after age 25 anyway, Millie was just an expensive companion for the animal park's star attraction, a thirteen-year-old male giraffe named Walter who was in his prime and cleared for breeding purposes.

"Even with everything that's happened," Daniel began, "I guess…it's like…somehow, we got away with something, ya know? Millie cheated death for a few more weeks, long enough to have her baby and not get chopped to pieces in the name of science, and that asshole zookeeper ain't never gonna work with animals again, not after this." He gestured towards the screen, re-reading the last paragraph about how the zookeeper was facing criminal charges for drinking on the job, and for organizing the public dissection and selling tickets to it after hours to curious veterinary students and aspiring taxidermists without the animal park's consent. There was no final comment about what had actually happened to the supposedly sick and senile giraffe, but it sounded as though the zookeeper was in serious trouble for years and years of animal neglect, and was likely the culprit for her disappearance.

That night, Daniel had nightmares about Millie, like he was back working at the animal park, but unable to help her. Then he dreamt of Dylan, revisiting the time they lived with a foster family who lived next to a trailer park where stray dogs roamed free. Finally, he dreamt of Jo, of her naked back and the rocky spine that divided her smooth planes of skin. He had so much on his mind, such a range of emotions all at once, even unconscious. On Wednesday, July 4th, Jo declared, "It's a holiday. I don't work on holidays."

"I guess I don't either," Daniel said, cozying up to her under the sheets.

As he began nibbling away on her precious earlobes, she explained, "The Hooker County Fair is today. This is the best day of the whole year."

They didn't make it to the fairgrounds till the early afternoon. Neither had much motivation to get out of bed these days. By the time they drove over to the sprawling land filled with stables, food carts, and rides and games for the family, they were drunk on sex and out of condoms. What a morning it had been. Jo let go of his hand as they approached the entrance, reminding him, "We're supposed to be cousins."

"We can be kissing cousins," he teased, giving her waist a squeeze.

"Stop," she playfully scolded. "We have to keep up the act. All of it. The whole thing about you being my cousin, my dad being alive and well, and turnips bringing in five grand a week. My eighteenth birthday is the 14thnd. Just ten more days and I can come clean and finally live a normal life."

"And pretty soon, the farm will be overrun with little piggies," Daniel added.

They paid the ticket man and passed through the gates. All of Hooker County was here today, sweating in the hot sun, getting sick stomachs from all the rich food. Morton, a small town just like all the other towns that made up Hooker County, didn't seem so small now. With all these fairly isolated people, farmers and such, when they all showed up at the same place at the same time, they made for quite an impact. Immediately, Jo and Daniel ran into the young doctor Holbrooke. The doctor gave her a nervous wave and eyed the brown-haired boy beside her.

"How's your father doing, Miss Josephine?" he asked after his patient.

"He's doing well. I can't thank you enough. He wanted to come today but I made him stay in bed. I'd hate to see him overexert himself too soon, especially since it's hot."

"That was good of you. No need to rush his recovery."

"He'll be out and about soon enough."

The doctor nodded, accepting this good news, then went about his business being awkward around the old guys eating barbecue. The whole fair smelled incredible. Freshly baked pies were lined up for the contest, whole pigs were turning on spits, funnel cake was being churned out by the mile, and kettle corn was popping non-stop from sun up to sun down.

Standing in line for the Ferris wheel, Mr. Ulrich, the master of the produce buying and selling in Morton, cut in line to greet Jo and ask if her daddy was here. She said, "No, but I'll tell him you said hello."

Disappointed, Mr. Ulrich said, "Missed seeing your cows this year. You two always had the best heifers in Hooker County. Sorry to see you give up the cattle side of things but I'm sure your daddy has a foolproof plan."

"Oh, yes. He does," she said with pride. "We're thinking about getting into pigs."

"Well," Mr. Ulrich said, contemplating this information. "Your daddy has a good sense about things so if he thinks pigs are the way to go, then that must be right. Just hope he keeps himself sober."

"Well, sober or not, he's always been a good daddy to me," Jo said, almost speaking her mind for a change.

Brenda Neilson, the lady who'd been selling the deceased Mr. Larsen cigarettes since December, caught up with Josephine and her companion as they treated themselves to corndogs and orange soda. "Darling, you're looking so pretty," Brenda said. "Is your daddy feeling better? Did he like the casserole I sent over? That's my great-grand momma's recipe."

"He did. He hardly shared any with us," Jo replied, lying her way to a future of freedom and that farmhouse she so desperately wanted to keep in her family.

"Now, this is your cousin? Is that right?" Brenda asked, inspecting the attractive young man at Jo's side.

"Yes, ma'am. This is Daniel."

"And what about the other one. There's two of you, isn't there?"

Daniel swallowed hard. "He's around here somewhere," he said, looking at the crowd as if Dylan had simply run off, never letting on otherwise.

Brenda swatted away a fly that took an interest in her hairspray and said something that almost knocked Daniel over. "Your brother came in the store just yesterday."

The town gossip, Ms. Brenda Neilson, was the one to ask if there was somebody's business that needed knowing. Looking for clues, curious what had become of Dylan, Jo inquired, "What did he buy?"

Brenda listed off a strange assortment of items, mostly toiletries, a toothbrush, a pair of sunglasses. Daniel knew this was Dylan's first time having a toothbrush all his own. He wondered if his brother savored this personal luxury. None of the things Brenda mentioned held much significance or hinted as to where Dylan may have gone with that stolen transport vehicle and several hundred dollars in cash. He was probably sleeping in the front seat, not too far away from Morton so he could go running back to his big brother if he woke up with bad dreams.

In the late afternoon, Jo led the way to the animal stalls. All the farm kids who'd been through the 4-H Youth Development

Program, home-schooled and taught an impressive work ethic, were watching with baited breath as the judges awarded ribbons for the black cows lined up in the center of the ring. The cows all looked the same to Daniel, but to the judges, there was a clear winner. As the ribbon was given to the sizable girl holding the lead of a massive black bovine, the crowd clapped and Jo nodded in approval with the judge's decisions.

Jo informed Daniel, "These are Angus. Aberdeen Angus. They were brought in from Scotland in the early 1870's. People thought they were freaks because they didn't have horns," like that should mean something to him.

"What was so great about that one compared to them others?" he asked, gesturing toward the winner, trying to learn more about the things she appreciated.

"Well, they're raised for beef so the judges are looking for nice meaty animals, but there's a lot to it. They start with the head, check to see if he has a good carriage, if his neck is broad and sits evenly on his shoulders. They look at the spine, if it's aligned well, if he's nice and long. The longer the cow, the more meat. He needs to have strong sturdy legs too, can't be bow-legged or sickle-hocked. Most cows that make it to show don't have structural problems like that."

Daniel couldn't help but smile, even though he had no idea what she was talking about. What in the world was sickle-hock? It didn't matter. Just listening to her talk while these big black animals paraded around the ring once more, made him as content as he'd ever been. Jo had a way about her, some calming effect. She wasn't like other girls, but that's exactly what he liked about her. Veronica, his last love interest, wouldn't have dirtied her shoes in a place like this. Veronica was into French films, French manicures and loud sex. Josephine, as it turned out, was much more his kind of girl, though he never knew it till a few weeks ago when he watched her corral a giraffe in a pickup truck.

"I have a question, and you're probably going to think it's a silly one," Daniel began. Jo raised an eyebrow, encouraging him to ask away. "Awhile back, you made a comment about your cow's wanting to mate the old fashioned way...if they're not doing things the old fashioned way, then how do they..."

"Artificial insemination. It's much safer, and much more effective."

Thinking through the logistics of this, not wanting to dwell on most of them, he teased, "Well that's no fun, is it?"

Jo led him over to the holy place where the swine waited for their chance to trot around the ring and hopefully win a prize before being sold for slaughter. It would be the shining moment in their little piggy lives, before their little piggy lives got cut short. Maybe they'd get to breed first, pass along their stellar genetics before meeting their end.

There was a pen where an enormous hog was laid out on her side while her nine piglets nursed. The little ones climbed over each other and pushed with their light fuzzy faces, feeding quickly and frantically, like their exhausted mother might actually have the energy to go anywhere else anytime soon. Jo smiled as she watched the family of pigs going about their business and, after asking permission, she reached down and scooped up one of the sweet-faced babies.

"That one's the runt," the owner of the pigs pointed out as Jo inspected the animal in her arms. "Wasn't sure she was gonna make it at first, but she seems okay now. Finally getting her place at meal time."

"She's just perfect," Jo said and she gently hoisted the piglet higher. "Aren't you?" she asked the little pig, tapping her own nose to the pig's snout.

Daniel reached out and touched the piglet's soft folded ear, wanting to join in Jo's admiration. The recently born creature looked naked to him, like it needed fur, or maybe a sweater. It was a perfect shade of light pink, almost human in tonality, and it was covered with fine hairs, just like a baby's head. It was pleasantly plump, especially the rear end where the curly tail quivered happily as Jo stroked the top of the pig's head. When the piglet started to squirm, Jo put her back down with the rest of her brothers and sisters, right in front of a vacant nipple so she wouldn't have trouble getting back to her lunch.

"Looks like we're getting started," the owner of the pigs said, nodding toward the judges table where the ribbons were set out in neat rows, ready for the next event. "I'll see you around, Miss Josephine. Wish us luck."

As they took a seat in the front row of the stands, Daniel breathed in, getting used to the aroma. He needed to get over it if he planned to stay on with Jo and help her raise stinky animals like these, so he might as well get over it now. He asked, "Don't you feel sad about raising up an animal just to kill it?"

She shrugged. "God gave us dominion over the animals. That's what they're for. I'll enjoy caring for them but I'll also enjoy what they'll become. I mean, bacon is amazing, right?"

What could he say to that? She wasn't the least bit squeamish, she respected the animals but didn't put them on some lofty pedestal, and she was a fan of bacon.

"Oh," she gasped in amazement. "Look at him. Look at that one."

Daniel followed her pointer finger to a gigantic pink and black hog. He wasn't sure he'd ever seen a pig in person before today, not one this large anyhow. Having grown up all over the place, bouncing from city to city, Daniel had missed out on this kind of American pride and these people who brought their livelihood here today to be scrutinized and judged, but mostly, appreciated by all. The man in the black cowboy hat and red plaid shirt inspected each pig in the ring. He felt their heads, their backs, their ribs, and hind legs too.

"These are Hampshires" Jo whispered, not taking her eyes off the line of animals. "I remember last year, when we were still showing our cows, somebody got disqualified for oiling their Hampshire."

"Say what now?" Daniel all but laughed. Oiling your Hampshire sounded like some sort of dirty joke to him.

She was serious as she explained, "Sometimes people powder their pigs, especially the lighter colored ones, or if they're dark, they add oil to their skin on the day of the show to make them look healthier. It's banned here. Been that way for almost ten years now. People should know better. It was a big scandal last year."

He couldn't help but lean over to kiss her cheek and he didn't care who saw this slip of affection. Right there, with Jo talking about stuff that made no sense to him, he found himself falling hard for this redheaded hog expert. Whatever she was interested in, he wanted to share that. For now, he was content to be her fellow pig critic, though when she asked him to try and pick the winner, he failed seven times in a row. Jo picked the winners six out of seven. She knew what to look for.

"What kind are you gonna raise?" he asked.

"Berkshires. They're good for bacon and pork but you can't let them get too big. They lose taste after they reach two-fifty live weight."

From behind them, a loud male voice called out, "Josephine Larsen, I'd recognize that ponytail anywhere!"

Jo turned to identify the voice, but by the uneasy look on her face, it seemed she already recognized it. Daniel watched her take a hard swallow as the color drained from her cheeks. Tiny sparkles of perspiration appeared at her hairline. Something about that booming voice was more than unsettling to her.

"Well, girl," the voice started up again, sounding closer this time, "Ain't you gonna say hi to me?"

She didn't correct his grammar, this barrel-chested man who looked to be in his early forties, judging by the rate at which his hair was evacuating the top of his head. He was tall, close to six foot five, and built as solid as one of the bulls in the adjacent livestock ring. The man had a nice-looking face even though it was a little swollen with extra weight. It was the sweat on his overheated face that gave him away. He was one of those guys who could sweat in a snowstorm just as well as on top of a seventeen-year-old girl.

Jo winced as he spoke to the back of her head once more, "Well, ain't you gonna say hi to me?"

"Hello, Hank," she managed, finally turning around since she'd been spotted and there was no easy escape route.

Daniel looked at Jo, then to this Hank person, then back at Jo. Yes, this had to be him, the sweaty man she slept with, just the one time, where she didn't think too highly of him or of the act itself. A little surprised in her odd choice in men, especially to lose her virginity to, Daniel looked the man over, from his sweaty brow, to his thick neck, to his Hooker Counter Water Services t-shirt which had some perspiration working its way through the center of his broad chest. The man had big arms, all the way down to his big hands. He had big fingers too, and the ring finger on his left hand bore a golden band. This man was a married man. Just seconds after Daniel realized this, the married man's wife and kids walked over, all cheerful-looking and blond, the descendants of Scandinavian pioneers for sure.

"How are you, sweetheart?" the wife asked, pleased to see Jo, despite how nervous Jo was to see her. The woman had a toddler yanking on one arm and a three-month old in the other. The lady was pretty, a little worn out looking, but still attractive. She had a short blond bob that showed off her pearl earrings. "Is your daddy here today? I haven't seen him in weeks," the woman continued, though it had been months since anybody had actually seen Jo's father.

"No, ma'am. He's at home today." Jo didn't look the woman in the eye. She couldn't. Even though there were two guilty parties standing here, only one of them looked remotely guilty. The married man looked proud, proud to have his wife and kids and that foolish young girl he'd had about six months ago, all standing there together.

"Well, you tell him we were asking after him," the woman said, shifting the baby higher on her hip when she started to fuss. The woman leaned in toward Jo, and spoke in a hushed voice as if to keep what she was about to say private. "I don't care what people say about his drinking," she began. "He raised you just fine, must be doing something right so I don't see why everyone's gotta be fishing around in his private affairs. A drunkard couldn't possibly raise a sweet angel like you. You're proof he's a good man."

Jo's gray eyes turned glossy. She bit her cheek and produced a manufactured smile of thanks, then walked away before her nose started to run and the tears fell freely. If she lost it now, in front of everyone, her dirty secret would be out. If she lost it now, Mrs. Winthrop would know she was no angel. If she lost it now, Mrs. Winthrop would realize this was the girl her husband was with that night when he came home late on New Years Day, a little sweatier than usual. Mrs. Winthrop, who was heavily pregnant at the time, knew he'd been up to something, she just didn't know who he'd been up to it with. Sweet Josephine Larsen, with her shining reputation, was dead last on the list of suspects. Jo was just a girl, for Heaven's sake.

Daniel followed after Jo's swinging red ponytail, keeping up with her as she desperately parted the crowd. He finally caught up with her under the grandstands near the rodeo. Fearful she'd keep up her quick pace and he'd have to start running to catch her, he grabbed her by the upper arm and spun her around.

Without asking a thing, she sobbed out an answer to his unspoken questions. "I was so stupid. I was so stupid and I never meant to hurt anyone. I wish I could make it right, but I can't face that woman. I can't face her and tell her what I did. I just can't. I was so, so stupid."

"Shh," he said. "Come here." Daniel opened his arms, pulling her in for a heavy heaving cry. She was beyond distraught, all broken up over her unwise decision involving this married man that took place in a cheap motel in Seneca right after her father died.

"Aren't you gonna ask me why I did it?" she asked, her voice muffled in his chest, right next to his heart.

"It doesn't matter, really. What's done is done."

"Ask me, Daniel. Ask me why I did it."

"Why did you do it?"

She took a quick sniffle and said, "I don't know."

Looking at her face now, Daniel believed her. She certainly wasn't an angel, like the wife of the unfaithful husband said, but she was still a good girl, a young woman with a promising future, who got all jumbled up in confusion and made a seriously bad call. Jo wiped both of her eyes at the same time, hiding from her grief.

"I'm so stupid," she whispered. "I just wasn't thinking straight. I never had beer before that night. I wasn't drunk, I only had two, but I wasn't myself either. Hank gave me the beer since I told him my daddy drove me there and he was just out for a smoke break. He said I was grown up enough anyhow. My dad had just died a few weeks before and I didn't want to be alone on New Years Eve so I drove out to the bar in Seneca where everyone was having a good time. I just didn't want to be alone, ya know? Hank was...always so nice to me...and he was telling me how his wife was about to have another baby, how they didn't mean for it to happen...and he started telling me how he always thought I was so pretty...and if he were younger, he'd take me out and treat me right...oh God, I'm so stupid. I was lonely and I just wanted someone to care about me for one night...and I thought maybe he did. But he...he just wanted to see if I would...and I did...and I wish I hadn't."

"It's over now. There's nothing you can do to take it back. But you can't think about it too much, it'll do bad things to you if you do."

Jo nodded regretfully and wiped her eyes once more. Going to that hourly-rate motel with Hank Winthrop was the biggest mistake of her life, during her most fragile of times. She started to feel nauseous as memories of that awful night crept back into her mind, how she curled up into a ball and cried herself senseless, puking up her Miller Lite in the dingy motel shower after the deed was done, and the way the second-hand beer swirled down the drain alongside a faint stream of blood. It was by far the worst night of her life, and she had nobody to confide in the next day, just a bag full of pregnancy tests she bought three towns over, a wretched pain between her legs, and a vow to never drink again.

"That's what's so horrible about it all. His wife doesn't know, nobody knows. I don't want anyone to know but...I wanna tell her I'm sorry, but I can't. He could go to jail, his wife might divorce him and those poor kids wouldn't have their daddy anymore, and besides all that, I'm just too ashamed. It's all my fault, it wasn't like he talked me into anything, I went along with it but...I don't know what I'd do if anyone found out about this...this horrible, repulsive, disgusting secret."

"Your horrible, repulsive, disgusting secret is safe with me," Daniel said, taking her by the wrist and kissing her on the underside, one of his favorite places to kiss her. It was such a tender spot, one Hank probably overlooked, but Daniel treasured. "Nobody's perfect, although you've got me pretty much fooled."

She sniffled out a laugh. "You must think I'm disgusting now, for what I did."

"Not even a little bit," he replied, squeezing her hand. Daniel's pulse was racing as he said, "There ain't nothing you can tell me that's gonna make me think less of you. I care so much for you, Jo. With you...it's kinda... I don't know. I'm not used to feeling this way about anyone. You kind of...messed me up a little." He closed his eyes and tried again. "That's not really what I mean. Um...shit...I...I don't really know how to say this. I don't want you to think I'm just saying this for the hell of it, or to make you feel better about things you wish you hadn't done, or because...we already...you know. I didn't mean for this to happen. I was content to like you a whole lot, and keep it to myself, but this...this just snuck up on me and now...well, it's there in a big way. I can't help it. You make me feel like...my stomach feels like...you know when you go out walking in the snow, and you get really, really cold? Then you come inside and you have a hot cup of tea with honey? You feel like that. You're the hot tea with honey. You warm me up. You thaw me out. And you smell fuckin' incredible, all the fuckin' time." Daniel quickly covered his mouth and mumbled, "Did I seriously just say that out loud?" He closed his eyes in embarrassment and tried again to spit it out. "I would do anything for you…God, I'm really bad at talking. I just want you to know…shit. Um. Shit. Shhhhhit. I sound like a blithering idiot right now. I just know it. This is why I should keep my mouth shut at all times. This little speech that's probably confusing the hell out of you, well, this is ridiculous. All this…all this shit coming out of my mouth right now, it ain't what I wanna say."

Jo chuckled while Daniel caught his breath. "Then what do you want to say?"

"I think I'm…pretty seriously in love with you."

Jo's brow wrinkled, her glossy eyes searched his face. Whatever it was she was searching for, sincerity or truth, she must have found it because she lifted her face to his and kissed his lips, without worry of who might see. She didn't say anything in return, but her kiss said all she needed to say. Josephine Larsen was a woman of few words.

CHAPTER SEVENTEEN

"Can I help you?" Josephine asked the strange man snooping around the side of her house at 8 a.m. on Friday morning. She'd never seen him before in her life. The man had dark hair, buzzed short. He wore a plain white dress shirt with gray slacks and looked unusually athletic under his commoner's uniform. For someone trespassing at such an early hour, in such a remote place, this man appeared mighty friendly when Jo approached him, even though her face was anything but friendly. She didn't like unexpected visitors in her barn in the middle of the night, and she didn't like them poking around her farmhouse first thing in the morning either. "What're you doing here?" she tried again, closing the distance between them. She set down her basket of dirty laundry.

He raised his clipboard and replied, "I'm with the insurance company. I was just taking a look at the storm damage. Hope I'm not disturbing you. Is your father at home?"

"He went into town," she said, crossing her arms suspiciously. "May I see some identification please?"

The man gave her a curious look. She waited, leaning on the side of the house, thankful Napoleon wasn't too stubborn this morning since they had very little warning of this so-called insurance agent's arrival. Daniel just happened to look out the window to see this man's silver sedan coming down the driveway and was alert enough to pull the giraffe inside before anyone spotted him. They were both in the bathroom now, Daniel and Napoleon, waiting for Jo to run off this unwanted visitor. It was Friday, after all, they had a lot to do to prepare for tonight.

"I don't carry a badge or anything," the man replied. "I'm just an agent."

"Do you have a business card?"

"Miss, I'm just looking at the storm damage. I'm with the insurance company."

"Yes. You said that already. But I didn't call anyone. I didn't report the damage."

"Your father must have."

"I assure you, he didn't. Which insurance company did you say you work for?"

"Travelers," he replied, after hesitating a little too long. The man clutched his clipboard tight to his chest.

"Wrong answer," she said, growing angry. "Beecher Carlson. That's the right answer. Let's try this again. What are you doing here?"

"Miss, I just need to take a quick look, and I'll be on my way," he started walking to the other side of the house now, continuing his tour without her permission. "Looks like some windows blew out, and I noticed the siding ripped off the front corner. What about the root cellar? Has there been any flooding with all the rain? Could you open this please?" He gestured towards the locked up doors leading underground.

"No. There hasn't been any flooding. Get off my property. Now!"

The man stared, as if to call her bluff. He was twice her size. Was she really yelling at him like this?

"NOW!" she yelled again, hitting a note that proved she meant it.

"Okay, Miss. Sorry for the trouble."

The man left. Jo watched his silver car drive up to the road and turn right, heading towards Morton. She wasn't sure he was who he said he was, but exactly who was he then? Some snoop sent by the pastors to chase her daddy back to church? A person from AA checking in to make sure Johan Larsen wasn't drinking again? Maybe he really was an insurance agent, just at the wrong farm. He could have been anybody and he was awfully close to the root cellar entrance, standing just a few yards away from nine hundred square feet of thriving marijuana plants.

"It's safe," she said, opening the bathroom door to let Napoleon and Daniel out.

"Who was he?" Daniel asked.

She shrugged.

After feeding Napoleon his ice cream, they got to work in the fields, quietly cutting through broccoli stalks. Jo was pensive while she worked, which Daniel found to be entirely endearing. She was concentrating so hard on that broccoli, she neglected to notice Napoleon eating from her basket. He was never big on stealing veggies before, only interested in ice cream. Today, for the first time, broccoli was on the menu. After eating his fill, Napoleon lowered himself to the ground, just a few feet from Jo, and curled up like a long-legged baby deer. It was clear he felt safe.

Wedged in between stalks, Daniel discovered a photograph, something that had been pinned up in the barn at some point, before the tornado rearranged everything. It was a close up photo of a baby calf being bottle-fed. A young girl's hand held the bottle, but the photo cut off at her elbow. Daniel handed it to Jo, the owner of the arm holding the bottle, he presumed, and she looked confused as to how the snapshot got there in the middle of the field, even though they'd discovered all sorts of random things on the property lately. "That's Theodore," she said.

"Did they all have names?"

She nodded, put the photo in her back pocket, and continued with her duties. He had hoped she might share one of her rare stories, the history of this farm she'd known her whole life, but she wasn't in a talkative mood today. Hours passed by, Napoleon eventually took a nap, and a swarm of starlings landed in the trees and made a deafening racket for a few minutes, then moved on, continuing their journey as a group of several hundred.

"What're you thinking?" Daniel asked some time later, keeping up his work.

"Nothing."

What a girl answer: nothing. He knew that was bullshit. No girl was ever thinking nothing. The thing that made Daniel grow nervous was all the possible things she could be thinking right then. Maybe his heartfelt words at the fair yesterday weren't sitting well. Maybe he scared her off. After all, she never said it back.

At lunchtime, they went inside for turkey sandwiches and lemonade, cooling off from the midday heat. They had lots of leaves waiting to be picked, weighed and bagged that afternoon. Jo was still in a funky mood, quiet, but not in her usual way. Something was bothering her but she wasn't up for discussing it. Afraid it was all his doing, Daniel reached out for her hand across the table.

"Will you please talk to me?"

"About what?" she said, faking a surprised smile.

"What's on our mind?"

"Nothing's on my mind."

"Does this have anything to do with…what I said yesterday? Cause you don't have to feel the same way or say anything back. That doesn't change a thing for me. I just wanted you to know how I felt, that's all. I was just being honest, I don't want you to feel any pressure and most of all, I never meant to scare you."

"Daniel McElroy, you don't scare me," she insisted, trying to sound playful.

Onto his next suspicion, he hesitantly asked, "Does this have anything to do with…this morning? Upstairs? I just thought…I thought you might like it."

Jo let go of his hand and started nervously playing with a strand of her hair. "I'm really sorry about your nose."

Daniel rubbed his sore sniffer and smiled. He was fine, just a little confused why she reacted so violently to something that supposedly felt so good. That morning, when he kissed her protruding hipbones and then a little lower, she snapped her knees shut and clobbered him in the face. His confidence more damaged than anything.

"Don't you trust me?" he asked, trying to get to the bottom of her strange reaction. Daniel simply couldn't come up with a reason for the awkward ending to their time under the sheets that morning, when he had to leave her to go deal with a bloody nose.

"I trust you," she swore. "I guess I was just a little...embarrassed."

"Why?"

"I don't know. Because...I don't know. I've never done that before." With very few friends growing up out here, and even fewer boyfriends, Jo relied on her dad to tell her everything she needed to know. Understandably, Johan might have left out a few things. "So it, um, it...it...it feels good?" she asked curiously.

"Well yeah," he said, trying to hide his grin.

Jo blushed, managed a sheepish smile, then stood up. She was by the sink now, washing up, pleased her leaky faucet fix had been successful. She looked out to see Napoleon slowly walking across the field, never in a hurry for anything. She smiled to herself, seeing that big baby of hers, how peaceful he was. Glancing back over at Daniel, who was wiping down the worn wooden table, she turned off the water.

"Daniel?" she started in a quiet voice, "I think I love you too. I mean. Yeah. I do. I do love you."

He looked up. He hadn't said anything. Was this her delayed answer from yesterday? Watching her face make a nervous little expression, like she couldn't believe she just said those words out loud, made Daniel the happiest man on Earth. "You do?" he asked, hardly able to speak.

She nodded her head then let out a giddy laugh.

With that, Daniel crossed the kitchen and picked her up off the ground. Jo wrapped her arms around his neck and her long legs around his waist. A hard kiss followed. Maybe that kiss was a little too hard because Daniel cried, "Nose! Nose! Ow!"

"Sorry!" she yelped, embarrassed.

It didn't take Daniel long to recover from the pain in his face. "I guess love really does hurt," he teased, playfully kissing her cheek.

"You're so cheesy sometimes. Good thing I love cheese."

After a brief make out session with Jo propped up on the sink, gentle on the nose this time, they finally got back to the task at hand. Daniel went back to cleaning the table, and Jo finished up the dishes. She glanced out the window again, seeing a flash of auburn. Napoleon started to run fast, galloping as if a predator startled him. Something was wrong. Jo had never seen him run like that. He ran straight for the trees, a place he'd never ventured before, and disappeared into the thick forest. He was still small enough to slip in through the curtain of trunks, unlike Millie, who turned back when she got to the trees. They were a fence for her, but not her baby. Nervous for Napoleon, curious what spooked him so badly, Josephine went outside to see for herself, and when she did, she couldn't quite believe what was coming down her driveway.

By the time Daniel went outside to join her, Jo was on her knees with her hands behind her head. There was an army of police cars parked on the driveway, the grass too, all silent with their lights flashing. Beyond the cars was a big black transport van, already unloaded. The twelve men from that van were in all black, wearing bulletproof vests and helmets, holding some serious looking weapons, like they weren't sure what to expect here on the Larsen farm. There were uniformed figures all around the house, guns drawn. An officer handcuffed Josephine while she remained on her knees. She looked completely dazed.

"On your knees! Hands behind your head!"

It took a moment for Daniel to realize that stern voice was talking to him. He was paralyzed in the doorway, unable to obey that command coming through the megaphone, unable to breathe.

"I said on your knees!"

Wide-eyed, Daniel dropped down to the gravel driveway. The man who was posing as an insurance agent that morning put cuffs on Daniel's wrists. Was this actually happening? He looked over at Jo, as if to confirm they were really getting busted right then and there. With tears in her eyes, she gave him a defeated smile. It was all over now. Everything was coming to an end. She had a good run.

Josephine mouthed something to him. He didn't get it right away, but when he realized she was telling him, "Don't say anything," he knew the kind of trouble they were about to face was as serious as it could be.

Daniel started to get lightheaded as he watched the raid. The team of men with the letters DEA printed in yellow on their backs use bolt cutters to open the chains to the root cellar. They knew exactly where to go, like someone drew them a map. A few cops went underground as well, just to see this with their own eyes. This wasn't the kind of thing they were used to finding out here in farm country. It was a sight to see, all those plants, all those hundred dollar bills growing out of the soil. This was one of the biggest non-cartel-related drug busts ever to take place in the state of Nebraska, and nobody suspected sweet little Josephine Larsen was behind it all, the start of the chain.

Two cops hoisted Jo up by her armpits, ready to take her away. She wasn't listening as they read her rights. All she could do was stare at Daniel, who was going down with her now. When a second pair of cops came for Daniel, Jo started screaming, "He doesn't know anything! He doesn't know anything! He had no part in this! Leave him alone! If he tells you anything, it's a lie! He doesn't know anything!"

Daniel and Jo were put in separate cars. He closed his eyes, trying to shut out the world of chaos around him. His thoughts were spinning, making him nauseous and tempting another seizure. How did they get caught? Where had they been sloppy? They only did one run together, last Friday, and all the rules were followed. They were so careful. Jo wouldn't have it any other way. Who could have possibly tipped off the police? His eyes snapped open. "Dylan," he gasped to himself.

Anger and disappointment spiked through his chest. His only brother ratted them out. What a way to get revenge. Dylan wanted the girl, and once he knew he couldn't have the girl, nothing else mattered to him. He just set off a minefield of events by snitching and he probably didn't realize how serious this was. Typical Dylan, he just wanted to make a statement, show his brother up, but what he'd done was unthinkable.

Daniel's suspicions were confirmed at the police station, two towns over. His brother had tattled, but only selectively. Dylan told them it was all Jo, the whole operation. He told them he and Daniel didn't know what she had growing in the root cellar or what they were helping her load into her truck. As difficult as it was, Daniel kept his mouth shut till he was appointed a public defender, since he couldn't afford to hire an attorney. He desperately wanted to tell the truth, help Jo out somehow, or at least get a fair punishment for his involvement, but he remained tight-lipped till his legal representation arrived, a man by the name of Howard Johns, who showed up with a brown leather brief case and a plan.

"I'm not telling you to lie, Mr. McElroy. I'm only suggesting you agree with what your brother and Ms. Larsen have already said. They both gave the same story, so all you have to do is say its true. Even if the details aren't exactly what you remember, if the story is close, then you will most likely be off the hook. Now tell me, Mr. McElroy. How important are those details? They're saying you didn't know anything about what she was doing down there. Maybe you knew a little something, but how important are those details? Are they important enough to bring up? Are they important enough to go to prison for?"

Ignoring Howard Johns and his leading words, Daniel asked, "How many years will she get?"

"Could be up to fifteen. Depends if they try Ms. Larsen as an adult."

"She's seventeen. She's minor for nine more days. She doesn't turn eighteen until the 14th of July. They can't try her as an adult if she's still a minor, can they?"

Howard Johns shifted in his plastic chair. "They can try her however they like. Her age won't have much sway, considering the amount she was producing. She's not a little kid if she can run an illegal operation of this magnitude."

Those words sunk in. Daniel started to feel numb, accepting there was no way out for Josephine. His vocal chords were wobbly as he asked, "Will I be able to visit her?"

"That depends. Are you going to agree to their story, that you didn't know anything? Or are you going to make a fuss over every conflicting detail? If you had anything to do with this, which they're both saying isn't the case, then I suggest you go along with that and you'll be released within forty-eight hours. If you go along with it, yes, you'll be able to visit her. Now if you go and start adding details and saying you knew more than they're saying you knew, you'll get jail time too, and no, you won't be able to visit her then. It's your call Daniel, I won't tell you what to do but…if you want to see her, your best bet is to validate the story that's already been accepted."

Daniel spent one night in a holding cell at the county jail. He wasn't sure if Jo was in the same building or not. Nobody would tell him anything. He barely slept, so much was running through his mind. To lie, or not to lie. Was it really lying? Both Dylan and Josephine provided a strikingly similar story and that story cleared Daniel of everything. But that story wasn't 100% true. It was definitely lying. He did know what she was doing in the root cellar. He participated. Could he live with himself if he let her take all the blame? She was likely to get the same punishment regardless of

Daniel's involvement, so by the time the morning came, Daniel knew what he had to do.

"I didn't know what she was doing down there. I helped her carry bags to the truck, but I didn't know what was in them," Daniel said his rehearsed words in a calm voice, sitting at a table in a small room with who knows how many people watching from the other side of the glass. He rubbed his bloodshot eyes and reached for the Styrofoam cup in front of him. With a sip of black coffee, his belly felt warm, though not the same way he felt when Jo was around. Still, it was a small reminder of why he just said what he said.

That evening, Daniel was released and no charges were pressed. They were all reserved for Josephine, who was looking at serious time for her dealings. She wouldn't get to raise pigs in a blue barn on her family's farm. The game was over and she lost. Her bail was astronomical, so she wouldn't even get to go home temporarily. Howard Johns explained to Daniel when and where Jo's court appearance would take place, if he wanted to be there to support her.

Daniel got a ride with Howard Johns back to the farmhouse. He had nowhere else to go. Besides, this was his home now, but it wasn't the same without Jo. It was such a beautiful day, a flawless, cloudless, day, but Daniel wished it were raining. How could the sun dare to shine on this farmhouse after what had happened? Inside, the house was mostly as they left it, even though it was searched for additional evidence after the root cellar was cleared out. In the kitchen, there were two sets of lunch plates drying on the wooden dish rack. The bread was still on the counter. Jo's glass of lemonade was sitting on the table, where she sat and ate a turkey sandwich just one day earlier, before she lost all freedom. Daniel took her seat at the table, felt the arms of the wooden chair, like a part of her was trapped inside. He sat there for three hours, barely blinking. What was he supposed to do now?

The sound of crunching gravel in the driveway startled him back into reality. For a moment, he felt the familiar panic about hiding Napoleon, because that was how he was wired now, but the giraffe was long gone. Daniel was surprised to see his brother driving the stolen transport vehicle, parking in front of the house, like he had any right. Furious, Daniel grabbed Jo's shotgun and approached the driver's side door.

"What're you doing here!" he screamed at Dylan, who looked like he hadn't slept in days, judging by the bags under his blue eyes where his youthful skin was tinged with the colors of insomnia.

Dylan got out, looking as calm as ever. "I could ask you the same thing," he replied. "This isn't your house."

Daniel lowered the gun. He wasn't going to shoot it, he just wanted to scare his brother into leaving. It seemed Dylan wasn't afraid of anything now. He was a changed man. He'd grown up in the last week. His young face had hardened just a bit. For the first time in his life, Dylan's face had a halo of stubble. In truth, he looked terrible.

"Where's Napoleon?" Dylan asked, seeing the empty front porch.

Daniel glanced back at the porch. It looked so bare now. "He ran off. When the cops came...he got spooked and ran to the forest."

"Oh."

"What the hell were you thinking, Dylan? Were you thinking at all?"

Dylan shrugged. "Now nobody gets Jo. Seems fair to me."

"No. It's not fair to her. She's gonna be in prison till after she's thirty!"

"Maybe she should have thought about that before she started growing weed."

"So you're not sorry, huh? There's not one bone in your body that regrets turning her in?" Daniel asked in disbelief.

Dylan explained, "Of course I'm sorry. I didn't mean for all this to happen. I didn't realize...by the time I realized what would happen, it was too late."

"What were you expecting, huh? Why did you go to the cops?"

"Because I wanted my brother back. She was getting in the way. She was pulling us apart. Now, nobody gets her and we can go back to the way things used to be. Just you and me. That's all I want. I want my brother back."

By the heartfelt expression on Dylan's face, Daniel couldn't help but believe him. His self-centered sibling just wanted to be a family again. But it wasn't so simple anymore. "Let's go inside," Daniel said, knowing they couldn't say everything they needed to say before the sun went down.

The boys sat at the kitchen table and had a difficult conversation. Each wanted something vastly different than the other, and there seemed to be no other way than to take separate roads. This would be the first time in his life that Daniel would choose his own path. He took a deep breath and explained, "I'm gonna stay here. I'm gonna wait for Jo."

"For fifteen years?" Dylan asked, eye brows high in disbelief.

"If it takes that long, then yes. I think she can get parole after seven. Till then, I'm gonna visit her as often as they'll let me. I'm staying right here."

"Why can't you come with me now, then come back when she's released?"

"I'm tired of wandering. I'm tired of waking up and having to remember where I am. I just want a home, a real home. This is the only place that has ever felt like home to me. It's not even this farmhouse or this land, it's Jo. She's home. I love her, I can't even explain how much I care for her."

"But…I was thinking we could…go to Mexico. We can try to find Mom. Maybe we can be a family again."

"I don't want to go to Mexico and I don't wanna find Mom."

"But…"

"You should go."

"Without you?"

"Yeah," Daniel said with a smile. "You'll be fine. You can take care of yourself. You don't need me telling you what to do all the time. If you find Mom, tell her I said hello and tell her I forgive her, even if she's not sorry. Will you do that?"

"Well…yeah. But…how will we…will you write to me?"

"Of course I'll write."

Dylan snickered as he said, "But will you write legibly?"

"I'll try my best," Daniel said, messing up his brother's hair one last time.

Daniel helped Dylan pack up his few belongings from the living room. They went outside together, ready to part ways. A piece of yellow police tape fluttered in the gentle breeze, interrupting the orchestra of insects. The boys loaded up the red pickup truck together, since the stolen transport vehicle had no plates and got terrible gas mileage. Jo wouldn't need the truck now and Daniel could get by without it for a while. After all, he was staying put.

The boys hugged goodbye.

"Are we still brothers?" Dylan asked, his voice muffled in Daniel's shoulder.

"We'll always be brothers."

CHAPTER EIGHTEEN

That night, lying in Jo's bed without her beside him, Daniel cried himself to sleep. The girl he loved was gone, the giraffe was missing, he wasn't sure when he'd see his brother again, and he had no idea what he was supposed to do with his life. He never had any hopes and dreams of his own, but Jo's sounded so good. He had adopted those same dreams over the last few weeks. Now, their collective dreams had been obliterated. The only thing he could think to do was go on living here for the next seven to fifteen years, surrounded by Josephine's things, her memory, and pretend she was there with him. That seemed to be the proper way of dealing with these kinds of losses in the Larsen household. He would see her in court in two days, and after that, he could visit her.

His simple plan of keeping things as they were was ruined the following morning. There were two strange men outside the house when Daniel awoke. He pulled on some clothes and approached them, asking, "What do you want?"

"Who are you?" the one with the beard asked, surprised anyone was home.

"I'm Daniel. I live here now. Who are you?"

"We're with the bank. My name's Kyle Newton. *You* live here?"

"I do."

Kyle exchanged a look with his associate, a dark-haired man with thick glasses. "Do you have some proof this property belongs to you?"

"Proof?" Daniel's heart sank. He had no proof of anything and this property definitely didn't belong to him. He was a squatter with the best intentions. The two men from the bank informed Daniel of the situation. The farmhouse wasn't even close to being paid off because a reverse mortgage had been taken out a few years ago when times got lean and the need for tuition money arose, and since Josephine wasn't old enough to inherit the place, and there was no other family on record, the bank owned it, regardless of her current legal problems. She had been making payments since her father's death, but for fear or tipping anyone off that things were not as they should be on the Larsen farm, she'd only been paying the minimum each month like her daddy had done, and at that rate, there was a long, long way to go.

"You can't take this away from her," Daniel said, grasping what they were saying.

"We'll give you a week to clear out any personal belongings."

"But she hasn't even been convicted yet," Daniel argued.

The dark-haired man took a turn to speak, saying, "I think we all know she's going to be convicted. Whether she gets two years or two hundred, she won't be keeping the house or the land. We knew her daddy, God rest his soul. We're all sorry it has to be like this, especially after everything she's been through all on her own. A week is more than enough time to vacate the property. We usually give less notice than that, so you best take our offer or we'll have to start the process of eviction. You understand, son?"

"Can I fight this? If I get a lawyer, can I fight this?"

"You can try," Kyle said, tipping his hat politely to say so long. "Son, you don't happen to know where her daddy's buried, do you?"

Daniel shook his head no, keeping his eyes focused on the man asking the question rather than letting them drift over to the woods where the bones of the farmer lay. Everyone in town knew Johan was deceased now, the charade was over, but that didn't stop them from asking about him.

Just minutes later, Daniel was on the phone with the only lawyer he'd ever met, the public defender who got stuck with him, Mr. Howard Johns. Howard explained that unless Daniel could pay for his services, he wouldn't be able to assist him this time. This new predicament wasn't like before, when Daniel was appointed a lawyer by the state because he couldn't afford one. Now, a few days later, he still couldn't afford one, even with all the money he'd earned in the last few weeks, plus whatever he counted that was stashed next to the oatmeal, and Howard didn't have any obligations to help him out. Daniel hung up discouraged, and looked around the house that was going to be sold off at auction. There was nothing he could do; he was utterly helpless.

Daniel was having one of the darkest days of his life. His appetite was gone, he hardly blinked. When he looked in the mirror, hateful green eyes looked back at him. He ran his fingertips along his jawline, wondering if this was his father's face, the face of a rapist. Daniel had his mom's unruly brown hair, he knew that for sure, but where did the rest of his features come from? Whose nose was this? Whose crooked smile? If he ever saw his mother again, would she be able to look him in the eye, would she be able to see her son all grown up, her own flesh and blood, or just a revised version of the man who ultimately ruined her world and forced her into motherhood at twenty-one years old. Daniel used a bar of soap to cloud up the bathroom mirror, forbidding reflections. He didn't want to see himself, he didn't want to exist anymore.

That hopeless afternoon, he searched the forest for Napoleon, but found nothing. That little guy had disappeared and unless there was an ice cream truck making secret runs out here, his young life was in danger. When Daniel set out looking again the next day, he had prepared himself for the worst, a giraffe corpse, but again he found nothing. It wasn't until the following morning when he was headed out for the courthouse, that he saw a set of large round hoof prints in the mud. There had been a visitor last night, who circled around the house a few times, left a rather large pile of pellet droppings near the root cellar, and then headed back toward the forest. That funny little fellow was still alive, eating *something*, surviving out there.

In the courtroom, among the dull cherry furniture, Daniel claimed a seat in the back and watched sweet Josephine Larsen cross the front of the room in handcuffs, escorted by two officers, one on each side. Her hair was in a ponytail, like it always was, but she looked exhausted. Even her ponytail didn't have its usual springiness. She stood up with her lawyer beside her, and received her punishment: Fifteen years. The judge went on to say she would be considered for parole after seven years, but that didn't feel like particularly good news.

The judge continued, telling Josephine due to her young age, she would stay at the Nebraska Correctional Center for Women, just west of York, until she was twenty-one. It was still a prison, but it was also a working farm. Jo would become the two hundred and eighty second inmate there. Then, when she was a little older, she'd be transferred to the Nebraska State Penitentiary for the remainder of her sentence. This was the best the judge could do, his own way of being merciful to the fragile-looking Josephine.

Knowing the judge had done something kind for her by giving her three years in the Correctional Facility before turning her over to the hardened criminals in the State Penitentiary, Josephine thanked him. Before exiting the courtroom, she met eyes with Daniel in the back and gave him a small defeated smile, like she knew she deserved this.

If it had just been one pot plant for personal use, she would have walked out the door that day with 50 hours of community service. But it was closer to 500 plants, all of which she intended to sell. She never once brought up the fact that her father was the one who planted them to begin with, that it was *his* side business she discovered after his death and decided to take over. There just wasn't much point in sharing any more details or passing the blame. It was done.

Daniel wasn't permitted to see Josephine the day of the trial. She was scheduled to be admitted into the Correctional Facility later that afternoon, and wouldn't be allowed visitations until the next day at noon. With nothing else to do, Daniel drove the stolen transport vehicle back to Morton. Before turning in for the night, he walked the perimeter of the fields holding a flashlight, shining it into the trees in case an auburn giraffe happened to be there. Nothing. Still no sign of Napoleon. But, in the morning, a fresh set of hoof prints gave him hope. The giraffe knew where home was, he was alive, but that's about all Daniel could be sure of.

The drive to the Correctional Center took an hour from Morton. During that time, Daniel made a list of questions in his head that he needed to ask Josephine during their twenty minutes today. That's all he was allowed. He could come see her for a maximum of twenty minutes, twice a week, and no more. When he got to his destination, he was pleasantly surprised. The building looked less like a prison and more like a school. There was a lot of grass, lots of wide-open space surrounded by a tall barbed wire fence. This place wouldn't be so bad for the next three years, but after that, the State Pen was likely to be a shock.

"Hey," Daniel said, watching Jo sit down across from him.

"Hey", she said, beaming a smile. It was good to see her in such high spirits. It made the gray jumpsuit with the prisoner ID numbers a little easier to take in. The black bracelet Daniel made for her was no longer around her wrist, she wasn't permitted to keep it.

They talked about Jo first, what she'd been through with the trial and how things went with her first day here. She said she'd be okay, that she'd get through this. There was a working dairy farm on the property and part of the inmate enrichment program was milking cows so Jo had something to look forward to. Being around animals, working hard, these were things she loved.

Josephine told him how most of the women at this location were only here a month or two, then transferred out. They weren't dangerous criminals, but they were lawbreakers for sure. She was by far the youngest female here, which could have been a bad thing, but it seemed some of the other women had taken pity on her already, taken her under their wing. She was a pleasant, likeable young lady, even in a setting like this.

Daniel let her talk, though he had a lot to ask her. When she finally ran out of things to tell him about the Correctional Center, they only had five minutes left. She had a few favors for him. In a hushed voice, she spoke, "There's money all over the house. Look in every container. Check the loose floorboard next to the couch too. And the ash bucket next to the fireplace. Oh, and there's a suitcase in my closet, look in there. And War and Peace...the book. There's another grand hidden inside. Take it all, okay? I want you to have it, do whatever you want with it. I'm so sorry I dragged you into all this. Oh, one more thing. Will you move the stone at my daddy's grave? People from Morton are asking where he's buried, and I know it's 'cause they want to dig him up and put him somewhere proper, like the church cemetery, but I know my daddy would want to stay right where he is. Just roll the stone somewhere else and nobody will be able to bother him. Will you do all of that?"

"Of course."

Next, she asked him, "So what are you gonna do?"

"Me?"

"My attorney told me about the house. I'm sorry...I wish you could stay there till you figure out what's next. I think the only reason they're moving so fast on the property is because Mr. Newton has a grandson who's been eyeing our land for years now and my daddy wouldn't sell it to him."

"I've got four more days, then I gotta be out. I know it meant a lot to you. I wish I could do something. I'm real sorry, Jo."

"Don't be," she said, shaking her head in understanding. "It's a steep price to pay on top of being stuck here, but it's not your fault. I knew this whole thing was risky. I knew that."

"But all you ever wanted was that farm and that house. That's why you did it in the first place, to make enough money to keep it."

"Well, I guess I learned my lesson, huh?"

After a long moment of silence, he told her, "Dylan came back and I have the transport vehicle with the trailer now. I can pack up some of the stuff from the house, but I can't fit everything. What do you want the most?"

She gave him a look, like this didn't make sense. "What are you going to do with the stuff? Get a storage unit or something?"

"I don't know yet, but if you tell me what to take, I'll be sure it's kept safe for you. It's the least I can do."

She listed off a few things, not much, mostly things that had been passed down through her family like the quilt her great grandmother had made, and the rocking chair in her bedroom that her mother sat in when she was still alive. She named a handful of other things that had some significance to her as well, things like her father's work boots, her favorite coffee mug, and some of the clothes from her mother's closet. When Daniel asked, "What about the books," she said, "As many as you can fit."

Daniel scribbled all these things down, unwilling to let a single detail slip. Then, onto his next question, he asked, "What was the name of the guy with the winning Berkshire at the county fair?"

Jo gave him a quizzical look. "Mr. Rooney. He lives in Seneca. Why?"

With just a few minutes left to talk, Daniel continued his questions without answering hers. "How many pigs is a good number to start off with?"

"I think somewhere between twenty and thirty. Why?"

"How many acres do you need to raise twenty or thirty pigs, keeping in mind future growth?"

"About fifteen. Why?"

"And about how big does the barn need to be?"

"Why are you asking me all this?"

"And what color blue do you want. Like…a navy blue? Or bright blue? Sky blue? You never said what shade."

Josephine looked him over. She cocked her head to the side. "I don't want you to do all that for me."

"You don't have a choice. This is what I want too and you can't tell me what I want."

"You have a life, don't waste it waiting for me. It's not worth it."

"I disagree. And I won't be wasting it. While you're in here, I'm gonna go see if Mr. Rooney can show me the ropes, teach me how to raise Berkshires. And I'm gonna work hard and save all the money, and I'm gonna buy some land, about fifteen acres. And I'm gonna work some more, two jobs, three jobs, I don't care. I'm gonna save up and buy a place to live, and I'm gonna build a barn. And I'm gonna paint the barn blue…and it would be great if I knew what shade to paint it. That's where you come in."

Daniel gave her a wink, since he couldn't reach out to squeeze her hand just then, like he wanted to. Jo's gray eyes were dripping salt water now, realizing this young man sitting in front of her was dead serious about all this. "Cobalt," she managed.

"Got it. Thank you."

"Time's up!" a guard announced.

Daniel and Jo took a long gaze at each other. It would have to last them till Saturday. Before he stood up to leave, Daniel said, "I love you, Jo. I love you no matter what."

"I know," she said, wiping her face. "I love you too. But I love you enough to let you go. It's not fair to you. This isn't gonna be easy. If you decide…this is too long to wait…I'll understand."

"I'll see you Saturday," he said, interrupting her. All those outs she was giving him, all those excuses she was prepared to accept, he didn't want them.

That night, Daniel got to work packing up the items Jo wanted to save. The transport vehicle would come in handy once more, but he refrained from packing it too full. Sure, he could fit the couch, the kitchen table too, but she didn't ask for those things and they took up a lot of space. On the off chance a certain giraffe reappeared from the forest, Daniel made sure there was enough room for the little fellow. He already knew what he would do should Napoleon show up in the next few days. Daniel had it all planned out, how he'd get the creature into the trailer with all those boxes and miscellaneous pieces, and which road he would take, and which zoo would be a good match, and how he would explain it all without causing further trouble. He had it all figured out, but that didn't guarantee the giraffe was going to make an appearance.

Going through her mother's clothing, Daniel collected what was hanging in the closet. They were all ugly, but Jo wanted them and they meant something to her. She was too young to have ever seen her mother wear these dresses, but perhaps having them helped her imagine. Daniel boxed up her father's pipe, his reading glasses, his work boots, his fatigue jacket, and the few framed photos from the bedroom. On the dresser, next to the wedding photo of Johan and his beautiful redheaded bride, sat a small jewelry box. Daniel lifted the lid. There wasn't much inside, just a few simple pieces, but there was one thing that caught his eye: an engagement ring. He pressed it between his thumb and forefinger, gazed at the tiny diamond, and knew this ring would be worn again someday.

It was the final night in the farmhouse. Daniel had packed the trailer half way, saving everything she asked for: the accordion, her dad's banjo, all of her 4H ribbons, plus all the books. Every last one was boxed up back there, he simply couldn't leave any volume behind. He also took a few things he might be able to use during the next few weeks, since he wasn't sure where he'd stay. He took a blanket and a pillow, some more of her father's clothes, some of Mr. Wessel's honey, and a few things to eat with too. Daniel had a feeling he might be sleeping in the back of that trailer in the near future, so he might as well make it as comfortable as possible.

Daniel went on a scavenger hunt all through the house, opening every container, every shoebox, searching the depths of every pocket, looking for Jo's cash savings. She wasn't kidding; there were rolls of money all over the place. She had some stashed in the house itself, hidden between its bones, while other rolls of money were in plain sight, like in the blue porcelain canister next to the oatmeal. He packed it all away in her suitcase, which he found in the back of her closet. The travel tag on the suitcase read Susanna Larsen, and it was clear by the condition of the bag she'd never traveled much of anywhere, and neither had Jo.

As the morning fog rolled away, Daniel took one last walk through the forest, holding an open gallon of mint chocolate chip ice cream. "Let's go! C'mon, Napoleon!" The forest was quiet. His voice seemed to carry on for miles. "C'mon! I'm gonna leave without you!" he said again. The men from the bank were coming at 9 a.m. to claim the keys, so this was Daniel's last chance, Napoleon's too.

He walked back to Johan Larsen's grave. The white rock with gray veining marked the spot. There was a pile of dead wildflowers placed below, plus some cigarette butts, right where she left them. Daniel crouched down and ran his hands over the rock as if to introduce himself. Quietly, he spoke to the man buried underneath. "I'm gonna take real good care of her, I promise. I've got a plan and I've got patience and…that's about it. I ain't nobody special, but I love her with all my heart. In a few years, when she gets released, when we're both old enough, I want to ask for her hand. I guess this is me askin' for your blessing."

A warm breeze fluttered overhead, sending a gentle whisper through the trees. Those old growth listeners were pleased and they rustled their leaves, encouraging him. Maybe it was the ghost of her daddy. Daniel tilted his head back, letting his face catch the breeze. That's when he knew it was all going to be okay. He felt peaceful, hopeful for the first time. Daniel rolled the rock away, just like Jo requested, so Johan could stay right where he was, the place he would want to be if he could say so. A snapping twig broke Daniel's calm trance. Somebody was watching him. It was Napoleon, walking through the woods several yards away. "There you are," Daniel said, slowly rising in order to keep the creature from getting spooked again. He took a careful step forward and raised up the gallon of ice cream he brought as a bribe. "Come here, you little devil," Daniel said, taking another step toward the mischievous giraffe whose camouflage didn't quite work with all the greenery around here.

Finally, the smell of his favorite treat lured the little guy. He was so hungry, pushing with his face, desperate for that cool creamy goodness. Daniel let him taste it and get some energy back, then he started walking. Napoleon followed, getting a taste every few yards as a reward for his progress. Eventually, Daniel climbed in the back of the trailer near the boxes of books and Jo's things, and set the ice cream down. Napoleon, standing outside the transport vehicle, stared in confusion with his big black eyes. All Daniel could do was hope the poor thing was hungry enough to go in after the ice cream. "C'mon, boy, it's okay."

Awkwardly, Napoleon took a step up the ramp and dragged his back legs into the square cavern. "Good boy," Daniel said, scratching his side while he polished off the ice cream. "You ready for a little bit of a drive?" Napoleon happily licked his face in response.

For the second time in his young life, Daniel drove down a long country road with a live giraffe in the back of a trailer that had a ceiling which could be conveniently raised and lowered when going under overpasses and bridges. Napoleon wasn't very tall yet, so there would be no need to adjust the roof during the course of this trip and that would buy a little time back on the road, since he wouldn't have to pull over at each overpass for the mechanical stuff. This time around, his brother wasn't in the passenger seat, his pockets were filled with about eight hundred dollars in cash plus the twenty-one-thousand in Jo's suitcase savings account, and he had a cooler of ice cream in the front seat to serve Napoleon every few hours. He'd given over the keys to the farmhouse and now it was time to move on from Morton.

By the time he made it to the Scottsbluff Zoo, it was midnight. He sat in the back of the trailer and gave Napoleon one more gallon of ice cream as a going away present. Jo couldn't take care of him now, neither could Daniel, but the giraffe deserved to be cared for. The two of them slept in the back of the vehicle together after Daniel recited his grandmother's poem and, at sun up, Daniel approached a zookeeper as she unlocked the back gate well before the crowds showed up.

"Um. Excuse me?" Daniel said, catching up to the woman.

"Yes?" she questioned, not used to seeing people hanging around the gates at this early hour. Her hair was graying, a little frizzy, but she had kind eyes.

"I've got someone who needs a home. It's a long story, how I got him, but if you promise to take care of him and not ask any questions, I'll give him to you, to the zoo."

"What?"

"He's five weeks old and he's taller than me already."

The woman's eyes lit up. "You've got a baby giraffe?"

"His name is Napoleon."

"How did you..."

"I can't answer that...all the way. Just know...*he* wasn't born in a zoo. He just sort of appeared. And now I want him to have a good home."

After a long moment, the woman agreed to take a look at the creature. That was a promising sign. One look at the sweet-faced baby standing in all his awkward glory won her over immediately. He flicked his ears, watching the zookeeper. The woman explained this was not the way these things should go, that this was wrong on many levels and she could get into a lot of trouble for doing this, but just as Daniel hoped, she accepted the giraffe and helped unload him. Daniel gave Napoleon a good scratch on the neck and said, "I'll come visit. You won't recognize me once you get tall. I'll look totally different from way up there, when you grow up to be as tall as a building."

When Daniel saw Josephine the next week, he had a newspaper article to show her. There, printed in black and white, was little Napoleon. The Scottsbluff Zoo had acquired him through "unusual circumstances" but he brought record-breaking crowds and was credited with saving the struggling zoo. Jo's eyes read over the story, about how the other giraffes in the exhibit had accepted the new edition right from the start. An older female named Zelda, who lost a calf a few years back, had adopted the young troublemaker, and although she couldn't nurse him like he wanted her to, she constantly attended to him and smothered him, just like any good mother would.

"Thank you for finding him a good home," Jo said, touching the image once more. "Now what about you? Did you find a good home for yourself?"

"Mr. Rooney hired me. After he found out I was sleeping in the trailer, he offered me a room too. He's hardly charging me any rent but he sure works me hard with the pigs. I don't think I'll be needing to find a second or third job at this rate. Did you know he's deaf in one ear?"

Jo chuckled. She cupped her right ear and leaned in, saying "What's that?" in a voice that was a pretty decent imitation of Mr. Rooney.

"How did your first class go?" Daniel asked.

"Good. I was thinking after I get my associate's degree, I'll just go right into getting my bachelor's. Might as well. It's not like there's anything else useful to do here."

"One thing at a time."

"Boring," she said with a wink. Jo was doing okay. Daniel recognized her old self was still in there, regardless of her current home.

"You're gonna have more degrees than you know what to do with, and then you'll ditch me and move to the city."

"Me? Move to the city?" Jo cackled. "I just can't picture that."

"Neither can I."

CHAPTER NINETEEN
(SEVEN YEARS LATER)

Daniel's phone rang. He'd been waiting all morning for it to do just that, and now that it was finally ringing, he was afraid to answer it. Jo's parole hearing was supposed to be conducted at 11:30 a.m. that morning, and after seven years of her model behavior, during which time she got two bachelor's degrees, started a prison literacy program, and learned to cook, they were keeping their fingers crossed for good news today. Looking around the farmhouse he purchased three years ago, about half way between Napoleon, at the Scottsbluff Zoo, and Josephine, who'd been transferred to the Penitentiary in Lincoln, he smiled to himself. The barn had been finished last year, and all it needed was some well-chosen pigs. He didn't dare pick them out. The only thing this farmhouse needed, besides a little more fixing up, was Josephine. Daniel took a deep breath and answered.

"Hello?"

"Well? Have you heard anything yet?"

"No, Dylan," Daniel snapped, a little disappointed it was his brother calling. "I gotta get off the line. She should be calling any minute now. I'll call you back as soon as I know, okay?"

"Okay. But there's something you gotta hear first."

"I don't have time. I gotta get off the line."

"Just wait, it'll take two seconds," Dylan swore. There were a lot of strange fumbling noises that followed. Daniel listened, waiting for something, knowing this call with his brother needed to end before he missed the important one he was waiting for. The McElroy brothers talked several times a month these days, made amends long ago and kept in touch from afar, but on this particular day, the only person Daniel wanted to hear from was Josephine. After more confusing sounds from the receiver, Daniel heard his brother whisper to someone near the phone, "C'mon. Say it. Just like you did before. Say...I love you, Uncle Daniel." After that little reminder, the child's voice belonging to two year-old Maria McElroy, said, "I wub you, unk Dambez."

Daniel smiled. He was a proud uncle indeed. Not only was he proud of his sweet little niece who had dark curly hair like her mother, Anna-Maria, but he was proud of his brother for making something of his life, all on his own. When Dylan went to Mexico in search of his long lost mother, he tracked down her last known address. She wasn't there, hadn't been for years. She was gone without a trace, but all hope was not lost. Living in that very same apartment was a beautiful woman with long curly hair and dark eyes you could drown in. Anna-Maria was a few years older, a woman with experience, and Dylan was hooked right from the start. He'd been hooked before, but this time, it was mutual. It didn't hurt that she had a great rack too. Not only had she made a man out of Dylan on the floor of her living room during the final minutes of the last World Cup match, but she made him an adoring husband after three years of dating. Exactly eleven months after their small seaside wedding where Daniel was the best man, she made a doting father out of him too. Dylan fainted when the doctor said, "Es una niña." At least he didn't throw up this time.

Dylan's voice came back on the line. "I've been trying to teach her that all morning. She can say it in Spanish perfectly. She has trouble with her L's in English."

"Keep working on it. She's almost there," Daniel reassured.

"Alright. I'll let you go. Call me as soon as you hear, okay?"

"I will."

"Love you, Daniel."

"Love you too."

Within seconds of hanging up the phone, it rang again. Daniel picked up, ready to fuss at his brother for calling back so soon. Dylan had to learn not to call Daniel every time little Maria did something cute, which was about every five minutes. He was a devoted father and Daniel was a proud uncle, but today, Daniel needed to keep the line open for Jo's call. Maybe this was it.

"Hello?"

"This is a collect call from the Nebraska State Penitentiary, inmate 192873, Josephine Larsen. Do you accept the charges?"

"Yes," he said, his voice growing nervous. Daniel sat down at the kitchen table, biting his nails. His breathing turned shallow, anxious to hear the news.

"Hey," Jo said, plain as ever. How could she do that? How could she sound so at ease after everything she'd been through? The State Pen had been a major shock, a totally different environment from the Correctional Center, but after four years in this place among hardened criminals, you'd never know how brave she had to be, judging by the even tone of her voice now.

"Hey," he replied. There was a long pause. "Well? What did they say?"

Josephine sniffled once. Was that a good sign or a bad sign? Her breathing was the only sound that traveled over the line. No words came just yet.

"Jo?" he tried again. "What did they say? What did they say?"

"Can you pick me up tomorrow at noon?"

Daniel started laughing. All his nervous energy, all his thankfulness, it exploded into a hearty cackle, an outburst of relief. Jo was laughing too, though much quieter. She was still in shock of it all. Her time was up. Parole would only require she stay in the state of Nebraska and check in with her parole officer three times a week for the remainder of her sentence. Easy. After seven years and five days, she was finally getting her freedom back. Tonight would be her last night in prison.

After ending the call with Jo, and phoning his brother to share the good news, Daniel got straight to work preparing the farmhouse for her arrival. Since this was her new home, one he had to create without much of her input other than what they could discuss during their visits, he needed to make a good first impression tomorrow. All the things he brought from her old house were in their proper places, plus a few new things he'd collected over the last few years like the framed piece of newspaper with Napoleon's picture from when he magically showed up at the Scottsbluff Zoo, saving the place from going under by doubling the number of visitors. Jo's favorite mug was in the cupboard. Her dad's boots had a spot by the front door, perpendicular with the wall. Even her mother's jewelry box found a home on the dresser Daniel bought at a secondhand shop a while back. The accordion sat beside the couch, as did the banjo, which Daniel had been teaching himself to play in the evenings after dinner. He'd already learned how to pluck out Doug Burr's 'Always Travel Light' and couldn't wait to show Jo.

Daniel changed the sheets on the bed, daydreaming about what they might do under them. Seven years was a long time to remain celibate. He cleaned the kitchen, curious how much she'd learned to cook in the prison foodservice program. He fluffed the pillows on the couch, wondering what book she might want to curl up with first. When the house was in good shape, he walked through the pristine blue barn. It still smelled of paint. The stalls were ready, everything was set up for the animals. He'd even found a spot to display all of Jo's 4H prize ribbons, so she'd remember where she came from and feel encouraged about the future. After working for Mr. Rooney for over six years, Daniel was prepared to care for a pig farm of his own. During the last year he'd done some odd jobs for other farmers in the area, keeping a bit of money coming in while he fixed up his own place. As he walked out to the edge of his property, near the white box beehives he put beside the small vegetable garden in honor of Johan Larsen, he picked some wild daisies, then brought them back inside and put them in a drinking glass on her nightstand.

Next, he drove into Wallace, the nearest town, and headed straight to the jewelry shop. There was something he needed to get shined up. Her mother's ring was thin and gold, very simple in ornamentation. The diamond was tiny, just a little speck of sparkle, but it was real and it had wooed a beautiful redheaded woman before. Daniel hoped this diamond would have a second life on the slender ring finger of his beloved's hand, and on the hand of their daughter or daughter-in-law, and their granddaughters too.

Lately, Daniel had been entertaining thoughts about how their wedding day might be. He had the perfect picture of it in his mind. Jo would have her long red hair in a ponytail, of course, and she'd be wearing her mother's simple sheath wedding dress, which Daniel had carefully packed up on that last day in the Larsen farmhouse. Although he knew nothing of women's fashion, he could tell from the style that the dress was from the 1960's, so it must have been passed down more than once. The ivory A-line dress would likely fall to just above Jo's knees, probably to where those sweet little dimples were set, the place his lips once kissed. Daniel treasured that image: his knobby-kneed bride. He wondered if Jo ever tried on her mother's wedding dress as a young girl, twirling around and daydreaming about who her prince might be. He hoped he could fill in for the prince okay. Although the dress was probably intended for the spring time, Daniel pictured him and Jo getting married in the middle of the snowy winter, sometime in January on the coldest day of the year, but he would be so warm inside, he wouldn't even need a suit jacket. He expected there wouldn't be many people there, just family, and that's all that really mattered anyway.

Daniel couldn't sleep that night. He kept turning on the bedside lamp, putting on his reading glasses, and looking at the ring, thinking over how he might propose. There were so many ways to do it. He could get down on his knees in the waiting area of the prison, ask her the second she stepped out into the free world. He could wait and bring her back to the farm, show her the new place, and propose in the big blue barn that sat toward the back of the property. He could wait till next week, when it was time to go pick out some Berkshires. Or the week after that, on her twenty-fifth birthday. Then, it hit him. He needed to do this at the zoo, with Napoleon watching over. Napoleon's mother, Millie the giraffe, was the most stubborn animal who ever lived, but she brought Daniel to Josephine's farm so many years ago.

In the morning, running on pure excitement and no sleep, Daniel trimmed his full beard and did what he could with his messy mop. Last week, he found his first gray hair, right in front of his left ear. Although he was tempted to pluck it out, since twenty-seven seemed awfully young for gray hair, he left it alone. He was older, a hell of a lot wiser too, so having a gray hair here and there was just fine by him. Daniel McElroy had never been healthier. He hadn't had a seizure since that day in Josephine's kitchen and he finally managed to put some muscle on his skin and bones. He really was doing well.

He hummed to himself as he made his final trek to the Nebraska State Penitentiary in Lincoln. He'd driven this stretch of road so many times, back and forth, back and forth, twice a week for several years, listening to Doug Burr most of time. He'd never driven it with Jo before. After today, he wouldn't have to drive two hours to see her beautiful face anymore. He'd be able to roll over and see it. What more could he want?

"Today's the day, huh sugar?" the guard said from behind the security window. She had to be the sweetest prison guard on the planet. She called Daniel all sorts of pet names over the years, but he always called her Ms. Geraldine.

"It sure is, Ms. Geraldine. All this time felt like it would never pass. But now...I feel like no time has passed at all."

"You take good care of my girl, you hear?" Ms. Geraldine warned in her usual playful way. She was just barely five feet tall and was pushing two hundred pounds, but she had the smile of a beauty queen. "Much as I'll miss her, I don't want to see her back here."

"You won't. I'm keeping her all to myself."

"Mmm hmm," Ms. Geraldine hummed with a wink. "All right, pumpkin. She'll be out in a minute. Have yourself a seat."

Daniel felt his stomach turn warm, like a cup of hot tea on a cold winter's day. The warmth spread to his chest, then his face and fingers. Sitting in the waiting room with a diamond ring burning a hole in his pocket, Daniel tried to stay calm.

"Hey you," Josephine said, walking through the door. She was wearing the clothes Daniel had bought for her, a pair of jeans and a plain white t-shirt. He was glad to see the jeans fit those long legs of hers. He had figured out the right length by holding them up to his own waist.

"You talking to me?" he teased, standing up to greet her.

Daniel was expecting a firm hug so when she jumped up and wrapped her arms around his neck and her legs around his waist, he stumbled a little. She was still lightweight as ever, just eager to see him. He inhaled her scent, right at her neck. She didn't smell like lemon lotion, or soil, or sweat. She just smelled like herself. Her hair was still long, even though she was strongly advised to cut it when she transferred here, because pulling hair was pretty common when it came to prisoner fights. Jo told them, "I don't plan on getting into any fights," and that was that. They let her keep her locks.

When he finally set her feet back down on the ground, he took a good long look at her face before kissing her. He'd seen her face twice a week for seven years from across a metal table that was bolted to the ground, but this was different. Somehow, Josephine Larsen had grown even more beautiful. She was awfully cute when she was a teenager, but now she was absolutely stunning. Prison hadn't robbed her of that.

"Sweet ride," Jo said, running her hands over the headlight of Daniel's truck. He bought this green pickup off of Mr. Rooney a few months after he started working on his pig farm. He ended up selling the transport vehicle to a scrap yard, mainly to get rid of it. It was kind of conspicuous to drive the thing around farm country, especially since it had no plates. It got crappy gas mileage too.

"It's got working AC and everything," he said, opening her door. "But you know what the best part is?"

"What?" she asked, climbing in.

"You. You, in the passenger seat, is the best thing about this truck."

Jo couldn't help but roll her eyes and smile. "You're so cheesy sometimes."

Daniel poked her in the nose once. He just couldn't help himself.

For the first time in a long time, they didn't have to rush through their conversation. There was no guard standing near, there was no clock ticking their time away, it was just the two of them in a green pickup truck, driving west. They were quiet now. They were themselves, the only two people in the world who could be comfortable with silence like this.

They passed through rolling farmland, lit up in pure sunshine. Jo took it all in, remembering what her homeland looked like. When they drove by a man on a tractor, a total stranger, Jo waved to him because that's just what you do. She looked so natural sitting there, watching the world go by outside.

Daniel reached for her hand. Curiously, she traced her fingers over his wrist, across the small tattoo she'd never seen before. It was still a little red with healing, a new feature on Daniel's skin. Jo asked, "What does it mean?" looking over the numbers and marks inked into his flesh.

"It's home."

Jo looked at the numbers and marks again. The top line read 40° 50' 18" N and the line just below that read 101° 9' 54" W. It was the longitude and latitude of their new home in the outskirts of Wallace, Nebraska, the place he hoped to grow old with Josephine raising pigs, and maybe one day, children. Daniel wouldn't be needing the compass rose tattooed on his shoulder anymore. His nomadic days were over.

"Is that where we're going?" she asked. "Home?"

"Yes. But…I was thinking we could go visit someone first, someone very, very tall. It's a few more hours but I think we can make it before the zoo closes. Is that okay?"

"It's perfect," she said, scooting over to rest her head on his shoulder. That was all the talking they did during the course of their four-hour drive. Silence suited them, and silence in the same place at the same time, suited them even better. They were the exact opposite of Dylan and Anna-Maria, who talked over each other most of the time.

The zoo was quiet. It was late in the day, the fieldtrips had come and gone, and only a few visitors filled the pathways and crowded around the exhibits. Many of the animals were sleeping, taking a long afternoon nap in the shade of a tree or man-made cliff. Daniel had been to this zoo by himself so many times over the years, even bought a membership so he could get in as many times as he cared to, which worked out to be about once a week. He knew the shortest path to Napoleon, but Jo, who'd been cooped up in prison for two thousand five hundred and sixty-one days, wasn't in such a hurry. She wanted to stop and visit each animal, take in the sights. Unaware of Daniel's urgent need to get to the giraffe exhibit and ask his burning question, Jo sat down to admire the flock of flamingos.

"They're so beautiful," she said, scanning over the almost-solid mass of pink winged creatures.

Daniel took a deep breath, desperate to get on his knees and ask Jo to be his forever, but he couldn't do it now, not with the flamingos. He took her hand, begging her to keep going. "C'mon. The African exhibits are this way."

"Why are you in such a hurry?"

"I just…I want you to see how big he is."

They made their way to the giraffes. Zelda, the oldest female who adopted Napoleon, was feeding on hay from a basket fixed to the side of the indoor enclosure. The other two giraffes were inside, not in the mood to be on display. At first, Napoleon was nowhere to be seen. Daniel started to get nervous. What happened to their giraffe? He was here just last week. How was he supposed to propose without Napoleon? His plan was ruined.

"There he is," Jo whispered, pointing to a tree and four giraffe legs that appeared to be growing out of it. "Oh, he's...enormous! Look at that," she went on, awestruck by the handsome creature.

Napoleon was just under seventeen feet tall now, weighing in at two thousand five hundred and fifty-nine pounds. He was fully grown, very healthy, and a strikingly beautiful animal. All his small-scale patterns of auburn and tan were spread out now, stretched to cover his huge body in maps of reddish brown. His funny little face was still the same, those big black eyes, those velvety lips and lopsided ears that were a little wider spread than they should be. He still looked like Yoda when it came to the ears. There was less white around his muzzle now, he'd gotten somewhat darker over the years. The nubby horns on his head were straight up and mostly free of hair, not like when he was a baby. He'd grown into his kneecaps too.

They stood watching him for a few minutes, waiting for him to come over to the railing, but he wasn't interested. From where he was over by the tree, there was nothing particularly fascinating about these two people observing him. They hadn't paid twenty-five cents to get a handful of pellets out of the machine to feed him either, so it wasn't worth the effort to walk over there just so these people could flash cameras in his face. He wasn't really fond of those pellets anyway.

Jo turned to Daniel and asked, "Do you think he remembers us?"

"Dunno," he replied.

Daniel put his hand in his pocket and found the ring, ready to proceed with his grand plan, even if Napoleon was being anti-social today, but Jo ran off. She was jogging toward the ice cream stand. Daniel let the ring fall back in his pocket and chased after her.

When he caught up, he heard her order, "Two scoops of mint chocolate chip on a waffle cone, please."

Daniel smirked, knowing exactly what she was up to. He paid for the ice cream and they returned to the railing, the closest they could get to that loner giraffe on the other side.

"You're gonna get us kicked out," he teased, tapping the sign that warned Do Not Feed the Animals Human Food. They probably had to put that sign there just for Napoleon, the little moocher.

Jo didn't care. She held out the ice cream cone, waiting. "Come here, Napoleon. C'mon," she said, letting her voice carry across the tiny parcel of Africa. "C'mon, boy!"

Finally, the giraffe moved. First, his tail swung, as if to gather energy. Then, his big hooves kicked up dust and he slowly walked across the man-made savannah. He no longer trotted around on old cattle fields or low-lying crops. His home was a grassland with some rocks, a small river, and a few trees for shade. He had everything he needed.

"Good boy," she encouraged, unconcerned with getting caught. She continued to hold out the dessert, even though it was starting to drip down her hand. Daniel kept a look out for zoo employees, security in particular, but the coast was clear for now.

Napoleon was at the railing, leaning his long neck over to get a sniff of whatever this young woman was holding out for him. It didn't look like those healthy pellets most tourists tried to give him from the machine beside the sign that warned against feeding him anything else he might actually want. His long blackish purple tongue took a curious taste. That cold sweet substance, minty and delicious, was familiar. He took another taste. His ears twitched in delight. Jo's smile was so wide, seeing her baby giraffe all grown up. She had helped him from his mother's womb, named him, cared for him, raised him on ice cream, and he was all grown up now, with hooves that were bigger than her head. After another lick, Napoleon snatched the whole thing from Jo's hand. He was so greedy. The waffle cone crunched in his mouth as he rolled his jaw in a slow circle, like a cow. When he finished, he moved his hungry face back to Jo's hand, searching for more, but it was empty. He licked the drips from her palm and wrist, letting his velvety lips clean her up. She loved it. She hadn't changed a bit.

Now was the perfect time for a proposal. Daniel couldn't have planned it better. Napoleon was there, close to them, and Jo was smiling, so he got on his knees and took her hand. It was still covered in sticky ice cream, but he slid the ring on anyway. He took a deep breath and just as he was about to ask his question, he felt someone chewing on his hair.

"Do you mind?" he aimed his voice upward, toward the curious giraffe. "Why do you always do this?" Napoleon searched Daniel's head for that brown hay-like stuff. That damn giraffe was just like his mother. "Can't you see this isn't the best time?"

"Still using girlie shampoo?" she teased, squeezing his hand a little.

Daniel, with his hair a mess, defended himself, "It just smells so good. I don't understand why guys can't use it. I mean, a coconut smells good to everyone, right? Not just girls."

"Apparently it does. Guys, girls…and giraffes."

Daniel chuckled. This was a strange tangent to go on just then, on his knees holding a diamond ring. "Cut it out!" he said playfully, swatting the animal away when he made another pass at his sweet-smelling hair.

"He likes you," she said.

"What about you? Do you like me?"

"I sure do," she replied with a grin, looking down at her mother's ring.

"Do you like me enough to spend the rest of your life with me?"

"I sure do," she whispered.

And so it was settled.

The End.

ABOUT THE AUTHOR

Sarah Mandell is a professionally trained artist with a background in commercial interior design. She's also the brains and busy hands behind a thriving indie craft business called Once Again Sam (www.onceagainsam.com) in Greenville, SC. Her first novel *Celia on the Run* was published in 2012 by Untreed Reads.

Newsletter: www.sarahmandell.com/newsletter
Website: www.sarahmandell.com
Facebook: www.facebook.com/AuthorSarahMandell
Twitter: www.twitter.com/theshyauthor
Instagram: www.instagram.com/authorsarahmandell

ACKNOWLEDGEMENTS

Thank you Jesus, for absolutely everything.

A huge thank you to my husband Josh Mandell, who took me to the zoo oh-so-many times to visit "my" giraffes, Autumn and Walter. Thank you for bringing the beautiful cover art for this book to life, and for all of your practical help getting this story out into the world. I love you, I like you too, and I truly appreciate your genuine encouragement day after day.

Thank you to my Dad, Dan Barchanowicz, for lending your editorial & proofreading talents to the final draft of this novel. I'll never be too grown up to ask you to check my homework. I'm lucky to have you as a Dad!

Thank you to the Mandell family for being endlessly supportive of all of my creative endeavors. It means the world to me!

Thank you to my friend and fellow author Shannon McCrimmon for offering such sincere encouragement during this whole process. I resisted self publishing at first, but seeing how you flourished all on your own, while I sat frustrated waiting on my former publisher for years and years, made me rethink everything. You're the reason I finally changed my mind and pulled the plug! Thanks for all of your advice as I step out into the indie author world.

Thank you to my friend Ana Duncan for being the very first reader of the giraffe story (even before my husband). I never once worried you would judge me when I shared my first draft with you back in 2011, and your excitement over the story was exactly what I needed to keep going.

Thank you to Keith Gilchrist at the Greenville Zoo for showing me what goes on behind the scenes, and for answering my endless (and probably bizarre) questions about normal non-fiction giraffe behavior.

Celia on the Run

Nick Novaczek is a cautious soul, a 17-year old with a quiet thirst for danger. On the eve of his grandmother's funeral, danger finds him by the motel swimming pool. Her name is Celia and she's everything he's not. This foul-mouthed beauty is hitchhiking across the country to make amends with her estranged father and doesn't carry an ounce of fear or hesitation in her tattered suitcase.

Hours after meeting Celia, Nick is hopelessly hooked and "borrows" his parents' car to join her mission, even though her story is full of holes. It's the mistake he's been waiting his whole life to make. After weeks of detours, with hundreds of miles left to go, their wild adventure unravels, but she won't turn back, no matter how desperate things get. Celia's got a charming smile to pay her way, a willing accomplice, and an endless supply of lies. Not to mention a gun.

Sarah Mandell's debut novel, *Celia on the Run*, is available for purchase on all ebook platforms.

Made in the USA
Lexington, KY
30 April 2017